DELIA'S DAUGHTER

CAROLE WILLIAMS

Amazon Paperback Edition

THE CANLEIGH SERIES

All available in ebook and paperback format

Rejection Runs Deep – Book 1
www.amazon.co.uk/dp/B076YZQW57/

Delia's Daughter – Book 2
www.amazon.com/dp/B076YZQW57/

Website: www.carolewilliamsbooks.com

Email: carole@carolewilliamsbooks.com

PROLOGUE

AUGUST 1978

Ruth could remember the terror she felt as the enormous black horse galloped towards her across the grass. She could remember her stepdaughter, Lady Delia Canleigh, on his back, shouting abuse at her and smashing her whip down on his rump as the pair approached. She could remember hearing the children screaming. She could remember the massive animal rearing high above her and as his front legs beat the air and came crashing down, how his left hoof had caught her head with a sharp blow. She couldn't remember anything else.

As she lay in her hospital bed, having been examined and diagnosed as suffering from concussion with a nasty gash on the side of her head, resulting in nine stitches; Ruth, the Duchess of Canleigh, re-played the ghastly scene of Delia, hell-bent on murdering her in her mind.

The beautiful sunny afternoon had started so well. Ruth had decided to take her four-year-old son, Stephen, along with Lucy, Delia's daughter of the same age, down to the lake at Canleigh for a picnic. Tina, their nanny, had accompanied them and it was just as well she had, as otherwise, Ruth might never have seen the light of day again.

It was Tina who placed Ruth in the recovery position after the attack and bandaged the wound on her head, having ripped up the tablecloth they had brought for their picnic to do the job. Tina had stayed with her, holding her hand while Ruth came round, shaking and feeling as cold as ice, having to pretend she was absolutely fine as the children, shook up and terrified by what they had seen, sobbed by her side.

"Demon was trying to kill you, Mummy," cried Stephen, pointing at the dead black horse lying motionless on the ground not far from them. "Why was Aunty Delia so angry and why did she make him rear up and his hoof hit you? I hate Aunty Delia. Are you all right, Mummy?"

His little face was a picture of concern and Ruth did her best to assure him that she was okay while little Lucy, her face as white as the tablecloth, sat stunned beside Tina. She saw Ruth looking at her and crept over to hold Ruth's other hand. "Please be all right, Granny Ruth. I don't know why Mummy and Demon were so angry but please be all right ... and that nasty gamekeeper ... Prit ... Prit."

"Pritchard," interjected Tina helpfully.

"Yes ... that horrid man ... he shot Demon. Mummy must be so upset."

Ruth tried to sit up but Tina wouldn't let her. "Stay there, Your Grace. Pritchard rushed back to the house for help. I expect an ambulance will turn up at any minute."

Ruth looked fearfully around. "Where's Delia? I know she was shouting something as she galloped Demon straight at me but I couldn't hear what she was saying ... oh, heavens ... Pritchard has killed him," she whispered tremulously, staring at the deceased animal.

"Yes, thank God," replied Tina grimly. "Luckily for you, Pritchard was out with his rifle and saw Demon rear up at you. He must have realised Lady Delia was encouraging him on to do you real harm so he shot him. Lady Delia managed to scramble off and

5

stumbled away towards the Hall. She looked stunned and shocked but I don't think she will come back down here. She will know help will arrive for you soon … and I do wish they would hurry up."

The ambulance seemed to take an age but Tina, calm and reassuring, cuddled the children, held Ruth's hand, and told them fairy stories she made up as she went along to take their minds off what had just occurred. Even so, the sound of the ambulance siren in the distance growing closer and closer was an enormous relief for them all, especially for Ruth, terrified Delia would return and finish her off.

Three-quarters of an hour later and Ruth was in the accident and emergency department of Leeds hospital, feeling distinctly safer surrounded by medical staff and policemen. Her only other concern was for the safety of the children. Tina had insisted she would stay with them and take them back to her house in Canleigh village until they all knew where Delia was and what she intended. Until then they were all at risk.

* * *

The pain in Philip's ribs, and his leg, in particular, was excruciating. He had passed in and out of consciousness a number of times and had no sense of time and no idea of how long he had been laying on the floor of Delia's drawing room at the Dower House. He tried to lift his head to look at the clock on the mantelpiece but dizziness overcame him and he slumped back onto the floor. His head appeared to be wet and he gingerly put a hand up to find that the back was soaked in blood and judging by the amount on the carpet, it was surprising he was still alive.

He began to panic. Where was she ... Delia? He could remember how she had been flirting with him, dressed in a flimsy negligee. How stupid he had been, coming back here for a drink after their ride. He might have known she had an ulterior motive. Although he had wanted to let her down gently, there was little option but to tell her he was now engaged to Ruth. The result had been disastrous. Delia went berserk, grabbing the poker and smashing it over his head. That was all he could recall but judging by the state of his ribs and his leg, she had carried on with her beating.

But where was she now? She had obviously left him for dead and he could only assume she had then gone after Ruth. God, he was so worried but there was absolutely nothing he could do ... and what if she did kill Ruth ... would she come back here to make sure he was dead and if he wasn't, ... ?

He shuddered. Delia in a rage was bloody unpleasant. She was vicious and nasty. It wasn't wise for anyone to put obstacles in the way of what she wanted ... and he had just put a big one in front of her. Telling her that he and Ruth were engaged ... but they couldn't keep it a secret forever. God, he hoped Ruth was all right. He was becoming frantic with fear, not only for his fiancé but also himself. Would anyone apart from Delia come to the Dower House? Would they find him alive or dead? His head had stopped bleeding but he couldn't bear the pain much longer. He was so cold too, desperately cold, and yet clammy and sweating at the same time.

He tried to move. If he could at least sit up, he might be able to reach the telephone on the table a few feet away and ring for an ambulance and the police. He managed a few inches but when a horrifying sharp pain, like no other he had experienced in his life, ripped through his damaged leg, he sunk blissfully into unconsciousness.

* * *

Tina loved her job as nanny to the Duchess of Canleigh, a position she had held since just after little Stephen Canleigh was born. She had worked for the aristocracy since she qualified but this was the job which suited her the best, enabling her to live in the village with her husband, Mark, and a menagerie of pets, work regular hours throughout the day and go home at night. She adored the Duchess and her small son, who was a delight to look after, and an even bigger responsibility since his father sadly died just a year after his birth, resulting in the baby becoming the Duke of Canleigh in his own right.

Tina and Mark hadn't any children, which was a deep sadness for both of them but they solved the problem by lavishing love on their pets and Tina being the best nanny she could be to any infant whom she was hired to care for. As a result, she was an extremely valued employee and loved deeply by the children.

As well as Stephen, she also had the pleasure of looking after Lucy Canleigh, Lady Delia's young daughter, since Lady Delia had moved into the Dower House last year, amid much apprehension on the part of the staff and Ruth. Up until now, all had been fine but today's display of utter venom on the part of Lady Delia was not only shocking but also highly alarming and once Ruth had departed in the ambulance, Tina hurried the two children to her terraced cottage in the heart of the village. She rang the Hardy's, the butler and housekeeper at Canleigh Hall, to tell them the children were safe and could remain with her until Ruth was discharged from hospital.

"Would you like me to bring some of His Grace's things down to you?" asked Hardy, realising that the Duchess would probably be kept in hospital overnight.

"Yes, please, Hardy. Do we know what's happened to Lady Delia? I need items for Lucy too but I'm terrified of going anywhere near the Dower House in case her mother is there."

"Mixed news on that score," replied Hardy. "After Pritchard rushed up to the Hall to phone for an ambulance and the police, apparently he saw Lady Delia making her way to the stables. He followed her . . . and found her . . . trying to hang herself in Demon's loosebox."

Tina drew in her breath sharply. "Oh, my God! Is she . . . is she dead?"

"No. He managed to cut her down just in time. The police have carted her off to hospital to be checked over and then they're taking her to the police station. She's been arrested for attempted murder."

"Oh, good heavens. What a terrible mess. Poor little Lucy. Whatever will happen to her now?"

"I shouldn't worry too much, Tina. Her Grace will make sure Lucy will be well cared for. Now, would you like me to come with you down to the Dower House? I have a spare key here at the Hall."

"Oh, that would be so kind, Hardy. Yes, please. I have my sister staying at the moment so she can look after the children while I come with you."

An hour later, Hardy collected Tina in the ancient old shooting brake, which thanks to the hard work of Tina's husband, managed to keep trundling around the estate. They were down at the Dower House in minutes and pulled up outside the front door. Hardy took the key out of his pocket but surprisingly they found the door wasn't locked and they entered tentatively. They knew Lady Delia wasn't there but even so, they both felt like trespassers.

The house had an ominous, eerie silence. They looked at each other, feeling uncomfortable and wanting to get back out as soon as possible.

"I'll go and find Lucy's room," said Tina, taking the stairs in front of her, two at a time.

Hardy looked at the doors on either side of the hall. To the right was the dining room. To the left was the drawing room. He opened the door and peered in. A moan from the direction of the fireplace, shielded from his view by a large sofa, made him step further into the room.

"Hardy . . . is that you?" whispered a male voice.

Hardy moved around the sofa quickly, aghast to see Philip Kershaw, their next-door neighbour, laid on his side, blood dribbling from a head wound and one of his legs stuck out at an odd angle.

"Master Philip! What on earth? Stay right there. I'm ringing for an ambulance," urged Hardy, hurrying towards the telephone on a table at the side of the room. Just as he replaced the receiver, relieved to hear the ambulance would be there in minutes, Tina appeared, carrying a pink suitcase and a grinning teddy bear.

"Right, Hardy. I think that's it," she said. "Should we get out of here?"

"Not just yet, Tina. We have to stay for now," Hardy replied from the other side of the sofa where he was kneeling on the floor. "I've just had to ring for an ambulance for Master Philip."

Tina stepped forward to see what he was doing, horrified to see Philip Kershaw, obviously having taken a severe beating. A poker was on the floor beside him, covered in blood.

Philip had slid into unconsciousness again but was breathing normally. Hardy sat beside him, holding his clean handkerchief to Philip's head. A considerable amount of blood had seeped into the carpet but the bleeding had ceased.

"He's in a bad way," whispered Hardy. "I don't like the look of that leg. I hope the ambulance isn't too long."

"It must have been Lady Delia," said Tina, sliding down onto the sofa, dropping the suitcase and teddy on the floor beside her. "Look, Hardy . . . the poker . . . it has blood on it. She must have beaten him half to death before riding down to the lake to try and kill Her Grace . . . but why?"

"I wouldn't mind guessing it's because Her Grace and Philip have become engaged. The news will have devastated Lady Delia. She's loved Master Philip intensely since she was a small child. It floored her when he jilted her only days before they were due to wed and married Sue Barrett instead. I had a suspicion when Sue died that Lady Delia would come back to Canleigh to try to ensnare him again. To find out he had just become engaged to Her Grace must have dealt her a mortal blow . . . and what's occurred today is obviously the result. Dear, oh dear. Where will it end?" he finished sadly.

"Well, she can't do any more harm, that's for sure," replied Tina, keeping her eyes on Philip's chest to make sure he was still breathing. His colour was ghastly and his eyes kept flickering but at least he was alive.

Hardy's expression was grim. "No. Now she's in custody, no doubt she'll be put away for a very long time."

* * *

Lady Delia Canleigh's neck was sore and sported a ghastly red burn mark but worst of all she was still alive and why? She had nothing to live for now. She had killed Philip, beating him furiously with the poker. Her darling, darling horse, whom she had watched being born and lavished so much care and attention on, was also dead. Shot by that dreadful gamekeeper. And then she had probably killed bloody, bloody Ruth. At least she hoped she had. She hated that woman so much. She was always standing in her way and she deserved to die.

Even so, there was no purpose to her own life any longer. No reason for her to go on. She would never get the estate now that bloody woman had spawned young Stephen and she would never, never feel Philip's arms around her again or his mouth on hers. There was just nothing, absolutely nothing left to live for. Why the hell did that damned Pritchard turn up, cut her down, and revive her? He had no business following her to the stables and interfering in the biggest decision she had ever made in her life. If she ever came across him again, he would be very, very sorry.

Delia rubbed her neck. She must only have been hanging in the noose for a brief moment but the rope had been thick and rough and in just a few more seconds, would have done its job.

"I think you can be discharged, Your Ladyship," said the accident and emergency doctor who had examined her. "Your neck will be a little sore for a few days but there is no lasting damage. You were very lucky."

Lucky? Lucky? What on earth was the stupid man talking about? Lucky to still be alive and having to face a murder charge ... again. She *had* been lucky last time but that was because she had planned it all out for months and managed to make the murder of her brother, Richard, the Marquess of Keighton look as if their half-brother had killed him. Instead, it had been she who had killed them both. Her careful attention to detail had resulted in the judge dismissing the case against her due to lack of evidence. But this time she had acted on impulse ... in anger and rage. She hadn't time to plan anything and now they would get her for it and she would go down ... for a very long time.

Prison. She couldn't bear the thought of being locked up, day in and day out with criminals, prostitutes, thieves and murderers. Not being able to gallop across the fields, not being able to remain outside for hours at a time, not being on Canleigh soil. How the hell was she going to bear it?

The two police officers standing behind the doctor moved towards her, one holding out a pair of handcuffs. Delia took one look at him and burst into tears.

CHAPTER 1

AUGUST 1995

"It's here," stated Ruth glumly, going through the post, Felix, the butler, had placed on the dining table.

She had known it would arrive. It always did, as regular as clockwork, exactly on Lucy's birthday every year, and they all tried to pretend it didn't matter but it did ... and this one was bulging, indicating it contained another long letter too. Until Lucy was eighteen years old, Lady Delia Canleigh had only sent cards but once her daughter attained adulthood, letters were enclosed, which upset Lucy for days. Ruth's heart plummeted at the thought of what the woman had to say this time.

Ignoring the bacon and eggs on her plate, Ruth looked out of the dining room window of Canleigh Hall and wondered, as she did every year, whether to hide the envelope but knew she couldn't. Lucy would know it was here. Apart from a Christmas card, it was the only communication she had with her mother and even though as a child Lucy hadn't been allowed any physical contact with Delia since she was imprisoned, she always accepted the cards, taking them up to her room to open. When the letters started accompanying the cards, Lucy showed them to Ruth. They were all the same, full of apologies and begging Lucy's forgiveness.

Lucy always kept them. A few years ago, Ruth had found a box in her wardrobe when she was checking on what items of school uniform needed replacing. It fell from a shelf as she opened the door, and she knelt down to gather up the contents, saddened by the sight of Delia's cards, heart bleeding for her step-granddaughter.

"Delia?" said Philip, looking up from perusing his latest edition of Horse and Hound magazine.

Ruth looked at her husband and nodded. Philip would never forgive Delia for what she had done and hated her name being mentioned, which was difficult at times as she was Lucy's mother. As far as he was concerned, the woman was pure evil and must never be allowed into their lives again but time was ticking on. Delia was due for release from prison on licence soon. Where would she go? What would she do? The very idea of her being at liberty again was horrifying.

"I wish the damned woman would rot in hell," Philip said angrily, wincing as he tried to stand up.

Ruth's heart turned over as she looked at him. She loved him so much and she often thought about how she so nearly came to lose him when Delia beat him so badly all those years ago. It had taken him a long while to recover. He had suffered from a cracked skull, a number of broken ribs, and his left hip and leg had been badly shattered. Apart from his bones, there had been no other internal damage but even so, he would never walk properly again, had to have an automatic car as he couldn't use a clutch any longer and relied heavily on a walking stick for support. The attack had also aged him. He looked far older than his forty-five years, with deep lines on his face and little left of his blonde hair.

Newly engaged to Ruth at the time, he had suggested they call it off, as he was reluctant for her to be shackled to a cripple for the rest of her life. Ruth had swept his doubts aside. She loved him. He loved her. They would create a full and happy life together, whatever his afflictions, and six months after the lengthy operations to fix his hip and leg, they married in St. Mary's, the tiny church nestled in the woods on the estate.

It hadn't been simple for Philip to manage his riding school and livery stables following Delia's battering either. He had inherited Tangles, the beautiful Tudor mansion bordering Canleigh land, from his grandparents, along with the business, which he had run successfully before Delia's assault. Afterwards, he tired easily and it was a long time before he felt confident to be on the back of a horse again and when he did, it wasn't long before he was in pain and had to dismount. His long hacks with his pupils over the Yorkshire countryside had to be curtailed and he had to be content with hiring more trained staff to take out groups while he resorted to teaching in the ring, shouting instructions from the sidelines.

Another regret for both Philip and Ruth was that it hadn't been possible for them to live at Tangles after their marriage. Ruth had promised Charles, her former husband, the Duke of Canleigh, that after his sad death from heart problems, she would live at Canleigh until Stephen, their one and only child, was of age to take up his inheritance and care for the estate properly. Once that time came they would move to Tangles but with Stephen's choice of career, joining the army at eighteen instead of attending university, it was placed on the backburner for a while longer. They couldn't leave the estate while he was away so much and as he was doing well, now a full Lieutenant, he had no intentions of giving up army life for the foreseeable future.

"I hope my demented half-sister isn't going to spoil Lucy's birthday," remarked Stephen, buttering a piece of toast. He was home on leave for a week especially for Lucy's twenty-first and didn't want the day ruined for her. She had been looking forward to it for months with a day of pampering and then a huge bash this evening in the marquee on the lawns in front of the Hall.

"So do I, darling. So do I," sighed Ruth heavily, giving Philip a wan smile as he placed a comforting hand on her shoulder and then limped out of the room. "What are you going to do with yourself today?" she asked Stephen. She loved having her son home and hoped he would want to spend it with her. Time with him was so precious now that he was away so much and she couldn't help worrying about his choice of career. The world was such a dangerous place and one never knew where he might be sent and what the outcome would be.

He smiled, his gorgeous big brown eyes twinkling at her. "I am going to spend it with you, Mother dear. I'm going to treat you to lunch somewhere nice ... how about popping over to that nice little pub you go to with Philip sometimes? I can give you a ride on the back of the bike," he laughed.

Ruth grinned back. "Lunch yes. Ride on that dratted bike, no. If you think you will ever get me on that, you had better think again. If we go anywhere, we will go in my car."

She hated that motorbike. It was big, it was noisy and offered no protection in an accident. She had been horrified when he had arrived home on it last year, having bought it while on duty in London. It had made the most awful racket coming down the drive and when the rider took his helmet off and she

17

discovered it was her one and only son, her only child, Ruth had been horrified. It was bad enough to be concerned about his army life but to know he was whizzing about the country on that awful machine was terrifying.

But, like his career, he wouldn't budge on getting rid of it. Stephen, once he had made up his mind about something, was stubborn and wouldn't back down, no matter how one tried to reason with him. The bike was here to stay and his poor mother just had to learn to live with it.

"Whatever you say, Mother," he grinned, buttering another piece of toast and spreading a thick layer of strawberry jam on it. He had a sweet tooth and never could resist their cook's homemade jams and jellies. "Anyway, it will take your mind off Delia for a while."

"Maybe ... but with her release imminent, I have a nasty feeling that this letter for Lucy is going to say she wants to see her. Goodness knows what Lucy will decide."

Ruth stared at the card with its first class stamp and spidery handwriting in black ink and shuddered. She wanted nothing more than to rip it up and burn it in the fireplace.

* * *

Lucy Canleigh lay in bed in her room on the first floor of Canleigh Hall, pondering on the realisation that today she had reached the grand old age of twenty-one and she was going to have a simply fabulous day. Later this morning and for the afternoon, there was a lot of pampering to look forward to, thanks to her lovely Aunt Vicky who owned the fabulously plush hotel, The Beeches, situated just outside of Harrogate, with Uncle Alex. For a birthday treat, they were paying for Lucy and her two best friends, Rosamund and Celia to enjoy a range of beauty treatments, swim, lay by the pool, and then have a scrumptious afternoon tea. Then there was the party tonight to look forward to. It was going to be fabulous with two hundred guests in the giant marquee on the lawn, dancing to Lucy's favourite band, the Commanders, and she was going to wear the most gorgeous rose-pink satin dress. It would be the best day of her life so far and she didn't want anything to spoil it but unfortunately, she was going to have to go down for breakfast and it would be there … the inevitable card … and probably a letter.

Lucy tossed around the bed, threw herself on her tummy, buried her head in the pillows, and groaned. Knowing her mother would soon be unconfined, Lucy was anticipating a request for them to meet and wouldn't be surprised to find a visiting order in with the card that would arrive today.

She was so confused. She would never forget witnessing that awful attack on Granny Ruth, her mother hitting Demon, making him rear and if it hadn't have been for Pritchard, the horse would have trampled her to death. Then there was what she had done to Philip, darling Steppie, whom Lucy loved to bits.

Her mother was a dangerous woman and would be out of prison in the very near future. What was going to happen then? Would she still bear a grudge? Would she come back here and try to finish what she had started all those years ago? Lucy was aware that her mother would be on licence and wouldn't be allowed to come anywhere near them otherwise she would be sent back to prison immediately but would that deter her?

Lucy was scared … mostly for Granny Ruth and Steppie, but also for herself because even though she was frightened of what her mother might do, beneath all that was her love.

She pressed her hand over her eyes, remembering what it had been like when she and Delia had lived at the Dower House when she was only tiny. Her mother had been wonderful then. Lucy had adored her. She was so beautiful, even with that funny mark all down her face … and the way she could ride. It was so exciting, watching her mother on Demon, streaking about. Lucy had been so in awe of her and so proud of her fearless parent. She had been utterly heartbroken, seeing that awful attack on Granny by the lake and then being told, albeit gently and kindly, that she wouldn't see Mummy again for a very long time as she had to go away.

Even though she had visited the Hall every day, playing there with Stephen and the nanny, the lovely Tina, it had been utterly strange to suddenly be plucked from the Dower House and given a bedroom of her own, near to Stephen's. Granny, Aunty Vicky and Tina had been wonderful, making a huge fuss of her, making sure she felt as secure and happy as they possibly could but she had cried every night for Mummy for months and months afterwards. It had been reasonably okay through the day because she was kept occupied and had Stephen to play with and once she started school and had lots more friends, it had been easier … but it was the nights. As soon as she got to bed, her mother was always in her thoughts and she wished and wished she would come home, they could return to the Dower House and live as they had done before that awful day.

Then, as time went on and as she grew up, she found out more and more about her mother. Granny Ruth told her everything, preferring to have Lucy hear the truth and not idle gossip. Granny relayed exactly why Delia had attacked her and Philip, and then informed her about the deaths of Uncle Richard and that other man, Rocky something, who was purported to be the illegitimate child of her proper grandmother, her grandfather's first wife, Margaret. Delia was rumoured to have killed them both, was arrested and charged, although her trial was abandoned due to lack of evidence, resulting in her name never being totally cleared and a big question mark over whether she did actually do it.

Then there had been the 'Daddy' question. Lucy had naturally always wanted to know who her father was. Granny hadn't told her much when Lucy was little, only that his name was Barrie and he had unfortunately died in a car crash. Later, when Lucy was around thirteen and started asking more questions and was old enough to understand, Granny gently told her how Delia had been having an affair with Aunty Vicky's husband, how he had helped her after her trial collapsed and brought her to Canleigh. They had drunk too much, had a row and he stormed out of the Hall in a temper, drove his car into a tree down the drive, and killed himself, having hit Delia before he left, sending her flying onto broken glass, which gave her the dreadful scar all down her cheek. A discarded cigarette in the bed sheets started a fire and her mother had been lucky to get out of her bedroom alive, hauled out by staff who arrived just as the blaze was taking a real hold.

Lucy had been so ashamed of her mother and so sorry for Aunty Vicky. It must have been utterly horrible for her, finding out that her own sister had not only had an affair with her husband but was also pregnant with his child. Yet she had always treated Lucy so well, never showing any signs of resentment. Instead, she was tremendously kind and thoughtful, always interested in Lucy's life and including her with anything her own family were up to, even offering her an Assistant Manager post at The Beeches now that Lucy had graduated from university and wanted a career in the hotel sector. What a truly remarkable woman Aunty Vicky was ... and she was giving her such a super day today.

Lucy smiled, stretched and flung herself out of bed and stared in the mirror. She should look older today but she didn't. She still had fresh, unlined, glowing skin, her long blonde hair, its natural colour a little darker but her hairdresser had lightened it for her, was thick and wavy, her eyes were a pretty blue and her figure was good. A few weeks ago, her tummy had been a bit of a problem but with the party looming and wanting to look good in *that* dress, she smiled at the garment hanging on the wardrobe door, she had made a special effort to swim in the Canleigh pool every day and it had worked. Her tummy was under control and she would look as good as she possibly could tonight and with Jeremy in attendance, that was particularly important.

Lucy had loved Jeremy ever since her Aunty Vicky and Uncle Alex had adopted him when he was six years old, along with his elder sister, Suzanne, who had been eight at the time. Lucy, just a few months older than Jeremy, had felt a strong attachment to him from the day he and Suzanne were

22

brought to tea at Canleigh. Suzanne was a reasonably confident little girl but Jeremy had looked such a pathetic little figure, pale and wan, unsure of himself, lacking in self-confidence and self-esteem after spending most of his short life living with a succession of foster carers. Lucy took him over instantly, persuading Stephen to show him all his toys, encouraging Jeremy to play and to talk.

Gradually, as he grew older and with the love, support and encouragement he received from Aunty Vicky and Uncle Alex, and the wider family, Jeremy came out of his shell and the happier and more confident he became, the more Lucy loved him. He was bright too, achieving good enough A-levels to go to Oxford and having decided years before that he wanted to study law, he went off two years ago with high hopes. They had all been stunned when he suddenly packed it all in just before last Christmas, with no proper explanation, returned to Harrogate, and announced he would like to be involved in the family business if Vicky and Alex would give him a job. Shocked as they were, they agreed, although insisting he commence with learning the ropes at The Beeches.

Lucy had been delighted to have him working alongside her. From the moment Aunty Vicky and Uncle Alex bought The Beeches and invited the family over to view it, she had fallen in love with the place and wanted nothing more than a career in the hotel industry. Having achieved good A-level grades too, Lucy had not long graduated from Leeds University with a business degree. To remain nearer home to study, had enabled her to work part-time at The Beeches and gain valuable experience at the same time. She had worked extremely hard and once her studies were complete, Aunty Vicky had given her a permanent full-time position.

While the rest of the family were flummoxed by Jeremy's decision not to continue with his studies, Lucy had been over the moon. It meant she could see much more of him and on their days off and weather permitting, they took to rambling over the nearby Yorkshire Moors and sometimes driving up to the Dales to walk for hours, seeking out lovely old pubs to eat and rest in. On bad weather days, they went to the cinema or the theatre or just lounged about either at The Beeches or at Canleigh. He had helped her plan the bash tonight too and was looking forward to it as much as she was.

Lucy hugged herself. They were going to have such fun tonight, she would look her very best after a day of pampering, and Jeremy wouldn't be able to resist her. She wanted nothing more than to have him propose and for him to do that tonight, would be the icing on the cake. She sighed heavily. She was so looking forward to today and she wasn't going to let anyone, let alone her miscreant mother, spoil it for her.

* * *

Lady Delia Canleigh turned over uncomfortably on the hard prison mattress in her cell in Holloway prison. She had been awake nearly all night and hadn't enjoyed any decent sleep since the first night of her twenty-two year sentence for attempted murder but that would soon change and she would have a nice, big comfortable bed to wallow in. She was due for release next week, albeit on licence, and would be allowed to journey up to Scotland, to Blairness castle, which her father bequeathed her when he died. It had originally belonged to her darling Granny's family, Granny had passed it on to Delia's father and he to her ..., and she would have to remain there for the remainder of her sentence, for five whole years, before she was free of the licensing restrictions.

Delia had inherited the castle when her father died but only visited it once before she was incarcerated as it held memories she found difficult to live with. School holidays with wonderful Granny, Father and her siblings, Vicky and Richard, her twin whom she had so successfully planned to kill so she could get her hands on the one place she loved the most, Canleigh. She had also been a dreadful mess when she was informed Blairness was hers, beaten and scarred by bloody Barrie, pregnant with his child and living a lonely life in London, desperate to get back to Canleigh, the only place in the world she wanted to be and to own.

So, with Delia reluctant to live in the wilds of Scotland, Blairness had ticked along with the old staff in place and the rooms covered with dust sheets. Then, three years into her sentence the old estate manager decided to leave for pastures new and Rathbones, the family solicitors, asked her permission to search for a replacement. Someone called Brian Hathaway, with impeccable references, had been appointed. All Delia knew about him was that he was the second son of an Earl, had a first class honours degree in Geography from Cambridge, and had been in the Army for years, many of which were served in the S.A.S. A year after the Falklands war, he left the army, wanting a somewhat less exciting career and as he had experience and knowledge of Scottish land and its owners, Derek Rathbone seemed to think he was just the man for the job when Brian's application landed on his desk. Delia had agreed. As long as Blairness was in profit, she wasn't too concerned and took little interest in the accounts and reports Rathbones sent her on a regular basis.

Now, with her release pending, she was having to give Blairness a lot more thought as she had no choice but to take up residence there and wondered what the hell she was going to do with herself in the wilds of Scotland. She would also be far away from Canleigh and would never be allowed back. She would never walk around the estate again, never ride around it, never enter the beautiful old Georgian Hall. Still, she would have to make the best of it. Anything was better than being holed up in here. Just to be able to breathe in the air unpolluted by prison smells, to feel the sun on her face and lay on the grass again was going to be absolute heaven after years and years of this hell.

But would she be content to live quietly at Blairness, and never darken the door of Canleigh again? She still didn't know. She had nursed a quiet anger towards Ruth and Philip for so long but now she was older, wiser and had paid a terrible price for her crimes. Had it all been worth it? They had still ended up together, living at Canleigh, while she had been rotting in jail … all because of her jealousy and uncontrolled temper … and because of that, she had also lost the love and respect of her child. Poor little Lucy had been an innocent victim in all that angst … and if it hadn't have been for Ruth and Philip taking the child in, bringing her up, goodness knows where she might have ended up. So, in a way, she had a lot to thank them for and that hurt. Really hurt.

She had attended anger management classes for the last couple of years. It helped more than she would have believed, as had the counselling. She hadn't wanted to attend either but it was pointed out to her that it was in her best interests to try to sort out her head. They had been right and she was much calmer these days and could think about Ruth and Philip without becoming het up. She had accepted that Philip was not for her and once she was released, she would have to move on with her life. Although there were going to be annoying restrictions on her movements and she wouldn't be allowed within ten miles of Canleigh or have contact with anyone there apart from Lucy, and that was only if the girl was willing ... and that was an almighty mountain she was going to have to climb.

Delia sighed and turned over once again. She had done her best with her last letter. How would it be received by her child, who wasn't a child any longer? She was twenty-one today and would no doubt have something wonderful planned, probably a big party ... at Canleigh. Delia slapped her head. She should have been there. She should have been the one planning it, paying for it, rejoicing in her child's birth. God, she had been so stupid!

CHAPTER 2

Lucy delayed going down to breakfast as long as she could but she was hungry and the smell of bacon and eggs wafting up from the dining room was exceedingly tempting. She showered, dressed, and ran down the stairs, to see Philip, her step-granddad, 'Steppie' as she liked to call him, hobbling painfully across the entrance hall towards the front door. He saw her and smiled.

"Morning, young Lucy. Happy birthday. I hope you have a fabulous day."

Lucy reached up and plonked a kiss onto his cheek. "Thank you, Steppie, darling. I fully intend to."

Philip grinned. He loved this girl as if she were his own and even though she looked similar to Delia, which was totally understandable as they were mother and daughter; her nature was so very different. She was kind, generous, funny and hadn't a malicious thought in her head ... but then Ruth and he had brought her up since the age of four. If she had been left with her mother, things might have been very different.

"Ruth is still in the dining room," Philip said, turning to the front door. "I must be off. I have a class to supervise in an hour and I want to be in the schooling ring with a coffee before then. I'll see you this evening, young lady."

Ruth was still in her chair in the dining room, coffee cup in hand, staring absentmindedly out of the window. She turned and smiled as Lucy entered the room and planted a kiss on her cheek.

"Morning, darling ... and congratulations. You are truly an adult today. My goodness, we will all have to watch out now."

Ruth's tone was flippant but she stared hard at the envelope at the side of Lucy's place at the table. Lucy followed her gaze, her heart missing a beat. It was there, just as she knew it would be ... and it obviously contained a letter again, a long one by the look of it, as it was so fat. Oh God. Perhaps she shouldn't read it today. It would only upset her.

She picked it up and placed it on the chair beside hers so she wouldn't have to look at it while she was eating. She helped herself to bacon, eggs, sausages and tomatoes from the hotplates on the sideboard, sat down at the table and picked up her knife and fork and glanced at Ruth.

"I wonder what she has to say this time ... more grovelling apologies I suppose."

Ruth sighed. "It's probably something to do with her release. It's very near now and I hate to say it, but she might want to meet up with you ... but it's up to you, of course. You don't have to have anything to do with her if you don't want to.

Lucy looked at Ruth. "To be honest, I'm not sure. I do and I don't. It was appalling ... what she did to you and Steppie and she didn't care what happened to me, did she? If she had, she wouldn't have done what she did. Leaving me, all alone. If it hadn't have been for the two of you, I would probably have ended up in care and that doesn't bear thinking about," she shuddered, having heard horrendous stories about what happened to some children when they ended up

29

under the control of the authorities. "Where will she live … when they release her?"

"I imagine it will be Blairness. It belongs to her and she has nowhere else to go."

"Well, at least that's far enough away for us to be out of harm's reach … and I suppose they will keep tabs on her."

"Yes. She will be on licence … and have to report regularly somewhere and if she does come anywhere near us, she will be whipped straight back into prison," said Ruth, having been alerted by the police a few days earlier of the exact date Delia would be freed and what would happen to keep them safe.

"Do you think she'll try and come here?" asked Lucy worriedly.

"No. I would imagine that after all these years in prison, she will have had plenty of time to think about the error of her ways and won't want to risk being sent back."

Lucy put down her knife and fork, picked up the envelope and examined her mother's spidery scrawl. "Right. I'm not going to mess about wondering what she has written. I'm going to open it now and deal with it."

Ruth sat chewing her lip as Lucy tore open the envelope bravely, took a quick look at the card which sported a lot of pink and white roses and a cringing message about a mother's love for her daughter, and unfolded the four sheets of white paper filled with Delia's handwriting. It only took her a few minutes to read and then she looked up at Ruth with horror.

"You're right. She wants to meet me. She actually wants me to stay with her at Blairness so we can get to know each other all over again. Oh God, Granny Ruth. What on earth shall I do? I don't know if I have the courage … don't know if I want to. It's full of apologies," she said, throwing the letter down on the table, "but how sincere is she? I don't know whether to trust her or not."

"The prison authorities seem to think she is dreadfully sorry for what she did. They say she shows tremendous remorse. She's attended anger management classes, had a great deal of counselling, and appears to regret what she did."

"Appears to but does she really? What would you do, Granny Ruth … if you were in my position? Would you meet her … or would you tell her to go to hell?"

"To be honest, darling, I have no idea … and it has to be your decision and yours alone. I don't want to influence you in any way."

"But you kept me away from her all these years … when she kept asking you to take me to visit her."

"Yes but that was because you were a child and I didn't want you to have to suffer the trauma of prison visits, or to have your mother confuse you in any way but now it's different. You are old enough, and have been for some time, to make your own decisions but whatever you decide, I shall always be there for you. You know that, don't you?"

Lucy nodded. "I know … and thank you … thank you so much for all you have done for me. Whatever happens with Mother, you know you and Steppie are the most important people in my life … apart from Jeremy," she grinned.

"Ah, yes. Jeremy," Ruth smiled knowingly.

* * *

31

Deep in thought, Philip drove his Volvo the couple of miles down to Tangles and by the time he arrived, couldn't remember one second of the journey. He pulled up outside the beautiful old Tudor house, turned off the engine and sat staring unseeingly at the ancient brickwork.

They had known it was going to happen and they had been dreading it for years ... not only him but Ruth, Lucy and Stephen. Then, of course, there was Vicky, Lady Victoria, Delia's sister. Delia had wronged her dreadfully and no doubt Vicky would be petrified now. He knew Ruth had told her Delia would be out shortly. The two women were very close and rang each other regularly.

Philip looked down at his bad leg and rubbed it. It hurt ... but then it always did. He tried to keep off the painkillers but now and again had to succumb, especially in the damp, cold winter months when the arthritis gave him terrible gip.

Delia had changed his life dramatically the day he had stupidly taken up her invitation to have coffee with her at the Dower House where she was living with Lucy at the time. He had been lulled into a false sense of security after an exhilarating ride over the fields and woods with Delia on her highly excitable Demon and him on Miranda, a newly acquired mare, and took up her invitation without thinking. He would never forget it. She had left him in the lounge, saying she was going to make coffee and then came back wearing some kind of floaty negligee and made a deliberate pass at him. Trying to withdraw from her advances he had told her, without any preamble, that he and Ruth had become engaged the night before. He would never forget the look on her face. Pure unadulterated evil. He couldn't remember her words now but knew she had screamed and screamed at him and then grabbed the poker from the fireplace and launched her crazy attack. He couldn't remember anything about it, apart from the first stinging blow on the back of his head but could recall coming round, finding he was alone and in the most awful pain all over his body, especially his leg and had never been so relieved in his life to hear Hardy and Tina when they arrived for Lucy's clothes.

The months afterwards had been some of the most difficult of his life. The first operation on his hip and leg had taken nearly ten hours and then he had to have a couple more after that. Hours and hours of physiotherapy and trying to walk properly again was a challenge but even so, he was left with a limp as the bad leg was now slightly shorter than the other due to the surgery.

Thanks to his automatic car, he was at least able to get around, even though he couldn't drive for long. After more than half an hour of sitting in the same position, he became stiff and the discomfort unbearable but the most upsetting result of the attack was that he was unable to ride for long. He could mount a horse with the aid of the mounting block in the yard, with one stirrup strap slightly shorter than the other, but as with driving, more than half an hour of activity and he was in agony, not only from his hip and leg but also his back. Long hacks with his pupils or just for his own pleasure were a thing of the past, which upset him badly. Riding had been one of his passions since his grandfather first placed him on a pony and having to make do with limping around the yard with the aid of a stick and supervising pupils from the sidelines was frustrating and depressing.

Thank God for Ruth. She had been an absolute brick and he loved her with every fibre of his being. She had helped nurse him during the long months of his recovery, bolstering his spirits, doing her best to make him laugh and to be grateful for what he had left. Yes, he might have lost the best use of his leg but he had her, his precious wife, whom Delia had tried to kill too. God, that woman, was wicked and however much he tried to hide it, Philip was terrified of her. Whatever the authorities said and thought, he knew her better than anyone. They had grown up together. They had been engaged. She had nearly killed him ... and Ruth. Even after all these years of incarceration, Philip knew she would still bear a grudge. She would never forgive him for marrying Ruth and would resent Stephen for inheriting Canleigh instead of her. That, alone, would make her mad. He would dearly like to know what she was thinking now and what she was planning to do once the prison gates slammed shut behind her and she was out in the big wide world.

* * *

The Beeches Hotel and Spa, a former stately home, was situated just outside Harrogate on the Skipton road, just a short drive from Fewston and Swinsty Reservoirs. When Lady Victoria and her husband, Alex, had discovered it four years ago, it was a crumbling wreck and hadn't been loved and cared for in a very long time. They had been staying at Canleigh for a weekend and were on their way for a drive up to the Dales when they noticed it, set back from the road with a big 'for sale' sign up at the entrance. Intrigued because the place looked empty

34

and forlorn, they stopped, parked the car, wandered around the grounds and the outside of the massive empty, crumbling, Georgian building, and fell in love. Six months later, it was theirs and cost them a small fortune in turning it into a thriving spa hotel with bookings for guests, weddings and functions for months ahead.

Not only did they own The Beeches, but clubs in Edinburgh and Cardiff, as well as their main residence and first club in Kensington. However, they both wanted to live outside of London and The Beeches was perfect for them and their family, with three floors, forty rooms, a massive function room, conference room, a restaurant, two bars, offices, and reception area. The business area covered the ground and first floor. The second was theirs, so big they could all spread out, with plenty of space for them all, unlike the cramped flat above the club in Kensington.

They had all been so happy here, with room to breathe, fabulous gardens, and beautiful countryside on their doorstep, with the added bonus of not being far from Canleigh, Ruth, Philip, Stephen and Lucy. She and Alex were horrendously busy of course but then they thrived on it and their hard work had paid off. Their businesses were booming, money was mounting in their bank accounts, even after the crippling amount they had paid to restore The Beeches to its former glory and the addition of the Spa ... and they had their family.

Having been told she couldn't have children during her first marriage to the cheating, bullying Barrie, Vicky had married Alex with little hope of ever having little ones to cherish but following a lengthy adoption process, and two years after their wedding, they were lucky enough to have siblings, 6-

year-old Jeremy and eight-year-old Suzanne, enter their lives. It had taken some getting used to, suddenly having two small, frightened little children to care for who had spent nearly six years of their short lives in one foster or care home after another and it certainly hadn't been easy, trying to make them finally feel secure and loved.

Then, to her enormous surprise and delight, Vicky discovered she was pregnant just over two years later and her happiness was complete when little Katrina was born. Their very own child. She loved Jeremy and Suzanne but could never feel the same kind of raw possessiveness and need to protect them as she did with Katrina, although she had tried hard to cover up her feelings and include the two youngsters in her newfound joy.

However, they were all growing up now and moving on. Her baby, Katrina, was twelve years old and attending Thistledown School in Harrogate. Suzanne had qualified as a hairdresser and beautician, managed to obtain a job on a cruise ship three years ago, met an Australian named Todd, had a lavish wedding at The Beeches, and was now living down under, pregnant with her first child. Vicky had been sad to see her go. Suzanne was a lovely girl, grateful for the loving home Vicky and Alex provided and not given them any problems. Indeed, she had been a huge help with Katrina when she was small, indicating that she was going to be a great mum when her time came and Vicky was looking forward to a prolonged stay in Australia once the baby was born.

Then there was Jeremy. He had been so easy when he first arrived at the age of six. He, like Suzanne, had been grateful, although wary to begin with. He had blossomed, keen to learn as he had an enquiring mind and loved to study, forever having his nose firmly in a book. It had all changed when Katrina was born and however much Vicky and Alex reassured him that they still loved him and Suzanne, he displayed jealousy of the new baby at every turn. His behaviour at school deteriorated and at home it was even worse, with temper tantrums frequent. Despairing, Vicky and Alex sent him for counselling sessions, which seemed to sort him out. He calmed down, his school reports improved and although he showed no real love for Katrina, he tolerated her.

She looked at him across the breakfast table. He was twenty now, nearly twenty-one and a good looking young man, with a well toned physique as he liked to swim and walk a lot, fairish hair, a long, thin face and cool, grey eyes. He spoke well, was confident and had a lovely, slightly effeminate manner, which had made Vicky wonder if he was gay, although a string of girlfriends since he reached puberty sent that theory out of the window … and there was Lucy. She and Jeremy were firm friends, spent a lot of time together and Vicky was positive Lucy had been in love with him since they first met as young children.

However, he had recently disappointed Vicky badly, having suddenly packed in University … which was a real puzzle. He had been doing so well, achieving great results in his A levels and obtaining a place at Oxford, choosing to read law. They had all been so proud of him and then, for some inexplicable reason he had arrived home just before Christmas, announced he wasn't going to continue with his studies and would she and Alex give him a job? They had naturally tried to talk him out of leaving Oxford but he had been adamant, stating firmly that he had decided law was not for him. His excuses didn't fool them but whatever the real reason, he wouldn't confide in them and they had to accept his decision.

However, that was of little consequence at this moment. Vicky had a far greater worry on her mind. She finished her one piece of lightly buttered toast and picked up her coffee cup. Jeremy, having finished his scrambled eggs, was glaring at Katrina, who was pulling rude faces at him as she scrambled to ram schoolbooks into her bag ready for the journey to school. Alex was helping himself to another coffee before he had to take her. It all looked and felt so normal but she didn't feel that way. She was shaking inside, tremors of fear rushing through her body. She felt sick and wished she hadn't eaten the toast ... and it was all because of blasted Delia, her elder sister, the one person in the world Vicky was terrified of.

She had felt this way for over a week now, ever since Ruth had rung with the news that Delia was about to be released. Vicky knew Ruth was just as scared. She didn't have to ask. Delia had scarred all of them badly and even though they did their best to push it to the back of their minds, it was always there and now Delia was about to regain her liberty, the fear would only intensify. Would she come back? Was she still harbouring a grudge? Would she try to hurt them all again?

Ruth tried reassuring Vicky that the authorities were confident Delia was no longer a threat as she would be taking up residence at Blairness, many miles away in the Highlands of Scotland but Vicky still felt a tremendous unease.

"You okay, darling?" asked Alex, noting her expression.

Vicky attempted a smile. "Not really. I can't get Delia out of my mind."

"Oh, is this the mad, bad Aunty Delia you don't tell us much about," queried Katrina, looking up from her school bag with interest.

"You simply have no idea how mad and bad she really is," replied Alex, looking at his wife with concern. She looked tired and drained. She had been working too hard lately and he had been away a lot, having to oversee their nightclubs so she had borne the brunt of it here. The last thing she needed right now was confirmation that Delia was about to be set free ... but then, they had all known it was coming.

"Do you think she will pay us a visit?" asked Katrina innocently.

Vicky gulped, her big brown eyes filling with tears. "God, no. She won't be allowed anywhere near us."

"Why?" queried Katrina, with eager curiosity. "She might have turned over a new leaf. After all, she has been put away for a long time. She might be a changed person and want to return to the bosom of her family."

Vicky stood up abruptly. "I have work to do ... and so do you, Jeremy. Don't be late downstairs, please."

Jeremy grimaced. He was on reception today, not one of his favourite duties. He could feel a headache coming on at the mere thought of it. "Okay," he replied with no hint of enthusiasm. "I shan't be a tick."

"You have five minutes," Vicky warned as she kissed Alex's cheek and patted Katrina on the head. "I'll see you both later. Don't forget we're all going to

Lucy's party at Canleigh tonight so make sure you're ready by seven thirty."

She left the room and crossed the hall to the bedroom she shared with Alex and headed straight to the bathroom, locking the door behind her. She gripped the sink and stared into the mirror above. Her eyes were full of fear. She hadn't smoked for years but desperately wanted a cigarette now. Her nerves were in shreds and she was finding it hard to pretend they weren't. Delia, her nemesis, would soon be free to harm people again … because she would. Vicky was damned sure of that. She tried to reason with herself, as Ruth had on the phone and Alex had when they went to bed last night, that Delia wouldn't have any reason to harm her or her family now. Her grudge, if she still possessed it, would still be with Ruth, Philip, and Stephen. There was no reason at all why Delia should want to interfere in Vicky's life again, even though she had so badly hurt her, both physically and mentally all those years ago. No. She had to pull herself together … for the sake of everyone. She had no need to fall to pieces, as she would never set eyes on her errant sister again.

CHAPTER 3

SEPTEMBER 1995

Delia stood outside the prison, looked up at the sky and breathed in the air. She could still smell stale cabbage and other unmentionable aromas but at least she was finally outside the walls and not inside. She was free and able to go where she wanted, more or less anyway. She had to have regular chinwags with a probation officer and had her first appointment at 9.00 a.m. tomorrow morning in Inverness, the nearest office to Blairness, from where she would be monitored for the next five years with a number of rules and regulations, including never going anywhere near Canleigh, Ruth, or Philip. Lucy was another matter. It was agreed if Lucy wanted a relationship with her mother, no-one would stand in her way.

She picked up her suitcase and walked across to the taxi waiting on the opposite side of the road. There was a man with a bicycle, leaning on the wall beside the vehicle. Delia took no notice. The taxi driver got out of the car, took her suitcase and flung it into the boot. Delia was just about to ease herself into the rear seat when the cyclist, who had left his bicycle by the wall, leapt in front of her brandishing a camera, shoved it in her face and clicked madly, the flash temporarily blinding her.

"Leave me alone," she screamed, pushing the camera out of the way and throwing herself into the taxi.

"Drive, man, drive," she shouted at the driver, who had quickly jumped into his seat. The car tyres screeched as they roared away, leaving the cyclist laughing on the pavement.

"Where to, lady?" asked the fat, balding man with glasses, looking at her in the rear view mirror.

"Kings Cross," replied Delia, trying to get her head back into gear. She hadn't expected bloody photographers outside the prison. No doubt her release would be all over the tabloids in the morning. She would be news again. Blast, blast, blast. She had wanted to avoid all of that. Get used to being free again. Get her life back. Return to some kind of normality.

"I need to catch the Edinburgh train. It leaves at ten so you better get your skates on."

As soon as she said which train she wanted, she knew she shouldn't have. She couldn't trust the man not to tell someone where she was headed but then, if anyone was interested in her whereabouts they would know she owned Blairness and she would have no-where else to go. At least as soon as the big castle gates were closed behind her, she would have peace and tranquillity to sort herself out and give her time to adjust and plan exactly what she was going to do and how she was going to do it.

She was lucky. The taxi driver was a kindly soul. He had seen many women emerging from Holloway over the years. Some he had known would return pretty promptly but this one ... he wasn't sure but he wouldn't be surprised. She looked fragile with her badly scarred face but she didn't fool him. He knew all about her, of course. He had recognised her immediately and remembered the whole ghastly scandal when she had been arrested for the attempted murder of her stepmother and her boyfriend at Canleigh. It had been all over the tabloids and on television for weeks. The trial had been covered thoroughly and the whole country was well informed about the doings of Lady Delia Canleigh.

On reaching Kings Cross, Delia jumped out of the car and gave the driver a ten pound note, telling him to keep the change. He removed her bag from the boot, she nodded to him and disappeared rapidly into the mass of people milling about outside the station. She walked into one entrance and hung around for a few minutes watching those around her to see if anyone was taking any interest in her. Satisfied they weren't, she walked back outside through another exit, hurried along the road and turned a corner into Platt Street. She kept walking, occasionally turning her head to see if she was being followed. After half an hour, she was positive she was on her own, in the middle of London, free as a bird, although she didn't intend to catch the train at 10.00 a.m, for which she had a ticket. If that blasted photographer outside the prison was aware she was being released today, there could be others who might guess her movements, although she had to be on the next train up to Inverness. The journey took just over eight hours if she caught the midday train, which would mean arriving just after 8.00 p.m. at the Maple Leaf guesthouse where she was booked into for the night so she wouldn't be late for her 9.00 a.m. appointment at the probation office in the morning. She could have gone straight home to Blairness but transport was a bit more sparse and unreliable in that neck of the woods and she didn't want to risk being late for her first interview with her probation officer, which could result in a swift return to Holloway.

So, she had nearly three hours to kill. She looked down at her clothes. She badly needed new ones. She headed back into the station and placed her case in a locker, first purchasing a Mars bar from W.H. Smiths to obtain some coins, having only been given ten pound notes on leaving prison. She jumped on the tube and headed for Oxford Street, feeling light-headed and dizzy with so many people pushing and shoving. It was like being in some kind of strange dream, surreal and odd, with no structure, no-one shouting and yelling at her and telling her what to do. A sense of jubilation made her grin at everyone who came close to her. She was free! No-one around her knew who she was or even cared. What a fabulous liberating feeling.

She was in need of a lot more money than was in her purse so a visit to a branch of her bank was necessary and then she could buy a few decent clothes, make-up, a wig and a pair of glasses. She found what she wanted fairly quickly. The bank, once she provided identification, were quick to provide her with a temporary cheque book and bank card so that she had enough means to kit herself out and get up to Scotland in comfort.

Oxford Street provided her with what she needed, which wasn't much really. Just a couple of pairs of jeans, new tops, and sweaters and a black leather jacket, along with boots and loafers. Everyone in the street seemed to be wearing white trainers but Delia couldn't imagine herself in a pair. They were too … white. She never did like white.

Two and half hours later she was back at Kings Cross, loaded down with carrier bags containing her purchases. She collected her suitcase and headed for the ticket office to buy a first class ticket in place of the standard one purchased via the prison authorities on her behalf before she left their care. She was becoming extremely hungry by the time she was seated on the train with her baggage stored neatly behind and above her seat. The lunch menu was highly tempting and while tucking into the best roast beef dinner she had eaten for longer than she cared to remember, accompanied by a bowl of strawberries and cream and a bottle of champagne, she watched the suburbs of London and the countryside flash by as the train headed northwards. Overcome with tiredness she closed her eyes and allowed the rhythmic sounds of the train to lull her into sleep, waking up just as the train pulled into Leeds, the worst moment of the journey. How badly she wanted to get off, jump into a taxi and roar up the drive of Canleigh. So near but yet so far. She could have cried as they pulled out of the station and headed for York but she would be back ... and if she had anything to do with it, it wouldn't be long.

Just after 8.00 p.m., the train pulled into Inverness station and Delia followed the throngs of people to the exit. Taxis were waiting outside and as she had no idea how to get to the Maple Leaf, she jumped into the first available one. Fifteen minutes later, she was alighting at the place where she would spend her first night out of prison. The woman who answered the door looked nice and homely and gave her a warm welcome, which made Delia smile. She was certain it wouldn't have been quite the same if she knew her guest was just out of prison and what she had been in for.

The room she was shown was clean and contained a single bed, which was going to be utter luxury after

45

sleeping in a prison bunk bed with someone snoring and moving about restlessly above her.

The woman left her with the information that breakfast was available from 7.00 a.m. which was perfect, providing ample time for her to arrive at the probation office on the dot.

Following the best eight hours sleep she had enjoyed for seventeen years, Delia tucked into a hearty full English breakfast. There was only one elderly couple in the dining room and as Delia had no desire to chat, they and the landlady left her alone to enjoy her food and read the novel she had purchased at Kings Cross. It was a murder mystery. How apt, she thought. Perhaps she should be starring in it.

Replete and heartened by the delicious breakfast, she paid the landlady, picked up her belongings and jumped into another taxi to take her to the probation office. Her new regime was about to begin.

* * *

Brian Hathaway wasn't sure how he felt about his employer, Lady Delia Canleigh, finally turning up at Blairness. Life had been comfortable, quiet and restful since he took up his post twelve years earlier and had been just what he needed after his long army career. After leaving Edinburgh university with a degree in geography, he had joined the Scots Guards, seeking excitement and danger and three years in, decided to try for the S.A.S. Following an exhausting and draining period of training, he was accepted and then followed a turbulent few years in the mountain troop, culminating in the Falklands War. Physically and mentally drained, he was discharged from the army in

1983, needing peace and quiet and a new perspective on life. He had found what he was seeking at Blairness, having seen the advertisement for an estate manager, and more than surprised and pleased when after a lengthy interview with Rathbones, Lady Delia's solicitors, he was appointed.

It was explained to him, in detail, that as Lady Delia wouldn't be physically present for a very long time, he would have to report regularly to Rathbones, which suited him admirably. Not to have an employer breathing down his neck was just what he needed after the strictness of army life and having grown up in the country as second son to the Earl of Glentagon, he was used to estate life and slipped easily into his role, diligent in his duties, and gaining the respect of estate staff and Rathbones.

The twelve years had slipped by quickly and he had hardly given Lady Delia a thought but that had to change now her arrival was imminent. He sincerely hoped they would get on because he didn't want to leave the estate unless absolutely necessary. He wasn't concerned about her reputation as a potential killer, having seen too much in his former career to concern himself with murderous outbursts from a disturbed woman and he could handle himself and wouldn't have anything to fear from her anyway. From all the information he had gleaned about her from Rathbones and old press cuttings he discovered in a filing cabinet in the estate office, she only threw tantrums when either Canleigh or her former boyfriend, Philip Kershaw, were involved. As both were many miles away and he knew she was banned from going anywhere near either of them, she would either totally flip or settle down when she took up residence here but if it was the former, or if they didn't get on, he would be able to obtain quality references from the solicitors and move on.

He left the attractive little tied cottage he had lived in since arriving at Blairness and called Meg, his chocolate Labrador. She was busy with her favourite pastime of ferreting beneath the bird table for any crumbs the birds had knocked to the ground but on his command, followed him to the Landrover, thick tail wagging and eyes smiling. She adored her master and as he lifted her onto the passenger seat now she was struggling with arthritis in her hips and couldn't jump in easily any longer, she gave him a big, wet lick on his face.

"Oh, Meg," he muttered, giving her a big hug. "We've had such a wonderful life here, haven't we, girl? I do hope it's not coming to an end."

He walked round to the driver's side, staring at the mountains and forests surrounding Blairness. He could just see the castle further down the valley, its turrets standing proudly against the awesome backdrop, the lake beside it, glistening in the sun. He would be terribly sad if he and Meg had to leave. He loved this estate. It had not only given him employment and a home but also the peace and tranquillity he had craved. He didn't socialise much but if he did feel the need for human contact, there were a couple of pubs in outlying villages where he could enjoy a good pint or two and spend a pleasant evening chatting with the locals, some of whom worked on the estate as gardeners, gamekeepers or maintenance staff.

His duties weren't exactly onerous as there were no shoots as on other Scottish estates and the castle wasn't open to the public so there was little need for any real security. There were several tenant farmers who mainly bred sheep and highland cattle but they were all hardworking, paid their rents on time, and gave him little cause for concern. So, his days were reasonably quiet. He had the Landrover to drive around in, a well-maintained cottage and a regular salary. His bills and expenses were small and few and far between so most of his money could be squirreled away into a high interest savings account for rainy days or his retirement. Overall, he was happy with his lot and hoped the arrival of his employer wouldn't upset the applecart.

He turned the key in the Landrover, the engine burst into life and Meg sat bolt upright by her window, eager to watch where they were going. He smiled. How many times had they done the same thing over the past few years? Please God, this woman who was about to come into their lives, wouldn't rock the boat and wouldn't give them cause to search for pastures new.

* * *

The McFrains, Angus the butler and his wife, Mary, who was the housekeeper, were wondering the same thing. They had worked at Blairness for much longer than Brian Hathaway, having been appointed by Lady Delia's father, the Duke of Canleigh. He had been a lovely man and they had enjoyed working for him on his long stays at the castle. He had almost lived here permanently at one time and it had been a real pleasure to look after him. Then he had married the lovely Ruth Barrett and she was simply delightful, always grateful for what they did, giving them lovely gifts and quietly pottering about in the room upstairs which had been turned into a studio for her painting.

49

Then there had been the child she had borne, young Lord Stephen, now the Duke of Canleigh, of course. He had been a lovely, happy baby but they had no idea what he was like now.

Lady Delia had inherited Blairness from her father on his death but apart from one brief visit, hadn't been seen in Scotland again. Neither had the rest of the family and life at the castle for the McFrains ticked quietly by. They kept the place clean and made sure it was well maintained but apart from that, had little to do as although the place was large, without anyone to look after, and with most of the rooms shut up and the furniture covered in dustsheets, they could easily manage.

However, with the impending arrival of Lady Delia to reside at Blairness on a permanent basis, they were a trifle nervous. They remembered her from her childhood, when the old Duke had brought the family up every summer. She had been a bright, enthusiastic child, eager to get out into the countryside and ride with her family and the friends they always brought with them. They remembered her laughing a lot, being boisterous, always engineering plans for trips out and if the weather was bad, games in the castle, but things would be different now. She was a hardened criminal. She had tried to kill people and could even have succeeded with Lord Richard and that Peter Percival, allegedly the old Duchess's illegitimate child and after seventeen years in prison, whatever would she be like now? They began to seriously consider retirement.

* * *

Delia arrived in Edinburgh. After her meeting with the grim faced Heather, the woman who would be monitoring her movements over the next few years, she needed to put off arriving at her final destination for a little longer ... and she craved sight of the sea. During her spell in prison, she had obtained a picture of a wide sandy beach, with sparkling azure blue water and dazzling white waves. She had hung it right next to her bunk bed and whenever she felt the ghastly prison claustrophobia, she would stare hard at the picture, imagining she was standing on that beach, listening to the crashing waves, hearing the seagulls, digging her bare toes into the warm sand and allowing the hot sun to soothe her body. It always calmed her but now she wanted to see it, in real life.

She had told Heather she was going to Edinburgh for a couple of days to shop for clothes and buy a car. Heather had looked at her over her gold-rimmed glasses.

"That's fine but I want to know which hotel you are going to stay in because I'm going to check you are actually there. Then, in a few days time, I'm going to pop over to Blairness for a chat. I shan't make an appointment. I shall just turn up."

Heather wasn't used to dealing with members of the aristocracy, who had no need to seek employment or find somewhere to live. She was a little out of her depth with Delia but was adamant her new client wasn't going to get the better of her or get away with anything if she could help it.

Delia left the probation office with a heavy heart and long list of what she could and couldn't do over the next five years of her licence. She needed to breathe. She needed wide-open spaces. She hurried back to the railway station with her baggage and caught the next train to Edinburgh, determined to buy a car at the first available opportunity. As far as she knew there was no vehicle at Blairness she could use and she badly wanted her independence back and needed to be able to get about without being noticed and at her own convenience.

The weather wasn't too bad. It actually wasn't raining and the sun was trying to make the day a little warmer. She took a taxi to Portobello and checked into the small guesthouse overlooking the beach, chosen in Heather's office and booked in her presence to shut the blasted woman up. Wearing a thick layer of make-up over her scar, the mousy coloured wig, and the glasses, she wandered down to the beach. No-one would guess she was Lady Delia Canleigh, newly released from prison. She looked just like any other nondescript woman in a thick padded jacket, meandering along, on a chilly September day.

It was quiet. The summer was over. The children were back to school and their parents back to work. One or two people were walking their dogs, letting them run in and out of the sea, chasing sticks or balls. It was good to see animals again. Perhaps she should get a dog now. It would be good to have some company in the chilly old castle she was now about to live in. It would curl up with her and help keep her warm. It was an idea. She would see if there was somewhere she could rescue one, the local RSPCA or whatever. She should consider a horse too … if she had the nerve to ride again. She would never forget Demon crashing down on top of her. How she had managed to wriggle free before his whole weight crushed her, was a mystery. Demon, her darling, darling horse. They had been as one, flying over the Canleigh acres. Would she ever experience that again with another horse? Did she want to? It was something else to think about.

She breathed in the fresh, clean air with relief. Finally, she could get the smell stale of cabbage and urine out of her nostrils. It was so good. So very good. She smiled at the scene before her, watching the waves dash in and out and finally began to relax. She had been so strung up for so many years, her body always tense, on the alert, waiting for someone in the prison to attack her. It had never happened. All the prisoners had been in awe of her. A real lady with a conviction for attempted murder and the possibility of having murdered two others. She was someone to be careful of and, apart from Crystal, they had either kept their distance or kowtowed to 'Lady D'.

Crystal. Delia smiled, wondering if she would ever see her cellmate again.

CHAPTER 4

Lucy was in a quandary and had no idea what to do. Since her birthday, her mother had sent her another three letters, all in the same vein, full of apologies and hope for a future meeting and even worse, suggesting she stay at Blairness … so they could get to know each other all over again.

So far, Lucy had ignored them all but it was becoming evident her mother wasn't going to let up and leave her alone until they met face to face and Lucy could tell her exactly how she felt about her. It had to be done. She wanted to get on with her life but this nonsense with her mother was dragging her down, making her feel depressed and low.

In fact, the whole family were living on a knife's edge since they received confirmation Delia was free and had taken up residence at Blairness. It was like waiting for a bomb to go off as they all tried to get on with their normal lives, but jumpy and anxious, especially if there was an unusual noise after dark, Philip taking to checking every downstairs window and door every night, even though Felix, the butler had already done so.

"I really don't know what to do," Lucy cried at breakfast that morning, throwing down Delia's letter onto the dining table. "Why won't she leave me alone?"

Ruth felt so sorry for Lucy and looked at her sympathetically.

"When all is said and done, darling, she is your mother. I know she has done us all terrible harm but she is human and no doubt has some deep feelings for you. She did love you very much when you were tiny," she said, remembering how Delia's eyes had lit up every time she looked at Lucy.

"Well, if she loved me now, she would leave me to get on with my life. I hate her for what she did to you … to Steppie … to me. I can still remember that dreadful day so clearly," she shuddered.

Ruth drew in a breath and looked at Philip, who was staring grimly back at her. None of them would forget it.

"I hate to say it, Lucy, but I think you need to see her," said Philip, taking a sip of his coffee. "I have a nasty feeling that if you don't, she just won't give up. Your mother has a dreadful stubborn streak and if she wants something, she is going to do her level best to get it. If she is now focusing on you, she won't stop until she receives some kind of reaction. So, the best thing to do, although I say this with complete reservation, is to meet up with her and tell her, right to her face, exactly how you feel. Then, if she persists, we can go to the authorities because she will have then gone against the terms of her licence."

Ruth nodded, seeing the wisdom of his words. She put out a hand and covered Lucy's. "Philip is right. I think you have to do this, Lucy. I am so sorry."

"I can't do it alone," Lucy whispered, her frightened eyes boring into Ruth's. "Someone will have to come with me."

Ruth gulped. She would have done anything for Lucy under normal circumstances but this was too big an ask. She really couldn't do it, not ever face Delia again. She was absolutely terrified of her and would be of no use to Lucy. Philip certainly couldn't go either. Goodness knows how Delia would react if he turned up.

"I know ... I know neither of you can come with me ... but what about Aunty Vicky?"

Ruth couldn't meet Lucy's eyes. If the girl knew what her father and Delia had done to Vicky she would never have said that but Ruth couldn't tell her. It was Vicky's secret and Ruth doubted very much if Vicky would ever want to divulge it to Lucy.

"I don't think so, darling," Ruth replied. "There was a lot of angst between Aunty Vicky and your mother ... but it might be better not to have a family member. How about Tina?"

Lucy pondered the suggestion. "Actually, Granny Ruth, that's not a bad idea. Do you think she would agree?"

"I know Tina was there that day and if it wasn't for her, I might not be here and Philip certainly wouldn't. She will have bad memories too but they won't be so deep rooted as ours and Tina is very resourceful and strong ... and she loves you. She won't like it very much but I am positive she will support you."

"I'll ask her then ... I think she's in today, isn't she?"

Ruth nodded. "Yes. We've decided to have a good check of the linen this morning. There's such a lot that can be thrown out."

"I'm so glad she decided to stay on as housekeeper after Stephen and I grew up. She was a wonderful nanny to us and the place wouldn't have seemed the same without her in it," Lucy remarked. "I suppose if Felix had been married, she wouldn't have been able to stay as his wife would probably have been the housekeeper."

Ruth grimaced at the mention of the butler who had replaced the Hardy's when they retired a couple of years ago. He hadn't been one of the best choices of staff. He was meticulous in his duties but she didn't like him, and often wished the lovely Hardy's were still butler and housekeeper. She missed them dreadfully, although they now lived in the village in a grace and favour cottage following their retirement and she saw them regularly at church and when she visited them occasionally.

"Where do you think we should meet ... Mother and I?" asked Lucy. "It certainly can't be here and I don't want to go up to Blairness."

"Somewhere in between then," said Philip, replacing his coffee cup and standing up, ready to go off to start his day at Tangles. "I would suggest a city or a large town, near to motorways, so that you can make a quick getaway."

"Philip!" warned Ruth. She knew he was scared and they both knew Lucy was, but there was no need to make it any worse.

"Sorry, darling. That was a bit stupid of me ... but we all have to remember we are dealing with Delia here ... and we all have to be extremely careful and not put ourselves into any danger if we can avoid it."

"She won't try to harm me, will she?" asked Lucy tremulously.

"No! Of course not," answered Ruth. "You are her daughter and whatever she has done, I am sure she loves you. She could never harm you. She would have absolutely nothing to gain by it anyway. You have never stood in her way or gone after something she wants. No, darling. You must get that thought out of your head immediately."

Philip moved round the table and kissed them both on the cheek. "Ruth's right, Lucy. Delia has no reason to harm you. I am sure you will be totally safe and once you have explained that you don't want anything to do with her, your mother will finally leave you alone. She has nothing to gain by pursuing you and she could end up back in prison again."

"Okay. I'll do it then. I'll talk to Tina first and then we can decide on exactly where we can meet her. Perhaps a service station on the motorway or something … where there are a lot of people about."

"That's not a bad idea," replied Ruth, standing up. She had a busy day ahead and wanted to crack on and all this talk of Delia was unsettling. "Let me know what Tina decides."

She and Philip left Lucy at the dining table, buttering another piece of toast. They walked out into the entrance hall and stood at the front door, looking out over the lawns towards the woods. It all looked so peaceful and tranquil but did little to calm their nerves.

"I'm not happy about this," said Ruth.

Philip threw an arm around her and hugged her close. "I know you're not, darling. Neither am I but if Delia isn't told, she could become a real pest. You know what she's like and the only person who can put her straight is Lucy. We will just have to pray Delia takes it on the chin and does leave Lucy alone. If she doesn't …"

"If she doesn't … I will get her sent back to prison so fast, her feet won't touch the ground," said Ruth through gritted teeth.

*　*　*

Delia was surprised to find she actually enjoyed living at Blairness, although a lot could be attributed to just having freedom after seventeen years. Being able to turn lights on and off at will, stay up late or have a lie in, have a shower in complete privacy, or even better, chill out in the bath with no-one yelling at her to get a move on and with no fear of attack. After a week of playing with the lights and walking through doors that weren't locked to her, the novelty slowly began to wear off and she started to relax and unwind.

She took to taking long walks. The weather was fine and she meandered through the countryside at leisure, occasionally straying off Blairness land. She had stopped at a couple of village pubs in the first few days but the reception she received, with polite but hostile and wary undertones, didn't contribute to a relaxing lunch and it was easier to take something with her. However, the solitude and the bracing Scottish air were gradually doing her good. The colour began to return to her cheeks after the prison pallor and she felt fitter than she had done for years.

She thought hard and long about buying a horse and a dog but was that being selfish? They would love her and she could end up letting them down. Her anger might explode one day and she might end up back in prison. Even though she felt calmer and more in control of her emotions than she had done for years, she still didn't entirely trust herself. No, she was better alone, with nothing and no-one dependent on her.

She thought about Lucy a lot … but then, she always had, guilty and remorseful for what she had done to the child. There was an awful lot to make up for … and it all rested on their coming meeting. God, she was so nervous … of seeing her child … but no, Lucy wasn't a child any longer. She was twenty-one. A grown woman with aspirations and ambitions of her own and Delia wanted to know what they were. She wanted to know her daughter, to love her, to cherish her, to atone for what she had done to her.

Delia had been elated but quite shocked when Lucy had finally agreed to meet her, assuming she wouldn't want anything to do with her. Early on in her sentence she had requested Lucy visit her in prison but Ruth and Philip had refused to allow it and after a few tantrums, which only resulted in privileges being withdrawn, Delia realised it was for the best. She didn't really want Lucy in such a place, as much as it hurt not to see her lovely little daughter.

However, Lucy could make her own decisions now and with the arrival of her letter this morning, obviously had. She had agreed to meet and Delia couldn't stop smiling. Her heart was lighter than it had been in a very long time and she wanted to jump for joy. She had grabbed her jacket, pulled on her walking boots and headed out of the castle with Lucy's letter tucked in her pocket, striding up to the top of the hill opposite Blairness, looking across at the castle and sighing with pleasure. It was beautiful. She had forgotten how much. Lucy had never seen it. What would she think of it? What would she think of her? How would their meeting go? Would it be a disaster or would it be the beginning of a completely new relationship? She was so nervous. She badly wanted it to go well. She had to get it right. She had to say the correct things or she could lose her child forever.

She pulled the letter from her jacket pocket and read it again. It was formal … no hint of love … no hint of excitement at meeting her mother after such a long time.

'Dear Mother', Lucy had written, her handwriting neat and small. 'Yes, I would like to see you, although a trip to Blairness might be a little too much for us both to begin with. I've had a look at the map and think it would be best to meet at a hotel. There's one, just off the A1 outside Edinburgh, The Bonnie Prince, which looks suitable. I can be there on Monday if that's okay with you … around 11.00 a.m?

She had just signed it 'Lucy'. Not 'love Lucy' or 'kind regards'. Just 'Lucy' … but she had said 'to begin with' which meant she was looking to forge a relationship again. It was a good sign and Delia had penned a note back quickly agreeing to be there and signing it 'with all my love'. She began to look forward to Monday with a real sense of hope in her heart.

A movement to her right, made her turn her head. The estate Landrover was meandering up the track towards her, driven by Brian Hathaway, with his gorgeous old Labrador, Meg, sitting upright by his side. Delia smiled. On the day she had finally arrived at Blairness and met Meg, she had fallen in love with her instantly. When the taxi arrived from the nearby railway station, Brian, the McFrain's and Meg had greeted her at the castle door. The atmosphere had been strained and uncomfortable with all three humans fully aware of her circumstances. Meg hadn't known or cared. All she knew was that the woman who had just arrived was making a huge fuss of her and Meg was always keen to have a new friend, who might, with a bit of luck, be carrying food.

Hathaway had introduced himself and they had arranged to meet in the estate office the next day to go over what had been done in Delia's absence and what was going to be done now that she was in situ. She had to admit, the man had been diligent and even without anyone to keep an eye on him from day to day, had kept the place in apple-pie order and the accounts were up to date and looking healthy from the rents from tenants farmers, along with a few holiday cottages dotted around the land. Even so, there wasn't room for complacency and although Delia was still a wealthy woman, her money would soon be eaten up. There were certain parts of the castle that needed urgent maintenance and it was going to be costly. She had begun to feel a frisson of excitement at the thought of being able to put all the thwarted plans she had for Canleigh into operation here. She could make the place hum, open the castle to the public, there were masses of grounds, which could be turned into a golf course, an exclusive caravan park could be hidden in the forest, many outbuildings that could be put to good use. Ideas began to form and take shape. She hadn't mentioned them to Hathaway yet, wanting to think it all through first, to decide exactly how she was going to get through the next five years of her life, still monitored and restricted by rules and regulations but it would be so good to be able to settle quietly at Blairness, live her life and hopefully have some contact with her daughter.

Hathaway pulled up when the vehicle reached her; Meg stood up, smiled a warm greeting and thumped her tail against her master behind her.

"Good morning, Your Ladyship. It's a lovely day."

Delia smiled. He was a handsome man. Five years older than her, according to his curriculum vitae, which would make him forty-nine. He was quite a bit taller than her, and she wasn't exactly tiny. He possessed a military bearing, projecting confidence with a commanding presence. His face was square, with a firm chin, a wide mouth, and a few wrinkles around his gorgeous blue eyes. His hair was dark and thick, greying slightly at the temples. For a second she wondered what it would feel like to run her fingers through it. She hadn't had a man for years and this one was single and lived alone in his little tied cottage with only Meg for company. Delia felt a stirring in the pit of her stomach and her mouth was going dry. She smiled up at him … and he smiled back.

* * *

Tina agreed to accompany Lucy to meet Delia but three days before the planned rendezvous, her mother was taken ill and she had to whiz down to Gloucester where her parents lived, to visit her in hospital.

"I'll be okay. I'll go and see Mother on my own," Lucy stated firmly at breakfast the next day.

"No. You won't," replied Ruth, breathing in deeply and squaring her shoulders. "I'll come."

"But you can't" gasped Lucy. "She tried to kill you. She might do it again."

"She won't see me. We'll drive up early, book a room and I'll stay in there … but I'll be close enough if you need me. You only have to pick up your mobile and I'll be at your side in an instant."

"And I'm coming too," said Philip, who had just entered the dining room, rested his stick against the table and sat down heavily in his chair.

"No," chorused Lucy and Ruth.

63

"Yes! I simply can't let you both go without me. I would never forgive myself if something happened to either of you and I had remained here. I need to be with you … but I certainly don't want to see her," he shuddered.

Ruth placed her hand over his. "Thank you, darling … but it goes without saying; Delia mustn't see either of us."

Philip looked at her and his voice softened. He loved her so much and would do anything to protect her. "She won't. We'll take the Range Rover just in case she expects us to turn up in a Volvo. We can drive up and stay in the hotel the night before and I suppose we had better book in under false names, just in case she tries to get sight of the register. She might guess we wouldn't allow Lucy to go on her own. See, its simple, really. Like a military operation," he tried to joke.

Lucy smiled with relief. She hadn't wanted to go up to Scotland on her own, hadn't wanted to push the two people she loved most in the world and who were in the most danger, to accompany her and this was a good solution. They would all be safe and she would know they were only yards from her should she need them.

"Thank you, Steppie, darling. That's a brilliant idea," she smiled.

* * *

The journey up to Edinburgh, even in the Range Rover, which purred along the A1 quickly and smoothly, seemed interminable. There were no hold ups, no long queues, or roadwork's but the five hours passed slowly. They were all nervous and worried and had little to say to each other. They watched the world go by, sitting in silence, thinking their own thoughts.

Ruth drove. It was too long a journey for Philip to be behind the wheel. As it was, he was uncomfortable and becoming stiff and would be glad when they finally arrived at their hotel and he could get out and walk about. They stopped at a service station to give him some relief, where they had coffee, examined items in the shop with little interest, and got back into the car. They all wanted this trip to be over with as soon as possible.

The Bonnie Prince turned out to be cheap and cheerless but would serve the purpose overnight. Lucy's room was next to theirs. They all had an early dinner and retired, supposedly to watch television or read but none of them did. Lucy lay in bed, worrying about the meeting ahead, her book unopened by her side. Ruth and Philip sat talking; unable to relax knowing Delia was going to be so close to them the next morning.

"I feel so sorry for Lucy," remarked Ruth, chewing her lower lip. "She's in a dreadful position, wanting a mother's love but wary of the mother she has ... and I bet Delia will pull out all the stops to gain her trust ... and not necessarily for the right reasons. What if ... what if she is only trying to ingratiate herself with Lucy so she can get to us?"

"Stop it, darling. Stop it," muttered Philip, pulling her close. "Lucy isn't stupid. If Delia is playacting, she'll realise it and tell us. She won't have to see Delia again and we can inform the authorities but don't let's get too ahead of ourselves. Delia's life has been turbulent to say the least but she could, just could, have turned the corner in prison. Having Lucy in her life could be all that she desires."

"You've changed your tune," Ruth said quietly. "You've never had a good word to say about Delia since she nearly killed us."

"I know and I'll never forgive her for what she's done to this family but everyone deserves a second chance ... and we have to be positive, while remaining cautious. It could just turn out okay. Lucy could regain her mother, Delia could regain her daughter, and we could all live in reasonable harmony."

Ruth gave a weak smile. "And pigs might fly."

* * *

Felix liked it when the Kershaw's were away. It didn't happen very often but when it did, it gave him ample opportunity to have a good scout through their things. Tina, the part-time housekeeper, was visiting her ill mother down in Gloucestershire so he didn't have her to worry about her and he waited for the cook and cleaning staff to finish their duties and depart for the day. They all lived in the village so with the family up in Scotland, he had the whole of Canleigh Hall to himself and he was going to make the most of it.

He made a meal in the kitchen first, delicious spaghetti bolognese with an ample dash of claret, then carried it up to the state dining room, to sit at the head of the grand oak table and enjoy a glass or two of the best Bordeaux from the cellar. He finished the bottle, held up his glass and toasted the oil paintings of the former Dukes and Duchesses of Canleigh on the walls. He giggled, wondering what they would say if they could see him now.

Stupid, arrogant lot. He was envious and jealous of the lifestyle of the aristocracy and had no time for them really. Life was damned unfair. Why had he been born to mere factory workers? Why hadn't he been someone like the present Duke, the young master Stephen? Lucky young bugger. He had inherited the whole shebang; the Hall, thousands of acres, hundreds of properties and office blocks in London and had millions in the bank ... and what did he do? Join the bloody army and risk his life. Stupid young devil. He could be idling his life away here, enjoying all the wealth his former family had built up over centuries. Felix would never understand it. If it had been him, he certainly wouldn't have signed up for years of military discipline and combat. Crazy. Just absolutely crazy.

Felix thought about the young Duke. Extremely handsome but unfortunately, straight. There would be no way Felix could encourage him to hop into his bed, which could have been proved to be most advantageous. The blasted boy had a most attractive girlfriend, Sarah Misperton-Evans. He had brought her back to Canleigh for a long weekend a few weeks ago and the whole family had fawned over her, no doubt thinking it was the wise thing to do as if she married Stephen, she would become the Duchess, and Mrs. Kershaw, the former Duchess, would be sent packing to live at Tangles with her husband. Good riddance as far as he was concerned. He couldn't stand the woman and knew the feeling was mutual. Ruth only tolerated him and their relationship was strained so he made sure she had no excuse to sack him but he was sure she wouldn't be too upset if he handed in his notice. However, in a few short years Stephen would take over the reins properly, with or without Miss Misperton-Evans. Would there still be a place for Felix here?

He emptied the bottle of wine into his glass, wondering on whether to treat himself to another but if he did, he would have a hangover and he couldn't abide hangovers ... and anyway, he wanted to get into the library and have a good old rifle through Mrs. Kershaw's drawers. He giggled. What an idea. A gay butler rifling through a former Duchess's drawers. He stood up abruptly. The wine was going to his head. He didn't have this opportunity very often and he was going to make the most of it.

He snuffed out the candles on the two Georgian candelabras in the middle of the table and left the room, walking unsteadily through to the library. He drew the curtains across the French windows and sat down heavily at the oak desk, smiling at the picture of Anne, the former Duchess of Canleigh over the fireplace, the present Duke's grandmother. She looked down at him haughtily. Snooty cow. He didn't think he would have liked her much either.

He turned to the desk, opening all three drawers on the right-hand side first. There was nothing of any great importance, mainly letters from friends and invitations, past and present. He supposed Susan Armitage, the household secretary, would have anything really important locked away in her filing cabinet in her office, in the old Duke's time apparently in the room next door to the library but after his death, moved upstairs, next to the nursery.

He tried his luck on the drawers on the left-hand side of the desk. The top one was full of pens, pencils, rubber bands and the general paraphernalia for writing. The second was empty but the third was intriguingly locked. He rummaged through the top one for a key. Nothing. He looked around the room, wondering where might be a good hiding place. He searched diligently but couldn't find it. Crafty cow. It was probably on her key ring, which she would have with her. Still, there was one other place he hadn't tried and she would never guess he would know how to get into it.

He looked at the picture of Filey Bay on the wall by the door. Behind it was the safe. He knew that because he had been in the room when Ruth Kershaw had opened it one day and stuffed some papers in. He only had to get the combination right and he would be in. It would be interesting to see what was kept in there.

He pulled the picture down and studied the combination dial. Now. What would she have used? Being a woman it was probably her birthday, Mr. Kershaw's birthday ..., or better still young Stephen's. He tried them all. Nothing worked. Who else was she close to? Lucy. It had to be her. He tried it, 100874. There was a click and the door moved. He grinned, turned the handle and opened the safe.

He didn't know what he had expected. Any valuable jewellery the family owned was stored at the bank in Leeds and now everyone used debit and credit cards these days, there probably wouldn't be any money, but to only find one big brown envelope was a bit disappointing ... and no key for the desk either.

He pulled out the envelope, franked by Rathbones of London, the family solicitors. He opened it, intrigued to find it was a copy of the final will and testament of Stephen, the Duke of Canleigh. He took it to the desk, sat down, and perused it with glee.

There were certain generous bequests to the Hardy's, the former butler and housekeeper, and Tina, who had been his nanny when Stephen was a child. Felix was furious to see there was no mention of him and as he obviously didn't count in the Duke's scheme of things, he certainly wouldn't be putting himself out for him in the future.

Then there was mention of sums of money and personal items for the Kershaws and Lady Victoria. However, the final paragraph, the most important one was to do with the all the investments, the estate and Canleigh Hall itself. In the event that the Duke didn't marry and have any issue, he was leaving it to Lucy Canleigh; lock, stock, and barrel.

Felix put his feet up on the desk and mulled the information over. That was interesting. Shouldn't Lady Delia Canleigh, Lucy's mother be next in line? Felix knew she had been in prison and what for but even so, surely she was entitled to the estate if anything happened to Stephen but then, he supposed the Duke had every right to bypass her. She was free now, of course, living up at Blairness Castle. Felix wondered what she would say if she knew Lucy was the Duke's heir. He had a feeling she wouldn't be too pleased.

CHAPTER 5

Delia reached the hotel an hour early; the butterflies in her stomach making her feel sick. This meeting with her daughter was so important and for the umpteenth time, she wondered what she was like now. She had been such a bonny, gorgeous baby, growing into an inquisitive child, so full of life, so full of questions.

Now, it was she who had the questions, wanting to know all about her daughter. She knew Lucy had done well at university, coming out with a first class degree in business but what was she going to do with it? What were her plans for the future, for a career? Then there was the question of what Lucy actually thought of her mother. Did she hate her? Did she love her? Was she ashamed of her? Questions, questions, questions. All of which Delia wanted answers to.

Delia sat in her newly acquired blue BMW in the car park and thought about the last time she had seen her daughter, by Canleigh lake. How much would Lucy be able to remember of that dreadful day?

Delia pressed her hand to her forehead and gulped. She could recall everything that happened that afternoon with clarity. It still hurt. Philip's last rejection, his admission he had asked Ruth to marry him and the rage, the uncontrollable rage as she had lashed out at him with the poker. Then, flying out of the Dower house, mounting darling Demon and forcing him to gallop towards the lake, heading straight for Ruth, that bloody, bloody woman who always stood in her way. Delia had wanted her dead. She had wanted Demon to trample her to death beneath his huge hoofs, there on the grassy bank by the lake in front of the nanny and the children. She could remember it well and she could feel it again, the jealousy, the fury, the despair.

She clasped her hands together tightly, hearing again the shot that rang out, realising what had happened and desperately scrambling to get clear before Demon fell and crushed her beneath him. She could remember little Stephen screaming at her, "what have you done to my Mummy?" She could remember staggering away, back to Canleigh Hall, wandering around the rooms, remembering her whole life there, limping down to the stables, throwing the rope over the beam, kicking the bucket away, then blackness and finally, waking up with bloody Pritchard by her side. Bloody man. If he had only been a few minutes later, it would all have been over. Her angst, her pain, her broken ambitions, her life.

But then, she wouldn't have had another chance with Lucy. She wouldn't be here, about to meet her child after seventeen long years.

She looked around the car park, wondering if Lucy had driven up or if she had come by train ... or if she was on her own or accompanied. Lucy hadn't mentioned anyone would be with her so Delia assumed she would be alone. She couldn't imagine either Ruth or Philip wanting to be here anyway ... and she was supposed to keep well away from them. No, her child was as brave as she was. She was coming on her own. The meeting might be a bit awkward at first but they would chat, remember how they had been before that dreadful day. How Delia had taught her to ride, the games they had played. Lucy would smile and they would become friends and eventually Lucy would want to move to Blairness to be with her and they would be a family again …, and they could forget all about Canleigh, Ruth, and Philip. They would have their own little paradise, up in Scotland.

* * *

"I feel sick," said Lucy, plopping onto the bed in Ruth and Philip's room. "I don't know whether or not I can do this."

Ruth sat down beside her, throwing an arm around Lucy's shoulders. "No-one is forcing you, Lucy. If you don't want to see your mother, you don't have to."

"No, you don't," agreed Philip, sitting on the chair by the window. They couldn't see the car park from there so he had no idea if Delia had arrived but as it was only five minutes before the appointed time for her to meet Lucy, she was probably downstairs now, waiting to see her daughter.

Lucy stood up and smiled grimly. "I know I don't have to but I must. It wouldn't be fair after she has travelled all this way."

"Fair!" exploded Philip. "Your mother has never been fair to anyone so I really shouldn't worry about her feelings."

"Philip," Ruth warned.

He put up a hand. "Sorry. I didn't mean to snap. Lucy, darling, you are too good to be your mother's child. Who you inherited your lovely nature from is a mystery as your father wasn't much better than Delia."

Lucy walked across and placed a hand on his shoulder. "I might have their genes but I have had your example to copy … you and Granny Ruth … and

73

Aunty Vicky and Uncle Alex. You have all kept me on the straight and narrow and shown me the way to lead my life."

Philip took her hand, squeezed it, and kissed it. "Go down there and be firm with her. Don't let her persuade you to do anything you don't want to do … and if you feel threatened or uneasy in any way, ring us immediately."

"I will," Lucy said, squeezing his hand back. She smiled woefully at Ruth. "Wish me luck."

"Oh, we do, darling. We do," said Ruth, watching with trepidation and terror in her heart as Lucy left the room.

* * *

Delia examined herself in the rear view mirror. It was just as well Barrie, Lucy's wayward father, had died, crashing his car into a tree, rounding a bend at full speed on the Canleigh drive after their furious row. If he had survived, his life wouldn't have been worth living after what he had done to her. Even after a number of operations following her fall onto broken glass when he hit her across her bedroom at Canleigh, her face would never be the same. Plastic surgery had moved on in the time she had been in Holloway and she could afford to undergo more operations but more surgery wasn't something she wanted to pursue at the moment. Even though the sight of the scar still made her angry, she had come to accept it now. It was part of her and she did forget about it most of the time. Once it was covered up by make-up, it wasn't that noticeable and she had learned to live with it, telling herself that if it offended others, it was their problem and not hers.

She looked at the wig and glasses on the seat beside her and deliberated about wearing them. She donned both whenever leaving the estate as there had been so much press interest in the days following her release and she didn't want anyone knowing her business and tracking her movements. Heather, her probation officer, had been told about the meeting with Lucy today as it was part of the rules that any contact with her daughter was to be recorded and she also had to report back tomorrow to tell Heather how it went. Apart from Heather, no-one else knew where she was at this moment, bar Lucy, and no doubt the Canleigh family, who were probably awaiting the outcome of this meeting with bated breath.

Deciding not to wear the wig and glasses as Lucy might not recognise her, she got out of the car and adjusted her clothing. She hadn't known what to put on. She didn't want to dress up and bring attention to herself and she didn't want to appear too laid back for the first meeting with her daughter for seventeen years. In the end, she had plumped for black trousers and sling back shoes with a cream blouse. She looked smart but wouldn't stand out in a crowd.

She locked the car and looked around the car park. It was full of cars and she wondered which one Lucy might have driven up in.

Bracing herself, she walked towards the gleaming glass doors of the hotel and into reception. People were milling about, heading for lifts, the stairs, talking on their mobiles, or paying their bills. The enticing aroma of bacon and eggs and coffee wafted out from the dining room. Delia's tummy rumbled. She hadn't been able to touch breakfast this morning but could kill for a coffee.

Nervously she walked into the lounge next to the dining room and studied the people sitting on leather sofas. There were a number of businessmen talking animatedly and shuffling papers and a few elderly couples sat reading newspapers and drinking coffee. A young couple, looking tired and frazzled, endeavoured to keep their two small infants quiet with juice and cake. There was no-one who could be Lucy. Delia's heart turned over. Had she driven all this way only to have to return to Blairness without seeing and talking to the one person she might be able to love again?

"Mum?" said a voice behind her.

Delia turned quickly, virtually colliding with the young woman standing behind her. For a few moments, she was speechless as she stared at the daughter she had longed to see. Lucy was beautiful. Exactly the same height as Delia, fair hair bouncing on her shoulders, clear young skin, and bright blue eyes, not as stunningly gorgeous as Brian's but certainly arresting. Dressed in designer jeans, trainers, a patterned blue top and a black leather jacket, there didn't appear to be an ounce of fat on her. She looked simply stunning. A daughter to be proud of.

Delia smiled warmly. She wanted to embrace Lucy but thought better of it. The girl looked worried and tense and that was to be expected.

Delia took a deep breath. "Lucy, darling. You look amazing. Let's get some coffee and have a good old chinwag. We have such a lot of catching up to do."

* * *

"Just look at you," smiled Delia, looking her beautiful daughter up and down as they waited for the coffee. "You are a real stunner, that's for sure."

Lucy wriggled uncomfortably on the sofa beside the window in the lounge. She hated the scrutiny her mother was giving her and she was annoyed with herself. She had wanted to march down to the bar and tell her mother in no uncertain terms that she never wanted to set eyes on her again but somehow the words wouldn't come. She felt almost tongue-tied now the moment was here and couldn't think what to say.

The coffee Delia had ordered was brought over by a pale-faced waitress, who didn't even bother to smile.

Delia dropped five lumps of sugar from the sugar bowl into hers and stirred it, amused by the surprise on Lucy's face.

"Habit now, darling. Prison coffee is simply ghastly without plenty of sugar to hide the foul taste."

Lucy wriggled again. She supposed there was no point in trying to ignore the fact that her mother had been in prison and not just away somewhere like other mothers ... on business or gadding about. No, trust her to have a mother who had spent a good part of her life in the care of Her Majesty.

"Now, darling. Tell me about yourself. What have you been up to? I want to know all about you. I know you did well with your A levels and achieved a first in business."

"How ... how did you know that," gasped Lucy, unaware that Delia had been keeping tabs on her.

Delia grinned. "Rathbones. They have been looking after my affairs, as well as Canleigh's, for … for a very long time. I had to have regular contact with them because of Blairness so I asked for regular updates on your progress at the same time."

"I see," said Lucy, taken aback. She hadn't thought her mother was interested.

"Now, darling," Delia continued eagerly. "What do you intend to do with your life now you are so well qualified … and is there any way I can help you achieve what you want?"

Lucy ignored the last bit. She didn't want her mother's help but she actually found she felt a little sorry for her. Delia looked genuinely interested and eager for information and Lucy didn't like to hurt anyone's feelings if she could help it.

"I'm working for Aunty Vicky."

Delia stiffened. "What! In a nightclub?"

Lucy managed a faint smile. "No. She and Uncle Alex have bought The Beeches just outside Harrogate. It's incredibly beautiful … and a bit creepy at night … but I love it. Aunt Vicky has done a tremendous job with it. It's a listed building but she's managed to renovate and redecorate and add a spa without causing any friction with the authorities and it's stunning … and exceedingly busy."

"I see," said Delia thoughtfully, staring hard at Lucy. As the girl spoke, she could see the likeness to Barrie, the girl's father, Vicky's former husband. She thought about Vicky, the sister she had so wronged all those years ago. How did she feel about Lucy? She must like her to offer her a job at her hotel so couldn't bear any grudges but then Vicky wasn't that kind of person. She was kind and gentle, even though she was obviously a damned good businesswoman.

"So what exactly will you be doing?"

"*Am* doing ... as I want a career in hotel management, I've been working there for a while ... on the days I didn't have to attend Uni. I'm a trainee manager as the best way to learn is to start at the bottom and work up. I waitress, serve behind the bar, clean bedrooms as well as helping in the office or on reception ... and since Jeremy packed in Oxford, he's doing the same."

"Who's Jeremy?"

"He's Aunt Vicky and Uncle Alex's adopted son. He also has an older sister, Suzanne who is living in Australia, is married and pregnant ... and then Aunty Vicky had Katrina. She's twelve now."

"Oh. What you mean Katrina is actually Vicky's child? I didn't think she could have children."

"Yes. She's a bit of a handful though." Lucy managed a wry smile. "I've heard them say she's a bit like you were."

"God! I hope not, for her sake. Poor child! Rathbones only kept me up to date with your life. I didn't know about all these children. How long ago did Vicky and Alex adopt?"

"Years ago. When I was little. Jeremy is a few months younger than I am and Suzanne is a couple of years older.

"Do I detect a romance with this Jeremy?" asked Delia with a grin. It was the way Lucy said his name and smiled almost secretively that had given her away.

Lucy blushed and took a sip of her coffee. She had adored Jeremy since they were very young but was never quite sure if her feelings were reciprocated. Sometimes he was attentive, at others he could be cold ... almost distant but when he did turn his attention full on her, she felt like a princess. She loved him. She knew she did. All she had to do was make him love her and now they were working together, seeing each other every day, it could become a possibility. She would do anything for him and eventually he would see that they just had to be together ... but she really didn't want to talk about this with her mother, who was a stranger to her. If she wanted to discuss it with anyone, it would be Ruth, whom Lucy adored and trusted implicitly.

Delia drank her coffee, sat back on the sofa and stared at Lucy. "That all sounds great ... having a career in hotel management but are you due any holiday at all?"

"I'm not sure," replied Lucy tentatively, worried as to where the question was leading.

"In that case, can I make a suggestion? We hardly know each other, darling ... and I genuinely want to try to make it up to you for all those years you have been without me ... will you, will you consider coming to stay with me at Blairness if you can get some time off? Please. Just for a few days and if you hate it, you can leave but I think we need to try to repair our relationship. I don't suppose for one moment we will ever be a normal mother and daughter but we can try. I can try. Please, Lucy. What do you think? Will you give me a chance?"

Now was the time. Now was the time to stand up and say straight out that she wanted nothing more to do with this pleading woman but there was something about her and Lucy was torn. She could remember how Delia had cuddled her as a child, how she had helped teach her to ride, how she had giggled with her, played with her. Until that moment, Lucy hadn't wanted to admit how much she had missed having her own mother, even after all those bedtime tears when she was little. Ruth was an absolute darling but when all was said and done, she wasn't her mother and whatever she had done, this woman was ... and she looked and sounded genuinely interested in a proper relationship. All the determination Lucy had felt for years slipped away. Perhaps she did want a relationship with her mother but once she said so, there was no going back, and the decision was going to hurt and worry Ruth and Philip, the two people she most loved in the world. She didn't want to upset them. She didn't want them to be frightened ... either for themselves or for her. She was torn but felt compelled to be true to her own wishes. She opened her mouth and shut it again. She looked around the room. Finally, she looked at Delia.

"Yes," she said.

CHAPTER 6

Crystal had first met Delia in the library at Holloway, both women having discovered reading was a great form of escapism from their surroundings.

"This one is good," said Crystal one morning, handing Delia a big, fat book with a woman on a horse on the cover. "Kept me riveted from the first page. Wouldn't mind reading some more of hers but can't seem to find any."

"Thanks," said Delia, taking the book. The woman and the horse could have been her and Demon. Her heart had missed a beat. More than anything in the world, she would have liked to be on his back, tearing madly across the countryside. Not holed up in bloody prison for years.

Although they were on different wings, Crystal and Delia often bumped into each other in the library and occasionally saw each other in the exercise yard. Not exactly becoming friends, they found they shared a love of the countryside and history and gradually grew close and sought each other out when the opportunity arose.

The prison, like all others, was badly overcrowded and it had been hard to find someone to share a cell with Lady D, which wouldn't cause massive trouble, and the Governor had been delighted when it was reported to her that Delia had finally become pally with someone who could reside with her and not cause a major problem. Crystal was duly moved in, enjoying the step up in status as companion to the aristocratic Lady D. She was due for release a few weeks prior to Delia and seeing a pathway to a much better life opening up to her, went to great lengths to explain to Delia, now she had a captive audience, how well qualified she was to assist her at Blairness and would love a job there at some point in the future. To her frustration, Delia never responded.

Crystal was disappointed and desperate. She didn't want to leave prison and have to take just any old job. She wanted one with status and preferably with a decent salary and accommodation thrown in ... and she had all the skills Delia could possibly need. After leaving school, Crystal had spent years at college, honing her skills to be the best P.A she could and hadn't been able to believe her luck when, straight after gaining some pretty impressive qualifications, she bagged a job as assistant to the P.A. for Lord and Lady Salis at Salis Hall in Norfolk, not far from Norwich where she had grown up.

She had loved that job, worked hard and steadily to gain more qualifications and took elocution lessons to disguise her regional accent to gain the respect of her employers and the team she was working with. When the P.A left to have a baby, she had presumed it would be a natural progression for her to be promoted but had been hugely disappointed. Lord and Lady Salis passed her over and appointed a thin-lipped woman, called Elizabeth, who had even more of a plumy accent than they did. Crystal was devastated, jealous, and full of resentment.

Then she had met the charismatic Roy Parker. He had waltzed into her office one rainy afternoon, offering the skills of his company to erect marquees for outside events. He had smiled, his eyes boring into hers, and when he spoke, his voice was like dark velvet. Crystal had never believed in love at first sight until that moment. She had taken the business card he had offered her and smiled back. He had asked her out for dinner that evening and she went home that night, deeply in love.

It had proved to be the worst encounter in her life, although she didn't realise it at the time. He had worked his charms on her well and even presented her with a diamond engagement ring. The romance had lasted all of three months and then, once he was positive he had ensnared her and she would do anything he asked, he put forward his plan to rob the house. Crystal had baulked at the idea at first, terrified they would be caught but the passion she felt for Roy, along with the resentment she felt towards her employers, won her over.

The plan had worked to begin with. She had given him the keys to the basement and turned off the alarms so he and his cronies could gain entry to the house and steal the jade and the two valuable Rembrandts. However, they hadn't planned on one of the gamekeepers being active in the middle of the night, noticing there was activity near to the house and calling the police. The black van the thieves had hired to cart their loot away was stopped by the police at the main gates to the estate and they were immediately arrested. Detectives had wanted to know how the men had gained entry to the house and Roy blabbed. Crystal was arrested in the early hours of the morning and later sentenced to four years for conspiracy. It became apparent in court a few weeks later that she had been neatly duped when Roy ignored her, making it quite plain he had no interest in her whatsoever. He had just used her to gain entry to the inner workings of the estate and she felt thoroughly stupid, humiliated, and angry that her career for the aristocracy was over … at least she thought it had been. Meeting Lady Delia Canleigh in prison was going to be the way back in and if Lady Delia didn't play ball, then she was in for a nasty shock.

Delia was released two weeks ahead of Crystal and even though she rang Blairness on a number of occasions, Crystal was repeatedly told Her Ladyship was too busy to take her call. By the time Crystal left prison, she still hadn't managed a conversation with Delia and no choice but to take up the only job offer the probation service had helped her obtain, working as a secretary in Norwich. It was with an engineering firm and she was bored to tears but as no other employer was keen to take her on, and she had to eat, pay her bills and have a roof over her head, she had to remain.

She heartily disliked the sales team she was working for; three brash young men who seemed to think it was hilarious when they learned their new secretary with a plumy accent was an ex-con. Crystal had no idea how they found out. Apart from the managing director and the human resources woman, no-one should have known as her time in prison was supposed to be completely confidential but somehow it got out and Crystal had to learn to deal with the constant ribbing. With that and the sheer boredom of typing long, tedious sales reports about inanimate machines, it was fast becoming one of the worst jobs she could ever imagine. Most evenings, after another long eight-hour day, she drifted back to her tiny bed-sit above an off-licence and wept. She wept because of her job, she wept because she was lonely and she wept because she actually missed Delia.

She went to the library and took out books about Scotland, the Highlands, and its castles, thrilled to discover any that mentioned Blairness. She poured over the pictures. It was a rambling old place, centuries old and looked amazing and she wanted nothing more than to work there, to work for Delia and she was going to focus on it. She was going to get there. She bought a writing pad and pinched a pen from work. She was going to write Delia a letter and Delia had better respond.

* * *

Jeremy sat by the open sash windows in his second storey bedroom overlooking the vast back garden of The Beeches. He flicked the ash from his cigarette outside, hoping it wouldn't catch anyone below. His mother would have a fit if she knew he was smoking so he daren't have an ashtray in his room. He rarely smoked up here anyway. It was too easy to be caught if she should come up. She would smell it right away. But this morning he felt defiant.

In half an hour, he would have to go down, present himself at the reception desk, and spend the next eight hours having to smile and be polite to anyone who came his way. It was more tedious and boring then he ever thought it would be and he was beginning to hate it. He would have much preferred to be involved in the nightclubs his mother and father owned across the country and have a bit of excitement but she, that woman who pretended to be his mother but wasn't really, not by blood anyway, refused.

"You're not mature enough yet,' she had said firmly. "When you are older, maybe, but for now, if you want to be involved in the business, you need to learn the ropes at The Beeches first ... and stay here in Harrogate, where I can keep an eye on you."

This was nine months ago, when he had jacked in his degree course in law at Oxford just before Christmas and returned to Harrogate unexpectedly. Vicky had been furious but Alex hadn't been surprised, although neither knew the real reason he had returned home and he hoped they would never find out. He still wasn't sure how he felt about what had happened. He was utterly confused and couldn't explain it to himself, let alone to his parents.

It was all Johnson's fault, of course. Jeremy hadn't wanted to go to that blasted party along the Cowley road. He had been suffering badly from a terrific hangover from the lunchtime session in the Mitre, from where he and his two best friends, Walters and Johnson, had been slung out after a drinking session that lasted for two hours. They then returned to their rooms to continue with the aid of ten bottles of Beaujolais, Johnson acquired when he did the Beaujolais run in France a few months before. They had all passed out but Johnson rallied in the early evening and harassed him into attending a party he had heard of where some female he was pursuing was going to be.

"Go on your own," Jeremy had groaned from the comfort of the sofa where he was nursing his sore head in the duck down cushions. "Leave me to die."

"I can't go on my own. I don't know anyone else there apart from Sarah and I shall feel a right Nellie if she decides not to go."

"Well, come back here then if she's not there."

"No. You have to come. I'll help you with your next assignments if you do," Johnson had urged.

That did the trick. Jeremy had been struggling of late and needed as much help as he could get.

He crawled into the bathroom and after a shower, felt a little better and after another glass of Beaujolais, felt ready to party the night away. The hair of the dog definitely worked.

Walters declined to come. He had taken himself off to bed with a pile of aspirins and refused to join them so Jeremy and Johnson weaved down the stairs from their rooms and out into the night to join the throngs of people enjoying the nightlife of Oxford. They didn't have far to go and they staggered along the pavements, drinking freely from another bottle of Beaujolais Johnson had brought with him. It kept them warm and happy and they joked, sang their way up the High Street on to the Cowley road, and then turned left into a road full of Victorian terraced houses. It was obvious where the party was. The noise of the music penetrated the night air and even though it was freezing, people sat outside on the pavement and in the small front garden, drinking, smoking, and talking loudly to make themselves heard above the music.

Sarah wasn't there, which was a huge disappointment for Johnson but he consoled himself with a female called Veronica and disappeared into a bedroom with her. Jeremy was left to find a drink and someone to talk to. He knew a few people from college but one person he certainly didn't want to bump into was in the kitchen, watching him carefully, his eyes never leaving Jeremy's face. Jeremy had been avoiding the youth for months. He made him feel distinctly uncomfortable and uneasy and he had no real idea why. They never spoke but whenever their paths crossed, he would stare relentlessly at Jeremy, which was positively disturbing.

Jeremy grabbed a bottle of beer from the table in the kitchen and turned to leave, avoiding the boy's eyes and was astounded when he made a quick movement and stood in front of him, preventing him leaving the room.

"Hello," the young man purred, his chestnut coloured eyes boring into Jeremy's. His voice was vaguely feminine, his skin was soft and moisturised, and his lips were full. "My name is Matthew. What's yours?"

* * *

Vicky was busy in her office at The Beeches. She glanced at her gold Cartier watch and sighed. It was 11.45 am. and through the glass door of her office, she could see the reception desk and that Gillian, the head receptionist was the only one on duty. Jeremy, who was supposed to have relieved her at 11.30 a.m., was nowhere to be seen, as usual. He was always late and it wasn't fair to the others who couldn't leave their posts until he made an appearance.

Just as her hand hovered over the telephone to ring his room, the lift doors opened and he wandered out, a look of vagueness on his face. He certainly didn't look alert and responsive to all about him, as she wanted him to be.

Vicky sighed again and turned back to the bookings sheet she had been studying. Business was good and getting better by the day and she was immensely pleased with what she and Alex had achieved with the hotel. The place had been quite decrepit when they purchased it but with their hard work and a hell of a lot of money, they had achieved something of which they could be immensely proud. It was becoming a top venue in the Harrogate area, rivalling all the other old, established hotels, and really giving them a run for their money. In fact, all their businesses were doing well. Every nightclub they had opened was booming. They seemed to have the formula just right and altogether were making pots of money.

She took a sip of the coffee on her desk and thought about what a fantastic team she and Alex were. It was a shame it wasn't quite the same with their family.

She had no concern for Suzanne. She was happy and settled in Australia, eagerly awaiting the arrival of her first child and Vicky was really looking forward to the day when she could visit. It was a pity it hadn't been so easy with Jeremy, seeing he had the same blood in his veins as Suzanne ... but then did he?

Lucy and Alex hadn't been given many details about the children's real parents when they adopted them, only that their mother lived in London, was a prostitute by trade and had dumped the children with social services when Jeremy was a tiny baby and Suzanne only two years old. Their father had apparently left the family home when Jeremy was born and hadn't been traced. Neither of the children had shown any interest in searching for their parents, although Jeremy had mentioned his mother once or twice lately, which was a little unsettling and Vicky did hope that he wasn't going to try to contact the woman and open a can of worms. She had enough problems at the moment helping him sort out his working life after his sudden departure from Oxford.

She had been puzzling for months as to why he suddenly jacked in his studies and returned to Harrogate, requesting a job in one of their nightclubs, preferably the one in London.

"But why?" Vicky had asked. "Why chuck it all in? I thought it was what you wanted ... a good degree, followed by a good career ... not look after drunks in a nightclub!"

He hadn't been able to come up with a good explanation and stuck to his guns. He wanted a job in a nightclub and nothing else would do. She had refused, naturally. She didn't want him hundreds of miles away in London. He was still young and easily influenced. Working in a nightclub was only going to bring him in touch with the wrong sort of people at this stage of his life. Although he was an intelligent lad, he wasn't mature enough to keep himself out of trouble ... and she wanted more for him than that. So, she and Alex insisted that if Jeremy wanted their help, he would have to remain in Harrogate, work at The Beeches, and learn the hotel trade from the bottom up. At some point in the future, he could become involved in the nightclubs and then one day, if he proved himself, and they wanted to take a back seat, he could be in a position to manage them all as Suzanne was settled with her life and Katrina had no desire to become involved. All she wanted was the money.

He reluctantly promised to give it a go but Vicky knew his heart wasn't in it. He didn't seem to be able to relate to the clientele, looking ill at ease and uncomfortable when he had to interact with them. He had no drive and no passion for the industry and she was worried about him. He had taken to going out on his nights off, which was fine and was to be expected from a twenty-year old but he would never say where he was going or who with. He was secretive and she didn't like it. He never brought friends back to the hotel, seemed to have lost touch with those he had made at school and the only person he openly spent any leisure time with was Lucy, which also made Vicky uneasy.

Ever since Jeremy had joined the family at six years old and Lucy was just a few months older, she had tagged around after him when they had a family get together, listening avidly to his every word, and gazing up at him with adoration. He, in turn, had appeared to return her devotion, although not quite so intensely, but while it wasn't a problem when they were small, Vicky had a nasty suspicion it was going to be now they were adults with Lucy also learning the hotel trade.

Lucy was ambitious. She had the passion and the drive to do well and would probably leave Jeremy standing and unable to keep up with her. She would also be a very wealthy woman at some point in her life with Delia owning Blairness, as no doubt Delia would bequeath it to her, which was probably attracting Jeremy for all the wrong reasons.

As much as she loved Jeremy, Vicky just knew he wasn't the right man for Lucy. He was floundering, secretive and becoming a liar and although he made a big show of being fond of Lucy, Vicky was detecting something else, something she had suspected for a number of years. She was sure he was gay and she was becoming positive that whatever made him leave Oxford so suddenly had something to do with a man. It annoyed her. If he were gay, she and Alex would be fine with it. They had gay patrons and gay friends. It wouldn't matter a hoot to them if Jeremy had no interest in females. She considered asking him outright but decided against it. It was his business and if he wanted her to know, he would tell her ... but she worried about Lucy. The girl was besotted with him and he should be straight with her and not lead her on.

Vicky sighed, finished her coffee, which was now cold, and glanced at the silver framed photograph of her three children on her desk.

Jeremy and Suzanne were smiling, their arms on each other's shoulders. Katrina stood in the middle, her hands on her hips, pouting and posing, pretending she was a famous film star. Since reaching puberty, she had started to play up more than normal. She was a bossy young madam and Vicky had to correct her on more than one occasion when she heard her with her friends, telling them what they should and shouldn't do.

"You won't have any friends left at this rate," Vicky repeated. "You really will have to learn to watch your tongue, young lady." Katrina listened and appeared to be contrite but it wasn't long before she was at it again, leaving Vicky wondering what on earth she was going to be like as she grew to adulthood. It was probably her fault. Alex was always telling her that she indulged Katrina too much. The girl had to have the best of everything, along with an en-suite bedroom. Jeremy and Suzanne, before she left home, had to share a bathroom. Thistledown School was more upmarket and expensive than the two private schools Jeremy and Suzanne had attended in London. Katrina enjoyed far more extra curricula activities than they had. She went riding, had ballet lessons, violin lessons, and her latest craze, acting lessons; insisting she was going to be the next

Catherine Zeta Jones, as she avidly watched 'The Darling Buds of May' on television.

Naturally, Suzanne and Jeremy had their own interests and were encouraged to follow them but Kristina always pushed herself to the fore, leaving no-one in any doubt that she was the important one ... she was their real child ... and had certainly made it clear to Jeremy a few months ago.

Vicky had been about to enter the family lounge one evening when she heard her daughter's remarks. Katrina and Jeremy were sitting on the sofa with their backs to her, arguing over what to watch on television. Katrina had the remote in her hand and a defiant tone in her voice.

"Remember who you are," she had said boldly, "the *adopted* child ... while I am the *wanted* one ... the *important* one ... the one who will inherit absolutely everything ... all the businesses, all the money. You are a nobody, Jeremy ... a failure ... a joke ... you can't even finish your college course ... and look what you are now ... just a good for nothing dogsbody in Mummy and Daddy's hotel. So, if you want to see your stupid silly gardening programme you will have to go to your room. 'Darling Buds of May' is on now and I'm going to watch it."

Vicky was shocked and aghast that her baby could behave so horribly, feeling sadness for Jeremy and annoyance with her daughter. As soon as Jeremy had sullenly wandered off to his room to see his programme on his smaller television, she headed straight into the lounge, ripped the remote from Katrina's hand, and pressed the off button. She then rounded on her daughter.

"You will never … never speak to Jeremy like that again, Katrina. I love Jeremy as much as I love you and it was a horrid, unkind thing for you to say."

"No, it wasn't. It's true. Don't pretend, Mummy. I know you love me best."

"Katrina!"

"Mummy! You do, you do. You have to. I love you much more than Jeremy and Suzanne ever could. They have their own mummy somewhere, so they have her … and they have you. It's not fair. I only have you." With that, she promptly burst into tears, cleverly reducing Vicky's anger, as she knew she would. She could wind her mother around her little finger easily.

After a final warning and a demand that Katrina apologise to Jeremy when 'Darling Buds of May' was finished, Vicky had relented, allowed her to switch the television on again and left her to it, intending to go straight to see Jeremy herself to apologise for Katrina's behaviour but diverted by a call on her mobile, the gesture was forgotten.

Vicky had no idea if Katrina had ever apologised to Jeremy. She had been so busy she forgot to ask but Katrina, her beautiful dark haired, attractive daughter, was becoming impossible, demanding more and more time and attention as she pursued her drama ambitions, taking the lead role in school productions and insisting she wanted to go to Rada once her A levels were behind her. She was certainly a demanding youngster and if she did achieve her ambitions in the acting world and became a star, she would probably prove to be impossible.

She also reminded Vicky uneasily of the young Delia. She had been horrendously bossy too, although her focus had been on Canleigh and Philip ... and look how that had turned out.

Thinking about Delia, Lucy remembered, with a nasty jolt, that the meeting they had all been dreading was today. She looked at her watch. It was just past midday. Lucy would be with Delia now, up in Scotland, and poor Ruth and Philip would be holed up in a hotel bedroom, worrying and waiting for the outcome. Vicky didn't envy them. Any contact with Delia, however remote, always led to disaster and misery. She fervently hoped Lucy would stick to her guns, inform Delia she wanted nothing more to do with her, and that would be the end of that but in her heart of hearts, she guessed it wouldn't be. Dealing with Delia was never simple and would probably be a dammed sight worse now that she had been living with the dregs of society for seventeen years. Goodness knows what other evil habits or desires she would have picked up. Vicky shuddered and looked at the tempting vodka bottle on the drinks tray in the corner of her office. Delia was making her want to drink again and she hadn't even set eyes on the blasted woman yet.

CHAPTER 7

Delia drove back to Blairness, unable to keep the smile off her face. The meeting with her beautiful daughter had gone far better than she could have imagined. Lucy had agreed to come and visit for a few days and that was a good start.

It was a two-hour drive back to Blairness but Delia didn't mind. She was happier than she had been for a very long time. Her daughter wanted a relationship with her, she had a beautiful home to live in and she was feeling a stirring of interest for the estate and how it could be improved. She had money in the bank even though it could soon be soaked up by Blairness if she wasn't careful so she had to find ways of making the estate more profitable and had to concentrate on that and put any hankering for Canleigh to the back of her mind. There was an alternative way to live her life now and the anger she had been harbouring for so long towards Ruth, Philip and the bloody Stephen, needn't be central to her very being. She could have a decent life up here in Scotland and finally put the past behind her. Lucy could help her … Brian Hathaway could help her.

Delia grinned. Her estate manager was certainly rather delicious, seemingly content to live on his own with his gorgeous old dog. Perhaps she should focus her attentions on him for a while although it probably wouldn't be wise. He was a damned good estate manager and it would be crazy to lose him if they fell out due to a sexual encounter but then … her eyes sparkled. When hadn't she lived dangerously? She knew he was interested in her. The vibes were all there from the sidelong glances he gave her when he thought she wasn't looking, how his eyes followed her, watching her movements. Yes, it probably wouldn't take much to get him into her bed.

As she swung the car through the open gates to Blairness estate and headed towards the castle, her heart was light. It was when she walked through the front door minutes later and saw the letter on the tray in the entrance hall her spirits plummeted. She had known it would come. Trying to avoid Crystal on the telephone was only delaying matters and she was going to have to deal with the blasted woman.

* * *

Ruth was horrified. Lucy wanted to go and stay with Delia. She couldn't believe it. Lucy had come up to Scotland, determined she was going to tell Delia she didn't want anything to do with her and exactly the opposite had happened. What the hell had Delia said to make Lucy change her mind?

"You can't," she whispered, her eyes wide with shock. "Please Lucy. Don't do it. Your mother is a dangerous woman. She simply isn't to be trusted. You know what she did to Philip ... and to me ... you witnessed that. She could so easily have killed us both. She's simply not stable."

They were all in the room Ruth and Philip had booked at the hotel. Philip was standing by the window, leaning on his walking stick with a glum look on his face. Ruth sat on the bed nursing a glass of brandy. There had only been a miniature bottle in the mini-bar. She could have done with an extra large one.

Lucy sat beside Ruth, holding her hand. "I am so sorry, Granny Ruth. I know how you both feel about Mother. Of course I do but I have to do this."

"But you said ... you have always said ..."

"I know but actually seeing her, talking to her, I hate to say this but I realised I still love her. She is my mother whatever she has done, and I need to find out whether we can actually have a decent relationship. I've said I'll spend a few days with her at Blairness and I will. If it all goes wrong, then of course, that will be that and I will never see her again. I promise."

"But ... but what if it doesn't go wrong. What if you hit it off?" asked Ruth tremulously. She was feeling so sick. Damn Delia. She was going to worm her way back into their lives. She just knew it ... and it was all going to end in disaster for them all. Delia wouldn't just be content to have a relationship with Lucy. She would lurk on the fringe of their lives, like a hovering eagle, waiting for the perfect moment to strike and kill her prey. Ruth had so hoped this meeting today would dash any hopes Delia had of re-entering their lives. She had banked on it. But she had been too complacent. Delia had triumphed. She must be utterly jubilant she had won her daughter over so easily. What else had the dratted woman got planned? Ruth's heart flipped over. Her hands were shaking and she felt so cold. So very cold, and she was absolutely and utterly terrified of what the future had in store.

* * *

They journeyed back to Canleigh in silence. Ruth drove, her eyes fixed on the road ahead, willing the miles to disappear behind them, wanting more than anything to be in her own bed with the covers over her face to shut out the horror of Delia re-entering their lives. She didn't know whether she could live with the fear. She was desperately scared for herself but what was it going to do to Philip? He had battled his way back to recovery from the awful bashing Delia had given him but he still had the occasional nightmare, when he would wake, shaking, sweating, and hitting out. He had slapped her hard in the face one night when she had been dead asleep. She would never forget the shock of being woken up in such a way. Philip had been traumatised that he could have done that to her and wanted to sleep in separate rooms in case he should do her some real injury. She had soon knocked that decision on the head.

"I love you, Philip. I don't want you to spend every night in another room. I want you beside me, cuddling me, loving me. It's only happened once. It might never happen again. No. You are remaining in this bedroom and that's that, darling," she had said with determination.

He had smiled, his lovely whimsical smile and she had loved him even more. He was so caring of her. She was a very lucky woman to have found wonderful Charles and then Philip. The only fly in the ointment in both relationships had been dratted Delia. It had been so peaceful for the last seventeen years, not having to worry about the awful woman, even though they had all known she would be released at some point and then they would all have to watch their backs, whatever rules and regulations the authorities put in place. Delia was devious and cunning and if she wanted to hurt them, hurt them she would. They were safe no longer.

* * *

Lucy sat in the backseat and felt more confused than she had ever done in her life. She twiddled with her long fair hair, twisting it round and round with her forefinger, something she always did when she was worried.

She couldn't believe she had gone up to Edinburgh with every intention of telling her mother to leave her alone and instead, ended up agreeing to spend a few days with her in two weeks time. She felt deeply upset she was hurting and worrying Granny Ruth and Steppie so badly. They had both been so good to her and she loved them deeply. They had been fantastic substitute parents and she would always be so grateful to them and hated upsetting them. But it had to be done. She could remember all the pain of missing her mother when she was little, all the crying under the pillows every night. They had been so happy at the Dower House, for the year or so they lived there before … before that dreadful incident by the lake.

That had been the last time Lucy had seen her mother. She and Stephen had been taken to Tina's house in the village until the following day, when Granny Ruth came home from the hospital and went straight to bed with a bandage around her head and a white face. Granny had looked so small and frail. Lucy had scrambled up to her and they had cuddled tightly. Then Granny told her that she wouldn't be seeing Mummy for a long while, as she had to go away.

"But … but I don't want to be at the Dower House on my own," Lucy had cried. "I want my Mummy!"

"Darling, you aren't going back to the Dower House. I am going to have a room next to Stephen's

101

made up for you and you are going to live here at the Hall with all of us. You'll like that, won't you?"

Lucy had nodded slowly. If she couldn't be with Mummy, Canleigh was the next best thing. She loved the old, grand house and the big, beautiful rooms. It was like living in a palace. She would be happy there, she knew she would but she did so want Mummy.

And she was happy. Ruth and Philip did all they could to make her life as comfortable as possible and Stephen had been brilliant. Ruth had explained to him what was going on and how Lucy would be missing her mother. Stephen was a sensitive soul and hated seeing anyone hurting or unhappy. They had been friends before the incident but afterwards and as young as he was, he went out of his way to make sure Lucy had everything she wanted and was never left alone to brood. He never knew about the sobbing that went on after Tina or Granny Ruth tucked them up for the night.

The yearning for her mother's love never really went away. It was always there, beneath the surface of her sunny smile and happy exterior. It was like a little knot in the middle of her tummy and then, today, it had suddenly unravelled and disappeared. It was when her mother had smiled at her for the first time and looked so interested in what she had been doing and what she wanted to achieve. Lucy had felt as if she had come home. Delia did love her and Lucy loved her too … and she was really looking forward to spending some time with her at Blairness and couldn't wait to get back to Canleigh and make the arrangements.

* * *

Crystal's letter was short and to the point.

'I've been trying to reach you on the telephone but am always told you are too busy to speak to me, hence this letter.

Delia, please, please will you give me some kind of job on the estate. I am so bloody miserable down here. I'm bored to death with the position I have but there is nothing else available to me as an ex-con and I can only afford a miserable little bed-sit. I'm going absolutely crazy and need to get away.

Please. I will do anything … and I promise I won't be any trouble and I'll work really hard at whatever you give me to do.

Much love, Crystal.'

Delia tore it up. She might have grown to like Crystal while they were in prison together but she didn't want any reminders of Holloway or anyone in it ever again.

CHAPTER 8

Delia was in her office in the castle, looking at the figures Brian had given her the day before for the bookings for the holiday cottages scattered over the estate. They were full for the rest of the year and it looked good but it could be better. Delia had thought hard and long about the idea of having a caravan park too. It wasn't the upmarket kind of venture she really wanted but it would be lucrative, could be sited well away from the castle, and wouldn't encroach on her life or the lives of other residents on the estate or the holidaymakers in the cottages. She was having a meeting with Brian later that day to have a tour of the estate and decide exactly where it should go and then they would have to contact the planning authorities for permission. It could be a year or so before it really got under way but it could help secure the future of Blairness and prevent her having to keep delving into her personal funds for the upkeep of the castle and estate.

She was also wondering seriously about the possibility of opening the castle to the public, perhaps a couple of days a week throughout the year or just for a few weeks during the peak periods of holiday season. It was a building of great interest to history buffs and even with the extra costs of toilets, car parking and staff, along with somewhere visitors could partake of refreshments, there could be a healthy profit in a year or two. She didn't like the idea of having hordes of people poking and prying into her private home but if her own quarters were roped off, and she kept herself occupied out on the estate during the few hours they were in her home, she could cope with it.

She heard a van coming along the drive and stood up to go outside and greet the postman. Jerry Hopkins was always on time, always cheerful and Delia liked him. Even though he must have known of her background, he never looked down on her or made her feel inferior.

"Morning, Your Ladyship," he chirped gaily with a grin. "It sure is a beautiful day today," he said, glancing up at the perfect deep blue sky. "Not much here for you, this morning," he added, handing her a few items held together with a large elastic band.

"Thank you, Gerry. Yes. It really is a lovely day," she agreed, smiling as he hopped back into his van, waved at her and drove back down the drive.

The phone was ringing as she turned to go back into the office and as she was the only one around at that time of the morning, she answered it.

"Mum. It's Lucy."

Delia's heart leapt with delight. "Hello, darling. It's lovely to hear from you."

"Mum ... I've looked up the train times for Friday. I can be in Inverness around 3.00 p.m. Would that be okay?"

Delia smiled widely. "Oh yes, darling. I'll be there to pick you up. I can't wait to see you. I'm having a lovely room prepared for you here. You'll simply love Blairness ... I can't wait to show it to you."

"I'm ... I'm looking forward to it. Bye, Mum. See you on Friday."

The conversation had been short and to the point but Delia was ecstatic. Lucy was definitely coming. Ruth and Philip hadn't been able to persuade her not to. Her daughter had a mind of her own. Thank goodness for that.

She sat down in Brian's chair and pulled off the elastic band holding the post together. The electricity and water bills made her grimace and the magazine on estate management made her smile, make a coffee and settle back for a read.

* * *

Crystal was desperate. If she couldn't leave her dreadful job in Norwich soon, she would curl up and die. Every second she was at work was a second too long. It was a nightmare. The work, which was so damned boring, typing about inanimate objects she had absolutely no interest in, with people who despised and looked down on her, was torment. She had never been so unhappy in her life, not even in prison, where at least she had commanded some respect, being a friend and cell mate of Lady Delia Canleigh. Every morning she woke with a sense of deep dread, and depression descended on her as she watched the clock tick towards the time she would have to get up, get washed and dressed and make her way to that miserable office on an even more miserable trading estate on the outskirts of the city.

She hadn't the funds for a car so had to catch the bus and sharing it with the hoi polloi was a thrill she could have done without. The shuffling, sniffling masses, pushing and shoving for the prize of a seat to journey at snails pace through the morning rush hour and then again on the return in the evening, was horrendous. Crystal hated it so much and it did nothing to ease her depression.

There was only Delia who could help her. Crystal's parents had disowned her after she was sent down for the robbery and wanted nothing more to do with her now. They were desperately ashamed of her after they had bigged her up to all their friends and relatives for working for Lord and Lady Salis. They couldn't bear to talk to her now, let alone allow her over their threshold. She was alone in the world ... apart from Delia ... and if Delia didn't play ball and give her a job just by asking, then she would have to show her ace card. Being in prison had taught Crystal a thing or two and she reckoned she could ease her situation greatly with a little blackmail. Yes, Lady Delia would have to give her a job; otherwise she just might find herself behind bars again very soon.

* * *

Delia was rudely interrupted from learning a lot more about grouse shooting than she had previously known from the magazine she was reading, when the telephone beside her rang again.

"Delia Canleigh" she said abruptly, annoyed to have been disturbed.

"Delia?"

Delia knew the voice instantly and inwardly groaned. Crystal was the last person she wanted to talk to and she really didn't want her here. That chapter of her life was truly finished with.

"Crystal. How are you?" she asked sunnily.

"Disappointed actually," came the reply.

"Oh?"

"Yes. This is the first time I have managed to speak to you after countless calls and you didn't answer my letter either.

"I'm sorry, Crystal. I'm just so busy at the moment and your letter must have been mixed up with the office post. I'll have to check." Delia lied easily but no doubt Crystal would see through it.

"Well, that's as maybe but I'm hoping so much that you can help me out, Delia. I really want to work for you. I shall work hard and make your life far easier than you could possibly imagine."

"Look Crystal. I am truly sorry but there just isn't anything here you can do. We already have a girl in the estate office who copes with everything admirably."

"Oh, I don't want to work in the estate office. I want to be your personal P.A."

"But I don't need a P.A, Crystal. I don't socialise and have no intentions of starting."

"You do need a P.A, Delia. I have to insist on that."

"Really, Crystal. You are being totally absurd. Now, please. Go away. I really don't think there is anything else we have to say to each other and I am busy. I have to get on," she added, flicking through the pages of the magazine.

"No, Delia. You have it quite, quite wrong. You need a P.A and it is going to be me. I can be on the train next week and can commence my duties a few days later, after I have settled in. I expect a nice room with a nice view, all my meals included, a monthly salary, a car and five weeks holiday every year."

"What! You are crazy! Now just clear off, Crystal … and don't contact me again."

Delia was just about to put the phone down when she heard Crystal's voice lower menacingly. "Do you want to go back to prison, Delia? So soon after you have been released. Did you like it so much?"

"What the hell are you talking about?" snapped Delia angrily.

"Can't you remember?" came the purring voice. "We got drunk one night. That smuggled in brandy that we bought ... or should I say you did. We got smashed that night, didn't we? It was fun. You got down off your high horse and actually talked to me, like an equal."

"So ... your point is?"

"Well, Delia. You let down your guard. You told me things. Things you have never told anyone else."

A sudden coldness entered Delia's core. She could remember that night, although that was amazing in itself. The strong Spanish brandy could have knocked a person's head off. They had nothing to water it down with and so had drunk it neat. Too much of it. Their heads were very bad the following morning and it had been torture trying to pretend they were fine to the prison staff. Getting rid of the bottle afterwards had been a challenge. Delia smuggled it down to the kitchen beneath a baggy jumper and left it in one of the bins. There had been a right furore when it was found but thankfully, it was never discovered who had placed it there, otherwise the parole board may have looked on her release date a little less favourably.

But what had she said to Crystal? What could she have revealed to have her former cellmate threatening to blackmail her?

"And what are these things?" she said.

"Your brother, Richard ... and that Rocky fellow ... you really did kill them. You told me exactly how

109

you planned it and how you carried it out. The gun, the duffle coat, the disguise. You got the gun from a chap who runs a nightclub in Soho … Benny, was his name? The police should be able to locate him fairly easily. Face it, Delia, you confessed it all …, and I have a tape to prove it. Remember that little cassette player I had? Well, it was on that night. You were drunker than I was and didn't notice me slip a blank tape in. I don't know why I did it. I had no idea what you were going to say."

Delia was silent. How could she have been so damned foolish? She had never spoken a word to anyone else about how she had plotted and schemed to get rid of her brother and Rocky. Why, the bloody hell had she spilled the beans in a drunken session in her cell? God! She was so bloody stupid and how the hell was she going to get herself out of this one? She had no choice really. She would have to give the flaming woman a job. What was the saying; keep your friends close but your enemies even closer. At least if the woman was here, she would know what she was up to … and could even get rid of her at some point. She could plan that too. The Scottish highlands were vast. There would be many opportunities to get rid of her somewhere where she would never be found. Her mind raced. The adrenalin flowed. She could deal with this.

"Well, Crystal. That was very clever of you. When did you say you could be here? I suppose I could find work for you … and provide you with all the things you require. I must warn you though; it is very quiet in the Scottish countryside. You might not like it."

"I shall simply love it, Delia … and you will love having me to chat to again. I simply can't wait. Thank you so much. I'll let you know exactly when I will arrive. I will go into work today, hand in my notice, and then inform the probation office. I suppose I shall have to report to the one you do. That will be fun, won't it? Going together. Just like old times."

The phone went dead. Delia sank back into her chair, desperately needing a drink. There was no alcohol in the office, only coffee. She got up, strode back to the dining room, grabbed the brandy decanter, and went back to the office, banging the door shut behind her. She drank more than she should … just like she had that damned night in that damned cell … but it dulled the fury. Then she remembered the meeting with Brian that afternoon. Sex always made her feel better and in control. Perhaps instead of touring the estate for a caravan site, they should have a steamy session in his cottage. That would make her feel loads better and let her subconscious deal with the dilemma she was now facing. Yes. That's what she would do. An afternoon with Brian would help her no end. He had no idea what was in store.

CHAPTER 9

"Come to dinner," urged Vicky. "I'm actually free tonight and so is Alex. It's a while since the four of us have had a proper get-together."

Ruth accepted readily, badly needing to be with members of the family who would provide the comfort and support she needed right now. Thank God for Vicky. She was always to be relied upon.

"We'll be there. What time would you like us?"

"Seven thirty for eight ... and don't be late," said Vicky with a smile, knowing Philip's tendency to leave everything until the last minute. Ruth had taken the trouble of altering the clock in their bedroom to half an hour later than it really was to fool him but it didn't always work.

"We won't. Thanks Vicky. Look forward to seeing you."

Vicky replaced her receiver thoughtfully. She knew what the main topic of conversation would probably be but having dinner together would be a good opportunity for them to air their concerns and decide how best to hearten and cheer up Lucy when they eventually had to pick up the pieces when Delia broke her heart. Because Vicky was damned sure that was what would happen in the near future. Delia never did anything unless it was to benefit her and even though Lucy was Delia's only child, Vicky harboured grave doubts that Delia would alter her ways. Still time would tell.

Vicky sat back in her chair and closed her eyes, thinking back on how Delia had nearly ruined her life and thanking God for Alex, who had done the opposite. He was her rock in all things and had been since her former husband, the charismatic, good looking, good for nothing Barrie, had nearly wrecked her life. She didn't think very often about that awful time but now it all came flooding back.

She remembered, with clarity, how excited she had been to marry Barrie, the love of her life at the time, and then with the patronage of her father, they had bought their first nightclub in Kensington with Alex. The three of them proved to be a great partnership and the club boomed but Barrie nearly finished it all, although all the warning signs had been there, even before they married, and how stupid and naïve she had been, thinking he loved her as much as she loved him and that she could trust him.

Delia had started the rot early on in Vicky and Barrie's relationship, long before they married. A fortnight before her wedding to Philip, Delia had wanted the whole family together for a weekend at Canleigh. Unfortunately Philip had broken off the engagement the day before but Delia had kept that information to herself and bitter and jealous of her sister's happiness, she had enticed Barrie into her bed when Vicky had disappeared into Leeds to do some shopping.

Vicky's life had been turned upside down by such raw betrayal. She had sent Barrie packing from Canleigh and didn't see him for months, even though it hurt like hell and she missed him badly but he grovelled and grovelled well, and eventually she relented to his persistent phone calls, cards and flowers. He professed how much he loved her and promised never to behave like that again. Foolishly, she was taken in and married him.

What a mistake that was. As soon as Delia beckoned, he was gone, enticed away again when she needed to be bailed after the deaths of Richard and Rocky. The crazy man had put their whole business at risk by putting up the bail money from company funds. Luckily, it hadn't been put to the test. Delia had remained in the country ... having an affair with Barrie until her trial and flaunting it at Vicky. Then, finally, there had been that awful, awful day when Delia's trial collapsed and Barrie took her back to their London flat over the club to celebrate ... and they attacked her.

Vicky closed her eyes. She could remember the fear, the pain, and the humiliation as the two of them grabbed her, ripped off her clothes, and threw her on the bed. It had almost been a blessing when Barrie had thumped her in the face and knocked her out. At least she couldn't remember the worst.

Barrie and Delia had fled to Canleigh and Ruth, on holiday at Blairness with Vicky's father and baby Stephen, and alerted by Alex, immediately travelled down to London to be with Vicky and nurse her through the following painful days and restore her faith in human nature. Vicky really didn't know what she would have done without Ruth and Alex. They had both been brilliant ... and still were.

But the dramatics hadn't stopped there. Delia and Barrie languished at Canleigh, drinking heavily and giving the staff a hard time. They rowed violently and Barrie had fled, leaving Delia in her room, the right side of her face embedded in broken glass and a fire starting in the bedclothes from her discarded cigarette. Well over the legal driving limit, Barrie hurtled down the drive in his car and crashed it into a tree. He was killed instantly. The staff managed to drag Delia clear of the fire in her room and she was rushed to hospital, her face a mess, resulting in a horrendous scar down her cheek but worse was to come. On a visit to Delia, Ruth discovered she was pregnant ... bearing Barrie's child.

Vicky, desperately wanting a child and unable to have one, was devastated and didn't know how she would react on meeting Lucy, the result of the affair between Barrie and Delia, for the first time. It had been daunting but Lucy had been delightful and Vicky loved her from the start. She was nothing like Delia, even her hair was a different colour, and her nature was kind. There were no hidden agendas with Lucy. What you saw was what you got. She was just a lovely young girl with serious ambitions in the hotel trade and Vicky wanted the best for her and would help her as best she could. It was a little unfortunate that when she smiled, she looked a bit like Barrie but it was something Vicky had to live with. She wasn't Barrie and that was that. Thankfully, she didn't have his nature either. In fact, Lucy was more like Vicky's own father, Charles, the 10th Duke of Canleigh. He had been a lovely man and Vicky could see a lot of him in Lucy. Which was an almighty blessing and must have been a real comfort to Ruth, who, without hesitation had taken Lucy to live with her as soon as Delia had been arrested after the horrendous attacks. Ruth was a real treasure in no mistake and now she was stressed out again over Delia. Vicky had no idea how she could help her but if there was anything she could do, she would do it. She didn't want Delia ruining their lives yet again.

* * *

"How is Lucy doing?" asked Ruth.

Vicky watched Alex refill their wine glasses with the excellent Merlot she had chosen for their dinner and smiled.

"Really well. She's a natural. Easy with people, efficient and quick. Everyone loves her … especially Jeremy. He only enjoys his stints on reception when she is working."

"Lucy adores him, you know."

"I know. She always has, hasn't she? Even when they were little. They have always been close. It worries me a little," confessed Vicky.

Ruth, Philip, and Alex all looked at her. They knew what she was going to say and they all agreed with her.

"I love Jeremy, of course I do. But there's something … I don't know what it is but although he's bright, I don't think he will make good husband material"

"Well, it might not come to that," said Philip, raising his glass to his lips. He applauded Vicky's decision on the wine. It was his favourite. It was just as well Ruth had to keep a clear head for driving home.

"No," interjected Alex, finishing his beef and placing his knife and fork neatly together. "You know what it's like in the hotel trade. Lucy will meet so many people and she is so young. She is bound to meet other, more suitable men. It's a dreadful thing to have to say but I wouldn't want to see her teamed up with Jeremy either. I love him too but …."

Ruth shifted uncomfortably in her seat. Vicky and Alex had been so delighted when they adopted

116

Jeremy and Suzanne and poured all their love and as much time as they could into making sure they had a fabulous life and wanted for nothing but perhaps they had gone too far and spoiled them, especially Jeremy, too much.

Then, lo and behold, Vicky had become pregnant. Her joy had been so lovely to see and they had all been enormously pleased for her, especially when she produced a bouncy daughter whom she and Alex named Katrina. She had turned out really well. She was a daughter of which to be very proud but had Jeremy's nose been pushed a little out of joint? He had known from the start that he was adopted and it must have been pretty galling for a young child to suddenly have a tiny sister intrude into his safe and loving environment. Vicky had appeared to treat them all the same but she never looked at Jeremy and Suzanne in the way she looked at Katrina, with deep, pure love in her eyes.

Ruth noticed Vicky glancing at the photograph of a smiling young woman with fair hair on the sideboard.

"How is Suzanne doing?" she asked. "Will you be able to get over to Australia this year to see her?"

"Oh, I do hope so. I do so want to be there when our first grandchild makes an appearance in October," replied Vicky. "I am glad, of course, that she has finished working on cruise ships but as lovely as Todd is, I do wish she hadn't married an Australian. We're going to see very little of her and her family now."

"Goodness, children are a worry," said Ruth, watching Alex top up everyone's wine glasses bar her own. She had enjoyed a small glass but couldn't have anymore seeing as she was driving home.

"You can always stay the night," urged Vicky, seeing Ruth's expression. Vicky knew how Ruth loved Merlot. "After all, we have plenty of rooms," she laughed.

"We could but Lucy will be on her own if we do. She's gone out with some friends but will be back by midnight. I don't like the thought of her being in the Hall all alone apart from Felix."

"Um. I know what you mean. The man is downright creepy," said Vicky with a shudder. "I honestly don't like him, Ruth. I don't know why you appointed him. There must have been other applicants who were far more congenial."

Ruth shrugged. "Probably but not with his credentials and you know me. I hate interviewing. I'm just not very good at it. I never seem to ask the right questions."

"If you change your mind and do decide to dispense with his services, I'll come and help you interview ... or Alex, won't you, darling?"

Alex nodded. "Of course. You know you only have to ask, Ruth."

"Well, I'll see. I have other, more important things to think about now with Lucy and Delia."

"Before we start talking about what we can do on that front, would you all like pudding?" Vicky asked, removing their empty plates.

"Yes, please," urged Philip. He loved dining with Vicky. She was a brilliant cook and as he had a sweet tooth, he always enjoyed her puddings.

Vicky smiled and left the room, looking forward to seeing Philip's face when she presented him with the baked Alaska.

"How is Stephen getting on?" asked Alex. "We see very little of him these days."

"Absolutely fine. He really loves the army … and he has a rather nice girlfriend too … they met at Sandhurst … Sarah Misperton-Evans. He brought her up for a weekend a while back and we all warmed to her."

"Oh good … perhaps we'll have a wedding in the family soon then," said Vicky, entering the room carrying an enormous baked Alaska, the top sparkling like frozen snow in the light of the chandelier above the dining table. Alex took a bottle of Sauternes from the ice bucket on the sideboard, removed the cork and filled their dessert wine glasses, just giving Ruth enough for a tiny sip.

"I think Stephen is a bit young to be thinking about marriage," remarked Ruth. "He might be training to kill people but marriage … no. Not just yet."

"Yes, you're probably right," said Vicky, deftly cutting a generous slice of Alaska for each of them, amused at Philip's delighted grin as he watched her. "But I expect Stephen, Jeremy and Lucy will all be costing us a fortune in the next few years when they do decide on their life partners. I know how much we spent on Suzanne's do. We're lucky having The Beeches and Canleigh to use for venues but even so, it is pretty costly."

"Which brings us full circle," said Ruth. "We started off talking about Lucy and here we are again. I do so worry about her … and …"

"Delia," they all chorused.

Ruth shuddered. "Yes … Delia … I do hope Lucy sees through her quickly. For all our sakes."

* * *

Lucy had enjoyed her evening out with the girls but she had to be on reception duty at The Beeches early in the morning so drove back to Canleigh Hall just after ten thirty. She didn't imagine Granny Ruth and Steppie would be long after her. Both liked to be in bed around eleven so would probably be well on their way back from Harrogate by now.

She turned off the Harrogate road and entered the estate. She never liked going down the drive at night. The enormous trees and massive rhododendron bushes gave her the creeps as she picked them up in the headlights of her car. She switched on the full beam to give her more courage.

It wasn't long before the Hall came into view. Felix had left the lights on in the entrance hall but no floodlights as he usually did when the family were out. As a result, the place didn't look particularly welcoming with no sign of life. With no dinner to serve, Felix had the night off and had probably gone out, and Tina and the rest of the staff would have returned to their homes in the village long ago.

She left the car by the front door, locked it, and ran up the front steps. The entrance hall was eerily quiet apart from the ticking of the grandfather clock. Lucy wasn't a fanciful girl. She had grown up in the Hall, was well aware of the ghost stories associated with it and they had never worried her but tonight, she felt a frisson of fear … no, that was too strong a word. Tense was more like it. Yes, she was tense. Perhaps it was because she was tired. She needed to get to bed. She ran up the stairs onto the first floor. Her lovely room was to her right. With relief, she turned the knob, stepped in, shut the door firmly behind her, and for some reason, locked it.

"That was a lovely evening," said Philip with satisfaction as they cruised through Harrogate and headed towards Leeds.

"Yes," Ruth agreed, putting her foot down on the accelerator now they were out into the countryside. "We really should all get together far more often … it's a pity we're all so busy."

"Well you needn't be, darling. You don't have to help out with all those charity events. You do far too much, you know. Those women take advantage of your good nature … you should spend more time with your art … you are so good at it. You should have an exhibition."

Ruth laughed. "Oh heavens, darling. I'm not that good … and no-one would want to buy anything of mine."

"You could be surprised, my dear. I really think you should give it a go. You know how painting relaxes you and it will give you something else to think about apart from Lucy and flaming Delia."

Ruth's good humour evaporated. "There's not much to be done there, is there? We'll just have to pray that Lucy's commonsense overcomes her desire for Delia to be a real mother to her … and if it doesn't, we will just have to be here to pick up the pieces."

"As usual," Philip commented dryly.

Ruth slowed down as they entered Canleigh village and turned up the drive for the Hall.

"Oh good," she said, as the building came into view. "Lucy is home. There's her car and her light is on in her room. I hope she had a nice evening."

She parked the car next to Lucy's and they walked up the steps to the front door and entered the house. Philip took the big key from its place behind a bust of the Emperor Nero, locked the door and followed Ruth up the main staircase. Neither of them noticed Felix standing motionless behind the library door.

CHAPTER 10

OCTOBER 1995

"I've been having a look at the area down by the river. I think that would make a much better site for a caravan park than the other valley," said Brian from the driver's seat of the Landrover as he pulled up outside the front door of the castle where Delia was waiting for him.

Dressed in clean jeans, green wellies and a forest green, fleecy jacket, Delia clambered onto the front seat next to him to have a great pink tongue poke out and lick her face.

"Meg. Behave," said Brian with a grin, pulling at the Labrador's collar, making her move closer to him to give Delia more room.

"I hope you don't mind Meg accompanying us, Your Ladyship."

"Good heavens, no," Delia smiled at the happy old dog, "she's very welcome."

She didn't mind a bit. With such a lovely animal and its even lovelier owner for company for a few hours, it would help relieve the bad taste she had in her mouth from Crystal's threatening telephone call and her imminent arrival. That could be placed to the back of her mind for now and she would concentrate on the task in hand.

Her earlier idea of enticing Brian into bed was knocked on the head now she was with him. She actually liked and respected him and was even a little in awe of him with his commanding, confident presence, which made her feel, unusually for her, a little shy. She was also beginning to realise how integral he was to the running of the estate. He knew it far better than she did and he was honest and reliable. She would be a fool to mess about with him. If she wanted uncomplicated sex, she could go to a bar in Edinburgh and find a willing man.

Brian drove straight to the site near the river. Delia had to agree it was a lovely spot. It would be a great shame to place row upon row of caravans here, with some sort of clubhouse and amenities for the holidaymakers, but needs must. Even though the estate was profitable, there was a great deal of maintenance work needed, especially on the castle, and another income stream to assist with future expenses was required, otherwise her personal funds would receive a serious dent.

They left the Landrover by the track at the top of the hill and walked down to the river, Meg trotting alongside, tail wagging and growing more and more excited as they approached the water. She loved to swim and suddenly with one almighty rush, she bounded down and was immersed in seconds, using her thick tail like a rudder as she cruised along, eyes shining happily.

Delia laughed. The dog looked so contented, the sun was shining, she had an interesting, handsome man by her side, and she was free to breathe in the fresh air. Bugger Crystal. Life was beginning to improve by the second with all of this and Lucy's imminent visit to look forward to. With just a tiny hope that she could actually be really happy now, Delia didn't want what was promising to be a far better life than she had imagined being disturbed. If she could push her hatred of Ruth and Philip right to the background and just concentrate on what she had here and Lucy, life could be really good. All that counselling and those anger management courses she had attended with such scepticism, had maybe done some good after all. She should think seriously about letting the past go and look forward to the future now she actually had one to look forward to.

"What do you think, Your Ladyship?" asked Brian, nibbling on a blade of grass and looking around with keen interest. "I thought the clubhouse could go over there," he pointed just behind him, "with full length windows all along one wall, it would have lovely views of the river and the hills beyond ..., and the caravans could go in lines over there," he nodded in the opposite direction. "It will be a small site, compared to most, and exclusive and upmarket, with good quality caravans. That will only attract those who just want to explore our stunning neck of the woods and local attractions, not the rowdy sort with cars full of rowdy kids."

"Perfect. We certainly don't want a damned theme park here, just a well run place with a clubhouse where they can go for a few drinks in the evenings and a meal if they don't want to cook or eat further afield. They will be nice people who will want to come to relax and unwind. In fact, we will make it for adults only, so we can guarantee they will have a peaceful time."

Brian smiled. He was pleased to hear there wouldn't be hordes of badly behaved children and teenagers careering all over the estate. He didn't mind the few who came to the holiday cottages. Their parents appreciated the landscape and taught their offspring properly. They kept to the country code, didn't leave litter, and made sure gates were shut

125

when crossing the fields. He enjoyed meeting them and chatting about the local area and what they should look out for in his beloved Highlands.

"I don't think we need to look at the other site," said Delia. "This will do well, providing we can get the planning permission. I would like it to be up and running by the spring so we need to get the plans drawn up as soon as possible. No doubt we will have to go through hoops to get it but it should be worth it in the end … and I like the fact that being in this valley, it won't be seen from other parts of the estate. It will be quite private. Yes, Brian. I like it. I like it very much. Now, how about somewhere we could plan a golf course and I've heard there are two cottages coming up for sale in Eastwick village. I believe that's only a few miles away so can we drive over there now and have a look, please? If they are any good, I think I'll buy them to add to the holiday cottages."

"No problem, Your Ladyship. Just let me get my errant dog out of the water and we'll set off. She'll have to get in the back now though otherwise she'll make a real mess of us," he grinned.

As reluctant as she was to end her enjoyment, Meg did as she was told and left her pool, shaking off great globules of liquid as she stood on the grass beside the river. Brian took an old towel from under his seat in the Landrover, gave her a coat a quick dry and then lifted her into the back of the Landrover, her tail still wagging.

They drove back down the track and out to the main road leading to Eastwick. Delia looked around eagerly. She could remember riding this way when the family came here in the summer holidays all those years ago. The countryside was so beautiful with massive mountains in the background, tall forests, and great valleys, with hardly anyone to be seen. It was refreshing and tranquil and she could actually feel her whole body relaxing properly for the first time in years. Her prison life seemed another world, light years away.

The two cottages Delia had heard about were on the edge of the village. One was semi-detached and the other was an end terrace. They were at least a couple of hundred years old, made of solid stone, had nicely cared for gardens and lawns, not big but adequate for a small family with a dog or two.

"The locals won't be too happy about you buying them for holiday cottages," stated Brian.

"Oh? And why is that?"

"With so many cottages being bought for holidaymakers, it's becoming difficult for locals to find a home."

"But these have been empty for months, according to the information I obtained. Surely if they were so desperate for homes, someone would have bought them by now."

"Unfortunately, they're being priced out of the market. Most of the population in these parts do manual labour. It doesn't pay well so they can't afford a mortgage."

"Well, that's that then. If they can't afford a mortgage, they can't buy it so should have no objection if I do."

"Yes, but if you bought them and then rented them out to locals, they would have homes here instead of having to move away and split up families."

"Oh. I see. I hadn't thought of that. But look how much I can command from holiday lets. I can't charge those sorts of rents for permanent residents."

127

"But it would be regular money, guaranteed. You might not be able to fill holidays cottages every week of the year, especially in the winter. You'll do all right over Christmas and New Year … just as the other cottages do but there are a lot of weeks in the winter, especially January through to Easter when the cottages stand empty and the heating still has to be on to stop them getting damp … and the insurance, etc still has to be paid."

Delia sat beside him and mulled it over. What he said made sense. If she had permanent residents they would pay all the bills and they would be in situ twelve months of the year … and she would only have to buy white goods for the kitchen. She wouldn't have to furnish them completely … and she would keep the goodwill of the locals.

"Yes. You're right. I'll give it some thought over the next few hours and get in touch with the estate agents tomorrow for a proper viewing. They look well-maintained cottages so we shouldn't have to do much to them, probably just a lick of paint. Then we could rent them out fairly quickly … now Mr. Hathaway, where should we site a golf course?"

* * *

Delia had thoroughly enjoyed her afternoon in the company of her estate manager and his dog. They rolled up back at the castle just before 5.00 p.m., Delia jumped out of the Landrover, patted Meg on the head, and watched Brian drive away, fully satisfied with their afternoon's scouting. The site for the caravan park was perfect, the cottages looked a good investment, and Brian had taken them up to Wethy

128

Ridge to look over the land he had suggested for a golf course. It wouldn't be huge but it would be an interesting one with ups and downs and plenty of room for little copses dotted about. It would be a draw for the caravanners and holiday cottage residents and locals would be able to play too. There was just the planning permission to sort out. Delia sighed. There was going to be plenty of work to do, that was for sure, but she was really enjoying herself. It was fantastic to be able to get her teeth into something about which she already had a passion ... and she had Lucy's visit to look forward to next week. She couldn't wait. She was going to spoil the girl rotten and try so hard to make up for all the lost years. It was such a damned shame her visit looked as if it was going to coincide with Crystal making an appearance. How she was going to deal with that, she still had no idea. She would have to play it by ear to begin with. See exactly what Crystal expected life to be like and how much she was going to get under her feet.

Then there was the question of those blasted tapes because Delia was pretty sure Crystal would have made a copy or two. Blast the woman. When things were going so well, why did she have to thrust herself in and cause problems? It was so bloody annoying!

CHAPTER 11

OCTOBER 1995

Jeremy drove his little red and white Mini-Cooper over to Canleigh Hall, having arranged to pick up Lucy so they could drive over to Ilkley for a walk over the moor and then have a meal in a nearby pub. It was one of their favourite outings. Ruth and Philip had taken them there when they were young, and they had loved it so much, they often returned as adults. Striding across the moor, with the spectacular view of Ilkley and the surrounding district far below them, the wide-open sky and then the fabulous old rocks to rest on, was so satisfying. It was a place to dispel all worries and all fears. One came away with a far more relaxed view of one's life and future.

Jeremy usually looked forward to their walks. Lucy would chat non-stop, she could talk for England if she was in the mood, and he would listen and throw in the odd comment. They would smile, laugh, and then stand looking in awe at the spectacular scenery below them, picking out the spots they recognised. If it were a nice day, they would take a picnic but if it were like today, overcast and threatening rain, they would eat in one of the nearby pubs. They particularly liked one in Ilkley itself, near to the river with the children's playground nearby. They could sit in the car after their meal and people watch. There were always plenty of folk about, walking their dogs, others just wanting an ice cream from the kiosk and then there were the children, screaming with pleasure as they were pushed higher and higher on the swings and running around in competition to be the first on the slides and other playground paraphernalia.

However, even though he was going through the motions, he didn't feel keen on an outing today. He had considered ringing Lucy to cry off but decided against it. She had emphasised how she wanted to talk to him before her first trip to Blairness and he didn't want to let her down... and he might feel better once he was up on the moor breathing in plenty of fresh air.

It was probably just tiredness. It had been jolly busy at The Beeches lately and Mother had been determined to keep him occupied. If he wasn't on reception duties, he was roped in for several shifts behind the bar and then there had been two weddings this week, which resulted in him having to be on duty as two key members of staff were off sick with the flu. So, this was his first day off in three weeks. He would have liked to spend it in bed but Lucy had persuaded him otherwise. He yawned as he turned down the drive to Canleigh Hall and wished he hadn't listened to her.

Lucy was waiting and tripped lightly down the front steps of the Hall with a wide grin on her face. She was dressed in a white sweater and a navy fleece and jogging bottoms, blue suede walking boots, and had a small blue rucksack on her back. Her long fair hair was tied back in a ponytail and apart from a coat of mascara, she wore no make-up. The result made her look far younger than her twenty-one years.

"Hello, Jeremy darling," she said cheerfully, "Thank you so much for this ... I know how tired you must be but I really need this today. I just want to get up on those hills and blow all my cobwebs away."

He smiled back, jumped out of the car, and went round to open the passenger door for her.

Even though she was wearing trousers, she slipped regally into the car as Ruth had taught her. Jeremy closed her door and went back to the driver's side. As he did so, he glanced up at the Hall. The butler, Felix, was just inside the front door. Jeremy could see him through the glass, watching them both. Felix smiled and nodded. Jeremy's jaw tightened. For some reason the man always made him feel uncomfortable. A bit like Matthew had on their first meeting. Jeremy shrugged the thought away. He wasn't going to think about either Matthew or Felix today. He had Lucy to entertain and she was right, they needed to blow the cobwebs away.

* * *

Full of envy, Felix watched them drive off. They were going to have a lovely day out while he was stuck here, having to prepare the dining room for lunch for Mr and Mrs. Kershaw and the young Duke, who was home for a couple of days. He had roared up the drive last night on his heavy, black Triumph motorbike, revving it up loudly beside the front steps with a big grin on his face. Mrs. Kershaw hadn't been amused. Felix knew she hadn't wanted the Duke to have a motorbike and to have him blatantly announcing his arrival on it, sent her into a right flap.

Felix walked through to the dining room and wrinkled his nose. There was still a nasty whiff of kippers from breakfast. He pulled a can of air freshener from a drawer in the sideboard and squirted it. Clean Linen, it was called. It didn't smell much like clean linen but at least it was better than kippers.

How anyone could eat the awful things, he had no idea. Yuk.

He cleared the breakfast things and made a start on laying up for luncheon, his thoughts drifting to Lucy and Jeremy. He supposed they would eat in a pub today, as it wasn't nice enough weather for a picnic up on the moors. He knew where they were going as he heard Lucy arranging it with Jeremy on the telephone yesterday.

He wondered about Jeremy. He wondered what his intentions were with Lucy and how she felt about him. Did she realise he was gay? Did Jeremy, for that matter? It was blatantly obvious to Felix but then he was older and had far more experience of the world than either of the two youngsters.

Felix had seen Jeremy look at him; the bashful, sidelong glances, the blushes, the hint of a smile. Did the boy know what he was doing? Almost, almost flirting with him … him, the butler. Felix was amused and pondered on trying his luck. He wasn't in a relationship and hadn't been for a couple of years. His last, with the chauffeur at Lord Patrick-Jones's palatial house in London, had resulted in a nasty break-up. Felix, with a couple of hours off, had walked eagerly down to the grace and favour cottage where his lover lived, to discover him in a passionate embrace with one of the gardeners. He hadn't spoken to him again and it wasn't long after that when he managed to procure the position he held now but he was lonely. There were few staff at Canleigh and none whom he could have a friendship with, let alone a relationship. Sometimes, on his evenings off, he went into Leeds, to the gay bars, but even though he ended up in bed with a couple of seemingly suitable young men, there was no follow up. They didn't

133

contact him and he didn't contact them but then he didn't fancy any of them as he did Jeremy. He had the added bonus of being young and ripe for the picking and Felix would very much like to teach him the ways of the world.

With a degree of satisfaction, he checked the table. Everything rested exactly where it should and then he looked at his watch. He had half an hour before he had to crack on with other duties so was going to make the most of it. Pru had made a gorgeous chocolate cake last night and that would go down very well with a coffee.

* * *

Pru, the cook, who had worked in the house for many years, looked at the solid old railway clock on the wall, put the kettle on, and then left the kitchen by the back entrance. She had need of a little wander to the garden to pick a few bay leaves for dinner tonight … and she didn't want to be in the kitchen at the same time as Felix. She found him morose and his company quite depressing … and he made her feel tense and on edge. She didn't like him and wished fervently that Mrs. Kershaw would get rid of him. How Pru longed for the days when the Hardy's were in charge. The household had been a happy ship then; at least it had when they all recovered from the trauma of Lady Delia trying to kill Mr. and Mrs. Kershaw. It had taken the whole household a long time to get over it. However, once the first year passed and Mr. Kershaw began a slow recovery from the awful injuries he had suffered at the hands of Lady Delia, the house had become a delightful place to work, especially with the

134

children; Stephen and Lucy, often joined by Suzanne and Jeremy romping around the place, and then the baby, Katrina.

Things changed again when the children turned into teenagers, going off to college or in the young Duke's case, into the army and then the Hardys retired. Prue missed them badly. All the household staff had been such good friends and at ease with each other, enjoying their breaks together when time allowed. The advent of Felix had put the damper on all of that. He was sharp with all the staff, dismissive of their problems and had no time for idle chat and they all took to avoiding him as much as possible.

Pru reached the kitchen garden. She could have phoned down to one of the gardeners to bring what she required up to the house but walking at a cracking pace past the stables, around the lake and to the kitchen garden by the Bothy during her coffee break was far preferable to sitting in the kitchen with that awful little man.

* * *

Felix sat at the table in the centre of the vast old kitchen and ate his chocolate cake with relish. There was no doubt about it, Pru could certainly bake. He sipped his coffee carefully. It was hot and he didn't want to burn his tongue.

His thoughts turned back to Jeremy. What a beautiful body the boy had. He was tall, slender, a neat little bum, hands with long, sensuous fingers, neatly cut brown hair and grey eyes. He was gorgeous and Felix felt a stirring in his groin. All his previous lovers had been older. Jeremy was quite a few years

135

younger. Would he play ball? Would he jump into bed with him? Felix didn't want to make the first move, just in case Jeremy's inexperience made him complain. Felix didn't want to lose his job. No, he would wait and see what happened, after all, Jeremy might look down on him seeing as he was a lowly butler? But then, Jeremy wasn't anything in his own right. He only happened to be adopted by wealthy parents. He wasn't clever or owned a lot of money himself ... as yet. He might do later, Felix supposed, if he inherited it from Lady Victoria and her husband but then there was an older sister somewhere in Australia and little Katrina and she would probably cop for most of it, as she was their real child. Still, it wouldn't hurt to ingratiate himself with Jeremy. Even if he didn't get him into bed, he might be able to make use of him in the future in some way.

He finished the chocolate cake, stood up, and left the kitchen. He had work to do.

* * *

They had walked for two hours and were tired. So far, the rain had held off but Lucy had a fold-up brollie in her rucksack, just in case.

"Let's have a perch for a while before we walk back," suggested Jeremy, pointing at a couple of rocks.

"Good idea," sighed Lucy. Her new boots were beginning to rub her heels but she daren't take them off to check as she might not be able to get them on again. She normally brought plasters but had forgotten them today. How daft was that?

"I've got something I want to run past you actually," said Jeremy. "Something that's been bugging me for a while."

"Oh?" said Lucy, trying to place her feet in a comfortable position to relieve the pressure on her heels.

"I'm … I'm thinking about trying to find my birth mother."

"Oh! Why … what's made you want to do that all of a sudden? I thought you were happy with Aunty Vicky and Uncle Alex."

Jeremy took a deep breath. "Well, yes. I am … but it's always been there … niggling at the back of my mind … the need to know my real mother … and father. It's like being a non-person, not knowing who your real parents are. It's never seemed to bother Suzanne … at least it didn't used to. We often talked about it … and she didn't feel the need to search them out as I did … as I do. Perhaps it's because she's a couple of years older than me and can remember a little of what went on and once we were adopted and settled, didn't want to think about it."

Lucy was giving his statement carefully consideration. "I think I would feel the same as you, wanting to find out where I came from. At least I've always known who my parents are, even if one ended up in prison for most of my life and the other killed himself by smashing his car into a tree along the drive at Canleigh. My parentage hasn't been too great, believe me."

Jeremy threw his arm around her and gave her a hug. "I know. It's been tough for you too. We're a right pair, aren't we?"

"We've also been incredibly lucky. You with Aunty Vicky and Uncle Alex and me with Granny

Ruth and Steppie. They didn't have to bring me up. They had Stephen so didn't need to add me to their family."

"Likewise, with Katrina. I know she came three years after us but at least she is theirs."

"Were you … are you jealous of Katrina?" asked Vicky, seeing the unhappy glint in his eye.

Jeremy sighed and finally admitted what he had known for years. "Yes. I suppose I am. Suzanne and I were the be all and end all for Mother but once Katrina arrived, I always felt we weren't quite good enough any longer … oh, Suzanne was okay as she wanted to help with Katrina so ingratiated herself that way but me … I felt I didn't quite measure up. I know Mother tried to treat us equally but she's never really been able to hide it. I'm not her real son and that's all there is to it and now Suzanne isn't with us any more, it's more obvious. Darling Katrina, can do no wrong, is doing marvellously well at school, always seems to get the best parts in school plays, is mentioned in the press for her budding acting skills, tipped for a career in the film industry … while I …"

Lucy squeezed his hand. "Aunt Vicky does love you very much you know. I think … I think she is just worried about you … chucking in Oxford without any warning … and you've been in a very strange mood since then … and you never talk about it … you can to me, you know."

Jeremy couldn't look at her. He stared blindly at the dark clouds above, getting darker by the second. It wouldn't be long before it was pouring. He glanced down below, at the cars snaking along the road, heading towards Ilkley and Skipton one way and to Leeds, the other. Full of people who knew who they were, what they were, where they were going. He wished he felt the same. He was so mixed up ... bewildered ... and floundering.

How could he tell Lucy what had happened in Oxford? He didn't want to tell anyone. He wanted to put it all behind him. It was degrading and shameful and should never have happened. But in a way it wasn't. In a way it had been an experience he had enjoyed. It was weird. He knew it had been wrong and everyone would be aghast if they knew the truth but it had been ... oh, he was so mixed up. He mustn't think about it and he was damned sure he could never tell Lucy. She thought he was some kind of God. He couldn't disillusion her.

"It was something ... and nothing ... to be concerned about. I suddenly realised Oxford and the academic life isn't for me and wanted a change of direction ... although I'm not sure hospitality is the right course to take ... I have been toying with horticulture ... you know how I like to be outdoors rather than in and there are some brilliant courses at Askham Bryan ...".

"If that's what you want, why don't you go for it then? I'm sure Aunty Vicky and Uncle Alex will support you."

Jeremy smiled wryly. "I'm not sure if they will after the Oxford debacle ... and to be honest, I am more interested in finding my real mother at the moment. I've been in touch with the authorities and she has agreed to meet me."

Lucy sat up abruptly. "Oh gosh. You have been busy. Where ... where does she live, what does she do, do you have any other brothers or sisters?"

Jeremy laughed. "Hold on ... I've only just discovered she is still alive ... I know no details apart

139

from that she wants to see me and she lives somewhere near Paddington Station in London."

"Wow. When are you going to meet her?"

"Next week."

"Oh no! I shan't be here. I shall be at Blairness with Mother."

"It doesn't matter. I want to see her alone anyway. It might not work out. We might dislike each other. I've some awkward questions to ask … why she gave me away is the most important one. I'm not sure I can forgive her whatever the reason is."

"She must have had a very good one. Surely, no mother could give a child away lightly. She will be overjoyed to see you, I expect."

"Um. Well, we'll see. I'm glad I've told you. I've been wanting to discuss it with someone but I don't want to mention it to your aunt and uncle until I've seen this woman … and also try and ascertain who my father is. If it doesn't work out, there's no real need for them to know."

Lucy thought about Aunty Vicky and Uncle Alex. They were level headed and forward thinking people and probably wouldn't be fazed by Jeremy's wish to find his real parents but she could understand his desire to keep his search private for now.

"Thanks so much, Lucy," Jeremy said suddenly. "I know I can always confide in you."

Lucy smiled and leaned against his shoulder, looking up at him adoringly. "I'll always be there for you, Jeremy. You do know that, don't you?"

Jeremy looked down at her. At her lovely face, her perfect, soft skin, her gorgeous eyes, the luscious mouth. He bent his head and brushed his lips across hers. It felt good. She raised her head higher, staring straight into his eyes. Their mouths met again.

Jeremy's spirits soared. He wasn't gay. He wasn't. He was kissing a woman. He was kissing Lucy. He wrapped his arms around her and held her close.

"I love you so much," she whispered, as Jeremy caressed her neck.

"And I love you too," he murmured back, closing his eyes tightly, trying to force away the image of another pair of eyes staring at him, another body in his embrace.

Lucy pulled away, staring at him with shock, not having expected such a declaration. "Do you, do you really?" she breathed with excitement.

Jeremy gulped. He had done it now. Committed himself. He supposed he did love her in a way. She had been his constant companion for years, always looking out for him, always there, eager to make sure he was safe and happy. He had learned to rely on her an awful lot. He looked at her. The one person who could help him lead a normal life, put that Oxford episode really behind him, help him blot it out. Who better than Lucy? And she loved him ... and he could learn to really love her. What could be better? Suddenly he felt a rush of overwhelming relief after months of anguish, despair, and soul searching. The answer to all that was here ... with Lucy. She would send his demons away. She would end all this confusion and angst ... and she could do it right now if he asked the right question. He already knew what her answer would be. Yes. He had to do it now, before he lost the courage. Then he would be truly committed and nothing and no-one could upset the applecart.

He turned to face her squarely, holding her hand tightly. "Lucy," he said thickly. "Will you ... will you marry me ... perhaps not now. We're probably too young … at least the whole family will think so … but at some time in the future when everyone has got used to the idea?"

Lucy flung her arms around him, her eyes full of unshed tears. She was so happy, she could burst. "Oh, Jeremy. I would like nothing more. You've been the only one for me ever since I can remember. I have adored you from the first time I set eyes on you when Aunty Vicky and Uncle Alex brought you to Canleigh to meet us all."

Jeremy laughed. "Oh yes, I remember. You stared and stared at me and then followed me everywhere, insisting Stephen show me all of his toys. Then you showed me that awful doll you had, really ugly looking thing, and I didn't like it. You were so offended but forgave me the next day and gave me your sweets. Lemon sherbets if I remember rightly."

They sat for another hour, arms around each other, reminiscing about their childhood, planning for their future. Lucy was ecstatic. Jeremy was feeling a massive relief, like a huge weight lifted from his shoulders. He could do this. He could marry Lucy and all would be well. He could be normal. He could be happy.

Realising they were famished and becoming chilly, they made their way back down the car park and then walked across to the Cow and Calf.

"Let's have some champagne," said Jeremy. "I know I haven't got you a ring … we'll go into Leeds or Harrogate and choose one on our next day off … but we are engaged. We need to celebrate."

Lucy giggled. "What a lovely idea … but you mustn't have too much. You're driving."

"Okay. One glass for me and if we linger over our food, I shall be fine to drive. We don't have to rush.

We can spend all evening here if we want to. I want to make this a night to remember. The start of our new lives. The start of our future happiness. Lucy Canleigh, you don't know how happy you have made me."

Lucy's eyes shone with pure love and adoration. She had expected to enjoy her day out with Jeremy but had no idea it was going to turn out like this. She was blissfully happy. She was in love and she was loved. How brilliant was that?

CHAPTER 12

OCTOBER 1995

"We've something to tell you," said Lucy, brimming with happiness.

Ruth and Philip were in the library at Canleigh Hall, the drapes drawn and a huge fire crackling with flames shooting up the chimney. Ruth was curled up on the sofa reading a family saga and Philip sat beside her, perusing the Leeds Times. Stephen was lounging on the sofa opposite them reading what looked to be an army manual.

They all looked up in surprise as Lucy burst through the door, hauling a hesitant Jeremy behind her.

"Oh, and what is that?" queried Ruth, placing her book on the coffee table, reluctantly dragging herself away from the doings of Margaret O'Donnelly in her quest to impress her new lover. She knew, from the look of pure joy on Lucy's face what the answer was going to be and she wasn't at all sure she was going to be ecstatically happy about it. Jeremy was a nice enough boy and she liked him but since leaving Oxford he had seemed troubled and all over the place and there was always this air of femininity about him, similar to Felix, the butler, making her wonder if Jeremy was gay too. Ruth stared at Lucy, praying she wasn't going to say what she thought she was going to. Her prayers weren't answered.

"We're engaged," announced Lucy triumphantly, turning to clutch onto Jeremy. "We haven't a ring yet because it was all such a surprise ... for both of us ...

but we'll get one on our next day off. Are you happy for us? Please say you are, Granny Ruth ... and Steppie ... Stephen."

Ruth stood up and smiled. Lucy looked so elated. Whatever her own misgivings, who was she to burst her bubble? She moved swiftly across the room, hugged her, and smiled at Jeremy. "Congratulations, darling. Of course I am happy for you ... for you both. I think this calls for champagne, don't you, Philip?"

"I certainly do," he replied, pushing hard on the arm of the sofa for support as he tried to stand up. His leg was playing up badly tonight and he was finding it difficult to make it work as it should. He straightened up and moved to the telephone on the desk. "I'll ring down to Felix and get him to bring some up."

Stephen rose to his feet, moved over to Lucy, planted a kiss on her cheek, and shook Jeremy's hand. "Well, you two are full of surprises."

Lucy smiled. "Aren't we just? I didn't expect to see you although I'm so pleased you're here to hear our news. When did you get here and how long are you home for?"

Stephen grimaced and looked anxiously at his mother. He hadn't told her why he had unexpectedly turned up this evening and he knew she was going to be terrified when he came clean. He took a deep breath. "I only arrived a couple of hours ago ... just for a couple of days. We're being deployed so they've given us some leave before we go."

Ruth's heart did a nosedive. She knew what he was referring to. Bosnia ... a horrifying war right on their doorstep so to speak, with reports of despicable things happening every day. She loathed watching the news, with more and more images of the intense suffering of so many people and it just seemed to be escalating. The world had to step in and try to stop it. For once, she agreed wholeheartedly with Tony Blair and his government. Something had to be done and soon but she so wished her own son wasn't going to have to be one of those involved. But then, she wouldn't be the only parent feeling this way. It was the price they had to pay for being enormously proud of what their children were contributing to the world.

"Oh God," whispered Lucy, with a look of horror. "Not Bosnia!"

Stephen shrugged and sat down again, smiling reassuringly at his mother and Lucy. "We're only going as peacekeepers. We're not actually fighting so there's nothing to worry about."

Ruth nearly choked. Nothing to worry about! He knew perfectly well that he and his fellow soldiers could be set upon or blown up at any moment. It was a war zone he was going to for goodness sake and she wouldn't stop worrying about him until she knew he had set foot back on British soil.

"So, when are you planning on a wedding?" she asked Lucy brightly, pushing her fear away, wanting to change the subject from the Bosnian war to a much happier one, albeit she hoped this marriage was going to be a few years away, in which time anything could happen and it might not go ahead.

"Christmas," said Lucy determinedly. "You married Granddad at Christmas, didn't you? In St. Mary's … and Christmas is such a romantic time for a wedding."

"Gosh," Ruth said, sinking back onto the sofa, "that's not long."

"Well, there's not much point in messing about. We don't need to get to know each other or anything

146

because we've been close for years and years and now we know what we want we might as well go ahead and do it. There's no need for a grand wedding and we won't invite too many guests … just family really and a few special friends so it shouldn't cost a lot," rambled Lucy, not wanting Granny to think the planned nuptials would make a severe dent in the Canleigh bank balance.

Felix, opening the library door and carrying a silver tray on which rested a silver ice bucket containing a magnum of Krug, and five champagne flutes, interrupted further discussion. He was curious to know what was being celebrated but from the excitement emanating from Lucy, he guessed immediately. So, the boy had popped the question. Mrs. Kershaw certainly didn't look too happy about it. She was smiling but her eyes had a glazed, pained look. Lucy obviously hadn't noticed. She was too excited and was hanging on to Jeremy as if her life depended on it. Jeremy, although trying to look thrilled, appeared somewhat dazed … as if he had done something wrong. Mr. Kershaw had sat down on the sofa. His back was to Hardy so he had no idea how he had taken the news but from what he could see, the man didn't appear to be exactly ecstatic.

Felix popped the cork on the champagne bottle, poured five glasses, and handed them around on the silver tray.

"We're celebrating the engagement of Lucy and Jeremy," explained Ruth needlessly. "Please take another bottle of champagne from the cellar and have a drink in the kitchen with the rest of the staff."

"That's very kind, madam." Felix turned to Lucy and Jeremy. "And congratulations to you both. I hope you'll be very happy." He smiled, gave a little bow,

147

and left the room, his eyes never leaving Jeremy's face.

He grimaced going down the stairs to the kitchen. Have a drink with the staff! Pompous woman. There was plenty of champagne in the cellar and she wouldn't miss a bottle or two. He would give the staff theirs and then retire to his room with another. He didn't feel in the mood for celebrating with a housekeeper, cook and cleaner. Anyway, what was there to celebrate? A silly young girl having been asked by an even sillier young man to marry him and how exactly was he going to get Jeremy into his bed now?

* * *

Ruth sat up in bed, trying to concentrate on her book but with little success. She kept reading the same paragraph repeatedly and none of it was sinking in. In despair, she turned to Philip, who was beside her, not pretending to read, just staring at the wall on the opposite side of the room.

"I'm so worried ... about both of them."

"I know you are, darling," replied Philip, taking her hand in his and giving it a squeeze.

"I can't bear the thought of Stephen being in Bosnia and not knowing what's happening. It's so appalling over there ... we hear so many awful things ... and there will be a lot we don't hear too. I feel so sick just thinking about him being mixed up in it all. He's so precious to me. What if something happens to him?"

Philip pushed himself up on the pillows, took the book from Ruth's hands, and cuddled her close. "Nothing is going to happen to him. He's well trained. He's sensible. He will be with commanding officers who know what they are doing."

"Oh, I know all that but …"

"No buts, darling. I know you are going to be anxious until he gets back but he's probably going to be out there for quite a while so you've got to be strong, otherwise you'll end up a nervous wreck."

Ruth brushed a tear away. Philip was right. She had to have faith in the British army and their commanders.

"Just concentrate on Lucy and her forthcoming wedding. You will enjoy yourself, planning for that."

"I do wish she wasn't in love with Jeremy," sighed Ruth, "He's not right for her. He seems such a mixed up boy and why did he come rushing back from Oxford, just before he was about to take his final exams? It was all very strange and Vicky has never received a satisfactory explanation. All he would say was that he had decided a career in law wasn't for him and he was wasting his time."

"Perhaps he was right. Perhaps he will do well in the hotel industry instead. With Vicky and Alex behind him, he should be able to … and Lucy loves it so she will keep his nose to the grindstone. They could both do very well if given the chance. Again, darling, you must stop worrying. Jeremy might not be the best catch in the world but he and Lucy have been close for years and he doesn't have two heads or anything."

Ruth punched him playfully and wrapped her arms around his neck, kissing him softly on the mouth. She loved her wonderful husband so much. Whatever happened she had him and she was so thankful.

* * *

Lucy lay in bed, turning over the events of the day in her mind repeatedly. She was deliriously happy about her engagement and then there was the trip to Blairness in a few days. Although she still had mixed feelings about that. She wanted to go. She wanted to spend time with her mother but underneath she was still a little scared ... a little wary. She wondered how Delia would take the news about the engagement, as it would be impossible to invite her to the wedding. Delia wasn't allowed anywhere near Canleigh and anyway, Grandma Ruth and Steppie certainly wouldn't want her here. Perhaps she and Jeremy could travel up to Scotland, spend some time with Delia after the wedding, and have their own little celebration.

Delia ... her mother. Lucy turned over, remembering all those nights after they had been ripped apart, sobbing herself to sleep. She had wanted her mother so badly and now she could have her again.

Ruth and Philip had given her a wonderful childhood. She had wanted for nothing, was loved and cared for, and had little to complain about. They were both exceedingly generous with their time, their love and their money and she had been exceptionally lucky to be given such a warm and caring environment in which to grow up ... and with Stephen, whom she adored. He was the big brother girls dreamed of having, never excluding her from any activity, encouraging her, helping her with her homework. She had missed him badly when he departed for Sandhurst, full of excitement and anticipation, more than keen to crack on with his officer training. His passing out parade had been wonderful. She had been so very proud of him, watching him march about, looking so handsome in his uniform. At the time, she hadn't given a thought as to why he was in the army and what it could mean. She hadn't thought of him going off to dangerous countries to fight and even though they weren't going in a combatant role, it was terrible to think he was now going to be in Bosnia. They would all be anxious but Grandma Ruth was going to be in a terrible state while he was away.

She tried to push the fear for Stephen away. There was no point in tormenting herself. He was going and there was nothing any of them could do about it. His regiment had undertaken several tours of Northern Ireland and as grim as the situation was there, he had returned unscathed. There was no reason to think the same wouldn't happen with Bosnia. The family would, as they had done in the past, resort to prayer, send him lots of letters and good thoughts and look forward to his homecoming.

During the conversation this evening, she hadn't thought to ask how long he would be away. She badly wanted him at her wedding and it would be a terrible shame if he missed it. Yes, the wedding. Lucy hugged herself, imagining a bright, crisp winters day, alighting at the entrance to St. Mary's from the Rolls, dressed in a bubble of white and floating regally down the aisle to where Jeremy awaited her. Her beam grew wider and wider in the darkness

*　*　*

Felix felt quite light-headed. He had definitely had one or two glasses of champagne too many. He was glad the family had gone to bed as he weaved his way around the downstairs rooms, pulling the window shutters closed and checking the front door was locked and bolted. Mr. Kershaw hadn't done his rounds tonight. He must have consumed too much champagne too.

He entered the library, placed the empty champagne flutes on the silver tray, and picked up the magnum of Krug hopefully but it was empty. They had drunk the lot. He nearly tripped on the Aubusson carpet as he left the room, just grabbing the tray as it threatened to slip out of his hands. He turned off the light, closed the door behind him, and made his way down to the kitchen.

He dumped the tray and its dirty contents near the sink in the kitchen, ready for the cleaner to deal with in the morning. He didn't feel tired and didn't want to go to bed. He looked out of the window. It was a clear night and the moon shone brightly. Feeling the need for fresh air and exercise, he quickly removed his black jacket, strode out into the vestibule where his parka hung, slipped it on, took a small torch from the top drawer of a cupboard housing odd bits of paraphernalia, and left the house by the kitchen door.

He felt better as soon as the chilly night air hit his lungs. It steadied him and cleared his head. The lake was gleaming in the moonlight and he wished he had remembered his camera. It looked a real picture and would have looked good in his album.

He moved across the parterre, eerie with the statue of Pegasus looking as if he was about to fly off into

152

the night sky. A quick glance up at the Hall satisfied him that everyone had gone to bed and wouldn't want him again tonight. Lucy's room was in darkness although there was a light on in Mr. and Mrs. Kershaw's. No doubt they were talking about the events of the evening. Felix would have loved to have been a fly on the wall and hear exactly what was said. He didn't think it would be ecstasy about the forthcoming wedding. Of that, he was certain.

He walked down to the stables, virtually redundant these days. Horses hadn't been stabled there for many years and although there were a couple of estate vehicles in the garages, there was talk of turning them into offices and renting them out, although Felix knew Ruth wasn't too keen. She had heard her say to Stephen that although she approved of the idea in principle, it would mean vehicles driving backwards and forwards, continuously passing the front entrance to the house. Their privacy would be destroyed. Stephen had suggested making one of the lanes coming up to the Hall from the side of the lake into a proper road so they wouldn't be disturbed by the traffic but as far as Felix knew, the whole idea had been shelved for the foreseeable future.

He walked slowly around the lake, enjoying the solitude. Owls hooted and there was serious rustling in the undergrowth as he passed. He surmised it was foxes or badgers. He didn't mind. He kept walking.

The path meandered around the lake until it reached the Bothy. No-one lived there now. The head gardener, Roy Fitzgerald, had a nice little terraced cottage in the village where he had resided all his life and therefore had no need to live on the actual estate. As a result, the Bothy's only function these days was as a restroom for the gardeners during their lunch and tea breaks and the old, rusty key, which hung just inside the door, was never used as there was nothing of any value inside. No-one would want to pinch the two ancient sofas and chairs in the lounge and tea making things in the kitchen.

Felix pushed open the front door and stepped inside, feeling confident enough to switch the light on. With everyone in bed at the Hall, no-one would notice.

He had only been inside the Bothy once before, not long after he became butler at Canleigh. He had taken a walk around the lake on one of his afternoons off and bumped into Roy turning up for a break. Roy tried to be friendly by inviting him to have a cup of tea but the meeting had been strained. Felix wasn't interested in gardening and Roy had no idea how to talk to a butler so Felix hadn't stayed long, making the excuse that he had to get back to the house, as he would soon be on duty.

Now he had the whole place to himself he decided to have a look around, heading up the stairs first where there were four bedrooms and a bathroom. All the bedrooms were empty and felt cold and damp. The bathroom had the luxury of soap encrusted with mud, a couple of grubby looking towels and toilet rolls. Felix grimaced and went back downstairs.

The only items on display in the kitchen were a stainless steel kettle and a few old mugs, surprisingly washed and left to dry on the draining board. There were cream coloured containers with a pretty pattern of green leaves half-full of coffee, teabags, and sugar standing by the kettle. The fridge contained an opened carton of milk.

It was an invitation Felix couldn't dismiss. He made himself a tea in the cleanest mug he could find and took it through to the lounge. The sofas looked a bit grubby but one of the chairs didn't appear too bad. He sat down and drank his tea, his thoughts turning to the family and in particular, Jeremy and Lucy.

He grinned. How naive they both were, thinking they could make a go of marriage and how could the silly girl not realise Jeremy could just as easily jump into bed with a man as a woman. It was plain as plain to Felix and although Jeremy was obviously in denial about his true sexuality, it would occur one day. Felix was sure of it ... and then what would happen? Miss Lucy would be horrified. Felix smiled, imagining how the young lady would take it. What would she say? What would she do? He didn't really care. All he knew was that at some point in the future, he was going to have a sexual encounter with the delicious Jeremy and Jeremy was going to enjoy it and want it again and again. Felix had no idea how he was going to achieve it but he was going to. Of that, he had no doubt.

CHAPTER 13

OCTOBER 1995

Delia woke up. The sun was shining through her bedroom window, straight onto her bed, bathing her in warmth. She remained motionless, savouring the tremendous realisation that she wasn't in prison. She was in her own bed, in her beautiful old castle, where all she could hear through the open window were the birds. There was no clanking of cell doors, no shouts from prison wardens, or yells and grumbles from the inmates. She could get out of bed when she wanted. She could do as she pleased all day. What a marvellous feeling after so many long years of torturous misery.

She hadn't been at Blairness long, only a few weeks, but things were definitely progressing nicely. Plans for increasing the estate's profitability were going well and her daughter was about to descend on her today for a whole week. A whole seven days in which to cement their adult relationship. Delia was looking forward to it so much and had spent quite a bit of money and a lot of time preparing Lucy's room. She did hope Lucy would like it, enjoy her stay, and want to come back. She had wronged Lucy so badly and wanted desperately to make it up to her. She looked at the clock. Lucy's train wouldn't be in until mid afternoon so there was still plenty of time to check everything was perfect for her visit.

The only fly in the ointment was that Crystal was also going to make an appearance sometime this week too. Delia had tried to persuade her to leave it for a few days but Crystal had been insistent, promising that she would turn up sometime midweek, after she had bought all she would need for life in Scotland for which Delia had been asked to contribute.

Delia sighed. The bloody woman and those dratted tapes she possessed would have to be dealt with, otherwise she would be bled dry in the coming months and years. Anyway, there was no way on earth she wanted to share her home with Crystal. They might have gotten along fairly well in prison but Blairness was very different. Delia had no idea how she was going to get rid of her but no doubt an idea would pop up in the near future. Meanwhile she had far more pleasant things to think about.

She stretched out her body languorously. The warmth of the sun making her feel lazy, relaxed and so very happy and that was an emotion she couldn't remember feeling since she had been engaged to Philip all those years ago and was about to be married. A shadow crossed her face. She didn't want to think about that episode of her life. Not now. She might have come out of prison still considering revenge on Philip and Ruth but now she had been in situ at Blairness for a few weeks, she began to wonder if she did still want to go down that path. Her freedom was so very precious and the anger she had been harbouring for what seemed like eternity was strangely fading. She would always love Canleigh but now she had Blairness, which was entirely hers without question and to do with as she saw fit, so did she really want Canleigh any longer?

But then, it could still be hers, quite naturally. Lucy had mentioned that Stephen was in the army and what more dangerous occupation could that be, especially with the situation in the Balkans? British troops would soon be embarking on a peacekeeping mission but even so, they could be ambushed, blown up, killed and even if it didn't happen there, it could somewhere else. She wondered how Ruth felt about her son being in the military. She wouldn't be too happy. What mother would? They might be proud of their offspring but it must be a dreadful concern.

Thank goodness Lucy was safely enjoying a job at this hotel Vicky and Alex owned in Harrogate. The Beeches, it was called. Delia had looked it up on the internet. It was just the kind of place she would like to stay, with a spa, nice big swimming pool, and luxurious rooms. She smiled, wondering what Vicky would say if she booked in but then she couldn't. She wasn't allowed anywhere near any of her family, with the exception of Lucy, who had been contacted by the probation service to make sure she was perfectly willing to stay with Delia.

Delia's thoughts turned to the impending arrival of her daughter. Lucy's train was due in at Inverness around three o'clock and Delia was going to meet her. Her tummy did somersaults. She was so looking forward to having Lucy all to herself, to showing her Blairness, the estate and the glorious Scottish countryside. She had already ascertained that like her, Lucy loved to immerse herself in history and the outdoors and where better than here? They were going to get along so well and it was going to be the best week of her life for a very, very long time and when Crystal turned up, she would just have to take a backseat until Lucy had gone. Delia wasn't going to have her former cellmate mess up what was promising to be a wonderful reunion with her daughter.

She stretched and eased her body out of bed, enjoying the sensation of the warm sunshine on her bare skin. She stood up and padded across the carpet to the full-length mirror on the old oak wardrobe. She still looked good, even after years of prison food and apart from a few sessions in the gym and walking endlessly around the exercise yard, no real exertion. Funnily enough, she had put on a few pounds since arriving here but that was down to the food. Her new Scottish cook, Mildred, was a marvel and it was difficult to refuse the gorgeous puddings, cakes, and biscuits she produced. Delia had succumbed for the first few weeks but eventually had very reluctantly put a stop to it, insisting that only fruit was provided for pudding and anything more fattening should never come her way unless she specifically asked for it or had guests. Those extra pounds disappeared with the new eating regime and the walks she took every afternoon, striding around the estate, enjoying the peace and tranquillity, usually alone but sometimes in the company of Brian.

Delia really liked her estate manager. They had been uneasy together at first while they sussed each other out. He hadn't shown it, but no doubt he had been nervous. He had looked after the estate admirably for many years and to have his employer, with her horrendous reputation, descend on him must have been somewhat disconcerting but he needn't have worried. With her knowledge of estate management she soon realised he did a terrific job of looking after Blairness. He was totally honest and the estate workers admired him, liked him, and as a result strove to do their best for him. She would be crazy to ignore all that and anyway, she really enjoyed his company too. He was damned good-looking and witty and was a mine of information and inspiration. Delia thoroughly enjoyed being with him and was pleased to see that their relationship was actually beginning to burgeon into a friendship. She hadn't been friends with a man before, at least not since Philip. All those she had met after they split up had been used as sex objects, just to allay the deep hurt she had felt at his betrayal. She didn't need that any longer. That was all in the distant past.

She wondered again about the possibility of luring Brian into her bed but did she really want to? She fancied him, that was true, but the burgeoning friendship between the two of them was becoming more important. She liked it. She liked knowing that she only had to pick up the phone and within minutes he would be by her side, helping her with whatever problem she had with the estate, reassuring her that nothing was insurmountable and with time and careful consideration, anything was possible. Delia smiled. Was she going soft? Was she ... was she falling in love? No! She was Delia Canleigh. The bad, notorious Lady Delia Canleigh. She didn't have room in her heart for love ... or did she?

* * *

Lucy was at Leeds railway station, Ruth by her side. Philip was parking the car.

Ruth looked at her watch. "We're nice and early. You have half an hour before your train leaves. Would you like a coffee?" she asked, looking at the variety of coffee shops to the left and right of them.

Lucy, dressed casually in jeans, a plain pink sweater and a black leather jacket, smiled at her

160

grandmother. "No, thank you. I think I'll buy a magazine and then get on the train. It's in ... look," she said pointing at the arrivals and departures board.

"Okay. If you're sure. Do you want me to come onto the platform with you?"

"No. You go off home. I know how busy you are today. I'll be fine, really I will."

Ruth threw her arms around Lucy. "Oh, darling. You know how I feel about this visit. If you are uncomfortable or worried at any time, just ring us. We'll be up there so fast ..."

Lucy hugged her back. "It will be fine, please don't worry. I'm a big girl now and she is my mother. I'm sure she won't be thinking of harming me."

Ruth pulled away and smiled weakly. "No. Of course not. I'm just being over-cautious ... but then can you blame me?"

"No. I quite understand. I do, really ... and if there are any problems ... well, I just shan't see her again. I promise."

Ruth hugged Lucy for the second time, forcing the tears back. Delia had caused Lucy so much distress over the years and Ruth would hate to see that continue. The girl had already suffered enough at her mother's hands. Ruth would never forget the anguish the tiny Lucy had endured after Delia had been imprisoned. The child had been distraught on many occasions and although she had coped with it well as she grew older, Ruth knew the pain of the separation from her mother was always with her. God help Delia if she hurt her again. Ruth wouldn't be responsible for her actions.

Lucy picked up her suitcase and they walked to the barrier beyond which the train for Edinburgh and Inverness was waiting. A few seconds later and she

161

was stepping onto it, beaming widely at Ruth and waving as she disappeared from view. Ruth turned and walked away, her heart heavy with dread.

* * *

Crystal was enjoying her shopping spree. Darling Delia had sent her a lovely big cheque, with the warning that it would be deducted from her wages but if she thought that, she was very much mistaken. This was a little sweetener and just the tip of the iceberg as far as Crystal was concerned. Delia was going to be her money pot from now on.

There had been a heart stopping moment when she had told her probation officer of her plan to move to Scotland, and then a ghastly day thinking it might not come to fruition. The probation office in Inverness had been contacted and discussions ensued, and then Delia was included in the conversation. However, to Crystal's delight, no objections were raised as Delia was offering her a home and employment, although it was requested Crystal report to the probation office the day after arriving at Blairness.

With it all settled, now came the fun bit and she walked happily around Norwich city centre, popping into the most expensive shops, exploring all the racks of clothes, wondering what were the most suitable items for her new life in Scotland, at Blairness Castle. Winter was approaching and it would be extremely cold up north. Old stately homes and castles were chilly even with central heating so she had to have thermals, thick sweaters, trousers, boots, and coats and she didn't want cheap ones either. Then there were toiletries to buy and she wanted a decent haircut and, of course, a new suitcase. She had wanted a real leather one for years and only ever ended up with the cheap imitations, like the nasty one in her depressing little bed-sit. God, she would be glad to leave that place behind. It wasn't much better than a prison cell, with its horrid wallpaper, ancient cooker and fridge and lumpy bed … and it was damp. The few clothes she did have were going mouldy and musty in the tatty old wardrobe. That's why she had left buying new stuff until the day before she left for Scotland. She didn't want her fresh, smart attire to smell ghastly when she arrived at Blairness.

She looked at the gold watch she had purchased half an hour ago. It was nearly lunchtime and she was already weighed down with packages. She would take them back to the flat, have a bit of lunch and then she had an afternoon of pampering to look forward to and a hairdressing appointment. Yes. Life was certainly looking up and becoming far more pleasurable and the best bit so far had been packing her job in. To be able to hold her head high and walk out of that God awful office with those nasty, simple headed men, had been so uplifting. Her spirits had soared and as soon as she could hand in the keys for that horrid little bed-sit, that would be even better. Thank God, she had met Lady Delia Canleigh in prison.

* * *

Brian Hathaway finished off his cooked breakfast with relish. If there was one thing he insisted on, it was a full Scottish start to the day and then he wouldn't need to eat again until he arrived home around sixish in the early evening. He downed two

163

cups of tea and then washed up in the kitchen, smiling at Meg's antics through the window. She had gobbled down her breakfast earlier and then went to lie out in the sun on the lawn but now she was chastising a sheep which had deigned to push its head through the rickety old fence and was trying to eat the grass. Meg didn't approve and told it so. The sheep took no notice and Meg became louder in her protestations.

"You silly old dog," murmured Brian, smiling broadly.

He finished the dishes and walked outside to join her. She stopped barking immediately and ambled up to him for a stroke.

"What a lovely day, girl," he remarked, looking around at the hills and mountains. A deep sense of satisfaction washed over him. He had been so content here for so many years and had been full of trepidation that the arrival of Lady Delia Canleigh would make his ideal life far less ideal, even maybe meaning a move to another estate. But it hadn't. She was all right, was Lady Delia. Obviously, he didn't approve of the fact that she had gone down for attempted murder of not only one, but two people but she had done her time, at least a good part of it. He knew she was out on licence but he hadn't seen any signs that she was harbouring old grudges. Far from it. She had been a bit aloof in the first couple of weeks but she had gradually thawed. It had helped that she had slipped into the lake by accident one day and he had to pull her out. They had tumbled back together, fell on the grass and both burst out laughing. That was when he discovered she had a reasonably good sense of humour and could be good company.

Yes, he liked his employer and he hoped she liked him. They were working well together, both keen on expanding the estate's profitability and he could see a rosy future if things remained as they were. He also knew she was massively excited about her daughter's arrival today. He hoped the visit would go well. He had a desire to see Delia happy. Delia, he thought. He wasn't thinking of her as Lady Delia any longer. She was Delia. Oh goodness. Surely he wasn't falling for her. That would be a huge mistake!

CHAPTER 14

OCTOBER 1995

Jeremy had said goodbye to Lucy the night before her trip to Scotland. They had taken the day off and gone into Leeds to buy the all-important engagement ring. It had cost him nearly all of his savings but from the look on Lucy's face, it had been worth every penny.

"I've always wanted emeralds," she had said when they entered the most prestigious jewellers in Leeds.

"I thought all girls wanted diamonds," he said.

"No. Not this one. Emeralds it is, please. If you don't mind."

Jeremy had laughed. "You have what you want, Lucy. It's going to be your ring and I like emeralds too as it happens."

The ring Lucy picked was beautiful; three emeralds in a row with tiny diamonds between each one.

"There, you see. You have emeralds *and* diamonds," Jeremy laughed.

Lucy face lit up spectacularly as he placed the ring on her finger. It fitted perfectly and she hugged him tight.

"Thank you so much, darling Jeremy. It's just perfect."

They celebrated with dinner at one of their favourite Italian restaurants before heading back to Canleigh. Lucy had to be up early to get ready for her journey to Scotland and he had to drive back to Harrogate, so they hadn't stayed in Leeds too late.

166

"I'm so excited about seeing mother but I do wish you could come too," Lucy said when they sat in the car outside Canleigh Hall.

"It's best you have this time with her on your own. I can always meet her on another occasion ... and anyway, you know what I am going to do tomorrow."

Lucy had sat up abruptly. "Oh yes. Oh goodness, Jeremy. I do hope it goes well for you. I shall be thinking of you and please ring me tomorrow evening. I shall want to know all about it."

Lucy had given him the telephone number for Blairness, they had kissed, she had jumped out of the car and headed into the Hall, waving goodbye as he drove away and now it was morning and Lucy was on her way to Scotland and he was on his way to London. Vicky and Alex didn't know where he was going. They thought he was spending a couple of days with a friend in Reading but in truth, he was heading for a hotel near to Paddington Station, which wasn't far from where his mother lived. Having examined a street map very carefully, he would be able to walk from his hotel to her home in around twenty minutes or so.

He arrived in London just after lunch. He could have caught the train but decided he wanted the freedom of having his car and the hotel had parking so it wouldn't be a problem.

He went to the hotel first and checked in. He hadn't much money, having spent most of his savings on Lucy's ring so he had gone for a budget hotel, which was pretty basic. 'The Excelsior' it was called. A grand name but not a grand place. Not a patch on The Beeches. His room was sparse without a picture on the wall, just a single bed, a wardrobe, and a chest of drawers. The bathroom was none too clean and he was glad he had showered before leaving The Beeches that morning. He didn't fancy stepping into this one. He even considered going to the nearest shop and buying some bleach to clean it but had other things on his mind.

His mother. He was finally going to meet the woman who had given birth to him and Suzanne. He had thought about her for years, visualising what she would look like, how pleased she would be to see him … but then if she was going to be pleased, why had she given him and Suzanne up in the first place? He had never received a proper explanation from Vicky. All she would say was that his mother hadn't been able to cope and couldn't give the children the life she felt they deserved. But that wasn't good enough. She shouldn't have had them in the first place if she couldn't cope.

He pondered on whether to ring Suzanne and tell her what he was doing but if he did, there was every chance she would tell Vicky and he didn't want her to know just yet. Not until he had seen his mother and ascertained exactly how the land lie between them and if there was any chance of some kind of relationship. Vicky might be hurt and he didn't want that to happen if it wasn't going anywhere. The less she knew the better.

He looked at the letter from the adoption society again. He had been surprised how easy it had been to find his mother. She had made no effort to cover her tracks, apparently still living at the address where she had been when she dumped her children and on his application to the society for contact with her, they had been able to reply to him fairly quickly and confirmed his mother had given her permission to visit her at her home at 3.30 p.m. that afternoon. He suddenly felt sick with nerves. What would she be like? Would she be pleased to see him? Would she like him? Would he like her? Questions, questions, questions … and in a few hours he would know the answers. Suddenly he wished Lucy was with him … or Suzanne … would he be able to do this without support? He shook himself. Of course, he would. He was a man, not a mouse. He looked at his watch for the umpteenth time. He was hungry, not having eaten since breakfast and then it had only been a couple of slices of toast and marmalade. Judging by the standard of the room he was in, he didn't think he wanted to eat here. The kitchens were probably filthy and he didn't want food poisoning.

He had a quick wash in the not too clean sink, brushed his teeth, slicked his hair back, put on a clean shirt, and left the room. The road outside was busy. There was a newsagent opposite and a small café. He crossed the road and looked in the window. It appeared to be clean and welcoming. There were two cheerful, smiling women behind the counter and a pretty waitress buzzing between tables. It was busy, which was a good sign and seeing a couple leaving their table in the window, he entered the café quickly and sat down. Within minutes, the waitress sprinted over, removed the dirty crockery, wiped the table and took his order, all with a welcoming smile. The place didn't do anything too fancy, which suited him. He liked plain, good old English cooking and wanted something filling so that he wouldn't have to eat much again that day. He chose a homemade Cornish pasty with peas and chips, along with a pot of tea. It was all delicious and he felt enormously better once he had finished, enjoying being able to people watch from his table. He actually felt quite cheerful as he left the café, realising that he ought to make his way towards his mother's street if he was to be on time for their appointment. Appointment. That was a strange word to have to associate with his own mother. He had never had to make an appointment to see Vicky.

The sun was disappearing behind big black clouds as he neared the street of terraced houses where his mother resided. Mrs. Beryl Porter her name was so she must have married since giving birth to him and Suzanne as their name was Seymour. He walked down the street, staring hard at the numbers. Some were hard to read or non-existent. None of the houses were particularly smart or well looked after. He wasn't sure if they were council houses or privately owned. If it was the latter, obviously the owners didn't care too much about keeping up appearances. The cars parked outside weren't exactly of the luxury class either, many old and battered and he noticed a couple didn't even display tax discs. Loud disco music emanated from one with a downstairs window wide open. Two small children played in the garden. Both had dirty faces and their clothes were shabby and black with grime. They stared at him as he passed.

"Oi, mister. What you doing here?" the elder of the two yelled.

"None of your business," he said quietly, quickening his steps. He certainly didn't want to get into conversation with two such disgusting looking kids.

They both poked their tongues out at him and he looked the other way. No. 39 he was looking for. He realised it would be on the other side of the street. He crossed over. The house in front of him was No. 23. It wasn't far now then. He strode along the pavement, pretending to anyone who was watching him and to himself that he was far more confident than he was actually feeling. His nerves were beginning to take over again and the meal he had just eaten was hitting the bottom of his stomach and making him feel full and heavy.

No. 39. He was there. Right in front of the house where his mother lived and where he and Suzanne had started their lives, although he couldn't remember it but then why would he? He had only been a baby when he and Suzanne were taken into care. He stared at it. Tatty yellowing net curtains adorned the front window, the wooden surround was old and rotten and the green paint on the front door was peeling badly. He only knew it was No. 39 because someone had stuck some white plastic numbers above the tarnished brass doorknocker.

As he stood staring at the house, he noticed the net curtain twitch. She knew he was here. His mother. He wanted to run away. He didn't want to go through with it now he was here. He wanted to be back in Harrogate with Vicky and Alex, at The Beeches, where there was clean linen and lovely food. What was he doing here, looking for a woman who had never wanted him, never come searching for him? It had been a stupid, crazy decision. He turned to walk back along the street but suddenly the front door opened and a grossly over-weight woman, dressed in a revealing black negligee, bosoms virtually hanging out, and a cigarette in her hand, stood on the threshold.

"Not coming in then?" she said with a slight slur. "You've come all the way from Harrogate haven't you? Don't you at least want a cup of tea with your old ma?"

171

Jeremy gulped. Surely this couldn't be his mother. It must be some other woman … a friend maybe. His mother would be inside.

The woman nodded towards the inside of the house. "Come on then. Come and have a cup of tea … or I've something stronger if you'd like."

"Tea … tea … will be fine, thank you," he uttered despairingly. He really didn't want tea. He didn't want to go inside but suddenly she moved towards him, grabbed his hand, and pulled him indoors. "If you don't get in here quickly, you'll get me a reputation, so you will," she giggled. "What will the neighbours say with a good looking young man hanging around on my doorstep?"

He followed her into what was the lounge. It was hard to make out if it was clean or not as there was so little light from the window with the thick net curtain. There were two black leather sofas, a big television standing on a black glass stand and a huge black glass coffee table in the middle of the room. The fireplace sported a gas fire and a row of cheap china ornaments on the mantle. Pictures in plastic frames adorned the walls; a hunting scene and a boat pulled up on the sand beside the sea. They looked incongruous on the wallpaper sporting a hideous red tulip pattern.

They were alone. His heart sank heavily. This woman must be his mother then.

"Milk and sugar, dearie?" she asked.

"Just black please."

"Sit yourself down … I won't be long with the tea and then we can get to know each other. My, you are a handsome lad, that's for sure."

Jeremy gulped again and watched her sashay out of the room, pulling the black wrap around her shoulders and stubbing out the cigarette in an overflowing ashtray on a sideboard near to the kitchen door.

He sank down onto one of the sofas and closed his eyes. He should go. He should leave now before she came back. He didn't want to get to know this woman. He had made a terrible mistake.

"There you are. Told you it wouldn't take long," she said suddenly, standing before him holding out a red mug with a chip in it. He took it but placed it straight onto the coffee table, beside two pornographic video tapes, 'All girls together' and 'Easy Rider'. It confirmed his fears. His mother was nothing more than a common hooker. He looked at her with distaste.

"What's the matter, dearie? Aren't you happy to see your old mum and why didn't the girl come with you ... your older sister?"

"She's in Australia ... she married an Australian ... she's pregnant," he uttered.

"Oh, that's nice. I like to think my children are doing well in life. What is it you do, dearie?"

"I work in a hotel ... in Harrogate."

"Oh, so it's a hotel, is it. A fancy one I expect, looking at your clothes ... and don't you talk nice ... they've brought you up proper haven't they, your adoptive parents? Much better than I could."

"You didn't even try!" he blurted out, his eyes misting over. "We were fostered out, time and time again, sometimes together but more often apart, we had to endure two ghastly children's homes ..."

"Yes, but you were safe, fed and clothed."

Jeremy nearly choked as he stood up and glared down at her. "How dare you! How dare you sit there and say that. We were both so bloody unhappy, had to endure so much bullying and we never knew who we

173

were and where we came from ... but looking at this little lot," he flung his arm in a circular motion around the room, "you did do us a favour. God knows what would have happened if we had stayed with you and where we would be now. No doubt you would have lured Suzanne into prostitution and I would be a bloody pimp!"

"Oh dearie me, you have got a temper," she said, with a smile. "Quite like your dad, you are ... and I had to chuck him out in the end. He put me in hospital more than once, I can tell you. Broke my arm, gave me countless black eyes and knocked me unconscious more times than I care to remember ... if I didn't do as I was told ... go out on the streets night after night, do it with man after man, just so your father could have a drink and laze about all day doing nothing. It was when I came home one morning and found him trying to fiddle with Suzanne that I snapped. I hit him over the head with a brandy bottle, got two of the neighbours to help me push him outside along with all his clothes and locked him out. He kicked up a hell of a racket when he came round but when I threatened to tell the police what he had done he buggered off. Never saw him again. Good riddance."

Jeremy stood with his mouth open. Thank goodness Suzanne couldn't remember what had happened to her; at least he didn't think she did. She was a well-adjusted woman and had never mentioned anything.

"That's when I had to give you two up. I knew I couldn't look after you properly. I didn't want to leave you at night while I was on the streets so I took to bringing men back here but I didn't like the looks they gave you both. I couldn't risk anything

174

happening to you ... so I took you to Social Services and left you."

"Couldn't you have found a proper job, got some childcare or something?"

She snorted. "Don't be ridiculous. I wasn't qualified for nuffin ... only to lay on me back with me legs open ... I was good at that ... still am," she said proudly, pushing up her ample breasts.

He looked away. He was shocked, embarrassed, humiliated. He had to get away from here. He wanted nothing to do with this woman ... or bother to look for a rubbish father. He wished fervently he had never come. It hadn't been his wisest decision.

"I've got to go," he mumbled, heading for the front door.

"Oh no, dearie. Please don't. Not yet. I want to know all about your posh life ... hear about your parents ... no doubt they have a lot of money," her eyes glazed over. "Maybe, maybe they would like to give me a little present ... for letting them have you."

"How dare you! You didn't let them have me! You left us to the mercies of the authorities. I despise you for what you did to us. I despise you for what you are. I want nothing more to do with you and don't you dare to contact my parents or me. If you do, you'll be sorry. I'll come back and finish off the job my ... my father started."

He didn't know how he got out of the front door but within minutes, he was flying up the road, passing the two dirty children who stared at him with open mouths and the house with the rowdy music bellowing out into the street. He ran for half an hour and when he did eventually stop, puffed and desperately wanting to burst into tears, he hadn't a clue where he was. It was a better street. Semi-detached houses; neat gardens, pristine white net curtains and no peeling paint here. Even the cars parked on the drives looked clean and in good condition. A different world from the one he had just left.

At the end of the road there was a little park with a couple of swings and a slide. There was no-one there so he walked over to a bench and sat down. He was trembling and felt sick but the thought of seeing that lovely Cornish pasty and chips again made him swallow hard and breathe deeply. He wasn't going to chuck up. He just wasn't.

He badly wanted to talk to someone. He looked at his watch. Lucy would just about be arriving in Scotland but he wouldn't be able to ring her until this evening. Even so, he didn't want to tell her about that … that … woman. He was utterly ashamed of her. What would Lucy think if she knew he came from such a family?

He sat on the bench for almost an hour, surprised out of his stupor by the sound of children rushing into the park to compete for the swings. They were in school uniform and carried swinging satchels. Obviously school was out for the day and he couldn't sit here any longer or someone would think he was a kiddie fiddler.

He stood up, his whole body feeling stiff and achy. He looked around, not having a clue which way to go to get back to Paddington and his hotel but didn't want to ask any of the mothers standing by the swings, eyeing him suspiciously.

He turned and walked up the street, the opposite way to which he had come. There was a tiny newsagents at the far end. The elderly Asian woman behind the counter was helpful, took his arm, led him outside, and pointed at the junction. "Go left," she said. "Keep going and you will see the signs for the station. It's not far."

He thanked her and walked in the direction she had indicated, desperate now to get back to the hotel, pay his bill, get into his car, and drive out of London. He wasn't sure where to. He didn't want to go back to Harrogate just yet but anywhere would do. He just wanted to get out of the capital and as far away from Beryl Porter as possible. That was funny. She hadn't mentioned marrying again after she had kicked out his father … perhaps Porter was her maiden name. He didn't care.

The Asian woman had directed him correctly. In a short time he was in sight of Paddington Station and from there it was only a few minutes to the hotel. He reached it with relief, rushed up to his room, threw his few belongings in his holdall, dashed back down, paid his bill, and went out to his car. It wasn't long before he was in heavy traffic leaving London. He looked for signs for somewhere he knew. Oxford. He was on the road for Oxford. He would go there. He didn't know what he would do when he arrived but it was somewhere he knew, somewhere he could hide up for a day or so until he got his head around what had occurred this afternoon.

Three hours later he was in the multi-storey car park in the town centre. It was reasonably quiet. Office workers had already collected their cars and gone home for the day. A few people were arriving for an evening out, dressed up and laughing happily.

For a few minutes he just sat in the car. He looked at his watch. It was seven oclock. Lucy would be expecting him to ring her. He pulled his mobile phone out of his bag. She hadn't rung him. He switched it off. He couldn't talk to her now. He wouldn't know what to say. Hopefully she would be so busy with her own mother she would forget all about him. He would ring her tomorrow.

He got out of the car and walked up the road onto the High Street. It was busy with students and townsfolk rushing off to their evening events. He remembered what it had been like when he was one of them. How exciting life had been … and then it all ended. Oh God. Was it another mistake … to have come back here?

His steps took him towards the Bike and Satchel. He wasn't surprised. It was their favourite café and where they all met on a regular basis … him, Warboys and Johnson. They wouldn't be there, of course. Being a year ahead of him, they had graduated a few months ago and were long gone, off to great careers, to earn good money, to have super lives. Not like him, a mere junior manager in a hotel, albeit a plush, luxury one, and painfully aware it wasn't what he wanted to do for the rest of his life. But then, law hadn't been right for him either. He sighed, thinking of all the wasted time he had spent in Oxford.

He opened the door of the café and walked in. The girl behind the counter was different. She hadn't been there when he frequented the place only months ago. Three tables were occupied by giggling girls and boys who ogled them. The table near to the window was empty. He ordered a coffee and sat down, staring out into the street, watching the traffic; the big red buses, the posh cars, the pedestrians heading into the centre of town.

The coffee arrived and he spooned in four heaps of sugar. It was good for shock. A few hours had gone by since that awful encounter with his mother but he still felt dazed and traumatised and hadn't any idea what he was going to do now. He supposed he would have to sleep in the car.

Absentmindedly stirring the sugar, he looked up. The door of the café was opening and there, on the threshold, stood Matthew. The boy who had changed Jeremy's life. They stared at each other and then Matthew gave a smile that lit up his whole face.

"Jeremy," he said. "It's so very good to see you again.

CHAPTER 15

OCTOBER 1995

The train was on time, pulling into Inverness railway station at exactly 3.00 p.m. Lucy had tried to read on the way but with the excitement and the beautiful Scottish scenery to gaze upon, she couldn't concentrate and hadn't reached further than chapter two of the new novel by Geraldine McCormick, whose books she usually devoured very quickly.

As the train slowed, she pushed the book into her large brown leather handbag, pulled her suitcase off the rack above her head, and made her way to the exit door.

She was exceedingly nervous. Although the meeting had gone well with Delia when they had met previously, going to stay with her so far away from home was a different ball game entirely. She knew there would be staff at the castle and it would be rare for her to be completely alone with her mother but was there any danger? She couldn't forget her mother was still on licence for attempted murder. She couldn't forget the rumour that she might well have killed Richard and Peter Percival so that she could get her hands on Canleigh. But then she couldn't forget how she had cried for her mother, night after night and how much she had wanted her for years, even though she pretended otherwise.

The train jerked to a halt, bringing her sharply into the present. The woman in front of her opened the door and stepped onto the platform. Lucy was next and for a second she hesitated but a gentleman behind her, grabbed her suitcase determinedly.

"Come on, love. Let me help you out with that," he said helpfully.

She had no choice but to get off the train, thanking him as he dropped the suitcase on the platform beside her before walking off with a smile. She looked around and saw her mother. Delia was standing just yards away, beautiful and elegant in designer jeans, a red fleecy jacket and her hair tied up in a knot on the top of her head. She wore a lot of make-up, no doubt to hide the scar, and looked simply stunning. She beamed at Lucy and sauntered towards her, putting out her arms to give her daughter a huge hug.

"Darling, Lucy. You don't know how much I've been looking forward to this and I'm so very glad you still wanted to come and didn't chicken out. With my reputation, I wouldn't have been surprised if you had."

"I nearly did," Lucy confessed with a grin. "I nearly stayed on the train."

"Well, I'm very pleased you didn't. I want to spend this week trying to make up for all those years we've missed. Now come," she said grabbing the suitcase, "we've got a bit of a journey to the castle and Mildred ... she's the cook, is making you a special afternoon tea so we don't want to be late."

An hour later, they turned up the drive for Blairness Castle and Lucy drew in her breath. It was simply magnificent and looked like something from a fairytale with turret upon turret, neat little windows, a big solid oak door, ivy growing all over the facade, huge rhododendron bushes at either side and big, big lawns wandering down to a vast lake.

"Oh wow," breathed Lucy. "This is incredible. I love Canleigh but this ... oh wow."

Delia smiled. "I'm so glad you like it. I can't wait to show you around. It's fascinating inside, lots and lots of lovely old rooms, and the entrance hall is massive and most impressive."

"It would make a fabulous country house hotel," said Lucy.

"Yes, I suppose it would," Delia replied, stopping the car on the gravel in front of the door. "But not in my lifetime. I couldn't bear to have hordes of people staying here with me. Although I am considering opening it to the public on certain days of the week but haven't done anything about it yet as there's such a lot to consider with health and safety, cafeteria, toilets, guides and goodness knows what else. It will require a lot of careful planning."

They stepped out of the car and Delia removed Lucy's suitcase from the boot. "McFrain, the butler, has a day off today. He's had to go to hospital to see about removing a cataract on his eye so I shall have to play butler for you."

Lucy followed Delia into the entrance hall and gazed around with admiration. The room was long and wide with a massive oak fireplace. On the walls were swords and other weaponry and two stuffed stags heads. An enormous oak table was in the centre of the room, and in the middle was a huge cut glass rose bowl filled with pink and white roses.

"Wow," said Lucy again, her eyes widening with delight.

"I do hope your vocabulary extends to more than 'wow'," Delia remarked with a grin.

"Oh, sorry. It's just ... I've never been in a Scottish castle before ... in fact I've never been to

Scotland. It's exceptional ... so full of character ... and charm."

"Well, you've a lot more to see, within the castle, the estate, and the surrounding countryside. We're going to have a busy week. Now, let's get you up to your room and settled in and then you can come down and have afternoon tea." Delia laughed. "And that will be an almighty treat, believe me. Mildred can bake a cake like no other and I would be terrifically fat if it were left to her. I've had to put a ban on her cake-making but she wanted to put on a special afternoon tea for you, so I had to relent for once and can guarantee we won't have much room for dinner later."

Lucy followed Delia up the solid oak stairs, on the left-hand side of the entrance hall, to the landing. They faced a long corridor but Delia strode to the door to their immediate left.

"This is yours," she stated, throwing open the door so that Lucy could enter first. "I do hope you like it. I know it's facing north east, which certainly isn't the warmest part of the castle to be in but you have magnificent views of the lake and the forests and mountains in the background and you will get the early morning sun. I'm afraid the furniture is very old but the bed has a new mattress and is comfortable. I slept in it last week, just to make sure," she smiled.

"It's lovely," replied Lucy, looking around. The room was decorated simply with whitewashed walls and ceiling, with a huge four-poster dominating the room, draped in dark green velvet, matching the curtains and the shaggy rugs on the polished oak floor. There was an impressive oak fireplace with matching wardrobes and a large dressing table with a mirror decorated with gilt edging. Lamps with gold shades were on the bedside table and the dressing table. It was like an historical film set. She walked to the window and looked out in awe at the lawns, the vast lake and the mountains in the distance.

"Your bathroom is through that door in the corner," Delia said, plopping the suitcase on the bed. "I'll leave you to freshen up and then come back down to enjoy this gorgeous afternoon tea Mildred is so eager for us to eat. When you reach the entrance hall, turn left and go through the music room and then into the red drawing room. That's where I shall be ... and if you needed me through the night for any reason, my room is at the end of this corridor."

She walked over to stand beside Lucy and placed an arm around her shoulders. "I can't tell you how pleased I am that you decided to come and stay, darling. I know it must have been a difficult decision for you but I promise I shall do my very best to make it all up to you for all those wasted, lost years ... and remember, whatever I may have done, I have always loved you and I still do. I messed up badly at being a mother but I am going to do my very best to rectify it now."

Lucy looked at Delia. "And you don't harbour any more grudges towards Grandma Ruth or Steppie ... Philip?" she asked. She hadn't wanted to be so blunt. The words had just slipped out of her mouth but she had to know. She had to be reassured that this woman would never again harm the two people she loved most. Then she would be free to love her as a daughter should. She really wanted her mother to be in her life but if there was one little flicker of doubt in her mind that Delia still meant harm to her loved ones, she would have no choice but to turn completely from Delia and never see her again.

184

Delia sighed deeply, took her arm from Lucy's shoulders, and turned to look at her. Their eyes met, Lucy's questioning, and Delia's forthright.

"I'm going to be brutally honest with you, Lucy. You deserve that much. For most of my time in prison, I *was* plotting and planning to finish them off. The hate I felt for both of them has been with me for many years and ..."

Lucy gasped and put a hand over her mouth. It was true. Everything Grandma and Steppie had warned her of. God, what had she done? How could she have been so naïve as to come up to Blairness, all alone?

"Don't panic, darling," said Delia quickly. "I don't feel like that any longer, please believe me. For the last year I've had to endure endless counselling sessions and lectures on how to control my anger which, although I didn't think so at the time, have obviously helped as since coming here ... to Blairness ... I've begun to feel quite different. I don't know what it is but I feel happier and more secure and settled than I have ever done. I really don't hanker after Canleigh any longer and as for Ruth and Philip, instead of hating them, I have them to thank for being there for you and bringing you up."

She shrugged and stroked Lucy's shoulder. "If I continue on the path I was on before I was sent to prison, I'm going to lose any hope of regaining your love and only see the inside of a cell for the rest of my days. So, no, darling. All that is behind me now. I can have a really good life here, I want you to be part of it, and I promise you faithfully, I bear no ill will towards Ruth and Philip and have only love for you. Do you ... do you believe me?" she asked shakily.

Lucy felt her body relax. She hadn't realised how tense she was until that moment. There was honesty in her mother's eyes and she did believe her. She had to if their relationship had any chance of cementing. She placed a hand on Delia's arm. "Yes ... yes. I do. Thank you for being so candid."

Delia brushed a tear away and gave a relieved smile. "Right, now hurry up so we can get our teeth into this delicious tea we've been promised."

* * *

Mildred had surpassed herself. There were dainty little sandwiches made of Scottish smoked salmon, cucumber with Mildred's special mayonnaise, which tasted like no other, and Aberdeen Angus beef. Then there was the pudding and cakes; a fresh raspberry pavlova with whipped cream, sultana scones with homemade strawberry jam and cream and a decorated fruitcake covered with marzipan and icing and with the words 'welcome to Blairness, Lucy' written in pink icing on the top. It was all displayed on the coffee table in the centre of the red drawing room, along with the best silver cutlery and Sevres porcelain china and a large, ornate silver teapot and accessories.

Lucy entered the room and opened her mouth.

"Don't ... don't say 'wow'," laughed Delia, who was sat on the sofa, patiently waiting for Lucy to join her.

Lucy grinned. "I wasn't going to. I was going to say how awesome it all looks ... even better than the afternoon tea Aunty Vicky offers at The Beeches ... and we rarely have such a treat at Canleigh."

For an instant, Delia's face clouded over but she bent to pour the tea and Lucy didn't notice.

186

"I'm sorry to interrupt, Your Ladyship," said a voice from the doorway. "But you have a telephone call from a Miss Crystal Delacroix."

"Oh, McFrain. Let me introduce my daughter, Lucy Canleigh. This is McFrain, Lucy. He and Mary, his lovely wife, have looked after Blairness ever since your grandfather lived here for part of the year, when I was a young girl."

McFrain nodded in acknowledgement and smiled at Lucy. "Welcome to Blairness, Miss Lucy. I do hope you are going to enjoy yourself here and if there is anything you need, don't hesitate to ask."

"Thank you, McFrain. That's very kind," replied Lucy, returning his smile.

How did you get on at the hospital, McFrain?" asked Delia, pausing with the teapot poised over an empty cup.

"Very well, Your Ladyship ... although I have to wait around six months before I can have the operation."

"Oh, why is that?"

"There are a lot of people ahead of me in the queue apparently. I shall just have to be patient."

"No, you shan't," stated Delia firmly. "We'll find a private hospital where you can have it done immediately ... and I shall pay for it. We can't have you risking life and limb because you can't see properly. It's absurd."

"That's very kind of Your Ladyship," said McFrain, unable to comprehend how generous his employer was. Whatever she may have done, she was certainly extremely good to her staff. He wondered how many other people in her position would have done the same.

"Nonsense. It's the least I can do, McFrain. You are a very important member of this household ... now ... this Miss Delacroix. Tell her I am busy please, McFrain."

"She said it was very important, Your Ladyship and she had to speak to you today."

"Oh, blast the woman," groaned Delia. "I'll take it in the office as I expect it's something to do with work." She knew Brian was out and about on the estate and Connie would have left at 4.00 p.m. as she had two small children to collect from nursery, which meant the conversation with Crystal wouldn't be overheard. "Tell her I'll be there directly."

McFrain nodded and left the room. Delia smiled at Lucy. "I shan't be long. Don't sit there salivating, waiting for me. Get stuck in," she said, waving at the food. "And when I get back I want to hear all about this young man of yours. I must say, your engagement ring is very pretty."

Lucy did as she was told. The sandwiches were utterly delicious and melted in the mouth and certainly calmed her tummy which had begun to rumble ominously.

The little gold clock on the mantelpiece struck, indicating it was five o'clock. Lucy's thoughts sprung to Jeremy and she rummaged in her bag for her mobile telephone. She had promised to ring him to find out how he had managed with his own mother, hoping it was as well as she was getting on with her own. She looked at the call list but he hadn't rung her. Perhaps she should leave it for now. He might be having a lovely time and she didn't want to interrupt. She would ring him later this evening and then they could swap stories about their respective mothers. She put the mobile back into her bag and took another sandwich, thinking Delia better hurry up or she would eat the lot.

* * *

Delia was livid, marched through to the office and grabbed the telephone.

"Thank you, McFrain," she said, picking up the telephone and waiting until she heard him replace the receiver in the entrance hall. "Crystal!" she said through gritted teeth. "What the devil do you want? I'm in the middle of entertaining my daughter."

"Don't worry, Delia. I'll only be a few minutes. I just wanted to let you know my train gets into Inverness at three o'clock on Monday and I expect you will be there to meet me."

"Really. Well, I don't know if I can. As I said, I have my daughter here for the week and I have to entertain her ... and to be honest, I told you I shan't have time for you this week. Why don't you leave it a few more days?"

"But it's all arranged now," Crystal wheedled. "I have to leave my flat on Monday morning so I have no-where else to go and I'm all packed and have bought my ticket so I have no alternative but to join you ... and you needn't worry. I shan't interfere with you and your daughter. I shall have plenty to do to settle in, after all, Blairness is going to be my home too, and hopefully for a long time, so I shall need time to acclimatise myself before commencing my duties."

Delia sighed, realising she had very little say in the matter at the moment but if Crystal thought she was going to have an easy ride when she got here, she had another think coming.

189

"Right. Well, come if you must but I can't promise to meet you. I will send the butler, Mcfrain, if I am out with Lucy and he can show you around the castle and to your room."

"Good. I knew you would agree," sang Crystal. "I'm really looking forward to being with you again, Delia. See you Monday."

The phone went dead and Delia replaced the receiver thoughtfully. It was a damned nuisance Crystal had decided to come to Blairness this week. She didn't want any distractions from Lucy and as she had no idea how Crystal was going to behave and what she would say, she didn't know exactly how she was going to deal with her or what the hell she was going to give her to do. There was nothing in the estate office as Connie had it all wrapped up and as the girl had been in situ for a few years and was good at her job, there was no reason to dismiss her ... and Delia liked her too. She was a pleasant, happy go lucky young lady who was always willing to do any task she was set and she also worked well with Brian. No, Connie's job was safe.

Crystal was insisting she was going to be Delia's social secretary but that was a laugh. She didn't have a social life. She didn't want one. She was quite content being here at Blairness on her own, just with the staff and Brian ... and maybe Lucy now and again. She didn't want to socialise with the landed gentry of Scotland and anyway, with her reputation now, they probably wouldn't want to know her. So that was that, so what exactly was she going to give Crystal to do? Damn the woman. Damn, damn, damn!

By the time she went to bed, Lucy was desperately worried about Jeremy. She checked her phone in case he had rung and she hadn't heard it but nothing. He hadn't even sent a text. She rang him. It went straight to voicemail. She left another message. She sent another text. 'Are you okay? Please let me know. I am worried about you. All my love, Lucy,' adding a row of crosses.

She tried to find excuses as to why she couldn't contact him. He was enjoying himself with his mother. Perhaps his phone was broken or he had lost it. It had to be one of those and she had to stop fretting. He would contact her as soon as he was able. Of course he would. No doubt, she would wake up in the morning to find a message from him.

She lay in the enormous four poster feeling ... oh, she didn't know how she was feeling really. Apart from the torment of not knowing what was going on with Jeremy, her mind was full of the afternoon and evening spent with her mother.

Lucy had to admit she liked her. Whatever anyone said, she was okay. She was attempting to be open and honest, talking about her prison sentence and the attack on Granny Ruth and Steppie with sorrow and Lucy was positive it was genuine and concluded that they were safe now. Mother didn't seem to harbour a grudge towards them any longer and indeed, had spoken about how grateful she was that they had taken her daughter under their wing and given her a home.

Then Delia had been so interested in her life, her job at The Beeches ... and Jeremy.

"I do want to meet this young man as soon as possible," Delia stated. "You must bring him up here ... as soon as possible. It's such a shame I won't be able to attend the wedding but we can have our own celebration here, what do you think?"

Lucy had nodded, sad that it wouldn't be possible for her own mother to be at what was going to be the most important day of her life. For a fleeting second she wondered about asking Ruth and Philip if they would agree but it would be a waste of time. Of course they wouldn't ... and anyway, it would be breaking the terms of her mother's licence. She wasn't allowed within miles of Canleigh and its occupants unless anything happened to Stephen and the estate reverted to her but that wasn't likely to happen. Stephen was young and fit ... although she wished he wasn't going to Bosnia but as Steppie had said, they had to put their faith in Stephen's superiors. They knew what they were doing, the troops weren't going out to fight, and he was superbly trained and sensible. No, he would be fine. Then, eventually, he would leave the army, settle back at Canleigh, get married to some lovely girl, raise a family, and then there would never be any question about Mother having Canleigh ... and anyway, she had Blairness, which was going to keep her well occupied.

"For the first time in my life I have something I can really get my teeth into," Delia had enthusiastically stated earlier. "The estate has been well looked after ... Rathbones ... the solicitors, excelled themselves when they appointed Brian to look after it in my absence. He has done a sterling job but now I want to put all my redundant business skills into making it hum ... I have plans for Blairness ... I am really going to put it on the map as a place people

192

can come and enjoy on their Scottish holidays … and make some more money in the process," she grinned. "A place this size eats up an incredible amount every month … it's really quite frightening. Luckily, Father installed a new roof and spent quite a bit on other maintenance jobs while he was alive but there are plenty of other things that need seeing to … and they are all expensive."

Delia's eyes had shone as she talked about her plans, her words quickened and her gestures became more exaggerated as she explained the layout of the estate and what she intended to do with it, with the help of her estate manager. However, she was almost coy when mentioning Brian Hathaway. Lucy could even detect a hint of a blush underneath that thick layer of makeup. Lucy was intrigued. She would meet this man tomorrow. It would be interesting to see how he and her mother responded to each other.

She glanced at her silent phone again. If she hadn't been so worried about Jeremy, she would be enjoying herself. She was surprised to find how much she liked her mother, wanted to spend more time with her, and was looking forward to exploring the estate and hearing more about Delia's ideas … and she absolutely adored the castle. Delia had given her a quick tour of the main rooms this evening, all elegant, old, and full of history. Not as grand as Canleigh with its fabulous ballroom and gold drawing room but it was comfortable and homely and she had fallen in love with it.

Lucy recalled Grandma Ruth saying with wistful eyes, how much she had loved Blairness when she spent time here with Grandfather. It was where she had taken up art in a serious way and had loved spending time out on the hills, painting to her hearts content. Lucy had seen the room Ruth had used. Delia had shown it to her but there was nothing left of Ruth any longer. All her paintings and art equipment had been moved to Canleigh years ago but it was a lovely room and Lucy could just imagine her grandmother spending hours in there, doing what made her happy. Canleigh was littered with her paintings and Steppie was always encouraging her to have an exhibition. He was positive there would be a lot of interest, as was Aunt Vicky who had offered The Beeches as a venue, but Granny Ruth was humble and refused, not believing anyone would want to gaze on her efforts, let alone buy them. Lucy thought she was wrong as her paintings were beautiful; rich and colourful landscapes, sucking one in, making one want to slide into the picture, to be part of it; to walk by the rivers, amble along the pathways, climb the hills but Granny Ruth was adamant and no-one could move her.

Lucy yawned, curled up in the feather duvet and pulled the lovely squashy pillows underneath her neck. She quickly checked her phone again to see if Jeremy had sent her a message and she hadn't heard the ping but there was nothing. He was out for the evening with his mother she reassured herself … but that left her with mixed feelings too. She had enjoyed herself with *her* mother today but she hadn't forgotten him. A pang of hurt rushed through her but she dismissed it quickly. Jeremy loved her. He wouldn't upset her needlessly. It was his phone. It had to be. He had definitely lost it or it wasn't working properly. He might have run out of credit or forgotten to take his charger. There was sure to be a very good explanation. He wasn't laying dead in a ditch somewhere. He hadn't had a car crash. He wasn't in

194

hospital severely injured and on a life support machine.

She yawned again. It had been quite a day and she was desperately tired and full of the lovely food Mildred had produced. She always slept with her window open. There was a light wind outside and with her bedroom overlooking the lake, she could hear the lapping of the water. It was soothing and restful. She laid the phone on the table beside the bed and turned off the light. It was like being home at Canleigh. Pitch black. No street lights and tonight there was no moon. She placed her hand in front of her face and couldn't see a thing in the inky blackness. She hoped there were no ghosts in the castle. No. She wasn't going there. She curled up in the foetal position, closed her eyes, and within seconds was fast asleep.

* * *

Jeremy couldn't believe what had happened. He couldn't believe he was here, in Matthew's flat in an old Victorian mansion in Oxford. In his bedroom. In his bed.

He laid perfectly still. It was three o'clock in the morning, the curtains were open, and a streetlight lit up the bedroom. He could see Matthew's tousled head beside him, an arm flung carelessly over Jeremy's waist.

What the hell had he done? How could he have been so brainless as to come back to Matthew's flat? After all, he was the person who had made him leave Oxford in the first place. How stupid he was. How utterly, utterly stupid. He was engaged to Lucy, for God's sake. He was supposed to be in love with *her*

195

... but there was Matthew. There had always been Matthew. He finally admitted it. He had fallen for Matthew in a big way last year but hadn't been able to deal with it then ... but could he now? God, what was he going to do? He was supposed to be marrying Lucy and he really did want to. He wanted a 'normal' life with her ... and children ... but now he had encountered Matthew again, he couldn't imagine a life without him. He had never felt such a burning desire to be with anyone else. He was totally 'in love' with Matthew ... or was it just sexual gratification? He wasn't sure. All he knew was that he had thoroughly enjoyed their coupling two hours ago. It had felt so right and he wanted more. He lay as still as he could, not wanting to disturb Matthew, watching the sky turn from black to inky blue and then a murky grey as rain clouds formed.

He bit his lip nervously. He had to ring Lucy today. She would be wondering what had happened to him. What the hell was he going to say?

CHAPTER 16

OCTOBER 1995

Surprisingly, considering she had such a lot on her mind, Lucy slept well in the grand old four-poster bed and when she awoke, lay for a few minutes luxuriating in the softness of the duvet and pillows. Then, with a sudden jolt, she remembered Jeremy and immediately checked her phone. Nothing. He hadn't called her and he hadn't sent a message. She would just have to pray that he was all right and it *was* just his phone playing up. But then, why hadn't he used a call box? He must know how much she would worry. It was terribly selfish of him.

Lucy's worry began to turn to anger and despair. If he thought so little of her and couldn't be bothered to put her out of her misery, what hope was there for their future marriage and life together?

Luckily, Delia's enthusiasm for having her daughter all to herself managed to push Jeremy's thoughtlessness to the back of Lucy's mind. They had breakfast together in the cosy dining room with seating for only around ten guests at the most but it was incredibly pleasant, overlooking the lawns and the lake with the sun streaming in the windows in the early mornings, bathing the diners in a warm glow. Delia had informed Lucy that the massive entrance hall was used to entertain larger parties for dining or the odd ceilidh.

McFrain had just finished placing all the dishes on the sideboard as Lucy entered the room. Delia was still to make an appearance.

The butler gave a little bow and waved a hand at the food. "Good morning, Miss Lucy. I hope you slept well and are hungry. You'll need a good Scottish breakfast inside you if you're going out on the hills with Lady Delia."

A laugh behind her made Lucy turn. Her mother walked into the room, smiling widely. She threw her arms around Lucy and kissed her on the cheek. "Morning, darling. Yes, McFrain is quite right. As beautiful as the weather is, it is October and can get chilly up on those hills. We can have a lovely long walk and then have lunch in one of the village pubs. I'm hoping Brian can join us as I would like you to meet him."

Lucy smiled. "That sounds lovely. I'm so looking forward to seeing the countryside. It looks so beautiful from my window."

McFrain smiled, gave another little bow, and left the two women to enjoy the hearty breakfast Mildred had produced.

"I shall go home a stone heavier," Lucy grinned. "Mildred certainly is a fabulous cook."

"I know. She's a gem. You will just have to go on a diet once you get back to Yorkshire ... after all, you don't want to waddle down the aisle."

Lucy gave a weak smile. That was if Jeremy still wanted to go through with it. Where the hell was he?

"I've just got a few things I want to check in the office before we go out," said Delia, spooning four teaspoons of sugar into her black coffee as they finished off breakfast. "I'll meet you in the hall in half an hour. I presume you have brought some sensible footwear as I suggested."

"Yes. I have my walking boots. Jeremy and I like to go out for hours over the moors at home so I have all the right gear."

They left the dining room, Delia, taking her coffee with her, heading off through a door on the opposite side of the entrance hall into the estate office and Lucy back upstairs to her room. The first thing she did was to check her phone again. Still nothing. It was now nine thirty. She hadn't spoken to Jeremy for a full twenty-four hours and had no solid idea of where he was and what was happening to him. She couldn't go a minute more without knowing.

In sheer desperation, she rang The Beeches, praying Vicky wouldn't be on reception, as occasionally she would give the staff a hand, especially during their breaks. There was no need to worry her unnecessarily. Lucy sighed with relief when she heard the familiar tones of Gillian.

"Gillian ... it's Lucy. Have you by any chance seen Jeremy this morning? I need to speak to him urgently and he's not answering his mobile."

"No. Lady Victoria was asking the same thing a few moments ago. She's not seen him either."

Lucy's heart plummeted, she felt sick, and for a second she was speechless.

"Lucy ... are you okay?"

Lucy cleared her throat. "Yes ... sorry, Gillian. Look, if he does turn up, will you please ask him to ring me as soon as possible?"

The conversation had made Lucy's fears far worse. If Aunty Vicky was looking for Jeremy, he certainly wasn't at the hotel. He couldn't have made it home from London. Oh, hell. How was she going to concentrate on having a nice day with her mother when she was so concerned about him? She didn't know whether to feel angry or sick with worry. Her thoughts began to turn wild again. He might be in a hospital somewhere. He might have been mugged. He might have had a car accident. He might be dead!

She walked to the window and looked out over the beautiful Scottish mountains beyond the lake. The scene was calming to the soul. She took a few deep breaths, trying to stop her mind from running out of control. If anything bad had happened to him, Aunty Vicky would have been informed and obviously she hadn't if she was asking the reception staff if they had seen him. So, nothing terrible had occurred. It was probably as she had first thought. It had to be his phone and he just hadn't thought to use a call box. He was probably on his way back to Harrogate now, having stayed in London overnight. Perhaps he had thoroughly enjoyed his mother's company, they had had a late night, he had drunk too much and was still in bed suffering with a gigantic hangover and daren't drive yet.

Even so, Lucy was incredibly miffed and was going to tell him so. She rang him again. It went straight to voicemail.

"Jeremy! Where are you?" She tried to keep the panic out of her voice but wasn't very successful. "Please ... ring me! You are being incredibly selfish and I am losing patience. If ... if you're having second thoughts about the engagement ... well, I will try to understand but this isn't fair of you to leave me dangling. I just want to know you're all right. I can't bear not knowing ... and Aunty Vicky is asking questions too. Please set our minds at rest. Please, darling ... please ring me."

Jeremy heard his phone but Matthew's caresses with his beautifully manicured hands prevented him even turning his head to see who it was, although he guessed it was Lucy … but he couldn't talk to her now. He was in heaven. Matthew was consuming him, not only his body but also his very soul. Jeremy had never felt like this before. He was on cloud nine, enveloped in the most glorious sexual encounter he had ever experienced. He had only had sex with a couple of girls while at college in Oxford and then Lucy but even with her it wasn't like this. The bliss, the ecstasy. He was drowning in it. He was in love … really, madly, deeply in love … and not with Lucy to whom he was engaged.

"God, you're fantastic," breathed Matthew in his ear. "I always knew you would be. I've wanted you for so long and now I've had you, I'm never letting you go."

Jeremy moaned as Mathew's hands drifted further down his body. He had never wanted anyone so much in his life. He reached out and pulled Matthew's head to his. Their lips met in a crushing kiss and all thoughts of Lucy left Jeremy's mind.

* * *

Despite not being able to contact Jeremy, Lucy enjoyed her first full day with her mother. They met in the hall, suitably attired in waterproof and windproof jackets and trousers. Lucy's were powder blue which set off her blonde hair and Delia was in

201

navy. She carried two black walking poles and gave one to Lucy.

"Believe me, you will need this at times. Once I became used to using one, I found it invaluable ... now, we'll walk round the castle first so you can see the grounds properly, then we'll pop into the office so you can meet Connie, the secretary, and Brian, if he's about and then we'll set off. We can get up to McCullen Top easily before midday and then drop down into Elvington village for lunch. The Black Horse has an excellent reputation for its food."

"That sounds great," replied Lucy, determinedly pushing Jeremy to the back of her mind. If he wanted to be so selfish, that was up to him. She wasn't going to let his lack of manners and concern for her ruin her first whole day with her mother. She had waited too long for this.

And despite Jeremy, she had a great time. They walked first around the outside of the castle, bordered by vast lawns leading down to the lake on the east side and then round to the magnificently laid out gardens on the south side, just outside the red drawing room and the library. On the west side of the castle stood the stables, with enough loose boxes for twenty-five horses. Beyond the gardens and the stables, wrought iron fencing kept out the sheep grazing on the adjacent fields.

"They all belong to one of the tenant farmers," explained Delia. "His family have been here since Granny's father was here ... gosh, Lucy, he would have been your great, great grandfather."

"What was your Granny like," asked Lucy. "I love that picture of her over the fireplace in the library at Canleigh. She was very beautiful."

Delia gulped. "Granny was wonderful. I loved her very much. I was devastated when she died."

Lucy was astonished to see tears springing up in Delia's eyes but she brushed them away quickly and looked up at the castle. "But living here is such a comfort. She loved this place and I am so privileged that even though she willed it to my father, she also put in a proviso that when he died, it was to be mine. She knew I could never have Canleigh, although I wanted it so badly, so she left me the next best thing."

Recovering her equilibrium, Delia linked her arm with Lucy's and smiled. "And I am going to make this place hum. I have the skills and the knowledge and with Brian to back me up, we are going to turn Blairness into one of the most sought after places for holidaymakers."

Lucy smiled back. Her mother's enthusiasm was good to see.

They potted around the gardens, admiring the clipped box hedges, the bronze chrysanthemums, the white hydrangeas, the delicate Acer trees turning into the most beautiful deep reds and gold, surrounded by great rhododendron bushes, not in flower now but with formed buds, ready to burst out into all their glory next spring. Then they moved onto the stable block on the west side of the castle.

"I've been wondering about buying a horse," admitted Delia, "but still haven't done anything about it ... but if you want to come and stay more often, perhaps I can get one for each of us and we will be able to go riding together ... that is, I presume you still ride. You were a brilliant little pupil when you were small ... remember all those lessons Philip and I gave you at Tangles on that little Shetland."

"Timmy ... yes, I do remember. I loved him, he was such a determined little thing ... he's still there ... in well-earned retirement. I take him a carrot now and again ... and yes, I still ride. I pop over to Tangles occasionally and go hacking with some of Steppie's clients ... those who can ride without supervision.

Lucy was surprised to find her mother could talk about Steppie and the past. She had thought it would be a subject they would have to steer well clear of, although it would be difficult not to mention either Granny or Steppie, or Canleigh, if Delia wanted to know about her life.

They left the stable block, walked along the west side of the house, waved at Mildred in the kitchen, headed past the staff sitting room, and the boot room, and finally reached the entrance to the office. Delia opened the door, and Lucy followed her into the spacious room in the north west corner of the castle. It was a light and airy room with double aspect windows overlooking the stables on one side and the front of the castle on the other, making it possible to see all along the drive to the main gates. Connie was sitting at a desk in the far corner of the room with a row of filing cabinets behind her, an open laptop in front of her, along with a pile of papers and a shorthand notebook covered with fascinating squiggles. There were two other desks, both in front of the windows with files, laptops and telephones arranged neatly.

"This is Connie," said Delia with a wide smile. "Connie, this is Lucy, my daughter," she added proudly.

Connie, an attractive young woman, dressed in black trousers and a blue sweater, stood up and shook Lucy's hand."

"Welcome to Blairness, Miss Lucy. I do hope you will enjoy your stay."

"Thank you," said Lucy, smiling back. "I'm sure I shall."

"Has Brian been in yet?" asked Delia.

"Yes. He's been and gone. Had a quick look through the post and now he's driven up to Glen Finnoch. He didn't say why but he will be back for lunch."

"It's a shame we missed him but we'll catch up later. Lucy and I are off up to McCullen Top and then having lunch at the Black Horse in Elvington. Perhaps you could ask Brian to join us. We should be there around one o'clock."

They left Connie to get on with her work and ambled back out into the stable yard and the sunshine. Their walk took the whole morning and Lucy enjoyed it far more than she had ever thought possible. Her mother was knowledgeable about all the flora and fauna and pointed out things of interest along the way. They even saw a golden eagle soaring majestically high in the sky above their heads and took the opportunity to sit on some well-placed rocks and enjoy the spectacle. The bird circled for quite a while, dipping and rising above them as if he were showing off to his human audience of two. Then suddenly, he rose higher in the sky and disappeared from view over the hill.

"That was awesome," sighed Lucy. "This is awesome," she said, sweeping her hand in front of her. "I think I am falling in love with Scotland."

"Well, it's in your blood, darling ... but I know what you mean. We all spent our summer holidays up here as children ... Richard, Vicky and I ... and we brought Philip and other friends." Delia's eyes had a far away look in them. "We had such a fabulous time … riding, walking, and playing crazy games in the castle. We all loved coming up here every year … the only fly in the ointment was our mother."

"Oh? I don't know much about her. What was she like?" Lucy had seen an odd photograph of Margaret when she was Duchess of Canleigh but Granny Ruth had never met her and Steppie didn't say much apart from what a terrible scandal she had caused which had resulted in making Delia very ill and upsetting Anne, the Dowager Duchess, so badly that she had a stroke and died.

"Awful. Quite, quite awful," said Delia quietly. "We all so wanted her to behave like a real mother but our wish was never granted. She spent weeks … months even, away from Canleigh, messing about with other men all over the world. Our interests and welfare were never important to her. She never wanted to spend time with us and when she came up here every summer, she was a nightmare. Just complained and moaned about how cold and dreary it was. She could never see the beauty in it. Then she took up with Parfitt … and cleared off. I saw him, you know. I found him in the Caribbean just after she had died. He was in a terrible state, drinking himself to death and had no money. He was desperate to get back to the UK so I gave him enough cash to catch a plane home. Whether or not he did I have no idea as I never heard of or saw him again."

"That was kind of you, considering he had broken up your family."

Delia gave a wry smile. "I suppose I felt sorry for him. Mother had ripped him to shreds, just as she did us. As long as she was all right, it didn't matter about anyone else. Dreadful woman … and," she said,

turning to face Lucy. "I have done the same to you …
not in quite the same way but I selfishly destroyed
your childhood because I was consumed with anger
and jealousy. It was so foolish of me … and
unforgivable. We had a good life. Ruth had kindly
allowed us to reside at the Dower House, which was
where Granny had lived for many years before her
death. I might not have been in charge of Canleigh but
we were actually living on the estate and we were
happy, darling, weren't we? Just us, in that lovely old
house."

Lucy thought back to that time when she had been
so young. She could remember it well … and yes, her
mother was right. It had been a marvellously idyllic
episode in their lives, abruptly ending with her
mother's horrendous attack on Steppie and Granny
Ruth. She shuddered, the scene at the lake as vivid as
the day it had happened.

Lucy nodded … if they were going to clear the air
completely, now was the time to do it. "Yes, we were
… so why … why did you do it … why did you go so
berserk that day?" She knew, of course. Ruth had
explained it to her very carefully many years ago but
she had never heard it from her mother and it was
from her lips that she wanted clarification.

Delia took in a sharp intake of breath. What she
said now was going to make or break her relationship
with her daughter but she knew she had to be as
truthful as she could be. This wasn't the time for
deceit or a cover up … at least not about Ruth and
Philip. Richard and Rocky were a different matter.

"You know I was engaged to Philip … your
Steppie as you call him."

Lucy nodded, biting her lip nervously.

"Well, he was the love of my life. We had grown up together and he was the boy ... the man that I wanted. I loved him passionately and couldn't wait to marry him ... then ... then he broke it off ... just a few days before the wedding ... for Sue Cartwright ... a woman who owned a tack shop in Harrogate." Delia's voice was hardening and Lucy looked at her anxiously.

"It nearly killed me, Lucy. The pain of losing Philip ... the boy ... the man ... I had loved and worshipped since I was a toddler ... the anguish, seeing him with someone else ... it was so brutal. I never had an inkling, no warning ... and to drop me like that, only days before our wedding ... I couldn't come to terms with it. There were other men, of course, but no-one who could compare with him. I thought of him as my soul mate. He was my best friend as well as my lover. I can't tell you how hard it was, knowing there was going to be another woman in my place, living at Tangles, sharing his life and his bed. I nearly went demented with despair."

Tears were welling up in Delia's eyes. It still hurt badly.

"I was away from the estate for quite a number of years and then I went back with you ... to the Dower House ... and Philip was on his own ... *she* had died. Philip had been good enough to care for Demon while I was away and we decided it was kinder for him to remain at Tangles instead of being stabled at Canleigh. Anyway, Ruth was terrified of him and wouldn't have wanted him on the estate. So, I took to riding every day at Tangles and Philip and I started to repair our friendship. I was determined he would eventually see we should be together and that was my plan ... to marry him. I always wanted to marry him. There was never anyone else but him for me."

Delia hesitated for a second, not quite knowing how to go on. Lucy was looking over the valley below but Delia knew her daughter was listening intently, waiting for the next words that would be absolutely shattering.

"Go on," urged Lucy, still not looking at her.

Delia took another deep breath. "I ... I invited Philip back to the Dower House that afternoon. We had been riding, just as we used to as kids ... as teenagers ... like we had when we were engaged ... I thought I could rekindle his love for me ... and then he told me ... he told me that he had asked Ruth to marry him the night before. I can't tell you how that felt. I was utterly shattered ... utterly broken that he could do it to me again ... crush all my hopes for a life with him a second time. I just saw red, darling. I'm sorry but that was how it was. I just wanted to hurt him for hurting me so badly. We were in the drawing room at the Dower House and the poker was there ... in front of me ... and before I knew what I was doing I had picked it up and was hitting him with it ... then I came after Ruth ... my nemesis ... she had thwarted my hopes of ever having Canleigh by producing Stephen ... although I had come to terms with that ... but to take Philip from me. I can't tell you, darling, how enraged I was. I was totally out of control and quite frankly, didn't realise or care what I was doing in those minutes. The agony ... the grief ... it was tearing me apart and was just unbearable. I loved Philip so very much and couldn't bear to see him with another woman for a second time. I was absolutely destroyed," she said, her voice breaking up.

Lucy turned. Delia had dissolved into tears, her shoulders shaking as the age-old grief for her lost lover took hold. She hadn't cried about Philip for a very long time and now she had started, she couldn't stop.

"I am so sorry, Lucy," she sobbed. "I am so very, very sorry for what I did to them ... to you ... to me ... can you ever forgive me?"

Lucy put her arms around her mother. "It was a dreadful thing you did but thank you for telling me ... I understand it better now ... but you have paid the price and done the time. Let's put it all behind us now and look to the future."

Delia smiled through her tears. "I haven't quite done my time. I am still on licence for a few years."

"Even so ... you are free to care for all this," Lucy waved an arm over the castle in the valley below. "And will have great fun putting all your plans in place ... and I'll come up often ... with Jeremy," she gulped, feeling a faint touch of guilt that he had been pushed from her mind for the morning.

"Will you ... will you, really, darling?"

Lucy nodded. "Yes. I will. I promise."

Delia fished in her pocket for a tissue to wipe the tears from her ravaged face. "God, Lucy. I have done some terrible things in my time, some of which I shall never tell a soul but I am truly sorry about the grief and anguish I must have caused you."

Lucy's interest was piqued. She knew about the rumour that Delia had killed her own brother and someone called Peter Percival who was supposed to be her half brother and feeling braver now that Delia appeared to be truly contrite, she ventured another question.

210

"Did you … did you kill your brother and that American chap?"

Delia pressed her hands to her head, unable to look Lucy in the face. "The trial collapsed. There was no evidence that I had," she muttered.

Lucy sat stock still, not knowing what to think. Her mother hadn't denied it but hadn't admitted it either. From her demeanour, Lucy surmised she might well have been guilty and suddenly she really wanted to know if her mother was an actual murderer. She had no idea what she would say if Delia did admit it but the question was there, between them.

"I know the trial collapsed but did you … did you kill them? Please tell me. I really need to know."

Delia turned, taking her hands away from her head. Her face was wet with tears and the ugly scar was showing underneath the layer of make-up. She looked defeated but her words were strong and bold.

"I shot Rocky. It was self-defence. He had shot Richard. I struggled with him to get the gun as he turned it on me and it went off. End of story."

"So you didn't plan it then … to kill Uncle Richard, as he was the heir to Canleigh and you wanted it?"

"No. Of course not. Richard was my twin. We had grown up together, played together. How could I hurt him?" Delia lied blatantly. "It was a terrible shock to me when Rocky brought out that gun and aimed it at Richard."

"But how did he get a gun? You had just flown over from America. How did he get it through Customs?"

"Apparently he sneaked out of the hotel we stayed in at Heathrow. He must have had a contact somewhere nearby that I knew nothing about. He

211

could easily have arranged it before we left the States."

"But why? Why did he want to kill Uncle Richard? It seems so bizarre."

"He was a druggie, darling. His brain was addled with cocaine and marijuana. I don't think he knew what he was doing, waving that gun around. I think he was as shocked as me when it actually went off and Richard keeled over and when he aimed it at me ... it was the most frightening moment of my life ... I had to get it off him and in the struggle ... it went off. God," she shuddered, "it was awful. I couldn't get out of that flat quickly enough."

"So, it really was all down to this Rocky chap ... your half brother."

"Yes ... and don't let anyone ever tell you any differently. The courts let me go. There was no evidence and that was that. There was no case to answer. My killing Rocky was purely self defence and no-one could prove otherwise."

"I see," said Lucy slowly, letting the words sink in. She badly wanted to believe her mother but there was something ... just a little niggle of doubt. She sounded sincere enough and obviously the judge had thought so otherwise the trial wouldn't have collapsed but ...

"You don't believe me, do you?" said Delia quietly, staring out over the landscape, avoiding eye contact with Lucy.

"To be honest, I'm not sure ... I want to, I really do, but it still seems odd to me, as to why this Rocky person would deliberately take a gun on his first visit to his half brother. Why? Why would he do that?"

"Money I expect. You see, darling, he might have had one hit single in the charts but the whole band let

212

it go to their heads. They drank and took drugs and wasted all the money they had made. Rocky was broke. He was relying on me to bail him out but I was pretending to be broke too as I really wanted him to pull himself together, get on with making more records and not relying on me for cash."

The lies tripped off Delia's tongue. She had rehearsed them so many times before she had pulled the trigger on her brothers and so many times afterwards. If she could pull the wool over the eyes of the court and that severe old judge, she should be able to do it to her own daughter.

"I had told Rocky about Canleigh, about Richard and how he had inherited a cool million from Granny and that if anything happened to Richard, I would get the lot. In his addled brain I suppose he thought if he killed Richard and I inherited everything … including Canleigh when Father died, he would be sitting pretty for the rest of his life as I would look after him."

"So why did he turn the gun on you?"

"I honestly don't know," Delia sighed. "But he did. I genuinely thought he was going to kill me. I had to save myself … and I did."

"I see," said Lucy, trying to picture the horrific scene.

"I'm sorry if it doesn't make perfect sense, darling but that was how it was. There was absolutely no evidence that I had planned anything and that was why I was set free … now please. Can we talk about something else? I hate to think about it. It was all so very upsetting. Richard was my twin and whatever anybody thought, I did love him … and have lost count of the times I have blamed myself for bringing Rocky over to the U.K and taking him to see Richard.

213

If I hadn't, he would still have been alive and we wouldn't be having this conversation."

Lucy looked at her mother, who was still staring at the beautiful scenery in front of them. What she said made sense and with a sudden wave of certainty, Lucy believed her. Of course she was telling the truth. Why would she lie? It had all happened years ago and the case dismissed.

"I'm sorry," she said. "I just wanted to clear it up. I really want our relationship to work and didn't want anything to be hovering around that needed to be said."

Delia turned to her and smiled, running a hand over her cheeks to wipe away the remaining tears she had shed earlier. "There's no need to apologise, darling. I don't want there to be anything lurking between us either. I want this relationship to work more than you will ever know. I've just spent seventeen years looking forward to having you back in my life again and am not going to mess it up. I promise you that ... so, while we're at it ... is there anything else you want to know about my lurid past ... although I can't promise to tell you absolutely everything," she laughed weakly. "There are some moments a woman has to keep private."

Lucy blushed. She certainly didn't want to know about her mother's exploits with men ... apart from one ... her own father.

"My father."

"Aah. I wondered when we would get round to him," Delia's voice hardened. She fingered the scar on her face. "That's what your lovely father left me with ... that ... and you," she squeezed Lucy's hand.

"What were you doing with him? He was Aunty Vicky's husband."

Delia sighed deeply. "Yes. I know … but he was the only one I could turn to when I was arrested after Richard and Rocky died. I needed to be bailed and he was the only person who would help. Father was in hospital with a heart attack and Ruth, who had just married him," Delia almost spat the words out, causing Lucy to look at her sharply, "she and your aunt were with him. They assumed I had planned the murder and had no inclination to help me. Barrie was the only person I could turn to … and he came up trumps. He didn't hesitate. We kept in touch during the period between my arrest and the actual trial and he was there to take me away afterwards."

"Kept in touch. You mean you had an affair … poor Aunty Vicky."

"Look, Lucy. Things aren't always black and white. Your Aunty Vicky was giving Barrie a hard time because she couldn't have children and he was fed up and thinking about a divorce. He was unhappy and I was unhappy. We just comforted each other, that's all."

"And you got pregnant … with me. Aunty Vicky must have been devastated … did my father know?"

"No. He died before I could tell him." She looked at Lucy, knowing she could face her now that she was telling the truth. "After the trial we went to Canleigh. We had a terrible row … we were drunk … and he hit me, sent me crashing down onto the floor onto a broken champagne bottle … that's how I ended up with this," she said, pointing at the scar on her cheek. "I had been smoking and the cigarette must have set the bedroom alight … I'm not sure exactly as I was knocked out. Apparently, he stormed out of Canleigh, got into his car, drove too fast down the drive, and crashed it into a tree. I was left unconscious in a bedroom which was on fire."

"God, how awful. How did you get out?"

"Anderson, the under-butler hauled me out apparently. It was very brave of him."

"So, when did you know you were pregnant with me?"

"I had guessed a few weeks before but hadn't had a test or told anyone. It was confirmed while I was in hospital after the fire."

"And you wanted me? You didn't consider a termination?"

"No! Of course not. I wanted you more than anything, darling. Barrie might not have been the person I would have wished for as your father but he had given me a gift … a very precious one … and I wasn't going to throw it away, believe me."

"Aunty Vicky must have been devastated … seeing as she couldn't have children."

"Yes, I believe she was … but there was nothing I could do about it and we all had to learn to live with it … how … how was she with you?"

"Marvellous. She's always been so kind and I admire her tremendously. She has achieved so much with the clubs and now the hotel," said Lucy with pride. "She's pretty remarkable."

"And you are now engaged to her adopted son," smiled Delia, touching Lucy's engagement ring.

Lucy's heart turned over. She hadn't given Jeremy a thought for most of the morning. Her phone was still switched on, and he still hadn't made any attempt at contact. She could kill him.

"Come on darling. I'm getting chilly sat here," said Delia, getting to her feet. "Let's wander down the other side of the hill into the village. Hopefully Brian will have received my message and will be there to meet us at the pub."

Lucy looked at her mother. She mentioned Brian a lot and always looked a bit ... not dreamy exactly ... but there was certainly something ... and Lucy had a feeling it was nothing to do with the fact that he was the estate manager. She stood up, eager to meet this man who her mother rated so highly.

Delia rose to her feet more slowly, checking Lucy's expression. She prayed her answers to her daughter's questions had satisfied her and they wouldn't have to have such a conversation again. Crystal ... bloody, bloody Crystal, was going to be another matter with her blasted tapes ... but she wasn't going to worry about that now. She had a nice lunch with her daughter and Brian to look forward to. She smiled brightly at Lucy and pointed to the path leading to the village.

CHAPTER 17

OCTOBER 1995

Jeremy found it hard to tear himself away from Oxford and Matthew. They had lain in bed in Matthew's flat for the second time in their lives, wrapped in each other's arms for hours, neither wanting to break the cosy bubble they found themselves in. Jeremy had turned his phone off, not wanting Lucy to invade what were the most beautiful moments of his life so far. He pushed the guilt to the back of his mind. Mathew was who mattered now. Matthew and no-one else.

"Don't go back to Harrogate," urged Matthew, running his hand through Jeremy's hair. "Don't run out on me again. I was shattered when you disappeared from Oxford last time and I could never understand why you fled. We had the most wonderful time together that evening."

Jeremy shifted his position, feeling incredibly foolish now, thinking of all the gratification they could have had if he hadn't rushed out of this flat and dashed home following their last encounter. It seemed ridiculous now but he was traumatised at the time, even though he had enjoyed the experience. Having sex with a man and wanting more had been a mind-blowing experience and sent him completely off balance for months. The angst of finding out he was gay was shocking. He hadn't wanted to be that way. He had wanted to be normal and the problem was made worse by not having anyone to talk to about it.

"I suppose ... I was ashamed ... confused ... totally bewildered."

"I do understand, you know, although I never had that problem. I seem to have known all my life that I'm gay. Anyway, I got you in the end. You see. We were meant to be together. So, don't leave. Stay here, with me."

"As much as I want to, I can't," sighed Jeremy, staring up at the white plastered ceiling with its Victorian rose in the middle. "There's my job for a start ..."

"Get one here. There are plenty of hotels in and around Oxford."

"Um. It's a possibility, I suppose. Although I don't think my parents would be too pleased if I did another bunk. They're already annoyed I chucked in Uni and they've been really good, giving me a job, although we all know that hospitality isn't really my cup of tea."

"Well, if law wasn't for you and the hotel trade isn't either, what do you like doing? Surely, you must be interested in something. Life's too short to waste it doing something you're not keen on."

"Well, there is something actually but you're going to laugh at this," smiled Jeremy wistfully, "it's ... it's gardening."

"Gardening!"

"Yes. We didn't have one in London ... oh, we went to the parks and stuff when we were small but I didn't take too much notice but when we moved to The Beeches five years ago and spent more time visiting Canleigh, I started taking notice of the grounds. Canleigh is exquisite ... and The Beeches ... well, it's just simply beautiful. Big lawns, herbaceous borders with an array of plants and bushes that come out at all times of the year … then there's a huge rockery and a fascinating little lake with cascades and weeping willows. It's simply gorgeous and I would love to be able to design something similar. I have lots of ideas."

He turned to Matthew, his eyes shining. "Oh, you should see them, Matthew. The lakes, the trees, the rhododendrons, the flowers, the roses, the parterre at Canleigh … and the kitchen garden. I just want to get out there and plant more, watch things grow, experiment with colour, change the landscape. My hero at the moment is Capability Brown. I'm reading everything I can about him. He was a pretty awesome man, you know."

"Blimey," Matthew grinned. "Do I have competition? I thought the man had been dead for a couple of hundred years or so."

Jeremy punched him playfully. "Don't be daft."

"Okay, but if you're that keen on gardening, why don't you do something about it?"

"Well, there are courses at Askham Bryan, that's a college not far from us … near York … but I hate to admit it, I haven't the bottle to ask my parents to support me again after leaving Oxford so abruptly. However, I was thinking, we have contractors coming in every week to tidy up the grounds, which costs a fortune, and I was going to ask if I could do it instead, which would save them a lot of money. Then, if they can see I'm really keen and want to get stuck in, they might look on a college course more favourably."

"Why don't you then? It's best keeping in with them. From what you've told me, they must be pretty rich with all the businesses they own … all those clubs and then the hotel … you could be damned well

220

off one day, when they pop their clogs," said Matthew, his dark eyes sparkling with speculation.

Jeremy grimaced. "Yes … possibly. Although there's Suzanne … my sister … and flaming little Katrina, who delights in telling me as often as she can, that she is the 'proper' child in the family and Suzanne and I are only adopted. She assumes she will get the lot."

"And will she?"

"I have no idea. It's something that's never discussed … after all, our parents aren't all that old … Mother is forty seven and Father … he's a bit older … and they're both in pretty good health, even though they work extremely hard."

"But one never knows what's around the corner … they might become ill or have an accident so you need to make sure you don't upset them in any way … play your cards right and don't take any notice of that silly child … Katrina. If your parents were good enough to adopt you, I'm pretty positive they will make decent provision for you if something should happen to them."

"Exactly … so you see why I can't afford to upset them too much."

"Then, I suppose, there is the delightful Lucy."

Jeremy looked at Matthew. His words had been sharp and spiteful. "I know … and we're engaged." He had told Mathew exactly how things were last night and didn't know why he repeated the fact.

"You can dump her for a start," said Matthew, pulling himself upright and lighting a cigarette. He exhaled. "The sooner everyone understands we are together, the better."

Jeremy lay still and thought about telling Lucy and his family. Everyone would be shocked and horrified,

Lucy most of all. Could he do it to them … to her? What would he say? Exactly how could he put it? 'I'm sorry but I'm gay'. How on earth would they react?

"You will dump her, won't you," urged Mathew, stubbing out his cigarette and slipping back beneath the bedcovers. He ran a finger down Jeremy's face. "Jeremy. Even if you don't come out … don't want to upset your family, you will abandon your engagement, won't you?"

Jeremy couldn't answer. The words stuck in his throat. He wanted to say he would but he couldn't. He knew how much Lucy loved him. She would be absolutely devastated, especially if he told her the truth. He went cold at the thought of doing it to her ... and the whole family would be shocked and horrified that he could be so uncaring of her feelings, whatever excuse he made up.

"And as for remaining up in Yorkshire … if you can't leave … which I can clearly see would be a foolish thing to do as there is so much at stake, I shall have to come up north more often."

Jeremy sat up abruptly. "No!"

"Oh? And why's that?" said Matthew, raising an eyebrow. "Ashamed of me, are you. Am I going to be your dirty little secret?"

Jeremy shook his head. "No. No … it's not that. I just need time, that's all. To get my head around what's happened. Everything … it's … it's all so fast. I can't quite take it in. I need to think about things and decide what to do. You must give me time," he said slowly. "Please, Matthew … that's all I need. Just some time."

* * *

Brian pulled up outside the Black Horse in the Landrover, Meg sitting upright beside him, just as Lucy and Delia reached the front door

Delia's face was wreathed in smiles as he got out of the vehicle, Meg following close behind. The dog wagged her tail enthusiastically and trotted over to Delia, who knelt down and cuddled her.

"This is darling Meg," she said, smiling up at Lucy. "The most spoilt Labrador ever."

"And why not? She's my closest friend and she deserves the very best I can give her," said Brian kindly, his eyes softening as he watched Delia making a fuss of his gentle old dog.

It gave Lucy a moment to study him and she liked what she saw. Dressed in a dark green wax jacket, brown corduroy trousers and green Wellingtons, he was tall and rangy with a shock of thick dark hair, a square face, beautiful blue eyes, and a wide mouth. For an older man, he was positively gorgeous and Lucy wondered why he wasn't married. He looked so ... dependable ... someone you could turn to in a crisis and he would deal with it and he obviously had a good heart the way he was looking at his dog ... and her mother. With surprise, Lucy realised this rather nice looking man might have feelings for Delia. Goodness. That was a turn up for the books.

Delia stood up and smiled at Brian, her eyes twinkling. "This is my daughter, Lucy," she said, placing an arm around Lucy's shoulders. "Lucy ... this is Brian ... to whom I have a lot to be thankful for

… he has looked after Blairness and its interests extremely well over the past few years."

Brian smiled warmly at Lucy and held out his hand for her to shake. It was big, warm, dry and firm, lending credence to her thoughts that he was a good person to know.

"Welcome to Blairness. I sincerely hope you will enjoy your stay. You couldn't have come to a better part of Scotland, that's for sure."

They settled in a corner table in the pub, the few locals already inside, smiling at Brian and nodding to Delia. Obviously, they were still wary of her and her reputation.

Lucy sat back, happy to listen to the conversation between her mother and Brian and stroked Meg, who lay on the floor, obviously hoping she would be able to have a little something come her way when the humans commenced eating.

Lucy was intrigued to see how her mother reacted to Brian. She could hardly take her eyes off him while listening intently to every word he said. As he spoke knowledgeably about the estate and the surrounding countryside, Lucy could understand why. The pair obviously shared a passion for it, along with improving the estate and its finances and then, there was their love of animals. Meg had lain happily at Delia's feet throughout the whole meal, Delia frequently putting out a hand to pat her, while Brian smiled at his dog now and again, even ordering a sausage so that she could enjoy her time in the pub too.

"I've heard there's a mare for sale … about four miles from here … just outside of Kinmoor. If you're interested I could take you over tomorrow," said Brian to Delia.

"I'm not sure," said Delia doubtfully. She had mentioned to Brian weeks ago that she would love to ride again but the last time she had been on a horse was when Demon was shot beneath her. Would it bring back the most painful memories that she would rather forget?

"It's the best way to see everything around here ... you know that," said Brian, aware that Delia had ridden there as a child and teenager. "Walking is great but you can cover more miles on a horse and you can get to places not accessible in a car ... that's why I hire a mount from Sutherlands, the local riding stables, occasionally ... and there's nothing stopping you doing that either, if you don't want the expense of keeping a horse of your own."

"True," said Delia quietly, mulling it over. It would be good to be able to gallop again, feel the wind in her hair and become exhilarated with the sheer pleasure of charging about at a crazy pace. Although no horse she could ever ride would ever touch her heart as Demon had. She smiled at Brian warmly. "Actually, that's a really good idea ... and I don't want to ride every day, especially in the winter so yes, I think that's what I'll do too."

"In that case," said Brian, as a waitress appeared at their table with their food, "I'm free for a couple of hours after lunch so why don't I drive you over to Sutherlands so you can have a look at their mounts and then take you both around the estate ... give Lucy a proper guided tour?"

"That sounds ideal, doesn't it Lucy?" Delia grinned at her daughter.

Lucy nodded enthusiastically. Anything that would make her mother happy at Blairness was worth encouraging. "Yes, it does."

"Good," said Brian, waving at the barman to bring them some more drinks. "That's what we'll do then."

Lucy watched her mother's smile broaden as she nodded her head in agreement. It was fascinating to watch. This strong, independent woman was actually letting her estate manager take charge. What was happening here? If she was right and her mother was becoming enamoured of Brian ... as he obviously was with her, then Granny Ruth and Steppie need fear no more. Lucy smiled. That would be a huge weight off everyone's mind, including her own ... the only thing she had to worry about now was Jeremy. She had checked her phone again when visiting the toilet on entering the pub. Still nothing.

"Perhaps Sutherlands will have a horse suitable for you too, Lucy. Then when you come up, we can ride together," Delia was saying. "In fact, we could even do it this week if they have a couple of horses free."

Lucy smiled at the barman as he approached with their drinks. She was so enjoying this time up in Scotland, despite her concern over Jeremy. She turned her smile on her mother, who was looking at Brian with a glazed expression. Goodness, she really was smitten.

"That's a lovely idea," said Lucy but didn't think either of her two companions heard her.

* * *

Jeremy dressed slowly. Matthew had left the flat half an hour earlier. He had a dental appointment he couldn't cancel as he had a loose filling, which had been playing him up all week. They said their goodbyes slowly and meaningfully.

"I want you to ring me every day," Matthew insisted. "I can't get through twenty-four hours without hearing from you and I want you to promise you will dispense with little Lucy as soon as you can. Meanwhile I'll see about finding somewhere to stay near Harrogate so I can come up often. Obviously I can't stay at The Beeches if it's going to cause problems ... at least until your family have had time to get used to the idea of us being together ... but I can manage most weekends."

"I regularly work at weekends. Don't forget it's a hotel I work in and we work shifts."

"Um. Right. Well, you must have a look at your rota and let me know when you're free so I can arrange accommodation ... somewhere where you can stay with me, away from prying eyes." His eyes had sparkled mischievously and Jeremy had to grin. Matthew's enthusiasm was infectious and Jeremy had visions of them entwined again. He groaned and reached out. He didn't want to go back to Harrogate. He didn't want to leave Matthew.

Matthew left the bedroom, kissing Jeremy firmly. "Ring me tonight," he said. "I'll be waiting."

Jeremy left the flat without checking his phone. He knew Lucy would have left more messages and he still couldn't deal with her. He would have to eventually but the drive back to Harrogate was going to take a few hours and would give him time to think about what he was going to say. God, what a mess his life was in. He slid into his car and headed out of Oxford.

* * *

"Jeremy!" exclaimed Lucy. "Where on earth have you been? I've been so worried about you. Why didn't you answer my calls or send me a message?"

"I'm so sorry, Lucy. I forgot to take my charger with me so my phone was dead."

Lucy's shoulders relaxed and she slumped back onto the feather pillows on her bed. She had just come up to her room to have a nap and then get ready for dinner tonight with her mother. Apart from the worry over Jeremy, which had now disintegrated, she was feeling happy and content after a lovely day exploring the estate and local area by foot, the welcome lunch in the pub with Brian and then all of them squashing into his Landrover, Meg relegated to the back much to her disgust, and bowling off to the Sutherlands to see their horses. That had proved a successful little trip as they had suitable mounts, a lively bay gelding for her mother and a gentle mare for her and they had booked a day's riding for tomorrow. They had then bowled along the lanes around the estate, Delia and Brian pointing out places of interest along the way. The scenery was breathtaking and Lucy was falling deeply in love with Scotland and certainly wanted to return.

"Well, thank goodness for that," she said with utter relief. "My mind was playing tricks. I was imagining all sorts of ghastly scenarios ... and how you might be badly injured or even dead. You have no idea how concerned I've been and if it hadn't have been for Mother and Brian, the estate manager, keeping me occupied, I don't know what I would have done."

"I'm so sorry, Lucy. I didn't mean to frighten you."

"Well you did so please, never do that again. Find a phone box or something. Where are you now?"

"Back at The Beeches."

"How did it go with your real mother? Was it … was it all right?"

"Well, not exactly. I shan't be seeing her again."

"Oh, dear. I take it she wasn't overly pleased to see you then."

"Yes, actually. She was very happy but … oh goodness, Lucy. She's absolutely awful. Common as muck, smokes like a trooper and greeted me in her flimsy nightclothes."

"Oh!"

"Yes. She's a hooker, Lucy, definitely on the game and doesn't appear to have a clue where our father is but from what she said, he sounds a good for nothing man anyway and not worth expending the energy trying to track him down. To be honest I couldn't get out of her house fast enough and I have no intentions of ever going back."

"I'm so very sorry," said Lucy sadly, thinking how the opposite was happening for her and her mother. They were getting on really well and she certainly wanted to spend more time with her.

"Where have you been since then? I rang The Beeches this morning and Gillian said you weren't there as Aunty Vicky was looking for you too."

"I … I spent the night in London … didn't feel like driving … I just wanted to be alone … to think," he lied blatantly. He couldn't tell her about Matthew. Not yet. He had to get used to the idea himself …, he hadn't a clue what he was going to say anyway, and when he did, he couldn't tell her over the phone.

229

"So didn't the hotel have a telephone you could use?" Lucy asked, still a little annoyed he hadn't made more effort to contact her.

"I couldn't remember your number … you know what these long mobile numbers are like. I find it difficult to even remember my own."

"You could have rung the castle … on the landline."

"Oh, Lucy. I suppose I could but to be honest I didn't even think of it. I was … I was in a bit of a state," he added, which was true. He had driven to Oxford in a daze, automatically driving but not having a clue how he got there, as he was so deep in thought about his rotten mother and how he would never find out where his father was.

"Oh, Jeremy, I'm sorry … I really am. Thank goodness you have Aunty Vicky and Uncle Alex, Suzanne, Katrina and … .me. We all love you so you don't need her."

"I know … and I am grateful … for you all … but it still hurts … anyway, how are you getting on with your mother? Is Lady Delia the ogre she is made out to be?"

Lucy laughed. "No, actually. At least she's not with me. We're getting on famously. We've had a super day today exploring, this morning on our own and then with Brian, the estate manager, this afternoon. He's really rather nice … and I think mother thinks so too."

"Really?"

"Yes," Lucy laughed. "I think she fancies him … and I'm pretty positive he fancies her."

"Oh, I say. A real Lady Chatterley scenario then," Jeremy joked, although it was the last thing he felt like doing but at least it was keeping Lucy away from

230

questioning him about his whereabouts during the last twenty-four hours.

Lucy giggled. "Well, he's rather a dish for an older man. I'm really surprised he's not been snapped up by some Scottish lassie but apparently he's never been married.

"If he keeps your mother happy, that's a good thing. She won't want to come down here and cause mayhem."

"That's what I've been thinking and she has loads of plans for Blairness so will have plenty to keep her occupied and away from Yorkshire."

"How has she been with you?"

"Lovely. Really lovely. I honestly can't believe she could have done all that she did but we had a good heart to heart this morning and I think she's told me the truth about everything and how she felt at the time. I can't condone what she did with Granny Ruth and Steppie, but I can understand it in a way and I can even feel sorry for her. She had an unhappy childhood with her mother causing such a dreadful scandal and leaving Canleigh, then she had a nervous breakdown and just before she was about to marry Steppie, he dumped her. Her father ... my grandfather ... refused to let her run the estate, then she ran away to the Caribbean to find her mother, only to discover she was dead. Then there was that episode when everyone thought she might have killed her own brothers but she clarified all that to me this morning ... and I can accept her explanation.

After that, she had an affair with my father ... Aunty Vicky's husband ... and ended up having a dreadful row with him. He hit her and sent her flying onto broken glass resulting in that horrendous scar on her face and leaving her pregnant with me. She must

231

have been in a terrible state and she had always loved Steppie deeply. Too deeply by the sound of it as when she managed to settle us into the Dower House at Canleigh and found out he was engaged to Granny Ruth, that's when she went berserk, tried to kill them and then herself.

Honestly, Jeremy, I do feel quite sorry for her. She's never had much luck with anything or anyone … and she's spent seventeen years banged up with all manner of people. It must have been dreadful for her."

"Blimey. She has got to you," said Jeremy with surprise. He really hadn't expected Lucy to feel sorry for Delia. He was damned certain no-one else did.

Lucy grinned. "Yes. I think she has … I find I actually like her and am more than happy to be up here with her … although I must say, I will be glad to get back to you. We have a lot to plan if we want the wedding to be at Christmas … it's only a few weeks away."

Jeremy fell silent. He was going to have to say something to her the moment she arrived back in Yorkshire and he was dreading it but Matthew wanted him to end it so end it he would. Although there was still a tiny part of him which didn't want to. He had liked the prospect of marrying Lucy and putting on a 'normal' front. Instead, he was going to have to cause her terrible pain and the family would be aghast, not only about him letting down Lucy but finding out why. With a shaky voice, he ended the call.

"Right. Yes. Well, I have to go. Aunty Vicky wants me on reception in an hour and I have to get changed. I'll ring you tomorrow, okay?"

"Okay … I'll …" but the phone was dead. He had gone without even saying he loved her. Lucy felt a pang of self-pity. She had so wanted to spend a little time telling him how much she loved him and wanted to hear the same from him but she might have been talking to an acquaintance, not the person she was soon to marry. Oh well. Perhaps he was just tired and still emotionally upset about his mother. He would be fine when she got back to Harrogate. She turned over, plumped up the gorgeously soft pillows, and rested her head gratefully. She was tired and now she knew Jeremy was safe and back at The Beeches, she could relax and enjoy the rest of her stay at Blairness. She closed her eyes and drifted off into a refreshing sleep.

CHAPTER 18

OCTOBER 1995

Matthew's dentist was only a few minutes walk away from his flat and he had hoped that if he wasn't long, Jeremy would still be there if he hurried back but he was wrong. Jeremy had gone.

He made a cup of coffee and settled on his brand new dark red leather sofa, which had cost far more than he should have spent on one item but he hadn't been able to resist buying it, considering that if one lived in Oxford, one had to keep up appearances even if one couldn't afford it.

His thoughts turned to his latest conquest. Jeremy had been an easy target when they had bumped into each other at that party last year. Matthew had fluttered his eyelashes and Jeremy was putty in his hands. Without protest, he had accompanied Matthew back here to his flat and within minutes was in his bed. It had been Jeremy's first time with a man but he had soon got into his stride and seemingly enjoyed the experience. It was afterwards when he disintegrated. He had cried piteously while Matthew had cuddled him, reassuring him that what they had done was quite natural, legal, and nothing to be ashamed of.

Jeremy hadn't listened. He had looked utterly shocked as he dressed hurriedly, unable to look Matthew in the eye as he stumbled out of the bedroom, downstairs and out into the night. Mathew hadn't seen him again ... until yesterday.

He had made enquiries about Jeremy following their first encounter and discovered he was reading law at Brasenose but that was as far as it went. He took to hanging around the college and eventually bumped into the chap Jeremy had accompanied to the party. On enquiring as to Jeremy's whereabouts, he was informed that the day after the party, he had jacked in his course and headed back to his family home in Yorkshire with no explanation to anyone.

Matthew was piqued. He had really fancied Jeremy and craved more than a brief fling but he was also lazy and couldn't be bothered to follow up the lead as to where he could be found. He was told that it was a big hotel somewhere in or around Harrogate but that was as far as it went and he took to consoling himself with the disappearance of Jeremy with other men who flittered in and out of his life with regular gay abandon.

However, this time it was different. This time there was more at stake. His finances were looking a bit grim and needed a rapid injection of cash if his present lifestyle was to continue. Matthew liked the good things in life but didn't particularly want to work for them. He had floundered through his English literature course at Oxford, supported with the profits of his parents grocery shop in Thame, and only just scraped through the exams to obtain his degree. Not wanting to work but obviously having to make a show of doing something, he asked his parents for a loan so he could rent a bookshop in Jericho, ignoring the fact that his father's business was on a downward spiral as he had an ongoing heart problem and had been recently diagnosed with Parkinson's disease.

Matthew opened the bookshop but once it was up and running, he grew bored quickly. Sitting there all day, waiting for customers, watching the clock tick by until he could lock up and spend the evening with friends in the city centre, soon grew tiresome. Regularly suffering from hangovers, he began to open up later and later in the mornings and close earlier and earlier in the evenings and as a result lost a lot of trade and the takings were miserly. He borrowed money from friends with rich parents and rarely paid them back and when an acquaintance gave him a tip for a race at Ascot and he placed as much as he could afford on the horse and it won, his interest in gambling came to the fore. He bet on everything now. He spent hours during the day in betting shops, placing large sums on horses and dogs and in the evenings, visited casinos, playing roulette and blackjack and pouring cash into fruit machines. Sometimes he won, sometimes he didn't but with the huge amount he collected at Ascot, he managed to coast along for a good few months without worrying too much but even that nice lump sum was beginning to fade away into nothing. He needed a more solid source of income and even though Jeremy wasn't wealthy, his parents were, so there might be an opportunity for a little skulduggery there … perhaps a little bit of blackmail if they didn't want the world to know that their precious adopted son was gay. It was an idea worth exploring anyway.

Matthew grinned. He hadn't been able to believe his luck when he had walked into the café last night and saw Jeremy sitting at a table. As soon as they looked at each other, he had known Jeremy would spend the night with him again … and it had been good … really good. Jeremy seemed to accept that if not totally gay, he was bisexual. He relished their love-making and Matthew guessed he was probably hooked now. Probably didn't mean definitely though. If Jeremy had stayed in Oxford their relationship would have been truly cemented but with him insisting on returning to Harrogate because of his work commitments, that was the danger ... once out of Matthew's grasp, he might revert for a second time ... become ashamed of what he had done again ... and that would be the end of that.

Then there was this damned Lucy woman to whom the silly chap had become engaged. She would have to be dealt with and got rid of, so the sooner he could get himself up to Harrogate and remind Jeremy of how good they were together, the better.

Matthew looked at his watch. It was eleven o'clock and no doubt Jeremy would be nearing Harrogate. At least he had his mobile number now. He would ring him later, when he had finished work. He rose to his feet. He really should open the shop for the afternoon but he couldn't hang around too long. He had a dinner date with Thomas early this evening and he didn't like to be kept waiting. They had been together for a couple of weeks but Matthew was growing bored of him. Thomas had no interest in gambling so wouldn't visit a casino and all he talked about was himself and his ambitions to become a famous actor in Hollywood at some point in his life. As he had only ever managed being an extra in a couple of Inspector Morse episodes, it was pretty doubtful he would ever attain his true ambition and until then would continue to be a frustrated barman in one of Oxford's seedier public houses. Matthew groaned at the thought of spending an evening with him, listening to his continual moans that no-one realised how much talent he possessed. He longed more for the educated mind of Jeremy, who could talk about and had opinions on things that mattered. It was time to get rid of Thomas out of his life. He would rather spend the evening alone, here in his flat, planning how he was going to see Jeremy again. He picked up his mobile and scrolled down for Thomas's name, determined to rid himself of all the dross in his life. He had someone far better in his sights.

* * *

Ruth was visiting The Beeches. She tried to get over to Harrogate at least once a week so she could pamper herself and spend some time with Vicky. A long, relaxing swim in Vicky's gorgeous pool, followed by a facial and back massage and then afternoon tea with Vicky herself was a treat she wouldn't do without and today they had plenty to talk about, what with the up and coming wedding and Lucy's trip up to see Delia. The girl was due home at the end of the week and Ruth would be jolly glad to have her safely back at Canleigh and away from her mother.

Blast Delia. Her release had put them all on edge, especially poor Vicky. Not that she had anything to worry about now. Delia would have no designs on anything Vicky possessed. She wasn't in line to inherit Canleigh and Alex was totally devoted to her and would never throw a glance Delia's way. He loathed her after what Delia and Barrie had done to Vicky, beating her up and raping her in a drunken, drug infused orgy of violence in their London flat. Alex would never forgive Delia for that.

Ruth did her regular forty lengths slowly, enjoying the gentle caress of the water lapping against her ears as she moved. An aquarobics class had just finished and only two other ladies remained in the pool so it was delightfully quiet and Ruth could allow her thoughts to wander. In an hour the place would be busy as doting parents brought their children for private swimming lessons so for now she could just enjoy the peace. It was only three o'clock and she had an hour before tea with Vicky so once she finished her last length, she moved to the sauna for ten minutes, followed by another ten minutes in the scented steam room. She showered and then lay back in the jacuzzi, allowing the force of the bubbles to relax her body even further.

"You look lovely and rosy," commented Vicky when Ruth knocked on the door of the flat later.

Ruth laughed. "I know. After a session here, I feel so very clean and new. I just love that new masseur. She gave my back a real going over today."

"Yes. She's very good. Now, I want you to try my new lime cake I've baked this morning. I've never made one before and I want to know what you think," enthused Vicky as they moved into the lounge.

Ruth smiled. Vicky was such a good cook and even though she was always busy with the business, she made sure she found some time for her favourite hobby and frequently produced fabulous mouth-watering treats for them all.

The cake was gorgeous and Ruth had two slices, ravenous after the afternoon's exercise. "This is crazy. I've just offloaded hundreds of calories and now I'm piling them in again," she laughed.

Vicky looked at her stepmother admirably. "I don't think you have anything to worry about. You have a super figure and you get plenty of exercise,

239

what with what you do here and then all the walking at Canleigh ... and you swim there every morning."

"True ... I always try and do forty lengths before breakfast every day. A habit I got into when I was married to your father. So, how are you, anyway? You don't seem your usually bubbly self today ... are you still worried about Delia?"

Vicky snorted. "While that woman is out of prison I shall always worry about her ... how on earth is Lucy getting on up there with her? I keep thinking about her."

"Apparently she's fine. She rang me yesterday and Delia is doing all she can to make Lucy's stay a good one."

"Oh, God. She's going to win the girl over. She's going to go into her play acting mode and pretend she's the one sinned against rather than the sinner. Lucy will be fooled into thinking Delia loves her and wants nothing but her happiness."

"Well, she probably does," said Ruth thoughtfully, stirring her tea. "After all, she is her mother ... and she did dote on Lucy when the girl was little. I saw it for myself when they lived at the Dower House and Lucy came up to the Hall every day to play with Stephen. Delia adored her and would have done anything for her."

Vicky nearly choked on her tea. "So much so, she ended up in prison for seventeen years. She wasn't too concerned about little Lucy then, was she? I just hope she's grateful to you and Philip for what you've done for her child."

Ruth smiled wryly. "Well, if she is, I certainly don't want her thanks. I love Lucy for herself. She has been a delightful child and we haven't regretted our decision for an instant."

Vicky frowned and rubbed her brow. "I wish ..."

Ruth threw a glance at Vicky. She looked so troubled and anxious. "Look, Vicky. We're all concerned about Delia but don't let it get to you. She'll do you no harm now."

Vicky smiled wryly. "Yes. I know ... but it's not just her. It's Jeremy. He disappeared down to London for a couple of days and has come back morose and unwilling to reveal where he has been. He won't talk to me ... in fact he's avoiding me ... and I can't understand it. He should be over the moon now he's engaged to Lucy and with the wedding to plan ... and then I had a funny phone call this morning."

"Oh? What do you mean ... funny phone call?"

"It was a young man ... on our private line ... asking for Jeremy. When I said he wasn't available as he was dealing with a guest and could I take a message, he slammed the phone down. Most peculiar ... especially as he knew our private number. As we're ex-directory, how on earth would he have obtained it, unless Jeremy has given it to him?"

"Have you asked Jeremy who it might be?"

"Yes ... and he went quite pale ... then blustered something about it being a friend who was probably looking for a job and he would ring him back later ... but I'm damned sure he was lying."

"Um. I see what you mean. What did he go down to London for, anyway?"

"To see friends I believe." Vicky bit her lip and sighed. "I have a nasty feeling about it ... and do hope it's nothing to do with why he packed in university so suddenly. I've never received a proper explanation for that either. I just wish I knew what he was up to. I hate all this secrecy."

Ruth didn't say a word as a sudden chill rushed down her spine. If Jeremy were up to something untoward, how would that impact on Lucy? Thank goodness they were only engaged and hadn't married yet but with the wedding arranged for Christmas, they hadn't long to find out what Jeremy was up to. Ruth wasn't particularly happy about this marriage in the first place but if Jeremy *was* up to no good and it affected Lucy or upset her in any way, he would certainly receive the full force of her fury.

* * *

Crystal stepped eagerly onto the train at the railway station in Norwich, her bag slung over her shoulder as she pulled two heavy black leather suitcases behind her. Luckily, the train wasn't too full and she managed to squash her luggage into the area set aside for suitcases near the door and slid into the empty seat in front of it, pleased it was forward facing, as she disliked watching the moving landscape from the opposite angle. It always made her feel a bit sick.

She removed her jacket and took out the novel she had bought especially for the long journey to Scotland. It was one of her favourite authors, Jenny Williams, who delighted her readers repeatedly with the investigations of her detective, Inspector Cartwright. Murders, bank robberies, rapes, and muggings. There was nothing Inspector Cartwright couldn't solve and, very often and quite ridiculously, almost single-handedly. It was all a load of baloney. Nothing like real life, if all the prison inmates Crystal had met were to be believed but it was good escapism when one wanted to retreat from the real world.

However, Crystal found that once the train moved out of Norwich and flashed through the Norfolk countryside, she couldn't concentrate on reading and her thoughts turned to Delia, Blairness and her new life. She knew she was blackmailing Delia into giving her a job and somewhere to live and didn't like herself very much for having to do it but the only other alternative was to put up with living the life the probation service had mapped out for her, working in dreary factory offices and residing in cramped little bedsits because she couldn't afford anything better.

From her bag, she pulled out another little book, a guide to Scotland, and its castles. Blairness was mentioned, not because it was open to the public but as it boosted holiday cottages to let. The picture of the actual castle was stunning with its pretty turrets and little windows. Crystal felt a thrill of excitement as she studied the photograph. She was going to live and work there. Her address would be Blairness Castle. How posh did that sound? Far better than Holloway prison or flat 1, Cinnamon Street, Norwich.

Crystal smiled, sat back in her seat, and stared out of the window, watching the landscape rush by. She was more excited than she had been for years … and she had Lady Delia Canleigh to thank for it.

* * *

"I have to go to the railway station to pick up Crystal in an hour," announced Delia as she and Lucy walked towards the castle. "Would you like to come with me?" She hoped Lucy would say no because she wanted to have Crystal all to herself, give her a good talking to and make sure that whatever the stupid woman thought, she wasn't going to blackmail her. However, as much as she didn't want Crystal at Blairness, the woman had been her only friend while in prison and life must be hard for her now. She could afford to be generous but Crystal must be made aware that Delia would not bow to her threats under any circumstances and if Crystal wanted to push it, her time at Blairness would be very short, whatever she may think she knew. Although there were those blasted tapes to find and dispose of. She might be able to persuade Crystal to hand them over. She might be able to threaten her. God, it had been totally stupid to get drunk that night and confess to the killing of Richard and Rocky. Under normal circumstances no-one would believe her cellmate but it was those blasted tapes. She had to get her hands on them.

"Actually, I feel pretty grubby" replied Lucy, looking down at her jacket and trousers, which were covered in mud, the result of taking a tumble down a bank. She hadn't hurt herself as the ground was soft but she couldn't wait to remove her clothes and get clean again. "Would you mind if I gave it a miss so I can have a bath?"

Delia's tension eased. "That's absolutely fine. You enjoy a nice long pamper. You can meet Crystal later."

"What's she like?"

"Oh, okay, I suppose. She was company for me in prison. We both read a lot and exchanged books and she shared my cell. She isn't aristocracy of course but she speaks very nicely and is well educated ... just a bit too gullible where the opposite sex are concerned ... having allowed herself to be dragged into a conspiracy to rob a stately home … all because she fell for a line some man fed her."

"Aren't you frightened she might do the same to you … steal your valuables?"

Delia gave a coarse laugh. "I don't think she would dare … and if she tried to, she would be very sorry, believe me."

Lucy looked at her mother sharply. Her harsh tones brought all the old doubts about her to the fore and she didn't want it to. The time they were spending together was far easier than she had imagined and they were growing closer by the hour. She didn't want the developing bond to be destroyed.

Delia saw the flicker of doubt cross her daughter's face and could have kicked herself. She had tried so hard to win Lucy over since she had arrived at Blairness and it was working. They were becoming friends, just as they should be. She had tried to be as truthful as she could so that Lucy would trust her and now, just because of her annoyance with Crystal, she had let down her guard. She threw an arm around her daughter as they walked through the back door of the castle into the boot room.

"Darling, ignore me. It's just a figure of speech. What I meant was that if Crystal did try anything, she would be arrested pretty damned quickly … not that I would personally do anything to her. Believe me?"

Lucy looked at Delia squarely. "I want to. I really do."

"Well you need have no fear then. I promise faithfully that I will never do anything to hurt Crystal. There. Will that do?" Delia grinned.

Lucy smiled back. Her mother looked and sounded sincere. She had to believe her otherwise every time she said something similar, there was going to be the same doubts enter her mind. "Okay, okay. I believe you," she said warmly.

"Good. That's settled then. Crystal will be fine in any case. She will be so grateful to have a decent roof over her head, a job she can enjoy and money in her pocket, she won't want to jeopardise it. It will all be fine. So," she said looking at her watch. "I better change too and go get her. I'll see you later, darling. Enjoy your bath."

Delia threw off her outdoor clothes and disappeared through the door to dash upstairs to change. Lucy removed hers more slowly, leaving the wet and muddy jacket near to the washing machine in the corner for one of the cleaning staff to see to. Luckily, she was the same size as her mother so could borrow one of her jackets in the morning if this one wasn't dry.

She had to keep her trousers on until she reached her room, as she couldn't pad through the castle in her underwear. Whatever would McFrain think if she should bump into him? She giggled as she ran up the stairs, just imagining the look on his face.

CHAPTER 19

OCTOBER 1995

Delia parked in the station car park. The train wasn't due in for another fifteen minutes and she sat in her car, mulling over exactly what she was going to say to Crystal. A few more vehicles entered the car park, their occupants obviously meeting people off the train as none of them hurried to leave their cars either.

The sun was streaming through her window and she opened it and closed her eyes, enjoying the warmth on her face. It made her want to go to sleep and she wished she were somewhere hot, where she could relax by a pool in a swimming costume with a drink by her side. Being an active person, she had never been one for those kind of holidays but at that moment, she would have welcomed it, rather than have to tackle a prison cellmate who was attempting to blackmail her.

She must have drifted off as someone slamming a car door shut nearby woke her up with a jolt and she realised with a sickening feeling that the train was in the station and people were beginning to swarm out of the entrance. She jumped out of the car, locked it quickly and moved towards them, looking for Crystal, hoping upon hope that she wouldn't be there. That she would have changed her mind.

Her luck wasn't in. Crystal stood on the platform, a bag slung over her shoulder and two bulging suitcases on the ground beside her. She smiled widely when she saw Delia.

"Hello. I thought you might have forgotten me."

Delia grabbed one of the suitcases. "Crystal. How the hell could I ever forget you … the car is in the car park. Follow me."

Crystal did as she was told, a wry smile on her face. She was here, in Scotland, about to go to live at Blairness Castle. For a second she was almost glad she had been to prison. If she hadn't, she wouldn't have met Lady Delia Canleigh or be here now.

Delia reached the car and slung the suitcase in the boot, waiting for Crystal to do the same with the one she was carrying. Delia jumped into the driver's seat and once Crystal was sat beside her, started the engine without a word and moved off into the traffic heading out of Inverness.

"No words of welcome, Delia?" asked Crystal, looking around her with interest. She had never been to Inverness before, it looked like a place she would like to explore, and a boat ride on Loch Ness looked most inviting as they drove past the sparkling water.

Delia didn't speak. She drove swiftly out of town, waiting until she could pull into a lay-by. She stopped the car abruptly, undid her seat belt, and turned to look at her passenger.

"Let's get one thing straight, Crystal. I didn't invite you here. I don't particularly want you here … but I do feel sorry for you. It must have been hard for you when you got out …"

Crystal snorted derisively. "That's a bit of an understatement. You simply have no idea how horrible it's been."

"No … but I can imagine. It hasn't exactly been a bed of roses for me either."

"Oh, come on! You have a bloody castle, pots of money … what the hell do you know about it?"

"It's the looks, the gossiping … whenever I go out. Everyone up here knows what I did and I can feel them talking about me, even if they aren't. It's not a nice feeling."

"Oh, poor you. My heart bleeds."

"Look Crystal. I am happy to give you a helping hand … after all, you were good to me in prison and probably saved my sanity at times but don't think you can blackmail me. Whatever I said that night when we got drunk on that ghastly alcohol … well, it's ridiculous. I had no idea what I was saying and you probably misinterpreted it anyway."

"But you did do it, didn't you? You did plan it all in cold blood. You did kill both your brothers. I have the tape, don't forget."

Delia looked away. The hills in front of them were covered with a great forest. It looked beautiful. She longed to be walking there, not confronting someone who wanted to be difficult.

"Crystal. Listen to me. I am more than willing to help you because I do owe you but please, don't think you are going to blackmail me. Tapes or no tapes, if you believe I am capable of murdering my brothers, and you know for certain I tried to kill two others, what the hell do you think I will do to you … up here … in my castle … in the wilds of Scotland? It would be damned easy, Crystal, for you to have an accident on the estate. It's pretty boggy, after all and there are numerous dangers out on the hills."

"Are you threatening me, Delia?" Crystal's voice was wobbly. She had thought she had the upper hand. To find she hadn't and her life could be in jeopardy, was more than a little disconcerting.

"Not threatening. Just warning. Now. If you have those tapes, hand them over. We can then get back to Blairness and never speak of this again."

"So, you'll still give me a home and a job?"

Delia sighed with exasperation. "Yes, you silly woman. Like I said, I owe you … so … the tapes please."

Crystal looked at her. "You absolutely promise? Honestly, Delia. I couldn't go back to Norwich again … that awful bed-sit, that dreadful job." She shuddered and her eyes filled up.

"Yes, for God's sake! I have a room made up for you on the top floor. You can eat your meals in the kitchen. You will have a monthly salary and can use my car when I don't need it. I'll try to find something for you to do, although we have Connie in the estate office who is more than competent and as I don't have a social life, I certainly don't need a secretary. However, there are going to be huge changes to the estate in the near future and I will probably need extra help, especially with opening the house to the public, and you are well qualified with your previous experience in a stately home. So, is that acceptable and are we quite clear? That is all I am going to offer you and all I'm going to say on the subject of my brothers. Do we understand each other?"

"Yes," smiled Crystal, unable to believe her luck. She rummaged in her bag and handed a white envelope, which contained the tape to Delia.

"Where are the copies?"

"There aren't any. I dropped my cassette player when I moved into my flat and I haven't been able to afford another so no, that's the only one."

"Are you absolutely sure, Crystal? You better not be lying to me." Delia's voice was severe and she was staring menacingly at Crystal.

Crystal gulped. "Honestly. I promise."

Delia took the tape and got out of the car. She dropped it on the tarmac and stamped hard until the plastic container was shattered. She pulled out the ribbon, ripped it into tiny pieces and then popped the whole lot into the envelope and threw it onto the back seat. It could be disposed of properly later. Pleased with herself, she slipped back into the car and smiled at Crystal.

"Right. Let's go home."

* * *

"This is my daughter, Lucy," Delia said proudly. They had reached the castle and were just getting out of the car as Lucy appeared at the front door, glowing from her warm bath and wearing clean jeans and a navy sweater

"Lucy, this is Crystal."

Lucy looked at the young woman, probably a couple of years older than her, who stood beside her mother at the rear of the car, pulling out one of two enormous suitcases. She was smaller than Delia, with a head of thick auburn hair pulled back into a ponytail and her round, unmade-up face was covered in freckles. She was wearing black trousers and a forest green fleecy jacket, which looked arresting with the colour of her hair and her wide, green eyes, complemented by the little gold studs in her ears.

Lucy smiled warmly and held out her hand.

"How do you do? I'm very pleased to meet you."

251

"Likewise," said the woman, shaking Lucy's hand. "And I am very pleased to be here."

From the rear of the car, Delia gave a grunt as she lifted the second suitcase out of the car. "What the hell have you got in here, Crystal? It weighs a ton."

"All my worldly possessions," said Crystal. "Absolutely all I possess in the world."

Lucy glanced at Delia. Their eyes met, Lucy's with surprise and Delia's with resignation.

"I'll show you to your room," said Delia. "I'm afraid we'll have to lug these upstairs ourselves. My butler, McFrain, has a problem with his eyes at the moment and I don't want him risking life and limb."

"A butler. My," murmured Crystal.

"Yes. A very loyal one. He's been with us for as long as I can remember. My grandmother appointed him when she was alive ... him and his wife ... Mary. She's on light duties at the moment too as she hasn't been well either."

"It sounds as if they need to retire and you need new and younger staff," commented Crystal.

"They will stay as long as they want. They know they will have a cottage on the estate to retire to when they are ready but not before. I won't push them out. If necessary, I will just hire extra staff to help them. In fact," Delia said, stopping in her tracks and looking straight at Crystal. "You could take over some of the housekeeping duties if you don't mind."

"Well, I am a secretary first and foremost," spluttered Crystal, not warming to the idea of being an assistant housekeeper. There was no kudos to that position.

"Yes ... but if you want to live here, you will have to help out. I thought I had made myself clear in the car," said Delia firmly.

Crystal appeared chastened and Lucy, who had stood in the hall while the two older women hauled the luggage up the stairs, was pleased her mother was taking a stand. She liked the McFrains. They had both been very pleasant and welcoming to her, telling her stories of what it was like in the old days when Delia and her siblings and friends used to stay at the castle every summer holidays. However, they were both becoming frail and it was obvious they needed help. Being young and healthy, Crystal could be of enormous assistance.

She heard Brian's Landrover pulling up outside and went out to say hello, as her mother and Crystal disappeared along the passageway at the top of the stairs.

* * *

"This will be your abode," announced Delia, puffing slightly after the exertion of dragging the suitcase up two flights of stairs to what was considered the nursery floor. Many of the rooms had been empty for many years but the McFrain's had a large flat the full length of the west side, while three rooms took up the old nursery on the south, partly above Delia's room below. There was a room for a nanny on the east side and what Delia considered the best, and furthest away from the McFrain's, was the large one in the north eastern corner, directly above Lucy's, and immediately to their left as they came up the stairs.

Delia threw open the door and Crystal stepped over the threshold and looked around eagerly. It wasn't bad, considering. It was sizeable, with a

253

double bed, a Victorian double wardrobe, chest of drawers and a heavy dressing table with a mirror on top. It certainly wasn't pretty but it was functional. There was a stone fireplace with a wooden mantelpiece, and the furnishings were a turquoise blue.

"The bathroom is through that door on your right," said Delia, pointing to the door. "Now, if we dump these flaming suitcases I'll take you down to the kitchens to meet the McFrains and Mildred, the cook. As you will be eating and working with them, you need to meet them as soon as possible. I can leave you with them to settle in. I'm taking Lucy for a drive shortly and we shan't be back until this evening so that will give you plenty of time to get your bearings. We'll meet tomorrow, after breakfast and decide exactly what your role is and what your duties will be."

"Yes, Delia," Crystal replied with a smirk.

"And that's another thing. I don't care about you calling me Delia in private but in public, it must be Lady Delia or Your Ladyship. Got it?"

"Yes, Your Ladyship. Anything you say, Your Ladyship," Crystal said, dipping a curtsy.

Delia sighed. "Pack it in, Crystal or you will be packing your bags quicker than you think."

But Crystal wasn't listening. She had moved to the open window and was looking out.

"Who is that gorgeous looking man down there, talking to Lucy?"

Delia hadn't heard the Landrover and walked over to the window, puzzled that her daughter should be talking to a man. Hardly anyone visited the estate. She looked out and saw the Landrover, Brian leaning on the bonnet while Lucy was making a fuss of Meg.

"That's Brian Hathaway, the estate manager," she said, annoyed that Crystal obviously found him attractive.

"Wow. Is he married?" breathed Crystal, her eyes not straying from Brian.

"No, but I think he may have a girlfriend," Delia added, knowing full well he hadn't but if Crystal was thinking of getting her claws into him, she would throttle her.

"That's a shame," replied Crystal, her eyes twinkling mischievously. "He's certainly a dish. I wouldn't mind getting him into bed, that's for sure."

Delia pretended she hadn't heard and marched towards the door. "Come on. I don't wait to keep Lucy waiting."

Crystal reluctantly peeled her eyes from the man below and followed Delia, wondering how deep this relationship with Brian and his girlfriend really was because if it wasn't too serious, she would certainly be setting her cap at him. He was simply gorgeous. The best looking man she had seen for a very long time!

* * *

Delia left Crystal with the McFrains and Mildred, shot back into the entrance hall and outside to find Lucy still chatting to Brian, Meg now lying at her feet.

"Hello," she said, smiling at Brian, her heart missing a beat. He was beginning to have a most peculiar effect on her and it was exhilarating to be in his company.

"Hello," he replied, smiling back. "I've just been telling Lucy all that you need to have a look at when you have your trip to Skye later in the week."

"Yes," enthused Lucy. "There's a lot to see. I don't think we're going to do it all in one day."

"Then we'll stay over. Find a nice guesthouse or something. I'm sure there must be some lovely ones there. It's a very popular tourist attraction after all."

"That would be nice," said Lucy. "It'll make a super end to my holiday up here."

Delia's face darkened for an instant. She had enjoyed having Lucy stay at Blairness more than she could ever say. The few days had passed so quickly and within a few more Lucy would be gone and goodness knows when she would come back. It was almost heartbreaking now that they were getting to know each other and getting on so well. She was going to hate seeing Lucy go.

Brian noticed the look on Delia's face and instantly sympathised. He had seen how much this visit had meant to Delia and he liked young Lucy. She was a lovely, sunny, thoughtful, and kind individual who listened avidly to all the information he provided in the time they spent together. He would also be sorry to see her leave but for her mother, it was going to a much bigger wrench.

"There's a lot of Scotland to see," he commented. "Perhaps after Lucy has gone home, I can show you some parts you haven't yet discovered." He was looking straight at Delia, hoping his words would help her adjust to life without Lucy and give her something to look forward to.

Delia looked at him gratefully. She guessed what he was doing and was touched he wanted to make her feel better. What a truly lovely man and yes, she

256

would love to spend more time in his company exploring Scotland but before she could tell him so, she was stopped in her tracks.

"So ... this is your estate manager, Delia. How do you do ... I'm Crystal," said a cultured voice behind them.

Delia turned and gave Crystal a withering look, which Crystal chose to ignore, her eyes straying over Brian's body with an expression of utter lust.

"Pleased to meet you," said Brian politely, holding out his hand for Crystal to shake. She took it, holding on to it longer than was necessary.

Lucy was fascinated to see that while Brian appeared faintly amused, Delia looked positively furious. Crystal, on the other hand, looked completely smitten and Lucy felt a vague sense of alarm and began to twirl her hair with her forefinger. If Crystal was going into competition with her mother over Brian, there was going to be an eruption and she doubted it would be very pleasant.

CHAPTER 20

OCTOBER 1995

Ruth looked around the dining table at Canleigh Hall and surveyed her family with pleasure. It was rare they could all get together but this weekend was an exception. Stephen, who sat opposite her at the far end of the table, laughing at something his girlfriend, Sarah Misperton-Evans was saying, was home on leave for a few days prior to being sent off to Bosnia but in twenty-four short hours he would have left Canleigh with no idea of when ... or if ... he would return. Even though she was constantly reassured he would survive, Ruth still felt a raging fear in the pit of her stomach and wouldn't be happy until he was back on British soil once more.

She felt sorry for Sarah too. She obviously loved Stephen. It was there, in the way she looked at him, spoke to him, and always had to be near him. She was a lovely girl, they made a lovely couple, and Ruth would be more than pleased if they decided to become engaged and marry at some point. Sarah would make an excellent partner for Stephen and a wonderful Duchess. She was also a lieutenant in the army, although not in the same regiment as Stephen. They had met at Sandhurst during training and had been close ever since, meeting up whenever duties allowed. Ruth wondered how Sarah felt about Stephen going off to Bosnia. Would she be as tense as she was? Would she lay awake at night, worrying herself sick about what was happening to him?

"Are you okay, Ruth? You look far away?" remarked Philip at her side, wincing as he tried to get comfortable on his chair. He had a special cushion at his back to provide more support but it had slipped and he was having difficulty placing it back into the right position.

Ruth put out a hand and adjusted it for him. "Yes, darling. I'm fine … just the age old constant worry about my son."

Philip placed his hand over hers but didn't say anything. He didn't need to. He knew how she felt and whatever happened, he would always be there to support her, love her, and listen to her woes. Ruth felt an overwhelming sense of love for him. She had been so very lucky, she thought, looking up at the portrait over the fireplace of Charles, the last Duke of Canleigh, her first husband. He was smiling down at her, just as he had when he had been alive. She wondered what he would have thought of his son, Stephen, being in the army, going off to help in a nation beset by the cruellest of wars. He would have been so very proud, just as she was, but he too would have been worried sick but would have done his best to allay her fears whilst stifling his. She smiled back up at him, comforted by the sight of him looking down on them. It gave her strength. She knew that while her precious son was overseas she would spend some time in this room, or at Charles's graveside in St. Mary's, talking to him, confiding in him about their son, gaining support from him, even though his physical presence was no more.

Felix had began to serve the pudding. Ruth watched him. She still didn't like him but still couldn't find a real reason to get rid of him. He was an exceedingly good butler. Nothing was ever

259

forgotten. All his duties were carried out with exemplary concentration. He never put a foot wrong but there was something … something not quite nice about him … and she didn't wholly trust him, although she had no reason whatsoever not to do so.

"We haven't much time now, before the wedding," Vicky was saying, further down the table. She looked divine tonight but then she always did. Her gorgeous thick head of dark hair was bouncing on her shoulders, gleaming in the candlelight. She was wearing a turquoise satin dress with a lot of lace, and flashing diamonds in her ears and on her fingers. She looked exquisite and so very happy as she gazed over at Lucy and Jeremy.

"I know," Lucy said, looking at Stephen. "I do hope you will be able to get home for it."

"So do I but we've not been told when we have leave again so be prepared, Lucy darling. I just might not be able to make it."

Lucy grimaced. "It won't be the same without you."

"But you will have the rest of us and when Stephen does get back, we can have another celebration," said Ruth, wanting to dispel the look of gloom on Lucy's face.

"Yes," added Vicky. "That's a lovely idea. We'll arrange something really special … so, Lucy. How are the preparations coming along?"

Lucy smiled quickly at Jeremy, who was sipping at his wine, looking decidedly not as a prospective bridegroom should, Ruth surmised. In fact, he didn't look too keen on the prospect at all.

"It's all in hand, isn't it Granny Ruth? St. Mary's is booked, as are the caterers who are going to prepare the wedding breakfast. We've a band booked for the evening shindig; the cake is being made, as is my dress. Invitations have been sent out and I think that's it really. All is under control and we just can't wait, can we Jeremy?"

"No, Lucy. No, we can't," said Jeremy quietly, attempting a bright smile.

Ruth wondered if anyone else had noticed his lack of enthusiasm. It worried her. Was Lucy about to make an almighty mistake? Jeremy was certainly acting strangely lately. It was ever since he vanished down to London that weekend when Lucy was up at Blairness. He hadn't been the same since and Ruth knew Vicky was concerned that he had disappeared overnight on a few occasions without a word as to where or whom he was with. It was certainly very odd and Ruth wondered if Lucy knew of his whereabouts at those times and if so, what she thought about it. Ruth would have liked to ask her but decided, for now, to keep her own counsel.

Felix was hovering over Jeremy with a pudding plate and Ruth could have sworn he actually touched the boy's shoulder as he moved away. Surely not. She shook herself. She was seeing things. Her mind was going a little crazy with all the worry about her family, which reminded her about something Perkins had mentioned to her earlier in the day.

"I was talking to Perkins today ... he's our gamekeeper," she explained to Sarah who looked puzzled, "he said that in the last few nights he has seen a light on in the Bothy but by the time he managed to get there, it was in darkness and no-one about."

"Perhaps it's a ghost," laughed Vicky. "You know what Canleigh is like ... we've had plenty of experiences with the white lady roaming the house and the headless coachman galloping up the drive. Perhaps one of them has moved down to the Bothy."

The whole table collapsed with mirth but only Ruth noticed how Felix, standing quietly at the sideboard, suddenly stiffened and looked even shiftier. Interesting, she thought. Was this mysterious night visitor to the Bothy something to do with him? But why would he go down there at night? What could he be up to? She realised he was gay, of course. Was it something to do with that? Was he meeting someone down there? If so, would it be an excuse to get rid of him? She would talk to Philip when they went up to bed and see what he thought. She would also have another word with Perkins to keep a closer eye on the place ... and see if Roy or one of his assistants would make sure the place was locked when they finished for the day. If, by any chance, it wasn't Felix down there, the last thing they needed were squatters moving onto the estate.

Felix noticed Ruth's scrutiny and had a nasty feeling his employer had guessed the nocturnal visitor to the Bothy was something to do with him. He would have to be more careful and not put a light on if he went there again. Although he would stay away for a while, just in case. It was a perfect place for an assignation ... almost romantic with the moonlight dancing on the lake on some nights. He found it peaceful and always came away refreshed and calmer but he didn't want the family to know about his strolls around the lake at night. They might not mind too much but he wanted to keep it secret just in case. He liked being out at night, all alone, watching and listening ... what for he didn't know but it did him good. He found he could get by on just four hours sleep a night so most nights he could be out and about from midnight for a couple of hours before turning in. He would miss his nightly strolls but wouldn't go for a week or so. He hadn't given a thought to Perkins doing nightly patrols and it was a damned nuisance. Although he supposed he could have a quiet word with him and then it wouldn't be a problem.

He checked the table to see who had finished pudding but so far it was only Jeremy. Felix was standing directly behind him and examined the back of Jeremy's head, fantasising on having an opportunity to run his hand through that gorgeous mop of hair, nuzzle his earlobes, kiss his mouth, pull off his clothes and ...

"Blairness has a lot of ghosts too," Lucy was saying. "But then you would probably know all about that Aunty Vicky."

Vicky finished her pudding and dabbed at her mouth with her napkin. "Not really. I was very young when we used to go there for the summer holidays and Daddy quashed any ghostly talk on the head straight away as he didn't want us to be frightened. He always allowed me to have a light on at night as well."

"Mother says that on some nights you can hear the cries of a little boy who was bricked into one of the walls in the green bedroom and there is a young girl who walks the upstairs corridors in her nightclothes carrying a teddy bear. I didn't see or hear anything while I was there but I am looking forward to seeing if Jeremy experiences anything when he comes up with me," she finished with a grin at her fiance.

Ruth exchanged a glance with Vicky. They both found it difficult that Lucy was getting along so well with Delia following a whole week up at Blairness. She had returned to Canleigh looking surprisingly

263

happy but knowing how much Ruth and Philip were concerned, said little about her few days in Scotland, apart from how much she had enjoyed herself and that she was going to go up as often as she possibly could. She also emphasised how her mother was actively engaged in improving the fortunes of Blairness and had no interest in Canleigh any longer.

"Will you be frightened?" Lucy teased Jeremy. "Will the Blairness ghosts scare you?"

Philip glanced at Ruth. "I don't know about ghosts … it's the living in that castle that I would be worried about," he said very quietly.

Jeremy was shaking his head and attempted a grin. "I don't think so. There's not much that frightens me and it's all a load of nonsense anyway."

"Too right," remarked Alex, sitting back in his chair with satisfaction. As usual, Pru had provided a fabulous dinner and he was quite replete. "I totally agree with you, Jeremy. Don't let young Lucy fill your head with such things. You will sleep like a top in that fresh Scottish air anyway. I can guarantee that," he added. On their sojourns to Edinburgh to oversee the club he and Vicky had bought four years ago, they had often took to the hills to do some walking, stopping an odd night or two in a guesthouse and always slept well, thanks to the fresh air and good Scottish fare.

"Yes, that's right, darling. You will," commented Vicky, smiling at her husband, remembering how much they enjoyed their trips up north. They hadn't been up there together this year and it was about time they had a romantic weekend away. She would make it a priority on her 'to do' list; only they wouldn't be visiting Blairness, that was for sure.

264

"Would you like coffee and liqueurs in here, Madam," asked Felix, "or in the library?"

Ruth looked around the table enquiringly. They had all finished pudding and occasionally, when dining together, they liked to remain at the table rather than dispersing but Philip was obviously in pain tonight and wanted to rest in a more comfortable chair.

"We'll go through to the library, thank you, Felix."

"Would you mind very much if we give it a miss?" asked Stephen, standing up and placing an arm around Sarah's shoulders. "It's a warm night for October, the moon is out, and Sarah and I fancy a walk down to the lake."

Ruth smiled. She didn't want to spend a single moment apart from her son but she couldn't deny him precious time alone with his girlfriend. "Of course not, darling but don't be too long. You might find it's chillier than you think and you don't want to go off to Bosnia with a cold."

"Don't worry, Mother dear, I'm a big boy now," Stephen grinned. "Come on, Sarah. I have something I want to talk to you about."

The family, intrigued by Stephen's words, watched the two leave the room, Stephen holding tight to Sarah's hand.

"Do you think he is about to propose?" whispered Vicky. "Oh, I do hope so. They make such a lovely couple."

Ruth nodded. "I hope so too. I was only thinking a few moments ago how much I like Sarah and what a great Duchess she would make and how she would keep Stephen on the straight and narrow."

"Whatever do you mean, Granny Ruth?" asked Lucy. "Stephen is one of the most stable people I have ever met."

"Yes, he is darling but whizzing around the countryside on that damned motorbike he insisted on purchasing does lend itself to reckless behaviour. Hopefully, Sarah can persuade him to get rid of the blasted thing and buy a decent car … goodness, children are such a worry," she added, smiling at Lucy as they all walked through to the library.

They settled on the sofas and chairs, Philip sitting in his favourite spot on the sofa nearest the fireplace, where he was able to put his feet on the brown velvet footstool to give his aching hip and leg a rest. Ruth took a couple of his painkillers from the desk drawer and handed them to him so he could have them with his coffee. He had only drunk one glass of wine at dinner and wouldn't have any more alcohol so he would be quite safe.

Ruth sat beside him, with Vicky next to her. Lucy, Jeremy, and Alex were grouped on the sofa opposite. Felix entered the room with a large silver tray on which sat a silver coffee pot, sugar bowl, milk jug and the pretty little Sevres porcelain cups and saucers, which Ruth liked to use for special occasions.

"Thank you, Felix. We can see to ourselves now."

"Very well, Madam. I'll just clear up the dining room and then I'll retire, if that's all right with you."

"Of course," nodded Ruth, breathing a sigh of relief as he left the room.

"Still not sure about him?" asked Vicky, noticing Ruth's sigh.

Ruth pulled a face. "Not really … but he is good at his job. Perhaps, with a bit of luck he'll get bored and leave."

Jeremy silently echoed Ruth's sentiments. He was becoming uncomfortable with Felix's attention; the sly looks, the odd touch, like that one on his shoulder at dinner. It was obvious that Felix had guessed his secret. He knew Jeremy wasn't completely 'normal' and it was obvious he fancied him but Jeremy had Matthew and certainly didn't want any more involvements, especially so close to home. So far, he had only managed to see Matthew a few times since their entanglement at Oxford, as it was difficult to find excuses to get away. He knew Vicky was worried by his absences but so far, Lucy had swallowed everything he had told her. Which was another problem. Matthew was still badgering him to cancel the engagement and whenever they were together, Matthew made it sound to easy to do but when it came to it, the words just wouldn't come and as the arrangements for the wedding moved further forward, it was becoming more and more difficult and Matthew, more and more annoyed.

"The longer you leave it, the more hurt and humiliated she will be when she does find out," he urged. "Ditch her, Jeremy, and let us set up home together … please … all your family will be fine with it once they get their heads around it and meet me, of course. Once they set eyes on me, they will know I only have your best interests at heart."

But he couldn't do it. He would lie in bed, rehearsing exactly what he was going to say but when he was in Lucy's presence the words wouldn't come and he ended up listening to her excited rambles about the wedding and their future together with gathering desperation. He was also aware that there was still a tiny part of him that wanted it to go ahead, wanted to pretend he could lead a normal life; be married, have children. He rubbed his brow and drank his Cognac in one hit. Why did life have to be so bloody complicated?

He envied Matthew. He had told his parents a long time ago that he was gay but being the only child, he was spoilt rotten and could do no wrong in their eyes. Therefore, they accepted it without question, just as they supported his lazy lifestyle by paying the rent on his flat, had given him a loan so he could rent a bookshop and make some kind of effort to work for a living, and often gave him generous handouts on request.

Yes, Matthew was lucky. He had an easy life, his family accepted his sexual preferences, and he had complete freedom to do as he wanted with no complications. Unlike him. He had family who would probably be shocked if they discovered he was bisexual and hadn't come clean to Lucy. He was still living with his parents and was about to get married for all the wrong reasons, and time was ticking on. The wedding was only two months away.

He took the coffee cup Ruth was holding out to him and without thinking took a big gulp. It burnt his tongue. It was just another thing to add to his misery.

CHAPTER 21

NOVEMBER 1995

Stephen never made it to Bosnia. A week after rejoining his regiment, he and two friends had a night out in London, rounding off the evening with a visit to Vicky and Alex's club in Kensington. They left to return to barracks, as happy as they could be, about to go off to a war- torn part of Europe. However, on entering the tube station, a gang of fifteen youths, decidedly the worse for wear, jumped onto the same train and took to taunting them relentlessly on the journey underground.

Terrified witnesses relayed that the drunken youths delivered the first punches and kicks and that the soldiers, as highly trained as they were, were vastly outnumbered and unprepared for such an attack on home soil. As the train pulled into the next underground station, the fight spilled out onto the platform but before the transport police could intervene, one of Stephen's friends was knocked unconscious, another sustained multiple fractures from a severe kicking and Stephen's head had been bashed with severe force on the hard concrete ground several times. The Duke of Canleigh was dead.

* * *

Ruth heard the car coming up the drive from the window upstairs and hoped it wasn't someone who wanted to talk to her. She had no appointments that day and had planned to spend most of it in her studio, finishing a scene of Canleigh from the far side of the lake. She and Philip had enjoyed a wander down there last week, she had taken a great number of photographs, and now wanted to get it onto canvas and it was coming on so well, she was reluctant to leave it.

"Come in," she called as Felix knocked on the door moments later. "Who is it, Felix? I really didn't want to be disturbed today."

"I … it's the Army, Madam. A Major Saunders and a Sergeant Whitaker."

Ruth froze, her hand hovering with the paintbrush. "Oh God," she whispered. "What do they want, Felix? Stephen hasn't gone to Bosnia yet."

"I'm sorry, Madam. They wouldn't tell me. They just want to talk to you."

Ruth gulped, staring around the familiar room, trying to force down the fear hitting her in the pit of her stomach. Stephen wasn't in Bosnia. He was okay. He was fine.

"Right. Well, tell them I'll be right down."

"Very well, Madam."

Felix left the room quietly, shutting the door behind him. Ruth made her way to the bathroom to wash the paint off her hands. They were trembling. She felt sick. She didn't want to go downstairs … but she had to. It was probably nothing, she reassured herself. It would be something silly, such as he had forgotten something and couldn't come home for it. She looked at herself in the mirror. She looked pale. Her eyes looked frightened.

"Pull yourself together, Ruth, for goodness sake," she told herself. "It will be nothing and you will be back up here finishing that painting shortly. Don't be so damned silly. Stephen is not in Bosnia."

She went downstairs. Felix had shown the two soldiers into the library. The Major was looking out of the French windows and the Sergeant was standing staring at the painting of the Dowager Duchess above the fireplace.

"Um. Good morning," Ruth attempted lightly. "What can I do for you?"

The Major turned. He walked towards her and held out his hand. "Good morning, Mrs. Kershaw. I'm Major Saunders and this is Sergeant Whitaker."

"Mam," said the Sergeant, removing his cap.

"Pleased to meet you both. Has my butler asked if you would like coffee?"

"Yes, he did but we declined. We don't want to keep you longer than necessary."

"Oh? So what is it I can do for you?" Ruth asked nervously, walking to the old oak desk that had belonged to Charles. She sat down in his chair, feeling his closeness, even his presence. She needed it but wondered why he had come to her now. Did he know what these men were going to impart?

"It's about Lieutenant Canleigh," said the Major with deep sadness etched on his face. He hated these duties. Hated having to tell parents that their precious children had died. It was bad enough when it was in combat but for this reason, it was horrific and he hoped the nasty little bastards who had so savagely attacked his men would be locked up for the rest of their miserable little lives. He had known Stephen well. He had been a damned good solider and would have gone far in the military. The Major also knew he was Mrs. Kershaw's only child so it was going to hit her doubly hard but he had to say it. Say the words that were going to destroy her life forever.

Ruth steeled herself for what was to come. She knew what he was going to say before he said it. She knew it in the bottom of her soul and she could feel the scream, threatening to leave her, threatening to shatter the peace of Canleigh.

"I am so very sorry, Mrs. Kershaw but I have to tell you that Stephen died last night."

It came. The scream. It pierced the stillness. It went on and on and on and the pain was so intense, Ruth fainted.

* * *

Vicky put down the telephone in her office and cried. Her lovely young brother, so full of life, was dead. In a senseless brawl on a platform in a London tube station. Vicky put her head in her hands and sobbed piteously. Stephen had so much to live for. He was the Duke of Canleigh, had a burgeoning army career and a really lovely girlfriend who they were all hoping to welcome as a permanent member of the family in the not too distant future. Oh God, poor Sarah. How was she taking the news? She would be devastated.

Vicky rooted in her handbag for a tissue as the tears flowed down her face. She had to pull herself together. She had to tell Lucy and then they had to get to Canleigh. She didn't know if she could drive though. She was too upset ... and Lucy certainly wouldn't be able to as she would be feeling the same. Alex was up in Edinburgh so it would have to be Jeremy. He wouldn't be in such a state. He would be saddened of course. He had grown up with Stephen

272

but he would be able to put his feelings aside and drive them the few miles down to the estate.

Lucy was on reception duties. Vicky could see her through the glass door of her office. The girl was smiling happily at a guest, handing him the key to his room. Vicky wiped her eyes, blew her nose and checked her face in the tiny mirror she kept in her handbag. She looked dreadful but it didn't matter. Her brother was dead. She would never see him again. God, it was hard to take in but Philip had been clear on the telephone. Ruth had received a visit from the army. Stephen had become embroiled in a fight and the result was that he was dead and laying on a slab in a morgue in London. Ruth was in a terrible state, which Vicky could quite believe. She had doted on Stephen and Vicky dreaded to think how this was going to affect her ... and she had to get to her as soon as possible. They had been through so many dreadful things together over the years, had always been there for each other and now she had to get to her again. Although what the hell she was going to say, she really didn't know.

Trying to compose herself, Vicky lifted the telephone and rang through to reception. She saw Lucy pick up the phone.

"Reception," she said briskly.

"Lucy, please ... can you ask Gillian to take over reception for you and then come into my office?"

"Okay," Lucy replied, throwing a puzzled glance at Vicky through the glass door. "I'll be right in."

Lucy didn't scream as her Granny did but she couldn't stop crying. She and Stephen had been so close since they were small and she had assumed he would always be there, acting as her big brother, even though he was officially her uncle, which had always

273

seemed somewhat ridiculous. To have lost him, and in such horrific circumstances, was so cruel and Lucy was inconsolable.

Vicky hugged Lucy tightly, letting her cry. "We must get to Canleigh as soon as possible. Ruth has collapsed and we must all be there for her."

Lucy gulped back the tears. "Oh, poor Granny Ruth. She must be distraught. She was so frightened for him ... going off to Bosnia ... and instead it's this, our own countrymen bashing him to death in a senseless attack in a London tube station."

"I know, I know. It's horrendous ... I honestly don't know how Ruth will come to terms with this. Look, Lucy. Go and get your bag and anything you need. Gillian can manage reception for a few hours. I'll go and tell Jeremy and he can take us to Canleigh. Luckily there are no functions today so he won't be missed too badly behind the bar."

An hour later they arrived at Canleigh. Philip's Volvo was parked outside and a sombre Felix met them at the front door, although his eyes roamed straight to Jeremy as soon as he stepped out of the car.

"I am so sorry for your loss, Your Ladyship," said Felix to Vicky, holding open the door.

"Thank you, Felix ... now ... where is ..."

"Oh, thank God you are here," said a crestfallen looking Philip, emerging from the library. "Ruth really needs you now, Vicky."

"Where ...?"

"In our bedroom ... in bed. I don't know what to do ... she didn't want me to stay with her so I've rung the doctor. Hopefully he can give her something to help."

Vicky headed for the stairs without another word.

"Do you want me to come with you?" called Lucy, clutching onto Philip, who looked as if he might topple over at any minute.

"No, darling. You two stay with Philip. I think he needs looking after too."

Lucy and Jeremy helped Philip back into the library, leaving Vicky to rush upstairs, dreading what she was going to find. It was strange Ruth didn't want Philip to be with her. She idolised him. They had been so good for each other. Vicky's heart bled for him. How he must be suffering at Ruth's rejection.

She reached the bedroom, knocked on the door and entered without waiting for Ruth's response.

"Oh, Ruth," she cried, rushing across the room and folding her stepmother in her arms. They sobbed together, for the gorgeous young man they had loved, who had made them laugh with his childish antics, had solemnly adjusted to the role of Duke of Canleigh, who had studied hard at school, had spent a lot of time with Philip at Tangles, helping him with the rescued animals, had roared around on his beloved motorbike, had fallen in love with the beautiful Sarah, had intended to help the beleagured people of the Baltic's and finally to fight for his country.

"Oh, Vicky. I didn't know what pain was until I lost your father but this ... this is something else. Stephen was my child. My blood. Apart from Philip, he was everything to me. I just can't believe he's gone ... and in such a terrible way, in such a sickening, revolting, senseless act."

"I know, I know. It just doesn't bear thinking about. Have they ... have they got the idiots who did this?"

Ruth nodded. "Major Saunders said they were arrested almost immediately and will probably get

275

life. The two lads who were with Stephen are in a pretty serious condition too … their poor parents. I should ring them."

"Do you know them?"

Ruth nodded, tearing tissues from the box beside the bed and dabbing at her eyes. "Yes. Stephen went through Sandhurst with them. They've been friends for a long time … all decent chaps … all wanting to do something worthwhile … unlike the yobs who … who."

She descended into another crescendo of weeping and Vicky hugged her close, the tears pouring down her cheeks too.

"Please don't shut Philip out, Ruth. He's suffering as well. He loved Stephen … we all did but they were good friends too and spent a lot of time together when Stephen was growing up. He will be grieving deeply."

"I know … but I can't deal with his grief too. Not at the moment. I have my own to deal with," Ruth cried. "I know I'm being selfish but I can't help it."

A knock on the door made Vicky rise to her feet. She quickly wiped her tears away with a tissue and crossed the room to open it. Malcolm Wyatt, the new doctor for the local area, stood on the threshold.

"Mr. Kershaw called me," he said quietly. "He wanted me to examine Mrs. Kershaw and give her something to help."

Vicky looked up at the tall, auburn haired doctor, who looked so kind and concerned. She managed a weak smile. "Thank you. She's terribly distressed, as you can imagine. I'll leave you to have a word."

She opened the door wider to let him in. "I'll be back soon, Ruth. I'll just check on Philip."

Vicky descended the stairs much slower than she had come up, her heart heavy with sorrow. It should have been such a lovely exciting time for the family with Lucy and Jeremy's wedding in the offing but now it would be sadness and a funeral. She wondered whether the wedding should be postponed for a while. None of them, especially Ruth, would be up to feeling jovial in just a few weeks time.

She entered the library. Philip was sitting on the sofa by the fire Felix had lit earlier but even so, the room felt chilly. Lucy and Jeremy were sitting opposite him, Lucy with silent tears coursing down her cheeks and Jeremy, sombre and quiet. They were all nursing brandy glasses.

"I don't know what to do," Philip said. "I just don't know what to do."

Vicky rushed over to him, sat down beside him, and took his hand. "Nothing. You don't have to do anything for now. Dr. Wyatt is with Ruth. Once he has given her some tranquilisers, you must go up to her and stay with her. Have one yourself if you need it. Just rest. The next few days are going to be gruelling but I am here, so are Lucy and Jeremy, and I have rung Alex and he will be here in a few hours. We'll see to anything that needs doing for the time being. I'll ask Felix to tell Tina to prepare a couple of guest rooms and Alex and I will stay here. I don't know what you will want to do, Jeremy … stay here or go back to the Beeches?"

"I'll stay here too," said Jeremy, glancing at Lucy who was looking at him beseechingly. He took her hand and kissed it. "Don't worry. I won't leave you."

"What about the hotel," asked Lucy with a quiver in her voice?

"Don't worry about that. Once the staff know what has happened I'm positive they will all rally and Alex can always pop back and make sure everything is in order."

Vicky had left the library door open and they could hear footsteps coming down the stairs into the entrance hall and then turn towards the library.

"Doctor," said Philip, stiffly getting to his feet. "How is she?"

Dr. Wyatt entered the room and pursed his mouth. "Not good but then that is to be expected, having just lost her only child. I've given her a sedative and here are a couple more," he handed a packet to Vicky. "Hopefully she won't need them but just in case. She will sleep now for a few hours but by the look of you, Mr. Kershaw, you also need to rest. Mrs. Kershaw is going to need you badly in the coming weeks and months. I suggest you go on up too."

Philip nodded, took his walking stick from where it was resting at the fireplace, and moved towards the door. "Thank you, Doctor. I'll ring you if we need you."

* * *

Philip found the pain in his hip excruciating as he made his way slowly upstairs to the bedroom he shared with Ruth. He had forgotten to take his painkillers this morning but he had some in his bedside cabinet and would have to take a couple as soon as he reached the bedroom. He winced every time he stood on his left leg and began to think that he would either have to start sleeping downstairs or have a lift installed.

He reached the bedroom and opened the door. Ruth was laying still, her eyes wide open, but she wasn't crying. He limped across the room and sat down beside her, taking her hand in his.

"I am so very sorry, darling. I loved him very much too. It's going to be pretty awful without him."

Ruth squeezed his hand and patted his side of the bed with her other. "Come and keep me company until I fall asleep ... the sedative is taking hold quickly ... why don't you have one ... you look done in too ... let's curl up and pretend this has never happened. It's just too painful to think about and I do need you, darling. I really do."

Philip didn't want any pills but removed his clothes and slid into bed next to her. She cuddled into the crook of his arm and promptly fell asleep while he lay staring at the ceiling, wondering what would happen now. The implications of Stephen's death put a completely new look on everything. Ruth and he had planned to move back to Tangles in the New Year, after Lucy's wedding, as she would be moving into The Beeches on a permanent basis with Jeremy. They had talked it over with Stephen and he had agreed there was no need for them to remain at Canleigh. The estate could easily be left in the hands of the estate manager and Ruth would only be at Tangles and could pop over at any time.

Philip was looking forward to moving back to his former home on a permanent basis. He hadn't minded living at Canleigh, which was what Charles had asked of Ruth when he had died, so that she would care for the place while Stephen was growing up, but it wasn't his real home. It was too big and formal. He loved Tangles and wanted to be there, where they would have the place to themselves without the fear of staff overhearing them or repeating anything they said, and he selfishly wanted Ruth completely to himself.

He longed for the day they could go but everything was up in the air now. He knew what was in Stephen's will. Lucy was going to inherit Canleigh, would be way out of her depth, and would need Ruth's help and assistance. Obviously, Lucy and Jeremy would reside at Canleigh once they were married but goodness knows if the wedding could go ahead just yet. Ruth certainly wouldn't be in the right frame of mind before Christmas and he doubted if the rest of the family would be either so it would have to be postponed. Lucy wouldn't want to live here by herself, Ruth would feel the need to stay here with her and, therefore, the move to Tangles in the near future wouldn't be possible.

Then there was Delia. Oh God, Delia. Once she found out that Stephen had died, she would assume Canleigh would go to her. She was in for a nasty shock when she found out she had been bypassed for Lucy. How the hell was she going to take that bit of news?

CHAPTER 22

Delia sat in the dining room at Blairness, drinking her coffee slowly, perusing the latest Horse and Hound magazine. She had given up on the idea of buying a horse. Hiring one from the Sutherlands was a much better idea. She didn't particularly want to ride every day and the upkeep of owning a horse and the inconvenience of having a box for it in the stables when she wanted to turn it into offices, was another consideration. The Sutherlands had won.

However, she was pondering on holding horse trials at Blairness. There were already venues across Scotland where it had proved a great success. It would be fabulous if that could happen here. She hadn't mentioned it to Brian yet. She wanted to give it some more thought first, likewise opening the castle to the public and anyway, they had enough on their plates with the caravan site, the golf course and the renovation of the stable block. That was more than enough to be going on with for the time being.

The dining room door was ajar and she heard the telephone ringing in the hall and McFrain answering it and then his footsteps as he came towards the dining room. She put down the magazine and looked up. "Who is it, McFrain?"

"It's Miss Lucy, your Ladyship. I must say, she sounds very upset."

Delia rose to her feet. "Oh dear. I do hope she's not going to tell me she and Jeremy can't come up this weekend. I was so looking forward to meeting him."

She moved quickly into the hall and picked up the telephone. "Lucy? Is something the matter, darling?"

"Oh, Mummy. It's simply awful," Lucy sobbed, taking great gulps of air.

"What is? What's happened? Is it Jeremy?" Delia asked, closing her eyes in anguish. From the pain in Lucy's voice, she surmised Jeremy had backed out of their engagement. She could just see herself, all those years ago, with Philip telling her it was off between them. She could feel the deep agony again. That awful, searing pain that ripped her heart to shreds. She would kill Jeremy if he had done that to Lucy.

"No ... no. It's Stephen."

"Stephen? What's he done ... surely he's not ... I thought you told me he wasn't going to Bosnia for another couple of weeks."

"He's not ... he isn't," Lucy cried. "He and his friends were out in London ... they got beaten up by a gang ... two of them are in hospital and Stephen ... Stephen is dead."

Delia gasped. "Oh, my God! How awful."

"I know. Granny Ruth is beside herself and Steppie is too. I'm so sorry, Mummy, but I'm going have to postpone our coming up to you this weekend. I can't leave here now. I am so sorry."

Delia felt the disappointment hit her. She had been so looking forward to having her daughter at Blairness again.

"No, of course not, darling. I quite understand. When will the funeral be, do you know?"

"Aunty Vicky is seeing to all the arrangements but there's no firm date yet, although it will probably be next week."

"I see. Well, darling. You look after yourself. Ring me if you want to talk and when the funeral is over,

282

we'll arrange another time for you and Jeremy to come up."

"Thank you, Mummy. I am so sorry. I'm really keen for you to meet Jeremy before the wedding so we'll come up soon, I promise."

"Okay, darling. Just remember I love you and will be thinking of you."

Delia replaced the receiver and walked back to the dining room, deep in thought. McFrain had disappeared down to the kitchens and she was alone. She poured another coffee and sat down. The Duke of Canleigh was dead. The Duke of Canleigh was dead! She couldn't believe it. The one person who had stood in her way of having Canleigh was no more. It would be hers now. Her precious, beautiful, wonderful Canleigh would rightfully be hers at last and she had done nothing to make it happen. She hadn't killed anyone. She hadn't plotted and schemed. It had just happened naturally ... by sheer luck. She felt sorry for the boy, of course. She had actually liked him as a child when he played with Lucy when they were tiny and no doubt he had grown up to be a very nice young man but even so, Ruth's sprog had always stood in her way.

Delia wondered when it would dawn on everyone that she would be returning to Canleigh as its rightful owner. How would they all feel ... bloody, bloody Ruth and ... Philip? She knew full well that the terms of her licence prevented her going anywhere near them but if Canleigh was hers, surely there would be no objection to her living there, provided she didn't go anywhere near Tangles. Anyway, the legalities could wait. She wanted to savour the thought of Canleigh being hers, after all these years, after all those tears of rage, after all that wishing and wishing.

She had finally achieved her dream. She was happy at Blairness. She had enjoyed more peace and tranquillity since being here than she had ever had ... but Canleigh, her beloved Canleigh. She felt dizzy with excitement. She was going to have them both, Canleigh and Blairness. God, she was so happy and actually smiled at Crystal as she entered the dining room.

* * *

Jeremy was in torment. After another agonising telephone conversation with Matthew, demanding he hurry up and break off the engagement with Lucy, he had very nearly found the courage to tell her but couldn't now. She was so upset about Stephen and he couldn't do it to her ... and the family would be absolutely furious if he piled on more distress. No. He had to keep his mouth shut for now and Matthew would have to understand but he didn't know if he would. Matthew was already angry that they couldn't meet for a week or so, not until after the funeral and had thrown a hissy fit.

"Jeremy, you can't do this to me! You simply can't. I have to see you. I will be up in York on Wednesday and you have to come to our little hotel. I'll ... I'll tell your flaming Lucy about us myself if you don't."

"But ..."

"There are no buts, Jeremy. I thought you wanted to be with me."

"I do ... but."

"There you go again. If you want to be with me, you will make the effort. You will, won't you? I'll be so angry if you don't and won't be responsible for my actions."

"Okay. Okay," said Jeremy, quickly thinking what was happening on Wednesday and whether he would be able to slip away, even if it was only for an hour or two during the night. He wanted to see Matthew just as much as Matthew wanted to see him. "I'll see what I can do. I'll ring you."

He had replaced the receiver just as his mother had entered The Beeches. He was in her office and could see her through the glass door, talking to Gillian on reception. She saw him too and waved. He held up a hand in acknowledgement and went out to join her. She reached up and kissed him on the cheek.

"I've some news, darling. I've managed to set a date for the funeral. I just hope Ruth will be up to it. Philip is walking around looking like a ghost but Ruth … she hasn't left the bedroom yet."

"When is it?" he asked. "The funeral."

"Wednesday … eleven o'clock at St. Mary's … on the estate. Then everyone can go back to Canleigh. I've so much to arrange. Ruth certainly isn't up to it and someone has to do it."

Wednesday. Oh, God. Why did it have to be Wednesday, Jeremy thought, panicking now that he would have to tell Matthew he couldn't see him … although, thinking about it rationally, he might well be able to. If the funeral were in the morning, it would all be over by the afternoon. Everyone would have gone home after the wake and he could get over to York. Lucy would remain at Canleigh and he could give her some excuse about having to be at The Beeches or something. Yes, it could actually be the perfect day.

"Right," he said to his mother as she stood at the reception desk, shuffling through a file she had brought back with her. "Well, if there is anything I can do," he said, with a helpful smile.

* * *

Felix chortled to himself as he drove Ruth's car towards Leeds to collect the curtains for the crimson drawing room, which he had taken to the dry cleaners last week. Lady Victoria was in a panic that they should be re-hung before the funeral and had also given him Mr. Kershaw's black suit to have refreshed.

He was a little sorry that the Duke of Canleigh was no more, especially having endured such a horrific, brutal end but Felix was well aware that Stephen hadn't liked him much and when he had retired from his army life, might well have given him the boot. Now he was relatively safe. With Miss Lucy about to become the legal owner of Canleigh, and with her marrying the delicious Jeremy, there would be no question of him leaving Canleigh. Miss Lucy was too timid and soft to dismiss staff as long as they were working hard and as for Jeremy ... well, with the pair residing in the Hall, he would have many opportunities to work on him ... to seduce him. Then he would be made for life. He could threaten to tell Lucy. Jeremy would be aghast and would give him money and presents ... much money and many presents. His spirits soared. Life was going to be so very good in the not too distant future.

* * *

Ruth opened her eyes, glanced at the window and watched the rain pouring down outside, hitting the glass with force while the wind howled around the Hall. The weather was simply horrendous and for some reason she felt horrendous too. Her body felt like lead and eyes were sore. For a second she couldn't understand why and then it hit her. Stephen was dead. Her darling, precious son would no longer be in her life. He would never dash through the door and hug and kiss her again. He would never again make her laugh. He would never again make her worry about where he was or what he was up to. She would never again have to shudder when she heard him roar off up the drive on that frightful motorbike, which she had feared would kill him. But it hadn't. It had been a gang of drunken yobs, in a London tube station. People she had never met and never would. People Stephen had probably never met either ... not until that night. Why, oh why, hadn't he remained in barracks? Why had he and his friends decided to go into London? If only they had gone to a local pub he might still be alive and his friends not in hospital.

She put a leg out of bed. She had to ring their parents ... see if their boys were recovering well. She knew they had rung her. Vicky had told her so but she was out of it at the time on the sedatives Dr. Wyatt had given her ... but she wasn't going to take any more. She wasn't going to collapse as she had done when Charles had died and then been unable to attend the funeral. She was going to pull herself together and take charge this time. She owed it to Stephen and it wasn't fair on Vicky. She had always drawn the short straw and seemed to have had to arrange all the family's funerals so far and she had a busy life too. No. She had to rally. She could collapse afterwards … after Stephen was interred.

She showered, letting her tears glide down with the water gushing down above her head and then dressed in a pair of old jeans and her favourite tatty blue cashmere sweater, which should have been thrown, but as it was such a favourite, remained. Charles had bought it for her many years ago and she always felt close to him when she wore it.

Opening the bedroom door, she stood and listened. She couldn't hear anyone moving about or talking but then as far as she knew Philip was at Tangles and Vicky and Lucy were at the undertakers. Felix must be down in the kitchens. She went down the backstairs to the boot room, donned her navy Barbour and wellingtons, and opened the back door.

The rain was pelting down but she pulled her hood up over her head and breathed in the air. It was fresh and damp and revived her a little. She strode around the Hall and across the grass towards St. Mary's. She needed more than anything to be in church. She wanted to talk to someone and it had to be God. In his house. She also wanted to be near to Charles. She usually took flowers to place on his grave every week. She had nothing today but he would understand; her kind, lovely first husband, the father of her son.

She reached the church gate and held onto it for support while a great cry of anguish ripped from her body and filled the air. Oh God! How was she going to cope without her son? She loved him so very much. Apart from the love she had for Charles and then Philip, Stephen had been her world, right from the moment he was placed in her arms as a tiny baby. The deep, overwhelming love for him that she had experienced at that moment had never left her and never would. She was utterly heartbroken.

"Mrs. Kershaw?" came a voice at her side.

Ruth turned, dashing a hand across her eyes, "Oh, Paul ..."

Reverend Paul Edwards, who had lived in the village vicarage for the last five years and conducted all the services at St. Mary's, took her arm. "Please ... come inside. You are soaking ... I can make you a coffee ... I always keep some in the vestry ... it helps when I'm numb with cold before the heating gets going properly."

Ruth allowed him to lead her up the path and into the pretty little church. He sat her down at the front pew which the Canleigh family had always used and left her to stare at the ancient stained glass windows and the alter. It looked particularly lovely today with two enormous arrangements of white and yellow flowers either side of the big brass cross in the centre. She couldn't make out what they were; her eyes were still misted over. She searched frantically for a tissue in the pocket of her jacket and eventually found a tatty one right at the bottom. She wiped her eyes and blew her nose, trying to regain some kind of composure before Paul returned.

"There," he said, emerging from the vestry a few moments later. "This should help make you feel a little better. It's only instant but it does on a cold day."

Ruth took the warm white mug he handed to her gratefully. She was shivering, inside and out, and the heat helped ease the tremors. It had been silly of her to come over in such a downpour but now she was here, she was already feeling a little calmer. The church always affected her that way. She loved to be here on her own. She would come every week, during the day, when no one was about. She would place the flowers on Charles's grave, have a word or two with him and then come and sit in the church, and always experienced a great sense of peace, which gave her strength. She needed it now, that strength and as she sat beside Paul, sipping the coffee, not speaking, but just being, she felt it come over her. As it was if God was recharging her body and her mind, which would keep her going until her next visit. A sense of stillness gradually settled on her.

"Did you want to talk?" asked the Reverend, finishing his coffee and placing his mug on the tiled floor beneath his feet.

"No ... not really ... there's nothing much to say. My son is gone and there's not a thing I can do bar learn to live without him in my life."

"I am so very sorry, Mrs. Kershaw. He was a grand, upstanding young man with a lot to offer. He will be sorely missed on the estate and no doubt with the military. I understand they will be involved in the funeral."

"Yes ... yes ... I believe they will be ... Lady Victoria said something to me about it but I couldn't quite take it in at the time."

"That's understandable."

"Thank you but I have to be strong now. I was so weak when Charles died ... I was in such a bad way I couldn't attend the funeral. I can't do that again. I have to be at Stephen's."

"And I am sure you will be. Just rest as much as you can. Let the remainder of the family help you. Don't take on too much. Don't feel guilty and I am sure God will guide you and will look over you at this difficult time. You will get through it with his help ... and ours."

Ruth touched his hand. "Thank you ... and thank you for the coffee ... it has certainly warmed me. Would you ... would you mind very much if I could be left alone for a while?"

The Reverend stood up and smiled warmly. "Of course not. I'll take the mugs through and leave by the vestry door. I shan't disturb you again but you do know where I am if you want to talk."

Ruth nodded as he picked up the mugs and disappeared into the vestry. She heard him shut the back door. She was alone with God. She bent her head to pray.

CHAPTER 23

NOVEMBER 1995

The day of the funeral, 10th November, was icy cold. There had been a sharp frost overnight and when Ruth awoke, crept out of bed so she wouldn't disturb Philip, and padded in her bare feet to the window, the grass between the Hall and St. Mary's was sparkling white. It was a beautiful scene and Stephen would have loved it. He had always liked the winter; playing in the snow, even as an adult he had loved snowball fights, skating on the lake if it was frozen hard enough and sliding down huge snowdrifts on his backside. He had revelled in it, coming indoors, his cheeks red from the exertion and the cold, but laughing … always laughing.

The sharp pain of deep grief hit her hard. She was becoming used to it now but she couldn't cry. She wasn't going to. Not today. She was going to be completely composed and dignified and keep a stiff upper lip. She had shed bucket loads of tears over the past few days and she would again but today, at least until after the funeral, she was determined to be in control of her emotions in front of so many people who were coming to pay their respects to the young Duke of Canleigh.

Wearing a black boat-necked cashmere dress, covered by a black woollen double-breasted coat, and the hat she had bought for Charles' funeral but never worn, Ruth gritted her teeth and bit back the tears as they approached St. Mary's, Felix driving the Rolls slowly … oh, so slowly. The support of her family, especially Philip, helped her enormously, as did the kindness of the villagers and estate workers, Stephen's school and college friends, and the military who turned up in full dress uniform and carried the coffin draped with the Union Jack, topped with Stephen's cap, into the church.

Ruth managed not to break down; trying to pretend it was someone else in the coffin and not her beloved son. Flanked by Philip, who held her hand throughout the service, unable to sing the hymns or say the prayers, frightened he would dissolve in front of the congregation, and a white-faced Lucy, Ruth held herself together, rigid with grief for the young man, her child, whom she would never see again.

Major Saunders gave a sparkling account of Stephen's army career, how well he had done in training, how he had been popular amongst his fellow officers and the men under his command. He mentioned how he was an outstanding soldier, earmarked for great success in the army.

Two of Stephen's friends stood up and recounted how close they had become with Stephen during their long months of training, along with some of the things they got up to when on leave, making the majority of the mourners smile. Ruth couldn't. She remained expressionless; willing the service to be over so she could get back to Canleigh and hide in the privacy of the bedroom she shared with Philip and let out the scream she could feel building up in her body again.

But the tributes went on. Alex told everyone what a valued member of the Canleigh family Stephen had been and what a great Duke he would have made. How kind, courteous, considerate, and loving he was and how much they would all miss him.

When Alex stood down, Ruth was surprised to feel Lucy make a sudden movement beside her, rise to her feet, and make her way to stand beside the coffin.

"I met Stephen when I was around three years old and right from that first day he became the big brother every girl would want in her life. He was funny, handsome, dependable, loving. He would do anything for anybody and didn't have a selfish bone in his body. He helped make my childhood safe and happy. He was always there for me, helping me with my homework, making me laugh when I was sad ... he had a marvellous sense of humour ... bolstering my confidence when I was afraid, and always urging me to strive to be the best I could in whatever I was doing. I badly wanted him to be at my wedding next month," her voice wavered, and she stopped to take a deep breath, "but even though he won't be there in person, I am sure he will be in spirit. I am going to miss him more than words can say. Darling Stephen," she finished, taking a step towards the coffin and placing a hand on his cap, "I love you so much. Rest in peace."

As Lucy returned to her seat beside Ruth, the Reverend looked at the rest of the congregation, waiting to see if anyone else wanted to say something but as no-one stood up, he nodded to the organist and the first bars of Abide With Me filled the church and the mourners rose to their feet. Ruth stood up but her legs turned to jelly and she had to sit down again. The whole scene in front of her began to swim. The beautiful stained glass window above the alter swayed, the intricately carved pulpit wouldn't keep still, the coffin ... that big solid box which contained the body of her son, draped in the Union Jack, seemed to be floating towards her. She wanted to break it open, pull out Stephen, tell him to wake up, to talk to her, to tell her it was all some silly dream. She wanted to shriek at him to stop pretending he was dead. It wasn't funny. It was a cruel, stupid joke and she wasn't amused. Then it all went black.

Ruth came to in the hard-backed chair in the vestry, Philip and Lucy by her side, both looking deeply concerned. Philip was holding her hand, stroking it, his eyes filled with unshed tears. Lucy was holding a glass of water.

"Drink this," she said, full of fear for her grandmother. "Then we'll get you back to the Hall and into bed."

"What … where is everyone?" asked Ruth shakily, taking the glass from Lucy's hand.

"Outside," replied Philip, as the strains of the Last Post from the military bugles filled the air.

"Oh, God," cried Ruth, dropping the glass on the black tiled floor, watching it smash into pieces. "I can't bear it. I really can't bear it."

Philip enveloped her into a big hug, holding her tight as she sobbed her heart out, while Lucy stood silent and shaking beside them, her heart breaking to see Granny Ruth so distraught.

It fell silent outside and Ruth raised her head, gulping back her sobs. "I'm so sorry," she whispered. "I was determined to be strong today."

"Don't be silly, darling. Everyone will understand," said Philip reassuringly.

Ruth took some tissues from the pocket of her coat, wiped away her tears, and blew her nose. "No doubt but I should be outside … I have to thank people for coming … there will be lots who won't be able to make it back to the Hall for the wake."

She rose to her feet, forcing a smile to her lips, pained she had caused more distress to Philip and Lucy. "I am okay. Really. I can get through the next half hour or so but I'm not sure about when we get back to the Hall. I don't think I can face entertaining people."

"You don't have to," said Lucy. "The rest of us can do that. You can go upstairs and rest."

Most people came back to the Hall for the wake, with only a few taking their leave immediately after the service, having to return to work. Ruth stood outside the church beside the Reverend, Philip, Lucy, Vicky and Alex, numbly shaking hands and trying to hold polite conversations, before sliding into the Rolls, which Felix had brought to the gate for the short journey back home.

"Do you ... do you want to see the grave before we go?" asked Vicky, who was accompanying her, while the rest of the family walked across the lawns with their guests to the Hall.

Ruth shook her head. "No. I'll come back later. On my own ... do you think anyone would miss me if I went upstairs straight away?"

"Of course not ... just go," Vicky urged as they alighted from the car and headed up the front steps to the Hall. She was concerned as to how fragile Ruth appeared, as if she might faint again at any moment. "I'll bring you some tea and something to eat."

Ruth tried hard to smile. "Actually, I think I would prefer something stronger. A brandy would be good."

"Are you intending to take any sedatives?"

"No. You needn't worry. I don't need them and anyway, I have to be wide awake for the reading of the will later."

"Oh yes. What time is Rathbone going to do it … you know he was at the church?"

Ruth nodded. "Yes. He's staying at the Canleigh Arms tonight. I offered him a bed here but he didn't want to intrude. He's coming at seven this evening to read the will."

"Oh, heavens. Lucy doesn't know Stephen left the estate to her, does she?"

Ruth shook her head. "No," she said slowly. "We've never told her because we didn't think it would happen … even when he joined the army. Goodness knows what she is going to say when she finds out."

Vicky looked up at Ruth who was ascending the stairs. "Well, all I can say is, thank God it's not going to be Delia!"

* * *

They all assembled in the library just before seven o'clock; Ruth, Philip, Lucy, Vicky, Alex and Jeremy, Tina and Prue. Felix was not invited, which didn't put him in too good a humour and he laid the table in the dining room for dinner with a sour look on his face and a burning annoyance that he wasn't to be included in the bequest.

An aging Derek Rathbone sat at Charles's desk with a sherry and ruffled the papers in front of him as the family filed in and sat down on the sofas, Tina and Prue standing behind. Ruth made sure she was sitting next to Lucy and held her hand tightly. The girl was in for such a surprise and Ruth had no idea how she was going to take it.

297

Rathbone read out Stephen's last wishes. It was the third time he had been called to Canleigh to carry out this task, the first for Charles, Stephen's esteemed father and then Richard, Stephen's uncle who had died at the hands of his sister, Lady Delia, if it was to be believed. That little saga hadn't been explained thoroughly as far as Rathbone was concerned, with the court case against her crumbling dramatically all those years ago. He had enormous respect for the members of the Canleigh family, had witnessed their suffering at her hands and was immensely pleased she wasn't inheriting the estate. Once she had been released from prison, and reluctant to have any personal contact with her again, he had handed over the Blairness account to his nephew, James Rathbone, to deal with.

He cleared his throat and looked around at his audience who were looking back at him expectantly. The first bequests to Tina and Prue were generous, five thousand pounds each, which made them both gasp with surprise and delight that the young Duke had thought so highly of them.

'I shall always be grateful to Tina for looking after me so very well as I was growing up. She made life such fun and was the best nanny a child could ever wish for. Prue made every mealtime a delight and I shall never forget sneaking down to the kitchen, when I could get away from Tina, to sample Prue's gorgeous homemade ice-cream, chocolate and cakes. Thank you, Prue. You are an absolute marvel.'

Vicky and Ruth smiled at the thoughtfulness of Stephen to include his two favourite members of staff. They both deserved it.

"All of my personal effects can be split between the family as my mother, Ruth Kershaw, feels is

298

appropriate," Rathbone continued and then he looked up. "Which leads me to the estate itself." Ruth glanced at Vicky and they both looked at Lucy, who was looking at Rathbone, interested to see who Stephen had appointed. She had considered her mother might be in the running but discounted it. With her record, that would be highly doubtful and anyway, Stephen hadn't liked Delia very much. He had told her so on more than one occasion that he had been wary of her when he was a child. No, it wouldn't be her mother. More probably his. Ruth would be the perfect person for Canleigh. After all, she had looked after it for Stephen for many years and was the former Duchess. She was the most appropriate person.

'I hereby bequeath the Canleigh estate to look after it to the best of her ability, as I know she will, to my niece, Lucy Canleigh.'

Lucy stared at Rathbone with shock. "What? No! Me? That can't be right."

Rathbone nodded. "Yes, it is, Lucy. You are now the rightful owner of Canleigh Hall and the estate, in its entirety, which also includes all the rental properties in London and elsewhere around the country."

"Oh!" Lucy gasped, not knowing whether to laugh or cry. "I can't believe it. Me?"

Ruth gripped Lucy's hand tighter. "It's going to be a huge responsibility, darling but I'll do everything I can to help, you know I will."

Lucy threw her arms around Ruth and hugged her tight. "Thank you, Granny. I know you will but ... but this means we will have to come and live here permanently ... Jeremy and I ... after the wedding." She looked across at Jeremy who was sitting on the sofa opposite her with a look of shock on his face.

299

"Gosh, Lucy. I suppose we will," he added slowly, not knowing how this dramatic change of direction in his life was going to affect him and what Matthew was going to say. This was going to put a completely new light on things and as much as he wanted to be with Matthew, if he stayed with Lucy, he would be able to live a life of luxury much quicker than having to wait for Vicky and Alex to expire and hope all they owned wouldn't be left to Katrina. No. He couldn't finish with Lucy now. It would be crazy.

"I'm going to need your support more than ever now," Lucy said to him, her eyes shining. "Blimey. Me. I can't quite get my head around it."

Jeremy couldn't either. He sat watching the family congratulate Lucy while Alex refilled their sherry glasses, Prue and Tina refusing and leaving the room as they had household duties to perform.

He looked at his watch. Dinner would be served at eight and would probably go on for a couple of hours. If he could get out of here by ten o'clock, it would give him an hour before he had to be in York. Everyone would think he was driving back to The Beeches but instead he would be miles away, meeting Matthew. He wondered what he would say to this turn of events because whatever Matthew said, Jeremy was going to find it doubly difficult to dump Lucy now. Even with Ruth and Philip to guide her, she was going to be out of her depth with the estate and suddenly the idea of playing the Lord of the Manor rather appealed to him. If he didn't want to, he wouldn't have to work again with all the millions Stephen had been worth, which now belonged to Lucy. He could have a rather nice life here. He could concentrate on his hobbies instead of having to work for a living. He could take up golf ... there was a particularly prestigious club in Leeds he had always fancied joining. He could have a more powerful car; they could have long, delightful holidays abroad or do cruises. He had always fancied that. A world cruise would be good. His thoughts rushed on, seeing a lifestyle that he could only have ever dreamed of becoming his for the taking. There was just one major problem. Matthew. The man was like a drug and Jeremy needed his fix regularly. He couldn't live without that … God. What a dilemma, he thought, rubbing his brow, dreading the scene he guessed would ensue later that night.

* * *

Lucy dashed up to her room, more excited than she had ever been in her life, overwhelmed that darling Stephen had thought her worthy enough of taking on Canleigh and the estate. She would do him proud. She would learn everything she possibly could and run it to the best of her ability. She knew she could rely on the family and Jeremy to support her but there was one person she knew whose advice she would really need. The one person who had the training, the skills and the knowledge and love for Canleigh that would really guide her to look after it in the best possible way.

She flung herself into the bedroom, slammed the door, picked up the telephone beside the bed, and rang Blairness, waiting impatiently for McFrain to answer.

"Blairness Castle," came his dulcet tones after an excruciating wait.

"McFrain … it's Lucy … please could you tell my mother I need to speak to her urgently."

301

"Yes. Miss Lucy. Just wait a few moments."

The few moments passed and then a few more. Lucy paced up and down with the telephone in her hand, looking out of the window at the parkland before her. Her parkland. It was all hers. Oh, heavens. It was unbelievable!

"Darling," Delia finally said. "How did it go … the funeral?"

"Sad. Very, very sad. Poor Granny Ruth was beside herself. The military looked pretty impressive in their uniforms though … Stephen would have loved it."

"You don't sound particularly upset," remarked Delia, puzzled as to why Lucy's tone was so light and happy."

"Well, I'm not … well, I am … about Stephen. Of course I am … but you'll never guess what he's done … in his will."

Delia didn't reply. She couldn't. Her mouth had gone dry and as she gripped the telephone, her knuckles turned white.

Lucy was so desperate to impart her news, she didn't notice her mother's silence.

"The estate, Mummy. Stephen has left me Canleigh and everything that goes with it … the whole shebang. It's mine. All mine. Isn't that absolutely fantastic?"

* * *

Delia didn't know how she managed to keep a lid on her emotions as Lucy prattled on, saying that after the wedding, she and Jeremy would take up permanent residence at Canleigh and that she would

302

want to listen to any advice from her mother as to how to improve it and keep it profitable, just as she was doing with Blairness.

Delia made the excuse that she had to go as she had a dental appointment but once the conversation had ended with a final 'I love you' from Lucy, she strode into the dining room, grabbed a glass and poured a big shot of brandy into it. She downed it in one and poured another. Then she sat down at the table and put her head in her hands.

Lucy. Her daughter. The one person she loved most in the world ... indeed the only person ... apart from the stirrings she was beginning to feel for Brian Hathaway but she couldn't think about that now.

She gulped down the brandy, letting the fiery liquid hurtle down inside her, warming her, adding fuel to the rage she was already feeling. She was astonished at herself. She had thought she was past all this angst for Canleigh, which she had suffered from since a toddler, ever since she and Richard had fought over the unfairness that it was to go to him and not her, even though she was the firstborn. She had been so much happier and more settled in her mind that ever before since she had been at Blairness and hadn't hankered after delivering a final blow to Ruth, Philip, or Stephen. She didn't know why. It could have been Scotland itself, which was calming, it could have been the peaceful atmosphere of the old castle, which had been balm to her soul after seventeen years of being locked up with the noisy scum of the earth, and then it could have been Brian. He was certainly having an incredible affect on her.

Then, when Lucy had told her that Stephen had died, for a split second her hopes had risen again. It had seemed so logical that Canleigh would pass to her. She hadn't, for one moment, thought he would have bequeathed it to Lucy, a mere slip of a girl. What the hell did she know about running an estate or looking after a Georgian mansion? All she did was work in a flaming hotel for her precious Aunty Vicky.

Delia rose to her feet, pacing the room and running her hands through her hair. She wanted to smash something up, hurt something or someone. The old rage she had felt years ago was flooding over her again.

"Delia … I'm bored … I was wondering if you fancied a chat," said Crystal from the doorway, dressed in a baby blue velvet leisure suit and yawning widely.

Delia grabbed the brass vase full of highly scented chrysanthemums from the centre of the dining table and hurled it at Crystal. Crystal ducked; it missed her and hit the wall, water and flowers spilling out over the cream paintwork. Crystal fled and Delia let out a howl of despair like a wolf baying for blood. It resounded all around the castle.

CHAPTER 24

Lucy was staying the night at Canleigh but walked Jeremy to his car before his drive back to Harrogate.

"I don't know why you won't stay here?" she said with disappointment.

"You know I have an early shift tomorrow," he insisted. "and I hate having to get up at silly o'clock and then deal with all the traffic. It will be much easier if I go now ... and it isn't as if you're on your own ... everyone else is here ... and you have lots to discuss with the family now you own this place."

He looked up at the Hall, resplendent and magnificent in the floodlights. He was still in shock himself. Lucy was now the owner of Canleigh and if they married, he would be entitled to share in all that she had inherited ... including all those millions. He ran his tongue over his lips. He couldn't get his head around it and wanted to get away from her as fast as possible so that he could mull it over ... think about what this could mean for his future ... for the future with Matthew ... and he still had to get to York to tell him. What the hell was he going to say? His head was spinning with it all.

"Yes but not tonight. Everyone is exhausted from the funeral. I think we all need an early night," Lucy was saying.

"There ... you see. You get to bed and spend tomorrow with the family here. I'll come over in the evening."

"Promise?"

"Yes. Definitely."

Lucy reached up and kissed his mouth. Feeling a rush of warmth for her, he responded, folding his arms around her in a big hug.

"I love you so much," Lucy whispered. "I can't wait for the wedding ... Aunt Vicky is talking about having to postpone it because of losing Stephen. I understand, of course, I do but I do hope we don't have to. I'll talk to Granny Ruth and Steppie in the morning and see what they think."

"Well, even if they don't want it to go ahead at Christmas, perhaps we can do it in the spring ... it would be nicer then ... with the weather warmer and everything," Jeremy added, thinking it would give him more time to talk Matthew round and find a solution to their spending more time together when he married Lucy. When, not if. His mind was obviously made up. He was definitely going to marry her. Oh, hell. He dreaded Matthew's reaction to the news.

"Yes," said Lucy, her face brightening. "Yes. It could, couldn't it? That might be a better idea after all."

"Look, it's getting chilly standing here ... go inside before you catch cold. I'll see you tomorrow," he said quickly, glancing at his watch. He had promised to be in York by eleven and it was now ten fifteen. He would have to drive pretty smartly to get there on time.

Lucy planted another kiss on his mouth, turned and dashed up the steps into the hall, shutting the door behind her and blowing him a kiss through the window. He waved, got into his Mini Cooper, and drove smartly along the drive to the main road, his head still spinning with the day's events.

Matthew was in the bar of the hotel on the edge of York where he always met Jeremy. He had just finished his third vodka and coke, lifted his empty glass, and gestured to the barman for a refill whilst glancing at the clock on the wall above the optics. It was five minutes to eleven. Jeremy was going to be late.

"Put a double in there," he said snappily at the barman, who lifted an eyebrow. He didn't like Matthew. He had encountered him on more than one occasion when he had stayed at the hotel and he was always rude. He hoped he wasn't going to sit there, get drunk, and become even ruder.

Matthew's mobile was in his pocket. He felt it vibrate, indicating a text message had come through. It was Jeremy. He was in the car park. Matthew felt himself relax. He was always so worried Jeremy wouldn't turn up, that he would let him down or finish with him.

He sent a message back. 'Will be in room 10 in five.'

They never met in the bar. Jeremy wasn't as well known in York as he was in Harrogate but even so, he always sneaked in the back entrance to the hotel and went straight up to whatever room Matthew had booked to avoid being seen.

Matthew downed the vodka and coke and made his way to the foyer and the stairs, the barman breathing a sigh of relief. Impatient for the lift to arrive quickly, Matthew ran up the stairs; his heart lighter than it had been all evening. With that blasted funeral at Canleigh, he had thought Jeremy would make the excuse that he couldn't come but he hadn't. He had put Matthew first. He was delighted.

He reached his room as Jeremy appeared at the far end of the corridor. They smiled at each other as Matthew opened the door and pulled Jeremy inside.

"God. I've been longing for this," Matthew breathed, pulling at Jeremy's clothing, virtually ripping off his shirt in his haste, buttons spinning across the room.

"So have I," whispered Jeremy, running his hands through Matthew's hair, feeling the familiar deep surge of sexual lust that always encompassed him when Matthew was near. He could never stop this. He needed it so badly. Whatever happened with Lucy, he couldn't imagine giving this up. His desire for Matthew was overwhelming. He was totally 'in love' with him.

An hour later, physically exhausted, they lay naked on the bed, bodies entwined as Matthew, ignoring the no smoking sign above the door, puffed hard on a cigarette, while trying to mentally digest Jeremy's account of the reading of the Duke of Canleigh's will.

"Christ! Canleigh now belongs to the precious Lucy! But it's worth millions … and she's probably going to have a load more too with all the property the Canleigh's own. Bloody hell, she must be worth a fortune now."

"Yes … millions and more millions," said Jeremy breathlessly. His heart was still pounding from the sexual exertion and he felt quite light-headed.

"Bloody, bloody, bloody hell!"

"I know. That's a serious amount of money … it's all those houses and office blocks in London, on the south coast … Bournemouth and Brighton and in

308

Leeds, as well as all the acreage at Canleigh and across Yorkshire. There will be enormous death duties of course but as there is an extensive and incredibly valuable art collection housed in the Hall, I am sure selling a painting or two will deal nicely with that."

"So ...," said Matthew thoughtfully, puffing deeply on his cigarette, "if you do marry the lovely Lucy, you will have access to all that lovely money."

"Yes," replied Jeremy simply, closing his eyes, waiting anxiously for what was to come. He didn't want a row. He felt too chilled, satiated, and content.

Matthew disentangled himself from Jeremy's limbs slowly, stubbed out his cigarette in the ashtray beside the bed and sat up, leaning back on the pale green satin headboard for support.

"So ... do you still want to dump her?" he said slowly, staring hard at Jeremy.

Jeremy opened his eyes but couldn't look at Matthew, aware of the tension in his partner's body as he waited for an answer. The atmosphere in the room was electric. His mouth was dry and he plucked at the duvet with his fingers, not sure what to say. He didn't want to admit that he wished to marry Lucy, searching wildly for the right words to say that wouldn't send Matthew into a frenzy. He still needed Matthew in his life and whatever he said now was going to have a massive impact on their lives one way or another.

He sighed deeply, deciding honesty was the best policy. "I don't know," he said. "I want to be with you more than anything ... you do know that, don't you," he turned his head and their eyes locked. "but blimey, Matthew, becoming Lucy's husband is a golden opportunity ... it would be crazy to throw that

309

away … and we could still see each other … I don't want to give you up … don't want to lose you. You're extremely important to me."

Matthew stubbed out his cigarette and stroked the hairs down Jeremy's arm with one finger. "I'm glad to hear it … you're very important to me too. So, we could both take advantage of this situation if we think it through properly."

Surprised that Matthew was taking it better than he had expected, Jeremy didn't answer, waiting anxiously for his next words.

"If you marry Lucy, you could ask for some kind of an allowance I suppose … what will you do about your job? Will you still work?"

"I shouldn't think so. It would look pretty silly, the husband of an heiress, working as a trainee in a hotel, even though it is a prestigious one."

"Then she would have to give you money of your own, wouldn't she? She can't expect you to have to beg for cash every time you want to buy something."

"That's true, I suppose. I hadn't got round to thinking it through properly … it's all such a shock … it's been a pretty peculiar day what with burying Stephen prematurely and then all this."

"Well, let's reflect on it now. If you marry Lucy, persuade her to give you a generous allowance for a year or two, and then cite for divorce, irreconcilable differences or something … unless you can catch her out with a man … you should get a damned good settlement, and then we can set up home together and have a pretty jammy life. There will be no need for either of us to work. We can just enjoy ourselves … travel, have a decent flat, etc., etc. In the meantime, you can give me a job on the estate. Find me one of those grace and favour cottages and then we can see each other as often as we like with no-one questioning it. How about a chauffeur's position or something … it must be something not too onerous … you know me … I'm not too keen on hard work. I'm fed up with the shop … it's not doing too well anyway and living in Oxford is pretty damned expensive so this would be a great opportunity for me too and I fancy doing something different. Driving would be good … I like cars and I like driving. Who is the chauffeur now?"

"Funnily enough there isn't one. Felix, the butler, he does anything that needs doing but all the family have their own cars and drive themselves mostly."

"Who will live there when Lucy takes up her inheritance?"

"To be honest, I'm not sure. Aunt Ruth and Uncle Philip had planned to move to Tangles … Uncle Philip's house a couple of miles away, when Stephen left the army, but I don't know what they will do now. Lucy will need a hell of a lot of help and guidance so they might decide to stay on for a bit."

"Not after you are married, surely."

"Um. Possibly not. Tangles is so near, they can drive over very easily. I know Uncle Philip has been desperate to move back to his home so there's every likelihood they will go."

"Well then, it will be just you and Lucy. You can easily persuade her you need a chauffeur to look after your cars and drive you about … and if she thinks that's not enough for me to do, I could perhaps help out in the butlering department. Always fancied myself in a penguin suit, serving at dinner."

Jeremy grinned. "I can't imagine that and anyway, I don't think Felix needs any help. He seems to have the butlering all sewn up," he shuddered. "He's a strange man … I think he fancies me actually. He looks at me funny every time I put in an appearance at the Hall and he even had the effrontery to touch me on the shoulder at dinner this evening."

"Oh, did he indeed," said Matthew with a grimace. "This Felix had better watch it or he'll have me to answer to ... well, if a chauffeuring position is out of the question, how about finding me a cottage on the estate to live in rent free? We can say I am a friend of yours ... which I am ... and I need some reason to lead a quiet lifestyle for a while ... perhaps I've had a nervous breakdown or some kind of serious illness and need time to recover ... you are worried about me and that's why you need to visit frequently, to make sure I am all right. Yes," mused Matthew, "that's it. That sounds plausible and I shan't have to do any work, which is even better."

"God, you are devious," smiled Jeremy, as Matthew nuzzled his ear and nibbled his earlobe.

"I know ... and don't you just love me for it, darling Jeremy. If we play this right, we could be rolling in it in a couple of years. What do you say ... are you in?"

Matthew slid down beneath the bedcovers, smiling up at Jeremy wickedly as he stroked and kissed his chest.

"Well?"

Jeremy stretched slowly and deliberately, allowing that wonderful feeling of sublime abandonment that accompanied Matthew's ardour to envelope him. Matthew. Matthew. He was all that mattered at this moment in time. "Oh, yes," he sighed. "I'm in."

* * *

Lucy was in bed at Canleigh. She couldn't sleep, even though she had taken up a hot chocolate, which usually lulled her into slumber very quickly. She tried to read but the book she had chosen from the library was too high-brow for her tastes and she couldn't take in the story. She rifled in the drawer beside the bed, knowing she had a pot of lavender cream which Granny Ruth had given her a year or two ago to use when she couldn't sleep because of examination worry. She found it and massaged it all over her face and hands, feeling the strong scent soothing her immediately. She replaced the pot in the drawer, turned off the light and lay back down, hoping the lavender would do the trick but her mind was too active, jumping from one thing to another, especially the sadness and sorrow of the funeral, which had been the first Lucy had ever attended. She still couldn't believe the lovely, funny, strong and reliable Stephen was no more ... couldn't quite comprehend he wouldn't roar up the drive on his powerful motorbike again, laughing, joking, and teasing Granny Ruth that he had managed a ton on the motorway. The tears slid silently down her cheeks as she remembered all the good times they had shared when growing up. She was going to miss him so very much. Even though he had been away such a lot such joining the army, he was still there for her and often rang to see how she was doing and chat about his exploits but although they had been close, she was still bowled over by him leaving her Canleigh. She felt a little guilty. It should have rightfully gone to her mother but no doubt Stephen had considered it would have been too risky for Granny Ruth and Steppie if Delia Canleigh took up residence here again and reside so close to them. So he did the next best thing and gave it to her.

313

Finally giving up on sleep, she turned the light back on and got out of bed. She was too wound up and wanted to talk to someone but as far as she knew, everyone in the house had retired. She wrapped her fleecy dressing gown around her and pulled on her slippers. She would go down to the kitchens and make another hot chocolate. Perhaps a second one would work.

The wind was rising outside and the house gave the odd creak and groan as Lucy padded down the main staircase into the entrance hall. She was surprised to see a light on the library and poked her head around the door to see who else was up.

"Hello, darling," said Philip, reclining on the sofa in his pyjamas, holding an empty brandy glass. "Can't you sleep either?"

Lucy shuffled over and kissed his head. "No. My mind is all over the place."

She sat down beside him and he took her hand. "I'm sure it must be. You have an awful lot to take in … how do you feel about it … inheriting Canleigh?"

"Frankly … terrified. I can't believe Stephen thought I would be the right person. It doesn't seem right somehow."

"Oh and why's that? You've lived here most of your life; you were like brother and sister … why wouldn't you think he would leave it to you?"

Lucy sighed, knowing he wasn't going to like her next words. "Mother. Surely she should have it."

Philip's expression remained passive. He had guessed she might feel some guilt. "The decision wasn't taken lightly," he said quietly. Your grandmother, Stephen, and I discussed it at length before the will was written up and we decided you were the most appropriate candidate. Delia gave up her right to Canleigh when she almost destroyed the family. She couldn't be allowed to come back and take up the reins as if nothing had happened. You, on the other hand, have always cared for the place and we knew that with support, you would do your best for it and we could all rest easy in our beds."

"I see," said Lucy slowly. She was flattered that the family had so much faith in her. She just hoped she could live up to it.

"And you will, you know," continued Philip. "Have lots of support. Ruth and me, Vicky and Alex ... and Jeremy, of course. Then there is all the staff, Rathbones and the accountants. You have a massive team behind you, all willing to give you any help and advice you need. You will never be alone, darling."

"And will you move back to Tangles? I know you were thinking about it ... I know you want to ... but it won't feel the same without you now. I had expected to be living at The Beeches, with Jeremy, after we marry ... or perhaps in a flat of our own in Harrogate. I certainly didn't think I would be living here."

"We'll stay for now and keep you company ... until the wedding at least. I shouldn't think Jeremy would want us hanging around once you are married."

"That's another thing. Do you think we should postpone the wedding? It's only a few weeks away and I don't want to put Granny Ruth under any more strain than necessary. Jeremy suggested we put it off until the spring."

"To be honest, darling, that would be a good idea, if you don't mind. I don't think Ruth will be up to partying so soon ... in fact I don't know if she ever will again ... Stephen ... this has hit her so very hard."

His face crumpled. He was devastated at the loss of the young man he had thought of as a son and to see Ruth so desperately lost was killing him too.

Lucy had never seen a man cry. It shocked her but she felt his pain and anguish. To lose such a precious member of the family was a severe and dreadful loss to them all.

"Would you ... would you like another brandy?" she asked.

Philip nodded. He rummaged in his pyjama trouser pocket for a handkerchief and blew his nose loudly.

Lucy took his glass and gave him a generous refill from the decanter on the sideboard, pouring a smaller one for herself.

"Thank you, darling. Sorry about that," Philip said sorrowfully.

"There's no need to apologise, Steppie darling. We all loved him so much."

He patted her hand. "You are a lovely girl, Lucy. Generous, loyal, and warm hearted ... and you will be good for Canleigh. You will look after the house, the estate, and its dependents to the best of your ability. I am sure of it. We are all sure of it ... and please don't ever feel guilty about your mother. She has her life back and she has Blairness. She should be thankful for that, get on with it, and never set foot near here again. Have you ... have you told her yet?"

Lucy nodded.

"And how did she take it?"

"Quite well actually. She didn't say much. In fact she was quite brief but she didn't yell or scream or get cross with me."

"Well, that's something to be thankful for. I just hope it stays that way," Philip remarked, wondering exactly what was going through Delia's head right now. Hearing Lucy was to inherit Canleigh must have been a massive blow for her and he felt a flurry of butterflies in his tummy. God help them all if she were in a rage about Lucy's inheritance.

* * *

Felix had gone for a walk after the debris in the ballroom and the dining room had been cleared up, following the wake. Extra staff had been drafted in from the village so it hadn't been too much of an arduous task but even so, he felt tired and wanted a bit of fresh air before he turned in.

The wind was strong and battered him as he walked in the darkness down to the lake. He had a torch in his pocket but didn't use it. He knew the way now and with a little moonlight could move fairly quickly. He didn't go as far as the Bothy, stopping at the first bench he came to on the path around the lake and looking back at Canleigh Hall. There was a light on in the library so someone was up but they wouldn't call him in the middle of the night so he wasn't concerned.

He sat and thought about the shattering day they had all endured. The funeral, the overwhelming sadness of the family, the sorrow of the guests at the wake, the exhaustion of the staff as they saw to the family's needs and then, finally, the reading of the will before dinner. He was still niggled he hadn't received a penny-farthing from the young Duke but had been intrigued to see the reaction of Jeremy after Rathbone departed and the family filed into the dining room for dinner. Jeremy had sat through the whole meal in a kind of stupor and had seemed in an awful hurry to leave Canleigh afterwards. Obviously the boy was reeling from the news that Lucy was to inherit the estate and how it would affect them both when they were married.

Felix mulled over how things were going to change at Canleigh and quite liked what was to come with Lucy and Jeremy, married and living at Canleigh without Mr. and Mrs. Kershaw, as they would no doubt move to Tangles. Felix had heard Mr. Kershaw say more than once that he was looking forward to the time when they could ... and there was no reason for them to stay at Canleigh following Lucy and Jeremy's wedding.

Then things could take an interesting turn. He would have access to Jeremy every day, be able to look after him personally, valet for him, look after his clothes, assist him with bathing, etc. He would be able to look on that Adonis- like body and salivate with sheer unadulterated lust. God. He could feel a stirring in his body at the mere thought of it, picturing a time when he could get Jeremy into his bed, or the other way around ... and by damned, it was going to happen at some point. He sighed deeply and pursed his lips. Yes. Jeremy was going to be his one day, by hook or by crook and then he would really be able to feather his own nest with all that lovely money Jeremy had access to. Felix was going to make sure some of that was definitely going to wend his way.

CHAPTER 25

Delia had hit the brandy bottle furiously following Lucy's phone call. It helped dull the ghastly pain of losing Canleigh yet again, this time to her own daughter, someone she loved unconditionally. She had managed to haul herself up the stairs with the bottle but drank so much, she passed out on the bed and woke up at daylight; stiff, cold, with a crashing hangover and the empty bottle on the carpet beside the bed. For a few moments she lay still, wondering why the hell she had become so inebriated and then, with a crashing sense of realisation she remembered. Canleigh was Lucy's.

She tried to sit up, holding her head in her hands as a searing pain shot through it. Her stomach was doing somersaults and as fast as her head would allow her, she hurried to her bathroom where she was violently sick. Christ! She hadn't felt like this for years but then it wasn't every day the house she had always coveted was whipped away again.

She splashed cold water on her face. It made her shudder even more. The temperature must have dropped dramatically through the night and as she didn't like heat in her bedroom, preferring to snuggle under the covers with a hot water bottle and leave the window open for fresh air, she was already freezing from passing out on the top of the bed instead of in it. She cleaned her teeth and gargled mouthwash, removing the vile taste left by the vomit. The image that peered back at her from the mirror over the washbasin was horrifying. She looked wild and unkempt with dark rings around her bleary eyes. Her hair was a messy tangle and the scar on her cheek stood out, red and angry, on her ashen face. She looked demented and she felt demented. The need to get out of the castle was overwhelming. The walls were closing in. She had to get out. She just had to.

She hurtled down the stairs, ignoring the pain in her head and strode across the lawns to the lake. The day was not a good one as far as the weather was concerned. The wind was fierce, swirling black clouds raced across the sky above her and rain sheeted down, soaking her in seconds. She had left the castle in haste, without thinking about the weather, still wearing the sweater and jeans from last night, which were soaked in seconds and the loafers she had pulled on were quickly sodden. It was just like being in the shower but colder, much colder but she didn't care. She was already freezing.

She reached the water, watching it smash furiously against the rocks. It looked mad and dangerous. Exactly like her. The rage and agitation inside her was at boiling point and she wanted to scream until she could scream no more but no sound came out. She stood, numb, and in deep shock, while the icy rain slapped her body and seemed to penetrate her very soul. She was in utter torment and distraught that she was so jealous. Of her own daughter. She didn't want to feel like this. Just when they were getting on so well. It wasn't right but she couldn't help it. To think that she had been rejected yet again ... for Lucy ... was utter torment. She had grown used to Stephen being the Duke and inheriting Canleigh and even though she didn't like it, had finally accepted it but to have Lucy gain what she had always wanted, just as she had her hopes raised it could finally be hers … it couldn't be. It wasn't right. It wasn't fair.

Suddenly the need to be on Canleigh land was overpowering. She had to go. She had to be there. It was the first time she had felt this strong desire since she had left prison and knew it would be foolish to go anywhere near the place but the pull was so intense, Delia knew she was going to act on it.

"Delia! What the hell are you doing?" The shout was behind her, almost carried away by the wind. "You'll catch your death dressed like that!"

Delia turned. Brian was striding towards her, in his heavy-duty waterproof clothing and Wellingtons. She remained immobile. She couldn't move. She couldn't speak. Tears joined the rain sliding down her face and she looked away, back at the black mountains in the distance, at the maddened lake and the swaying trees. The world was like a dark, crazy place and she felt her mind going with it, sinking down into a terrible abyss of despair and misery.

"Delia … what the hell is the matter? Please. Come inside. This is not the sort of Highland day to be out dressed as you are."

He moved in front of her, growing more worried by the second. Her eyes were glazed and full of tears, and without the make-up she usually wore, that awful scar on her cheek was highly conspicuous on her pasty white skin. She was shaking uncontrollably and when he touched her hand, it felt like a lump of ice.

He took her firmly by the shoulders and turned her around, propelling her towards the castle. Something was obviously badly wrong but now wasn't the time to ask. He had to get her indoors before she made herself really ill.

They reached the boot room, Delia still in a daze, unable to do anything for herself. Her teeth were chattering uncontrollably and her whole body was shaking.

Brian quickly removed his outdoor clothing and then took off her shoes before pulling her through the entrance hall and up the stairs to her room.

"Sit there," he directed, pushing her down on the bed. He darted into the bathroom, turned the bath taps on and threw a generous amount of a strong, sweet-smelling bath foam into the water. He grabbed a towel and went back to Delia, rubbing her hair and wiping her face. She sat, impassive, allowing him to minister to her. She still couldn't speak.

"Do you want me to get Crystal," he asked. "Do you want me to ring anyone?"

Delia shook her head. "No," she croaked. "No. I don't want anyone ... no-one wants me. They all hate me. They always have. No-one has ever loved me. They said they did but they didn't. I might as well be dead."

"Delia," said Brian softly, kneeling by her side and brushing her hair back from her face. "That's not true. Lucy loves you. You know she does ... and I ..."

"Don't say it. I don't want to hear it ... it wouldn't be true anyway. No-one can love me. I'm just not loveable. I'm bitter and nasty, I've been to prison for attempted murder. I've done terrible, ghastly things. I'm the worst kind of sinner there can possibly be. How on earth could anyone love me?"

She started to cry, her slim figure shaking with cold and emotion. Brian pulled her to her feet, into the steaming bathroom, gently peeled off her sodden top, jeans and underclothes, and lifted her into the water, watching carefully as the heat penetrated her bones

322

and the shaking subsided. She laid her head back and closed her eyes but he daren't leave her. He didn't trust her not to sink down and drown herself. He sat quietly on the chair beside the bath, wondering how he had managed to get into the position of undressing his employer and dumping her into the bath, as naked as the day she was born.

But he knew why. He loved her. He had from the moment he set eyes on her. He had been so worried about his position at Blairness with a woman who had gone down for seventeen years for attempted murder but once they met and talked, he had been swept away by his feelings. Even after all those years of a prison diet and lack of real exercise, she had looked good. Tall, slim, thick black hair, a fabulous face, even with that scar which she tried so hard to conceal but it was her courage and capacity for hard work that he admired the most and the way she listened avidly to everything he told her about the estate, about Scotland and about himself. She was interested and willing to learn. She might have been haughty with everyone else but with him, on their long rambles and drives around the estate, she had been natural. No airs or graces. Just solid, good company, ready for a laugh, able to giggle at herself when she slipped in mud or water and fell over, and even telling him the odd dirty joke she had heard in prison.

They had lunched often, sometimes at various village inns and sometimes taking sandwiches and a flask. They had parked the Landrover at special viewing platforms and sat staring silently in awe at the fabulous Scottish scenery, the acres and acres of open ground, forests, and mountains without a single person in sight.

"Gosh," Delia had sighed on one occasion. "Just think of all the poor people living in cities, all on top of each other and yet here we are," she said, waving a hand at the landscape, "in all this and no other person to be seen for miles. It's incredible. We are so lucky."

Over the weeks, they had grown to know and like each other and even though he still called her 'Her Ladyship' when in company, somehow he had slipped into using Delia when they were alone and she never corrected him. Her status as his employer, and even her time in prison and why she went there, seemed irrelevant as they grew closer and closer. He had no idea where it was all heading but he did want to remain at her side. She was far more vulnerable than people realised and he felt an overwhelming urge to protect her and look after her and even make her happy. If she would let him.

"Are you still here?" Delia whispered, raising a hand out of the water and brushing the hair from her face, uncaring that the side with the scar was nearest to him.

He smiled, relieved to see that she had the hint of a wry smile on her face. He nodded. "I'm not going anywhere until I know you are okay."

"You take a lot on yourself," she said.

"Yes. I know."

Their eyes locked for a second and Brian resisted the urge to bend down and kiss her. He knew she wanted him to but she was in a vulnerable state and he didn't want to take advantage.

"Are you going to tell me what sent you out there in that appalling weather, in totally unsuitable clothing?" he asked.

Delia sighed. With the heat of the water, her rage was disappearing. She felt calmer and with the reassuring presence of Brian at her side, quite light-headed. "If you must know, Lucy has inherited Canleigh."

"Oh? So, is that a bad thing?"

Delia lay in the water, considering the question. Was it such a bad thing after all? Did it really matter if Canleigh didn't come to her? She had Blairness now. She had Lucy's love and then there was this man. This gorgeous handsome, strong and honest man whom she had begun to have real feelings for. So, could she let it go? All that deep-rooted desire for an estate that was never meant to be hers.

"I'm ... I'm not sure," she said finally. "I've considered Canleigh should rightfully be mine since I was a small child. Richard ... my twin ... stood in my way and then young Stephen and now my very own daughter. I loved ... I love the place so much ...

"Yes but you haven't seen it or lived there for years. You've managed to get through life without it ... and you have Blairness and I know you are falling in love with it here. I think it's time, Delia ... it's time to let go. Canleigh and your passion for it have ruined a good deal of your life. Don't let it ruin the rest."

Delia looked up at him. His dear, kind, concerned face. What he said made perfect sense. She did love Blairness. She did love Scotland and she was beginning to think she loved him.

"Take me to bed," she whispered, holding out a hand. He gripped it firmly and pulled her to her feet, soapsuds cascading down her body. He grabbed a bath towel, wrapped it around her, and stood back.

"No," he said firmly. "Now isn't the time ...

"But I'm your employer, Brian," she said with a wry smile. "You have to do as I say."

Brian cleared his throat. She had no idea what she was doing to him, standing there, her bare skin glistening, her gorgeous figure wrapped in that towel. He wanted more than anything to take her to bed but it would be wrong.

"I need you ... I really need you," she said sadly. "Even if we don't have sex. Please, Brian. I just want you to hold me ... no-one has done that for a very long time."

He stepped forward and placed his hands on her bare shoulders. "I'll sit with you for a while but there will be no sex ... not on this occasion at least," he said with a hint of a smile.

Delia sighed deeply and allowed him to fold her into a warm, loving embrace. She felt as if she had come home.

* * *

Last week, Delia had informed Crystal she was considering opening the castle to the public and would need someone to run that side of things, looking straight at her former cellmate.

"I'm going to give you a real chance, Crystal, to prove yourself. I know how you want and need to get your teeth into something and I can't think of anything better. It's going to be damned hard work and a hell of a lot of responsibility but I think you could do it, especially with your interest in anything historical. I can offer you a real future now, if you want it but no more silly blackmail threats, no more lazing about pretending you are in control. I'm offering you the chance to run the house opening side of things ... it will be hectic, but with your prior knowledge of how things are done in a stately home, you should be able to cope with anything thrown your way and naturally, Brian and I will back you up. You will have a proper salary, a good one, and you can have a cottage on the estate, if you would prefer, rather than living here in the castle. You can also have my car as I am thinking of buying a Range Rover, as it's far more practical for me. How does that sound?"

Crystal had been amazed ... and exceedingly grateful. She had never wanted to blackmail Delia in the first place but she had been desperate and jealous and Delia knew that. She was growing to love Blairness, fascinated with the art and architecture and Scotland was getting under her skin. She adored the peace and tranquillity and wanted, more than anything, to remain. The idea of her own cottage and car, and a real job with real responsibility was more than appealing. It was the best thing that had happened to her for years and something she hadn't imagined in her wildest dreams.

"I don't deserve it," she breathed, her eyes shining with hope.

Delia gave a caustic laugh. "No, you don't but we've been through a lot together and I don't know what I would have done without your company in prison. You kept me sane ... so I do owe you for that. So, how about it? Do you accept? However, I must warn you, it's not going to be a picnic in the park?"

Crystal beamed. "Of course I accept ... and believe me, Delia; I will do absolutely everything I can to help you make a success of it. You can depend on me, I promise ... and I am truly sorry for trying to blackmail you ... I really am. It was unforgivable of me."

"Forget it," said Delia generously. "We all do crazy things when we're desperate. Let's just move on ... and make a great future for ourselves here."

Crystal had planted a kiss on Delia's cheek, eyes shining with unshed tears, eager to get cracking and determined she would be do all she could to help Delia from now on.

* * *

Crystal left her room carrying a book on the history of the Highlands, a pen and a shorthand notebook full of jottings about different aspects of Blairness she considered could be included in any forthcoming tours of the castle.

She plodded downstairs in search of breakfast, intending to mull over her ideas with Delia, having no idea of the drama that was unfolding in the bedroom along the landing.

She loved living at Blairness Castle, even on those dark, dreary days in the gloomy old building with the black, satanic mountains in the distance. It was far colder up here than down in Norfolk, even though the chilly winds of the North Sea could be bracing at times but with the aid of the brand new thermals she had bought before travelling up, she was warm enough.

Delia's decision to open the castle to the public and allow Crystal to become the manager was a generous one but it was going to take a while to gain the necessary permissions and do the alterations needed for the safety and enjoyment of the public. In the meantime, Delia had suggested Crystal study the castle and its contents, along with the Highlands, and prepare notes for the tours she would undertake when the time came, which Crystal was finding delightful. She was thoroughly enjoying exploring all the rooms that might be shown to the public; researching the paintings, the sculptures, the furniture, the history, even the ghosts. She sat for hours with the McFrains, the longest serving staff members, asking question after question concerning all they had gleaned about the castle during their long years of service. She also ordered book after book from the library in Inverness in her quest for knowledge of this part of Scotland and any reference to Blairness.

Prior to Crystal's promotion, Delia had insisted Crystal have her meals with the staff in the kitchens but eventually relented on breakfast, which now turned into an hour every morning when Crystal joined her and they could discuss what she had found out and how it could be incorporated into the forthcoming tours.

Crystal had also been given the spare desk in the office, and Connie had cleared out one of the filing cabinets for her to use, although there was nothing much in it yet, only her typed up notes on the history of the castle, along with minutes of any relevant meetings she had with Delia and Brian.

So, Crystal was settling in and beginning to look forward to when she would be run off her feet with organising the guides, the reception, car parking and café staff and making sure the general public had an interesting and enjoyable time during their visit to the castle.

There was only one huge disappointment in living in the Highlands. Scotland seemed to be lacking in decent single men, at least near Blairness. All those she encountered were too old, too young, were married or in a close relationship. Apart from Brian. He was perfectly delicious and she fancied him rotten … but for some reason she couldn't seem to catch his eye. She always made sure she was dressed beautifully when he was about, that her make-up was perfect, that she wore the best perfume she could buy but as much as she smiled and chattered gaily when he was near, he remained pleasant, kept conversation to the point and that was that. No progress. No hint of a possible romance. The obvious conclusion was that he must have a woman somewhere but who or where she had no idea. She had certainly never seen him with one, only Delia. They spent long hours together, driving off in the Landrover, ostensibly to see to estate matters. Surely not, she thought as the possibility struck her. Surely Delia wasn't another Lady Chatterley. Crystal was damned envious of her, if she was.

She wandered into the dining room and helped herself to scrambled eggs and a couple of sausages from the hotplates on the sideboard. She wished Delia would hurry up. There was a lot to discuss this morning. She had mapped out a route through the castle for visitors, which would include all the most interesting ground floor rooms and a few of the bedrooms, and wanted her approval. She was also eager to divulge what she had learned about the ghosts and was seriously wondering on whether it would be possible to run occasional evening ghost tours, which would bring in much needed revenue. Delia probably wouldn't want people tramping through the house at that time of day but Crystal was going to suggest it, nevertheless.

She sat down and pushed her knife into a sausage. She had left the dining room door open and heard a door close at the top of the stairs but it couldn't be Delia. The footsteps on the stone stairs were heavier. Surely not a man, coming out of Delia's room!

Crystal waited with bated breath as the footsteps came nearer, heading towards her and her mouth fell open as Brian appeared, tucking his shirt into his trousers.

"Oh, morning," he said pleasantly, surprised to see Crystal at the table. "I've had to put Her Ladyship to bed. She's had some disturbing news and got herself soaked outside. She's had a hot bath but needs something hot inside her too so I'll take her up some food and coffee."

Crystal sat still, her astonishment preventing her saying anything coherent. She watched as Brian busied himself heaping cornflakes into a bowl and bacon, a sausage and a couple of fried eggs and mushrooms onto a plate. He poured coffee into a cup and then piled the lot onto a silver tray.

"I don't think she will be well enough to come down today. She needs to stay in bed if she doesn't want to catch a chill," he said, moving towards the door.

"Oh, right," Crystal mumbled as he left the room, her eyes glazing over with speculation. So, her employer *was* having a relationship with the estate manager. That was certainly a turn up for the books. She wondered how far it had gone … if they had enjoyed rampant sex together. She clamped her teeth together with jealousy. Christ. Delia was a bloody lucky woman. She had so much materially while Crystal had so little and now she had the best man in the Highlands. Bugger, bugger, bugger.

* * *

Brian pushed open Delia's door with his foot. She was in bed, dressed in satin pyjamas, her hair flowing

331

over her shoulders. He had dried it earlier with her hairdryer, while she sat impassively on the bed, allowing him to run his fingers through her mane of silky, brunette hair. She had loved every second of it. Apart from male hairdressers, she had never had a man dry her hair before and she thrilled at his touch.

He placed the tray on the bed beside her and stood looking down at her. "You certainly look a lot better," he remarked.

"And I feel better ... thank you ... thank you for looking after me," she said, gradually regaining her equilibrium.

"You're welcome," he replied gruffly, taking his eyes off her. More than anything, he wanted to hold her in his arms again. It had seemed so right earlier, cuddling her, feeling her warm, sexy body close to his. It had been hard, keeping his feelings in check, to push down the desire, to stop himself kissing her passionately. He couldn't believe how much he wanted her and couldn't remember ever feeling like this about another woman in his life. He had enjoyed relationships, two that had come close to marriage but nothing like this ... this deep, burgeoning love, this meeting of minds.

"Right. I better get on," he said, turning away from her. "Connie will be wondering where I am. We were having a correspondence session at nine and I'm an hour late. I'll get a right telling off," he grinned, knowing what a bossy boots Connie could be with anything to do with the office. She ran a tight ship and she expected everyone else to feel the same about her domain.

"Tell her it was all my fault," Delia said, eyeing the cornflakes. She loved them, often snacking on them throughout the day but they weren't doing it for her this morning. In fact none of the items on the tray were, apart from the coffee.

Brian watched the expression on her face. "You must eat something ... the eggs and sausages look and smell delicious. Get some of them down you ... and that coffee ... while it's hot. Now I must go. If you need me, you can get me on my mobile ..., which is in the Landrover. I left it there when I saw you by the lake. No doubt there will be a lot of messages from Connie." He pulled a face.

"Okay ... and thanks again. I do appreciate it," she said, as he walked to the door. God, he was gorgeous but somehow she was pleased, although confused, that he had refused her advances. He was an honourable man and wouldn't have wanted to take advantage of her in her distress ... but ... and it was a depressing thought ... perhaps he wasn't attracted to her, not like she was to him. The scar might put him off, or her prison record, or her status as his employer. The odds were stacked against her. She knew that but she also knew, from the looks he gave her, that there was something there but whether or not it would ever come to fruition was another story. As he closed the door softly behind him, she slid down the bed and cried. The whole world was against her. She was so miserable she could die.

* * *

Brian strode back downstairs in his socks, across the entrance hall and into the office, apologising profusely as he opened the door.

"It was Lady Delia … she required my services … and I'm really sorry but I left my phone in the Landrover," he said quickly, to pacify his enquiring secretary.

"Well, you are here now … should we get on with the dictation?" she asked, raising an eyebrow as she noticed he wasn't wearing any shoes. "I've the wages to see to today as well so there's a lot to do."

An hour later, the dictation session finished and Connie in a lighter mood now she could be left to get on with her work, he strode into the boot room next door to the office, pulled on his waterproofs and Wellingtons, and went outside to the Landrover. The day had improved. The wind had dropped and the sky was lighter. He glanced over at the lake. Instead of crashing waves, there were now only ripples. The whole world seemed a great deal calmer than it had earlier this morning. He hoped Delia was feeling the same way, would have stayed in bed and gone back to sleep.

He drove out of the castle gates and drove back down to his cottage to fetch Meg. He had left her at home this morning as she hated the rain and preferred to stay in her basket until it had passed. Peculiar really, for a dog who loved to swim and couldn't throw herself in the lake fast enough. If she were caught in the rain, she was a different dog, tiptoeing through puddles and her tail down, miserable as sin. Daft old thing.

Meg was eager to be helped into the Landrover, having sniffed the air to make sure there were no threatening droplets about to land on her head and sighing with contentment as she nestled down on the passenger seat beside her master.

They drove down to the site of the new caravan park. Since planning permission had come through, work had started before the full onset of winter and Brian wanted to see how it was coming along, although he doubted much would have been done this morning with such atrocious weather.

He thought about Delia, remembering how her slight body had nestled in his arms as he placed her in the bath, how her hair had felt as he ran his hands through it to dry it. Her quietness and then ... her invitation into her bed.

No matter how he tried to ignore it, she was in his skin, in his heart and in his mind, twenty-four hours a day. He even dreamed about her. He had never felt like this about a woman before and had no idea why he should about this one and with her violent record, he would normally have steered well clear of any entanglement ... but he didn't want to. He loved his job on the estate and he had to acknowledge it, he loved her. He loved her smile, her laugh, her beautiful deep brown eyes, her luscious mouth, her thick, glossy hair, and her body. Oh, her body. He wanted to stroke it, kiss it, embrace it. He wanted, more than anything, to experience wild, passionate encounters with her.

He gulped, pushing away the images in his mind. It was stupid to think like that. She was an enigma, was Lady Delia Canleigh and if they did eventually fall into bed together, it was bound to end badly. He was just kidding himself that it could turn out otherwise. He had to pull himself together and find another woman to take his mind of off Delia ... but who? There was simply no-one he was interested in in the local area ... and then he remembered Crystal. She had been making a definite play for him for the last few weeks. Perhaps he should ask her out … but that was an even crazier idea. She was another ex-con and he didn't fancy her enough. No. He would just have to keep reminding himself that Delia was his employer and leave it at that. He would have to be very, very firm with himself.

CHAPTER 26

Delia went to Canleigh. She couldn't help herself. She rose from her bed at midday, her mind still in a whirl with Lucy's news that she was to inherit Canleigh and then the scene with Brian earlier this morning. She was so mixed up about it all and felt the walls of Blairness closing in again. She didn't want to be in the castle. She didn't want to be in Scotland. All she wanted was to be at Canleigh … even if it was only to say goodbye to it. She just had to be there … now … today … and hang the consequences. Luckily, she had paid her fortnightly visit to the probation office yesterday and didn't have to worry about that for a while and she didn't intend to stay in Yorkshire for long anyway. To avoid being recognised she could wear her wig and glasses and a great deal of clothing to make her look fatter … and if she only went out after dark, she should be able to get away with it.

Her laptop was on the chest of drawers. She took it back to bed and turned it on, searching for holiday cottages somewhere between Harrogate and York. She certainly couldn't stay in a hotel or guesthouse. It had to be somewhere completely private where she wouldn't run into other people. To be on the safe side, she chose a detached bungalow on the outskirts of York, only around 45 minutes drive to Canleigh. She had to book for the whole week but wouldn't be there that long. A couple of days would suffice as the longer she was in Yorkshire, the more chance she had of being seen.

She left the castle, throwing a hastily packed canvas bag containing a few clothes, the wig, glasses and makeup into the back of her car and drove smartly out of the castle grounds. A mile down the road she stopped, took out her mobile from her handbag and rang Connie, asking her to inform everyone she was going away for a couple of days.

"Where shall I say you are, Your Ladyship ... just in case there is an emergency while you are away?"

"Um ... Edinburgh," Delia said quickly. "I just want to do a bit of shopping. I'm not sure where I'm staying. I'll let you know."

With that, she switched off the phone and started the car, hoping she wouldn't bump into Brian until she was well clear of the estate. If he saw her, he might guess where she really intended going and she didn't want to risk him trying to stop her. She was going home and that was that. She was going back to Canleigh.

* * *

Brian always popped into the office at the end of the day to check his messages and sign any post Connie had left for him. Connie had already departed for home by the time he arrived, the office was in darkness, and there weren't many lights on in the castle either. Perhaps Delia was still in bed but he noticed her car wasn't standing on the castle forecourt where it had been that morning. She never went out at night so he was puzzled as to why it wasn't there ... unless Crystal was using it this evening.

Not too concerned, he entered the office and sat down to sign the heap of correspondence Connie had prepared earlier from their dictation session. She was an excellent typist and there were no errors so he signed them all quickly and put them back on her desk for her to deal with in the morning. Then he checked his messages. Reception for his mobile was a little patchy when he was out and about so at times it was difficult for anyone to talk to him. Today had been no exception and Connie had typed out a list of people who were trying to get hold of him and finally, at the end, she had left a note to say Lady Delia had decided to visit Edinburgh for a couple of days but hadn't said where she was staying.

Brian sat still, frozen to his seat, fear for Delia uppermost in his mind. She had been reasonably calm when he had left her this morning but goodness knows what had gone through her mind when she was alone. Had she gone doolally again? She had been so distressed about Lucy inheriting Canleigh. Surely, she wouldn't have gone down there. No, she would be risking prison again if she did. Surely, she wasn't that stupid ... but then he had seen her anguish this morning. She hadn't been thinking straight and the thought had crossed his mind that she might have thrown herself in the lake if he hadn't come along.

He picked up the phone and dialled her mobile. It went straight to voicemail, deepening his anxiety. He didn't know what else to do but keep ringing her. He couldn't go after her as he had no real idea of where she was. He wanted to believe it was Edinburgh but he had a nasty feeling it wasn't but then he couldn't swear she would go to Canleigh. He wondered if he should warn Lucy, just in case ... but why frighten the girl if there was no need?

He ran his fingers through his hair with agitation. He was deeply worried but thinking about it logically, there was nothing he could do but wait for her to either get in touch or return home. She loved

Edinburgh so she might well have gone there for a couple of days rest and recuperation ... see a play or shop ... or something. He tried to persuade himself that there was absolutely no way she would have gone down to Yorkshire. He would kick himself if she had. He had seen the state she was in this morning. He should have kept a firmer eye on her, or asked Crystal or the McFrains to. Christ! If she had gone down to Yorkshire and was caught ... he groaned and placed his head in his hands. He would be devastated if she was sent back to prison again. He couldn't imagine life here at Blairness without her now. He picked up his mobile and rang her again, willing her to answer. It went straight to voicemail.

* * *

The motorway was quiet and the car hummed along with Delia at the wheel, eager to reach Yorkshire as fast as possible. It took her just over six hours as she only stopped once at a service station for a coffee and a quick trip to the loo, although she made sure she donned the wig and glasses before leaving the car.

When, eventually, the 'Welcome to Yorkshire' sign came into view, her excitement grew. She was home. She loved Scotland and Blairness but this was her real home, where she had been born and grew up ... and in her adult years, suffered. She gripped the steering wheel tightly as she remembered how much she had loved Philip and how he had let her down, not once but twice. How differently things would have turned out if he had loved her as much as she loved him; if he hadn't spurned her, almost at the alter.

340

Even if her father hadn't allowed her to run Canleigh, at least she would have been nearby, at charming, lovely old Tangles. She and Philip would have been happy. They would have had children together and life would have been perfect. She would never have had to murder Richard and Rocky, try and kill Ruth and him or attempt suicide. It was all his fault. She had never thought of it that way before, but it was. His decision to dump her only days before their wedding and marry that awful Sue woman had been the catalyst for her to go completely off the rails. She hadn't even slept with another man before that. She had never wanted to. All she had wanted was Philip and to be his wife. God, how she hated him now.

She could feel it, the old rage and jealousy returning. She had to stop the car in the nearest lay-by and get a grip of her feelings. She wound down the window and breathed in the night air. It steadied her. She looked at the clock on the dashboard. It was nearly seven thirty and she was growing tired. It had been a highly emotionally charged day and then a long journey. The cottage wasn't far away and the sooner she got there the better but Canleigh was only a few miles in the opposite direction. She couldn't resist it. She turned the car and headed towards it, elated as soon as she knew she was on Canleigh land. Her land. Her home.

She didn't head for the village and the front gates, she went via Killington, and through the rear entrance to the estate, driving slowly now, not wanting to attract any attention as she neared the Dower House. Lucy had mentioned it was empty these days. Someone had rented it for a while but had moved out and they couldn't find another tenant who was willing to pay an exorbitant rent.

Delia pulled up in front of it and turned off the car lights, knowing the house could be seen for miles and didn't want anyone querying why there was a night visitor. She took her torch out of the glove compartment, got out of the car and walked towards the building. Even in torchlight, it looked just as it had the day she ran out, having belted Philip hard with the poker in the lounge and then leaping onto Demon to tear down to the lake after Ruth. It all came flooding back, how angry she had been, how demented with rage. She took in deep breaths, trying to steady herself, trying to force down the wave of nausea and the tears. Perhaps she shouldn't have come. Perhaps this had all been a brainless idea. She was tired. She couldn't deal with it. How barmy she had been ... was being.

She returned to the car and drove back down the track to Killington. She half wanted to go the other way and gaze on the Hall but she couldn't now. It was too painful. She had to get to the bungalow. Have something to eat and then sleep. She then had all day tomorrow to plan what she was going to do. She had no idea at the moment. She couldn't think clearly.

She reached the bungalow half an hour later. The instructions she had been given were easy to follow. It was down a side street of similar properties. Number twenty-three. She pulled up on the drive, took her handbag and canvas bag from the car, found the key to the bungalow under the flowerpot by the door, and stepped inside. It was warm and welcoming. The heating was on, a bottle of red wine stood in a prominent position on the coffee table in the lounge with a note of welcome and there was coffee, tea, and sugar in the tiny kitchen, along with a carton of milk in the fridge.

She drew the thick damask curtains in the lounge, pulled the blinds down in the kitchen, locked the door, and sank into the old-fashioned chintzy sofa with a glass and the wine.

Here she was. In Yorkshire. Only a few miles from Canleigh. What on earth would people think if they found out? Would anyone report her? God, she had to be careful now.

She rifled in her handbag for her mobile phone. She had turned it off when leaving Blairness, not wanting anyone to ring her ... or persuade her to return. Brian, of course. No-one else would bother. The McFrains wouldn't think it their place and Crystal wouldn't care. No, if anyone would be concerned it would be Brian. At least she would like to think so.

The familiar phone information lit up the mobile and then indicated she had five missed phone calls and three voicemail messages. All were from Brian. He sounded desperately concerned and for a second she felt a pang of guilt, not used to anyone worrying about her. It was an unusual feeling. She debated on whether to ring him but fought against the desire to hear his voice. He would guess where she had gone and would try to persuade her to return immediately and she didn't want that. Not yet. She had to spend a day or so here first. She resorted to sending a text message.

'Am quite safe. Please don't worry. Will be back in two days. D'

That would have to suffice. She switched off the phone again quickly before he had time to answer. She couldn't think about him now. She was physically and mentally exhausted and needed sleep. She picked up her bags and went through to the bedroom. It wasn't exactly luxurious but it would do. A double bed with a pine headboard and matching wardrobe and dressing table. All the furnishings were in a sickly pale green, which wouldn't help if one was feeling a bit ill, she surmised. A quick shower relaxed her and she slid into bed and within minutes, was fast asleep.

* * *

It was ten o'clock in the morning when Delia opened her eyes and for a second lay wondering where the hell she was and then it all came flooding back. Lucy's phone call to say that Canleigh was now hers, crying by the lake, Brian guiding her indoors, putting her in the bath, drying her hair, the crazy journey down here and then the visit to the Dower House. Tears threatened but she gulped them back. She hated feeling sorry for herself. It was pathetic. Anger, yes, but not self-pity. That she loathed ... in others and herself.

She pulled on some clothes and drew back the curtains cautiously. It was a quiet road and at this time of the morning, most people had gone to work. Two people were chatting on the opposite side of the road while their dogs stood looking bored by their sides, a postman hurried past with a heavy bag slung over his back but he didn't turn up her drive. Nothing to worry about there then. No-one appeared to be taking any notice of what was going on at number 23.

She realised her car was on full view. There was a garage, which she had access to, and as soon as she had nipped to the nearest shop to buy a few supplies, which by the instructions left by the owner was only a mile away, she would put it away until tonight. She couldn't go to Canleigh until after dark so it could stay there all day.

She carefully placed and adjusted the wig on her head, plastered on make-up to hide the scar and then put on the glasses. No-one would recognise her like this and luckily, it was chilly outside so she could pull the hood of her coat up too. She took another peek outside. The people who had been chatting on the opposite side of the road had gone and there was no-one in the street at all.

The shop was easy to find, she parked outside and dashed in, wanting to spend as little time inside as possible. She grabbed a basket and threw in bread, more milk, cheese, eggs, butter, yoghurts, cornflakes, two big bars of chocolate, a couple of frozen meals and paid in cash at the counter.

Minutes later, she was back at the bungalow, found the key for the garage, and tucked the car away. Hurrying back indoors, she felt an immense sense of relief as she locked the front door behind her. She was safe for now. No-one knew where she was and she liked it that way.

The day went by slowly. She hadn't brought anything to read with her and the books the owner had left weren't to her taste, being mostly science fiction, which she wasn't remotely interested in. Daytime television didn't float her boat either; quiz shows and old drama series, which had been repeated umpteen times were utterly boring.

She had a long, hot bath and lay back in the water, thinking about Canleigh, wishing it were possible to just drive over there now, in daylight, without worrying who she might bump into and if they would report her. As it was, she couldn't do anything until after dark and even then, not in the early evening. She had to wait until around midnight ... until the chance of anyone being up and about was pretty remote. Then it would be reasonably safe to drive over, park somewhere discreet along the lane near the Dower House and walk down to the lake; wander up to the Hall, the stables, the gardens. She would have until around six in the morning as that was when the staff and tenant farmers would start to rise and commence their duties, which would give her six hours to have a good scout around and renew her acquaintance with her old home.

With nothing else to do and feeling relaxed after her bath, she went back to bed and slept all afternoon, hauling herself out half way through the evening and into the kitchen to eat a huge bowl of cornflakes and one of the frozen meals which advertised in big letters that it was cottage pie with vegetables. What had happened to the vegetables she had no idea as they were so few and far between and the mashed potato on top was revolting and the meat content even more so. It was the first time she had prepared a frozen meal and it would be the last. It reminded her of prison food. Another bowl of cornflakes and then a chocolate bar, along with a glass of red wine went down much better. She shoved the remaining chocolate bar in her jacket pocket in case she grew hungry through the night.

At eleven thirty she was ready, disguise in place and wearing black jeans, a black leather jacket, a black check woollen scarf around her neck and leather gloves. She also wore her thermals. The night could get cold and she didn't want it seeping into her bones. She decided to dispense with a bag. She took out her purse and mobile and pushed them down into the pocket of her jacket with the chocolate, picked up her car keys and left the bungalow. Five minutes later, she was heading for Canleigh, heady with excitement.

The roads were empty and it only took just over half an hour before she was driving through Killington towards the back entrance to the estate. She drove past the Dower House this time, and down the lane until she was in sight of the Hall, took a right turn down a sidetrack into a field, and parked behind the hedge. Hopefully no-one would see the car for the next few hours and wonder what it was doing there.

Having killed the engine, she sat for a few moments with the window open, listening to the stillness of the night. An owl hooted. She smiled. How often had she heard the owls at night here?

She got out of the car, remembering to take out the torch, locked the door, pushed the keys into an inside pocket of her jacket and zipped it up. Whatever happened she mustn't lose them or she would really be in trouble. She walked back onto the lane and looked across the fields at Canleigh Hall. Dark clouds glided overhead, parting now and again so that the moon could show up the land before her ... and the Hall. Oh, God. The Hall. Her heart leapt as she set eyes on it for the first time in seventeen years. It still looked as splendid as ever, the huge Georgian pile that should have been hers to queen over. Instead, she was risking going back to prison just to obtain a glimpse of it.

She meandered down the lane towards the lake, loving the peace and quiet, not scared at being alone at night. She was on her own land. She felt confident and ambled along, enjoying the sounds of rustling in the bushes as she passed. A fox stood in her path, his eyes lit up by the moonlight. He stood his ground until she was nearly up to him and then scarpered quickly into nearby woods. A rat charged across the lane, which did make her shudder, and a couple of sheep resting behind a hedge, gave a pathetic bleat and moved away quickly.

She reached the far side of the lake to the Hall and looked across to her former home. It looked much bigger now she was nearer. Only ten minutes and she could be standing at the front door if she hurried. She reached the old Bothy first and the bench outside. Wanting to rest her legs for a few moments, she sat down and stared across the lake in the dappled moonlight. She could make out the swans on the far side, tucked up tight for the night on the grass beside the boathouse. They had always liked to sleep there. The ducks were on the bank further along. She remembered how, when she was tiny, she and Granny had strolled down to the lake nearly every day to feed them. More memories of Granny came flooding back. She had been the best person in the world when she was alive. Delia's rock. Until that day her parents had that awful row after her mother disgraced herself so badly in a London park, romping around with Simon Parfitt, and Granny had suffered a severe stroke and died. Delia would never forget it. She had never been able to forgive her mother for what she had done, nor her father for putting her brother and sister before her and disappearing down to their schools in the south of England to advise them what had happened. He had blatantly ignored her needs, not even bothering to talk to her, to reassure her or to show her that he cared about her welfare. Thank God for the Kershaw's who had taken her in and cared for her for months. Philip and his lovely grandparents had saved her sanity.

Sitting still for so long was making her cold, even with the addition of thermals. She stood up and

348

moved along the path around the lake, a movement behind a tree in front of her making her stop for a second but it was nothing, just a night creature scurrying out of her way again.

She walked up to the stables. Little had changed since she had last seen it; the day she had tried to hang herself in Demon's loosebox following her attempt to kill Philip and Ruth, and after that blasted gamekeeper had shot and killed her darling Demon.

She walked straight across to his loosebox, shut the door and switched on her torch. She couldn't resist looking up at the beam from which she had thrown the rope and then placed it around her neck. She shuddered. What a ghastly frame of mind she had been in. She wasn't much better now but not that bad. She had been truly desperate and heartbroken then.

For a second she shut her eyes and thought about her horse who had spent so many hours of his early life in here. She could feel his presence, and it was almost possible to believe that if she put out her hand, she could touch him. She could hear his whinny of welcome, feel the warmth of his breath on her face. A tear slid down her face as the searing pain of his loss hit her. God help Pritchard, that bloody gamekeeper who had shot him … if she came across him tonight.

She brushed away her tears and looked at the wall in front of her, shining the torch down the brickwork, running her hand along to find the loose brick. It was still there and came away in her hand and inside the cavity, she saw it. The piece of paper that had made her so very happy when she was only thirteen years old, which had kept her motivated and content for all of her teens, giving her something to work for, to aim for. She pulled it out and read it again, the words written by her twin brother, whom she had killed years later because he had reneged on this promise.

'I, Richard Canleigh, Marquess of Keighton, do solemnly declare that on the day I inherit Canleigh Hall, I will give up all rights to the estate and it will pass to Lady Delia Canleigh for her to do with as she pleases.' And there, beneath the declaration was Richard's signature, bold and firm. What a chump she had been to believe him but then she had only been thirteen, still a child in the eyes of the law.

She didn't know what to do with the note, whether to put it back or take it with her. It had no purpose now. She tore it into pieces and stuffed it back behind the brick. That's what she thought of her brother's promises!

She didn't stay long in the stables. There were no horses, only a couple of cars. Perkins, the old stable hand whose domain this had been when horses played a large part in the life of the Canleigh family and who had taught her to ride, had retired long ago. His flat above the stables was empty, as was the tack room and his office. Just big empty spaces now and it made Delia wonder why Ruth and Stephen hadn't made better use of the block. She was going to rent her unused outbuildings at Blairness as office space. Surely the same could be done here? It was a wasted opportunity to say the least. She would mention it to Lucy. Perhaps she would do something about it.

She walked quietly and quickly up the hill towards the house, through the side gardens and to the parterre in front of the south terrace. It looked ghostly in the moonlight with the topiary and stone ornaments, along with the massive statue of Pegasus in the middle.

She crept up to the house and looked in the library window. The curtains hadn't been drawn and in the dim light she could just make out the furniture, exactly the same as it had been when she had lived there. Ruth obviously wasn't one for change then.

She badly wanted to go inside. She knew where there would be a key to the boot room door, if no-one had thought to move it, but it would be risking too much. If someone should catch her, she really would be for the high jump. It was bad enough that she was standing outside. Even so, she made her way to the boot room and fiddled about under the window. She could remember Perkins having made a little ledge beneath the bigger one where a key was always kept. She couldn't believe it. After all this time it was still there. She turned it over in her fingers, itching to use it and go inside but commonsense prevailed. She put it back.

She turned away from the Hall and crossed the lawns silently. There was no shelter from prying eyes. She was totally out in the open and prayed no-one would wake up, look out of the window, and see her.

Minutes later she was standing outside the gate to the churchyard where most of her family were buried. Taking deep breaths she entered, moving swiftly round the side of the church to where her grandfather, granny, father, and brother all lay. They all possessed well-cared for headstones and fresh flowers. She was pleased, glad that those she had loved hadn't been forgotten in her absence.

Then she looked at the new grave beside them, still covered in wreaths and flowers but as yet, no headstone. This had to be Stephen. Poor chap. She was sorry he had been killed in such a dreadful way. He had been a nice little boy and was no doubt a nice

351

man. Certainly someone to be proud of. Suddenly Delia, as a mother herself, felt desperately sad for Ruth and was surprised by such a strong emotion. Ruth and Stephen had been top of her hit list for so long but now one was dead and the other grieving and it was nothing short of tragic.

She wanted to say something to Stephen ... to all of her departed family ... but didn't know what. She had said sorry so many times in her prayers and in her thoughts and now she was here, right in front of their graves, she had no words. Just tears. Tears for what might have been, tears for their lives, tears because she missed them and would never see them again ... and because some of them had their lives shortened because of her. Granny had suffered that awful stroke, not just because of the row between her mother and father but because of the wilful act of violence Delia had perpetrated against Simon Parfitt's car afterwards. Granny had died only minutes later. Richard had reneged on his promise and she shot him. That had caused her father to suffer a heart attack. Weakened considerably afterwards, he had then suffered a fatal one after hearing her conversation with Ruth about how she wasn't going to abort Lucy and how much she hated her family. Yes, so many of them were in their graves, earlier than they should have been, all because of her. God, what a bloody awful person she was.

Startled out of her reverie by a twig snapping nearby, she moved back to the wall of the church. Someone was in the churchyard and she was about to be discovered. Panic overtook her and she moved too quickly, tripping over a small headstone. She went flying, landing with a thud on the hard ground.

"Well, well. May I help Your Ladyship up?" said a cultured male voice she didn't recognise. Who the hell was he and how the hell did he know who she was? Her heart was in her mouth and she could feel the prison walls around her again, could hear the harsh clang of the big doors as they were locked and bolted behind her. God, what an idiot she had been to come back to Canleigh.

CHAPTER 27

Felix was exultant. He couldn't believe he had caught the famous Lady Delia Canleigh sneaking around Canleigh grounds. He had seen her coming towards him on the path around the lake and darted behind a tree, wondering why a strange woman was walking around the lake at this time of night. He knew it wasn't Ruth or Lucy. They wouldn't have dreamt of doing such a thing on their own.

He watched the woman closely as she came nearer to him along the path. She had paused for a second and then as she continued on up to the stables and then to the house, obviously knowing exactly where she was going, it struck him who she was. Her hair was short and she wore glasses but she was tall enough to be Lady Delia and from the confident way in which she was walking, it had to be her. There could be no other reason why any other woman would be in the Canleigh grounds at this time of night but then, why was she?

He followed her, adept at creeping about, both in and out of the house. When she entered the stable block, he was intrigued to see her walk straight across to a loose box on the opposite side to the entrance. He watched from behind Mrs. Kershaw's estate car and then it came to him that someone had said Delia had tried to hang herself in there. The thought crossed his mind that she was intending to finish the job tonight but just before he decided to go and investigate, she emerged and strode across the stable yard and up the hill towards the Hall.

Flabbergasted, he continued stalking her, watching her stand on the south steps looking down at the parterre and then through the library window, before heading to the boot room door and fiddling around under the window ledge. In the moonlight, he could see she had something in her hand. It looked like a key. For one horrified moment he thought she was going to enter the Hall but she replaced the key under the ledge and moved away, round to the front of the building and then across the lawns to the church. He waited until she was in the churchyard and then he darted behind her, carefully closing the gate quietly behind him. He stood silently behind an enormous Yew tree, watching her at the graves of her family. He knew perfectly well she was only out of prison on licence and one of the conditions was that she never set foot on Canleigh soil or came near its occupants again. To come here was foolish in the extreme and he couldn't help but wonder what she was up to.

Always on the lookout for an opportunity, Felix realised one was being given to him on a plate and before she left the estate, he was going to take advantage of it. He moved towards her but accidentally stepped on a twig. It snapped and alerted her. She moved quickly but didn't look where she was going and crashed onto the ground. He was standing above her before she could rise to her feet.

"Well, well. May I help Your Ladyship up?" he asked, unable to prevent a smile of satisfaction creep across his face.

Delia scrambled to her feet, shrugging off his outstretched arm. "No. Don't touch me," she commanded. "Who the hell are you anyway?"

"The butler, Your Ladyship. Felix Bamford"

"Oh ... and why, pray, are you sneaking about the churchyard in the middle of the night? I'm sure Mr. and Mrs. Kershaw wouldn't be too happy if they knew what you were up to," replied Delia frostily, desperately trying to regain her poise and the upper hand.

"Well, I could say the same about you, Your Ladyship. After all, you have much more to lose than I do."

Delia swallowed. She wished she had a weapon of some kind as she could have happily battered this horrid little man to death. Lucy had mentioned he was a bit of a weasel and gave them all the creeps and she could see why now. She wouldn't have employed him for a second.

As she hadn't answered him, he continued. "Now, Your Ladyship, I think we need to come to some sort of arrangement, don't you ... that is, if you don't want me to tell the world you have been here."

Delia sneered. Yet another attempt at blackmailing her. She had sorted Crystal. She would do the same for this creature ... but exactly how, she had no idea. "Blackmail ... just because I wanted to see the graves of my family. You really are despicable."

"The same could be said about you, Your Ladyship. After all, you have a far worse reputation. I haven't tried to kill anyone and haven't spent one day in prison, unlike yourself ... seventeen years I believe ..., and then you are only out on licence."

"Well, that should tell you something, you stupid little man. I'm not frightened of you and I'm not going to be blackmailed by you. No-one would believe you, anyway. As far as everyone is concerned I'm tucked up in bed at Blairness," she bluffed, hoping and praying he wouldn't check.

"Um. So, if I ring the castle early in the morning, your staff would confirm that, would they?"

Delia didn't answer. Her brain was working overtime to find a way out of this blasted awful dilemma she had found herself in, while her eyes were searching for something, anything that she could use to bash him over the head but then that wouldn't be very wise. If he survived an attack, he would tell all, they would descend on her like a ton of bricks, and she would be whisked back to prison immediately. If she killed him, it probably wouldn't take them long to put two and two together and she would be arrested anyway. Whatever she did, she couldn't do anything physical to him ... not at this moment in time ... but in the future, maybe.

"Okay," she said slowly. "So, what do you want? I only have a couple of twenty pound notes with me and I don't suppose for one moment that will be enough."

"Ah. That's better, your Ladyship. I knew you would see sense. I'll ring you in a couple of days and give you a bank account number. Then I want you to deposit £500 in there every month for the remainder of my life."

"£500! You must be joking. You might think I'm a wealthy woman but I have a huge estate to run and staff to pay. I can't keep up that sort of regular outlay."

"Oh, I think you can, Your Ladyship. I think you can. As I say, I'll ring you in a couple of days, once I have set up the account. Now, I'll say goodnight and what a pleasure it was to meet you, having heard so much about you ... most of which wasn't very good," he chuckled.

Delia clenched her fists in her jacket pockets, desperately wanting to lash out but not daring. She watched him walk out of the churchyard and disappear across the lawns back to the Hall. It was just as well she couldn't see the wide grin on his face.

* * *

Delia remained in the churchyard for a while, angry with herself for having been caught out and now in the situation where someone was trying to blackmail her again. She sat on a bench by the front door of the church and looked across at Canleigh in the moonlight. It looked stunning with the clouds whirling above, like something from a gothic painting. Eerie and frightening to people who didn't know it like she did.

How she loved it. How she had wanted it but looking at it now, she wondered if she still did. She had hankered after it for so long, for so many years and that yearning had nearly destroyed her … and all for nothing. It would never be hers. The instant jealousy she had felt when Lucy had told her that she had inherited it, was fading. If anyone was to have it, Lucy was the best person. She would look after it, treasure it and love it and with her guidance, could make the place hum.

And she had Blairness now and was excited about its future. It was totally hers, without question, and she could do what she liked with it, make it one of the most desired tourist attractions in Scotland, which was a tantalising prospect. She looked across at Canleigh again. Brian was right. She had to let it go. Help and advise Lucy if she wanted it but that would be it. She had to concentrate on Blairness now ... and then there was Brian ... that was another exciting possibility.

She moved her legs and discovered, even wearing her thermals, she was becoming stiff with cold again. It was nearly two in the morning and time to head back to the car. She could do with a hot coffee and something to eat, while she pondered on what to do with that little creep who wanted £500 out of her every month to keep his mouth shut.

As she moved quickly through the woods at the side of the church, she stopped briefly to blow a kiss at the Hall. It would probably be the last time she would set eyes on it and it was her final goodbye but surprisingly she didn't feel as sad as she had thought she would. She turned and headed up the track on the side of the woods, which would eventually run into the lane where she had left the car, warming up a little as she strode along.

She stopped when she reached the turning for Tangles on her right. It would only take a few minutes to walk to the lovely old house she had loved so much and where she had always been so happy. She felt far warmer with the exercise and there was plenty of time before daylight. She headed for Tangles. She was well aware the house would be empty at night as Philip lived at Canleigh with Ruth and apparently, according to Lucy, just used the house during the day when he was working. She wondered if he still left a key under one of the flowerpots edging the back lawn. His grandparents always had and as Philip was a creature of habit, she could take a bet that it was still there.

She could have burst into tears when she saw the Tudor building before her. She had loved it as much as Canleigh. It had played such a huge part in her young life and she had always assumed she would be its mistress. What a dreadful blow that had been to find out that she never would be. Philip had been so bloody cruel.

The place was in darkness and there were no signs of any of the stable hands stirring from their quarters further down the lane. She walked round to the back. The flowerpot was still there and so was the key. She slid it into the keyhole in the back door, wondering if Philip had ever had the locks changed but no. The key turned and she slipped inside, whisking the torch out of her pocket.

Locking the door behind her, not wanting to be discovered by anyone else, she went through into the kitchen, always the hub of the house when Constance, Philip's grandmother, was alive. She had been a fabulous cook and prepared succulent meals every day. A lovely woman, a second mum to Delia and much preferable to her own mother, who had been nothing but a common tart.

The old rocking chair by the aga was still there and the room was warm. Seeing the coffee container sitting by the kettle she couldn't resist and made herself one, sitting down in the old familiar chair, letting the warmth from the aga and the coffee do their work. Her eyes started to close and she jerked herself awake. It would never do to fall asleep and for Philip to find her in the morning. That really would be disastrous.

She washed up the coffee cup and then wandered around the rest of the house, nostalgia for the past overwhelming her at times. She went from room to room, pleased that even though Philip had been married to that Sue woman, he had kept it exactly as it had always been. It was as if Constance and Ralph were still alive and would appear at any moment and welcome her back to Tangles. She smiled. How lovely that would have been. How happy that would have made her.

She paused at the bottom of the stairs. Did she dare to go up ... look in his bedroom ... the room where they had made wild, passionate love nearly every day once she was of age and before he dumped her so cruelly? Scenes of their lovemaking flooded back to her and she groaned. Philip had been her first love and she would have done anything for him, even dressing up in costumes to keep him interested and entertained. It had been a joyous time when she had everything to live for. She was studying at Askham Bryan so that she would have adequate knowledge to run Canleigh and she had Philip, the wedding and the move to Tangles to look forward to. She had Demon, her beloved horse and she had ambitions. It had been a perfect time and then it had all come crashing down around her ears.

Before she knew what she was doing, her feet were marching up the stairs. She peered into all the other bedrooms and saw nothing much had changed there either and then she reached his. Gingerly she pushed the door open and stood on the threshold, staring at the bed. It was made, which was unusual. Philip had a tendency to be slovenly and throw his things around the room and rarely made the bed. It was obvious it hadn't been slept in for an age and how she longed to get in it, curl up, and pretend she was there as Philip's wife. How it should have been ... but she couldn't. The temptation to fall asleep was too great. She did a grin. It would be a little like Goldilocks and the three bears if Philip was to find her in his bed.

She walked to the window and looked across the darkened front lawn, surprised to see car headlights heading down the lane towards the house. She darted back from the window and drew in a short, sharp breath. Who the hell was it? Surely that little Felix creep hadn't told someone she was sniffing about. No. It wouldn't be worth his while and she had been so quiet, she was positive no-one else had seen her ... but then it could be someone going past the house down to the stable block where all the staff had quarters. It could be one of them returning from a late night at one of the clubs in Leeds or Harrogate.

She tried not to panic but when the car drew up at the front door, her whole body started to tremble. There was only one person it could be. It had to be Philip. She looked out of the window quickly as the car lights went off and the security light sprang into action. He took an age to get out of the car, holding onto the door for support and placing a walking stick before him. She gasped when he eventually stood up. He looked so old. His hair, going thin when she had last seen him, was now almost non-existent. His face was lined and he seemed to be finding great difficulty in walking. She had done that to him.

The shock at his appearance had overcome the need to escape for a second but then, as he put his key in the front door, she jerked herself upright. Oh, God. He mustn't find her in here.

She crept stealthily out of the bedroom and into one of the guest rooms where it was very doubtful he would enter and stood behind the door, listening to his movements, praying he wouldn't make himself a drink and discover the kettle was still warm. Still, she had one advantage over him. She could move quickly.

If she ran, he would never be able to catch up with her.

But he didn't go into the kitchen. From the sound of it, he had headed straight for the room which she had noticed he used as an office. She could hear him shuffling papers and the faint whirring of the laptop as it warmed up. Waiting until she heard him typing, she took off her shoes and walked soundlessly down the stairs, the key to the back door in her hand. Luckily, it was in the opposite part of the house to Philip's office and she crept along the corridor, praying that he wouldn't stop typing. Tap, tap, tap, went the keys. Just keep it up, she thought. Please, don't stop.

She reached the back door, unlocked it slowly, and drew in a deep breath of relief as she closed it behind her, not bothering to lock it in case it made a noise. She shoved the key back under the flowerpot. Philip would probably wonder why the door was unlocked but hopefully, would think it was an oversight by one of the stable hands as they were frequent visitors during the day. Anyhow, there was no reason to link it to her.

She hurried back to the lane, taking a wide turn to avoid the front of the house and the security light, and then started to run. He might not intend to remain at Tangles for long and she didn't want him to find her along the lane. Why one earth was he coming down to work in the middle of the night anyway? Perhaps everything in the Kershaw household wasn't as lovely as it would seem. He should be tucked up in bed with his precious Ruth, not down here working. Strange, very strange.

She reached the car without any more drama and headed back off the estate towards York, locking it in the garage and entering the bungalow quickly, not wanting to be seen by any nosy neighbours.

Peeling off her clothes until she was down to her thermals, she grabbed a glass and the wine and threw herself on the sofa. What a night! She couldn't believe how it had turned out. She had only gone there to ... to what? What had she hoped to achieve? Why had she risked her very freedom just to set eyes on Canleigh again? She must have been utterly mad and now look how her desire had turned out. She had another bloody blackmailer to get off her back and she had no idea what she was going to do about him. She would have to pay up for a while until she could think of something. Thank goodness she had sorted Crystal. She had been a pushover but this nasty little Felix. He was a different kettle of fish.

Then she had seen Philip ... and she had known, as soon as she set eyes on him, that any feelings for him were gone. She felt nothing ... no desire ... no longing. He was old, feeble and of no use to her. Not like Brian. Her lips curled into a smile. Brian. She checked her phone. He had rung her three times today, each time leaving a message asking her to ring him as he was worried about her. That was such a nice feeling and she loved him for it. Yes. Love. She did love him and it wasn't just about passion. She respected him. She liked him. He was great company, knowledgeable, funny, considerate and quite, quite gorgeous.

Suddenly she couldn't wait to get back to Blairness to see him again. She looked at the clock. It was four thirty in the morning. She couldn't drive now. She had been up all night, was tired and then, of course, she had just been drinking. She would turn in, have a few hours sleep and then drive home this evening … and they could have dinner … she didn't care where … it could be at Blairness, it could be at his cottage or it could be in a pub. All she knew was that she wanted to be with him this evening. She wanted to hear him laugh, watch his face crinkle into a smile, hear those deep, sexy tones which made her toes curl.

She flicked on her mobile and sent him a text. 'Am coming home later today. Am absolutely fine. Let's have dinner'.

Smiling happily, she headed off to bed, curled up in a tight ball and slept solidly for five hours.

CHAPTER 28

Brian read the text message with enormous relief. He had been so worried about Delia and where she might be. To know for certain that she was returning to Blairness later and wanted to have dinner with him was the end of a nightmare couple of days worrying about whether she had gone somewhere to top herself. Obviously not and she even sounded chirpy, wanting to eat with him this evening.

"Do you know the name of that new restaurant in Kinmoor?" he asked Connie five minutes later as he strode into the estate office, mildly annoyed to see Crystal sitting at his desk, thumbing through his telephone directory.

"The Magpie ... and it's lovely. We ate there last week," said Connie with a smile. "Would you like me to book you a table?"

"Please ... around 8.30 p.m. should be okay. It's for two."

Crystal looked up from the directory; highly envious of the woman he was taking out. "Who's the lucky lady, Brian?"

"Lady Delia actually. I've just heard from her and she's coming home today and wants to have a working dinner ... so it's nothing to get silly about ... and could I have my chair back please, Crystal."

"Sorry," she said, standing up abruptly, moving over to her own desk, taking the directory with her. "I'm glad Delia is coming back and I can have the car again as I'm just trying to find a decent hairdresser in Inverness and thought I was going to have to go on that old bus that trundles through the villages."

Connie and Brian exchanged a glance and then Brian bent his head to concentrate on the paperwork Connie had left on his desk, his heart feeling lighter than it had for days. He was so looking forward to setting eyes on Delia again. Not only had he been worried about her but he had actually missed her presence more than he would have guessed. She was an integral part of his life now and he couldn't imagine being without her. Her reputation and history might be pretty dreadful but he had seen another side to Delia on their discussions and outings around the local area and he wanted that to continue. If she were whipped back to prison he really didn't think he could bear it. Life without her wouldn't be a life any longer. She had managed to wiggle her way under his skin and into his blood and he was desperately, madly, insanely in love with her.

* * *

Delia woke just after noon, excited at the prospect of returning to Blairness ... and seeing Brian. On turning on her mobile, she had discovered a text from him to say he had booked a table at the Magpie for 8.30 p.m. She smiled widely. To spend precious time alone with him this evening was a tantalising prospect.

She packed quickly, throwing her things into the canvas bag, locking up the cottage and putting the key back through the door as instructed. She jumped into the car and drove smartly northwards, eager to get back to Scotland as soon as possible.

Her tummy lurched as she passed the signpost for Canleigh but only for a second. She had done with it now. Her future was in Scotland, at Blairness … and possibly with Brian … and she couldn't wait to get home. She grinned. Home. It sounded good. On the way down, she had been thinking of Canleigh as her home but it wasn't any longer. Blairness was and she was longing to get back there and really concentrate on her future.

However, even though she had managed to get herself into more hot water with that blasted Felix, she was glad she had come down to Canleigh. She felt as if a huge weight had been lifted from her very soul and she was finally free of her obsession with the place, feeling more at peace than she had ever done. She would always love it, of course but after all these years she had finally accepted it would never be hers and nor would Philip. Seeing him last night had killed any lingering passion. He was nothing like the man she had used to know, old and almost wizened, looking as if he carried the weight of the world on his shoulders. She felt terribly guilty for her part in making him that way but there was little point in regretting something one had done. At the time, he had deserved it, hurting her as badly as he had, not once but twice … and anyway, if Lucy was to be believed, he was idolised by darling Ruth so he wasn't unhappy and she needn't give him another thought, not now she had another man in her life … someone she could look up to. When all was said and done, Philip had let her bully him. She couldn't do that with Brian. She might be his employer but with his military air, he commanded absolute respect and was certainly no pushover.

She smiled as she turned onto the slip road for the A1, neatly edging in between two cars in the slow lane as she headed back up to Scotland. Gosh, she couldn't wait to see Brian again. Her tummy flipped over at the thought of being with him, seeing him smile, just being close to him. She felt almost sick with excitement and desire. God. She really did have it bad this time.

* * *

Delia bounced into Blairness six hours later. The roads had been reasonably clear and she had been so keen to get back home as quickly as possible, she hadn't stopped once. As a result, she was starving and craving a bowl of cornflakes.

McFrain met her in the hall, having heard the car approaching. "Welcome home, Lady Delia. I trust you have enjoyed your time away," he said politely.

"Well, let's say it's been interesting," she smiled. "I shan't require dinner, McFrain. I'm eating out with Brian ... we have a lot of estate matters to discuss but I wouldn't mind a bowl of cornflakes to keep me going while I have a bath and change."

McFrain smiled. "I'll bring some up to your room, Your Ladyship."

Delia dashed up the stairs, wondering what to wear for dinner at the Magpie. Time was getting on and she hadn't long to get ready but the place didn't look particularly posh so there was no need to go overboard. She opened the wardrobe in her room and checked her clothes, knowing she didn't possess anything very sexy as she never went anywhere that didn't require jeans or outdoor wear. All her good clothes, which had been at the Dower House when she had been arrested, were all in boxes in the dressing room, no doubt badly creased and way out of fashion. She really would have to have a look. She

369

had only put it off as they would remind her of her unhappy past life. She could deal with them now. In fact, she might not even bother. They could all be dumped and she could buy a completely new wardrobe ... go to Edinburgh and spend some money on herself.

She found a pair of black trousers and a forest green cashmere sweater she hadn't worn. Practical and smart with a pair of black leather high heels ... and she wouldn't look like she was trying to entice Brian into her bed. Perfect attire for a business meeting and wouldn't raise any eyebrows.

Freshened up by a long bath, munching on the cornflakes McFrain had brought up, and then carefully applying her makeup and dressing in the chosen outfit, Delia examined herself in the full-length mirror on the wall. She looked good. All signs of that dreadful misery she had felt just a few short days ago had completely disappeared. She looked like a woman hell bent on enjoying the rest of her life and making a real future for herself in this lovely old castle which her grandmother had loved so much. Perhaps she could finally become the granddaughter she should always have been. She couldn't erase all the dreadful things she had done but she had spent a hell of an amount of time in prison and could work now to atone for her misdemeanours by making a success of Blairness and giving lots of work to lots of people ... and then there was Brian. She hoped there would always be Brian ... to help her ... to guide her ... to even love her. Her heart flipped over and as she walked downstairs to meet him in the hall and saw him smiling up at her, her knees trembled and her hands shook. God, she was smitten. Totally and utterly smitten and she hoped desperately he felt the same way.

* * *

Brian couldn't stop smiling. He didn't want to. He wanted to get hold of Delia and shake her hard. He wanted to tell her how scared he had been for her … how scared he had been that he wouldn't see her anymore but he couldn't. He was so pleased to see her, and to see her looking so well and bonny, it actually hurt.

She moved towards him and her perfume made his senses reel. "Brian," she said softly.

"Your Ladyship," he nodded, as McFrain moved towards her, holding out her black wool coat for her to slip into.

"Don't wait up for us, McFrain. I don't know how long we shall be."

"Very well, Your Ladyship. Have a good evening," he replied, holding open the front door.

Brian stepped aside for Delia to go through first, watching her perfect figure with pleasure as she moved out into the night air, tossing her hair back with one hand, giving him another hint of her expensive perfume. He wasn't sure what it was but it suited her. Earthy, strong, bold.

He had dispensed with the Landrover tonight as it was covered in mud and dog hair. Instead, he had driven up to the castle in his newly acquired black Volvo estate car.

"Um. Smart," Delia said with appreciation, admiring it in the castle floodlights.

Brian held open the passenger door for her. "Glad you approve, Your Ladyship."

Delia slid into the car and Brian closed the door behind her. For some reason he felt slightly shy, an emotion somewhat alien to him. He was usually totally in command of any situation he found himself in but now, here with Delia, he was feeling ... oh, he didn't know how he was feeling, apart from being enormously pleased she was back at Blairness, in one piece and looking far happier than she had a couple of days ago. With butterflies fluttering about in his stomach, he got into the driver's seat and started the car. Delia threw him a smile and his heart melted. Whatever was this woman doing to him?

* * *

The meal was superb. They both ordered duck pate, followed by Aberdeen Angus steaks and chocolate gateau but wine was dispensed with. "I want to keep a clear head tonight," announced Delia. "There's a lot to discuss and as I am going to be extremely busy in the morning, I don't want a hangover. I think I must be growing up at long last," she said with a grin.

"Okay ... so what would you like to drink?" he asked, surprised by her statement.

"Just mineral water please, Brian ... and coffee after ... lots of coffee."

Order placed with the waitress and settled in a corner of the restaurant in site of a crackling log fire, Delia leaned forward towards him, a look of eager anticipation on her face. He had never seen her look so animated and was intrigued. Wherever she had

372

been, whatever she had been doing had obviously done her the world of good, and he couldn't wait to find out what exactly she had been up to and wondered if she would tell him. He didn't have long to wait.

"I've been to Canleigh," she announced breathlessly. "I know, I know," she put up her hands to ward off his protest. "I know it was stupid and I shouldn't have gone and I was risking being incarcerated again but I had to … I needed to get it out of my system."

Brian was staring wide-eyed at her, angry and scared at what she had done, placing herself in serious jeopardy. He had prayed so hard and convinced himself that she was spending time in Edinburgh, even though deep down he had known where she would go. He was so furious he found it hard to speak.

"And did you?" he asked coolly. "Did you get it out of your system … because I do hope so …for your sake … if anyone …"

"It's okay, Brian, really," she said, pushing the memory of Felix's monetary demands from her mind. "I wore a wig and glasses and only went there after dark … in the middle of the night actually."

"Oh Christ! I don't believe this." He felt cold with fear. Had this woman fooled him in the past few months? Had she led him into thinking she might not be the woman portrayed by the world as evil and cunning. Had she duped him too? If she had, he would have to leave Blairness. He couldn't remain here if she was just a scheming, cold-blooded bitch. He had thought he had seen something else in her for months, a person who had been let down badly over the years, hurt and vulnerable beneath that hard, over-confident exterior. He had wanted to try to make things better for her. He had wanted to love her, cherish her, and protect her but was it all in vain? He looked at her, watching her beautiful brown eyes sparkle as she talked, her lovely hands gesticulating, that long, thick mane of hair swirling around her face and that mouth, that gorgeous mouth with wide lips and so very kissable. Oh God, was she going to be the death of him?

She had been chattering on while his mind was in a whirl and he hadn't taken in half of what she said, until her last words. "Ghost tours ... horse trials?" he asked, with a puzzled frown.

"Yes, Brian, ghost tours and horse trials," she laughed. "Haven't you been listening to what I am saying?"

He pulled himself upright, trying to clear his head and concentrate on what she was talking about. "I know you are opening the castle to the public but ghost tours ... have you thought this through? They will have to be at night ... think of the disruption and all those silly people, screaming and yelling if there is the slightest noise or movement ... and as for horse trials ... that will entail a hell of a lot of organising. What on earth has brought this on?"

Her face took on a sombre look. "I experienced a ... an epiphany if you like, while I was at Canleigh. It's hard to explain but you know my history, you were filled in when you applied to be estate manager and it was naturally all in the papers for weeks. You know I always hankered after Canleigh ... and Philip ... but it's all gone now, Brian. Seeing the house and the grounds ... albeit in the moonlight ... I finally realised I have been following a pipedream since I was a child. Canleigh was never meant to be mine and

374

never will be and I have to let it go and leave my child in peace to care for it and love it as I do ... and she will. Lucy has a good, sensible head on her shoulders ... she will be absolutely fine ... after all, look whose genes she has in her body," she grinned.

Brian shifted in his seat, incredibly relieved at Delia's words. If she felt this way, perhaps it hadn't been such a bad thing she had paid the Canleigh estate a visit.

"And as for Philip. I did see him ..."

"What!" exclaimed Brian with alarm.

"No, he didn't see me but I saw him. He is nothing like the man I remember and have wanted ... again since I was a small child. All that passion for him has disappeared ... faded away. I know now that although I thought it was, it wasn't real love. I was too possessive ... too bossy. The poor man must have had a dreadful time with me ... and then look what I ended up doing to him. I have a lot to answer for," she said, her eyes filling with tears as she looked up at Brian's surprised expression.

"So," she continued, taking a sip of her water, "I have finally rid my system of Canleigh and Philip ... and I have Blairness to concentrate on now, totally and utterly. I am one hundred percent committed to improving this place and making it hum ... we're definitely going to open the castle to the public and if we can get the toilet block, café and shop up and running as soon as possible, we might ... just might, be able to open by August, even earlier if we're lucky. All the other outbuildings and the stables are going to be rented out for office accommodation and can command some pretty impressive rents. Oh, and Crystal came up with the idea for ghost tours for the castle and I think it's a good one. We'll only do them once or twice a month and then I can disappear for the night. Go and stay in a hotel or something. We can have lots of events ... dog shows, classic car shows, evening concerts, etc, etc. As for horse trials ... I always wanted to have them at Canleigh but Blairness will be every bit as good a venue. It's going to need a lot of research but we can do it, I know we can ... oh, and then there are weddings. Blairness would be a fabulous backdrop and the ceremonies can be held in the entrance hall, along with splendid buffets ... or we can put up marquees in the summer."

"Christ, Delia. You don't let the grass grow," he grinned. "We're still sorting out the caravan park and golf course. We'll be working all hours at this rate."

"I didn't think you were frightened of hard work," she teased.

"You know I'm not ... I'm fully behind you on this, you know I am ... but it's going to be hard getting it all organised. We're going to need a lot of help ... extra staff."

"Yes we will. Someone will have to manage the café and the shop too. Crystal is going to be too busy, being in charge of everything that's going to happen in the house and as it's her idea, she can sort the ghost tours too."

Brian looked concerned. "Can you trust her? Look what she did at her last stately home ... I'm surprised you allowed her to live here with her background."

"Well, I had my reasons," Delia said quietly. "She was finding it really difficult to get a decent job when she came out of prison and couldn't afford anywhere nice to live either. She had been good to me when we were inside and I just felt I had to help her out."

Brian sighed. "You do like taking risks."

Delia laughed. "Yes, I do."

Brian smiled. Delia looked so animated, her eyes were sparkling, and she looked more alive than he had ever seen her. He felt her excitement and revelled in it. The woman in front of him was nothing like the one who had screamed and cried by the lake just days ago, the one who had frightened the hell out of him as she launched towards madness. Whatever had happened to her at Canleigh had done her the world of good and he thanked God she had finally seen sense and where her future really was ... at Blairness ... and with him ... as his employer ... or more. Whichever it was, he didn't care. He was just so glad she had come back, safely and happy and still in his life. The dreadful tension he had been feeling for days slipped away. He sat back in his chair and smiled as Delia's enthusiasm for the transformation of Blairness spilled out of her. It was infectious and he too, felt a rising excitement for what lay ahead ... for the castle and for them. The future looked brighter than it had for a long time. He loved his position at Blairness, he loved this dynamic, enigma of a woman ..., and he knew, he just knew, she loved him. His very soul filled with sheer pleasure at the thought of what was to come ... of what they could do, together. He smiled as the fire beside them crackled and glowed and Delia smiled back. He was so happy he could burst.

CHAPTER 29

SEVEN MONTHS LATER
MAY 1996

Lucy was more excited than she had ever been in her life. It was Saturday, 4th May, her wedding day and she was ecstatically happy. She had woken up at dawn. Her bedroom window was open and she could clearly hear the birds chirping merrily as a beautifully promising day broke in the sky.

Her wedding dress hung on the wardrobe door. A fabulous creation by Felicity Pargiter, an up and coming designer taking the London fashion scene by storm. Lucy had seen one of her designs in a magazine, had been bowled over by its beauty and contacted Felicity immediately. The end result was amazing. She couldn't wait to drift down the aisle in the strapless ivory gown, made of Duchess satin with a pleated cross-over bodice, a band covered in pearls at her waist and a floor length skirt, along with a silk tulle veil and six foot train. She just hoped she would be able to cope with the satin shoes. They had six inch heels, much higher than she was used to and she had spent a lot of time trying to walk sedately around the bedroom, trying to break them in without wobbling all over the place. She had considered buying more sensible shoes with lower heels but she had fallen in love with these and they looked so perfect with the dress, she was determined to persevere.

She looked at the clock. It was only six a.m., so there was plenty of time to idle away. Her hairdresser and beautician were arriving at nine to help prepare her for the wedding at noon, although Aunty Vicky and Granny Ruth had insisted they would bring her breakfast at eight. How spoilt was that? The only other time she received such attention was if she were ill.

She lay still, thinking about Jeremy, her lovely new husband to be. In just a few hours, she would be Mrs. Seymour. She hugged herself with pleasure. She was so looking forward to the day ahead, her only regret being that her mother couldn't attend but it was impossible and she and Delia had accepted it. Lucy had taken Jeremy up to Blairness but the visit hadn't been a huge success. Jeremy seemed ill at ease with her mother, which Lucy put down to nerves as Lady Delia Canleigh did have a somewhat formidable reputation but she was disappointed when her mother came to her room later that first evening of their visit, wanting to talk to her.

"Are you sure? Are you really sure you want to marry Jeremy?" Delia urged.

Lucy could remember the surprise at her mother's words. "Of course I do," she had answered, staring at her with shock. "Why? Don't you like him?"

"I'm not sure, if I'm truthful," Delia replied. "I honestly don't believe he is as in love with you as you are with him ... and I'm worried about you, darling. Now that you are the owner of Canleigh and all that goes with it, this marriage is going to be somewhat advantageous for him and I don't want to see you make a big mistake."

Wounded by Delia's words, Lucy had sprung up from the bed. "You're wrong. He loves me deeply. Don't forget we've known each other for years, ever since we were children, long before we knew I was going to end up with Canleigh. No-one expected that. If Stephen had married and had children, it would never have happened. No, Mother. Jeremy and I have always looked out for each other. He adores me. I just know he does and I adore him and we are going to be extremely happy."

Delia's lips had smiled but her eyes hadn't. "All right, darling. I just hope you are right. I want nothing more than for you to have a successful marriage. I've said my piece and now I'll shut up but I do want to give you this ... I know I can't come to the wedding but I can give you a fabulous honeymoon."

Lucy had torn open the large white envelope Delia handed her and cried out with delight as she read the contents.

"Oh, my goodness. A whole month cruising the Med and then four weeks exploring Italy and staying in five star hotels. Oh, my! Jeremy will be thrilled. Thank you so very much," she said, throwing her arms around a laughing Delia, who was delighted to have given her daughter so much pleasure.

Surprisingly enough, Jeremy hadn't seemed as pleased as Lucy thought he would be. He had thanked Delia warmly the next morning but even though Lucy had waved the cheque Delia had written out in Lucy's name for an incredible amount of spending money, a shadow crossed his face when Lucy confirmed that the honeymoon was to take two months.

She had puzzled over that look ever since, especially when he repeatedly said two months was a long time to be away and couldn't they cut it short?

"Why? It's perfect ... and what do we have to rush back for? Granny Ruth and Steppie will continue to look after Canleigh and Aunty Vicky isn't going to worry and will keep your job open for you."

That was becoming a bone of contention too. Obviously, she didn't have to work once she was married and she would have to concentrate on Canleigh for a while anyway and get her head around being in complete control so reluctantly she had told Aunt Vicky that she would have to forgo a career in the hotel trade. But Jeremy had been another matter. He had suggested he give up his position at the Beeches too but Aunt Vicky had been appalled. "You can't live off Lucy for the rest of your life ... and what would you do all day. No, Jeremy. You have to work and keep your self-respect. I insist on it."

Lucy had overheard the conversation and wasn't surprised when Jeremy had sulked for days afterwards and then admitted to her that he didn't want to continue working at the Beeches once they were married.

"What would you like to do instead?" she asked.

"Horticulture," he said firmly. "I want to study it properly ... and there's ample space for me to experiment at Canleigh."

"Okay. Let's talk about it while we're on honeymoon," Lucy suggested. "Between us, we can probably come up with a proper plan and placate Aunty Vicky."

Then there was this Matthew chap who had suddenly entered their lives. It was after that time when Jeremy had popped down to London to see his birth mother, whom strangely enough he never mentioned again. Lucy didn't know what to make of Matthew. She had only met him once, when he turned up at The Beeches when she and Jeremy were both on reception duty, not long after Stephen's funeral. Jeremy had actually flushed and stumbled over his words when Matthew approached the desk with a weird smile on his face. For a split second, the thought crossed her mind that the two were lovers but she threw it away immediately. Jeremy certainly wasn't gay. It wasn't often they had the opportunity to make love but when they did, it was always perfect, so she had no worries on that score. Even so, she didn't take to Matthew. Jeremy introduced him as a friend from his Oxford college days but he struck Lucy as being someone not very nice to know and she hoped Jeremy would give him a wide berth in the future.

However, Matthew seemed to be making a habit of popping up to York every couple of weeks for the rest of the winter and every time he did, Jeremy insisted on going over to see him and didn't return until the next day and was always in a funny mood for days afterwards. Then he stated that he wanted Matthew to be his best man. Lucy hid her dismay well but Aunty Vicky, already perturbed by the friendship between the two men, took the opportunity to admonish Jeremy for spending time in York with Matthew when he should have been with Lucy.

"It's only one night every couple of weeks," Jeremy insisted. "Matthew is my only real friend and it's good to get together and have a chat about our Oxford days. He's a very interesting chap ... surely you don't begrudge me a little me time?" He had looked belligerently at both Vicky and Lucy. They glanced at each other despairingly and Vicky sighed. "No. I suppose not."

It was never mentioned again. Jeremy disappeared every couple of weeks and neither Vicky nor Lucy said another word, although both were uneasy and wished Jeremy could have picked someone else to be his best man.

Never mind, thought Lucy. This evening they would be heading off on their honeymoon and she wouldn't have to see or think about the ghastly Matthew for eight long weeks. It would be just her and Jeremy, indulging themselves and spending glorious hours making love. They were spending the first night of their married life together at the Randolph in Oxford and then driving down to Southampton tomorrow to board their cruise ship. She hugged herself again. She was going to put all thoughts of niggling problems out of her mind. This was her wedding day and she was so happy, she could die. She rolled over and lay in the sun streaming through the window and allowed it to send her back to sleep.

At exactly eight o'clock, there was a tap on the door and Ruth and Vicky, both with beaming grins, stood on the threshold; Ruth bearing a tray laden with boiled eggs, buttered wholemeal bread, fresh orange juice, a bowl of cornflakes and a pot of tea. Vicky was carrying a posy of gold roses, a bottle of champagne, and three crystal glasses.

"This is the best way to start your wedding day," she announced, placing the glasses on Lucy's dressing table by the window and popping the champagne cork expertly. She handed Lucy and Ruth their glasses and raised hers. 'Here's to a wonderful day and a wonderful life for you and Jeremy," she said, smiling at Lucy. "I hope you'll both be very happy darling."

"Thank you, Aunty Vicky. I'm sure we will," Lucy replied as Ruth raised her glass and added her good wishes.

"Thank you for postponing the wedding, Lucy," she said quietly. "I know it must have been hard for you but I don't think I could have been very jolly at Christmas."

Ruth had walked around the house like a ghost following Stephen's funeral and Christmas had come and gone without her even taking in what time of year it was. It was only in the last couple of weeks, with the warmer weather and the excitement of Lucy's impending nuptials that she made a supreme effort to appear interested and happy. It had been Vicky who had helped Lucy with all the planning and preparation, as Ruth certainly hadn't been capable.

Lucy placed a hand on Ruth's arm. "It doesn't matter a bit. It's much nicer at this time of the year anyway … just look at the weather outside. We're going to have a fabulous day."

They all glanced out of the window at the beautiful blue sky and Ruth moved closer to look outside. The great white canvas marquee was up on the lawn in front of the house, ready to seat two hundred people for the wedding breakfast and the staff hired especially for the occasion were hurrying about, preparing the tables and the decorations. The ballroom had been considered for the event but it was decided that as so many of the guests were young and quite liable to get more than a little tipsy, it would be safer to entertain them outside where they couldn't do any damage.

Vicky was refilling their glasses and noticed the travel documents on the dressing table. "Italy," she said dreamily, "I do so love it and miss it … it was with a heavy heart I sold the villa near Lake Como which Father left to me but we needed the money to help buy The Beeches and that was that."

"We all had some lovely times there," agreed Ruth, remembering long holidays at the villa when she was married to Vicky's father and was Duchess of Canleigh. "What a lovely honeymoon you will have, Lucy. I do envy you. How romantic."

Lucy's eyes shone with excitement. "I know. I can't wait. Four weeks cruising the Med and then four weeks staying at some of the best hotels in Italy ... and we're going to do absolutely everything. I can't wait to see Rome ... the Vatican, the Colosseum, the Forum, Trevi Fountain, Spanish Steps ... all the fabulous art in Florence and Venice ... gondola rides ... San Marco, the Doge's palace ... the music, the art, the food ... that will be the icing on the cake."

Ruth and Vicky smiled at Lucy's enthusiasm but both their faces grew solemn at her next words. "And then we're going to Scotland ... to see Mother. As she can't come to the wedding, we must go to her for a separate celebration and as she's paid for the honeymoon, I shall want to tell her about our travels and show her the photographs. I'm sorry you're both not happy with our relationship but we are getting on well and that's the way it is, I'm afraid."

Ruth and Vicky glanced at each other. They were both incredibly apprehensive about Lucy's friendship with Delia but there was nothing they could do about it, and at least the woman couldn't come to Canleigh for the wedding. That was a tremendous relief.

As if on cue, the telephone beside Lucy's bed began to tinkle and Lucy answered it, thankful it interrupted the conversation. The atmosphere always became tense with members of her family when her mother was mentioned.

"Lucy, darling," came Delia's voice down the line, light and cheerful. "I'm calling to wish you all the luck in the world, for today and in the future."

385

"Thank you, Mummy. That's very kind of you," replied Lucy, noticing the despairing glances between Vicky and Granny Ruth.

"And enjoy that honeymoon. I want to hear all about it ... well, perhaps not all," Delia laughed. "I'm so looking forward to seeing you when you get back. Now, I better leave you to it. No doubt, you have to start getting ready for your big day. All the very best, my love. I shall be thinking of you. Enjoy it ... and be happy."

* * *

Jeremy was nervous. He wrestled with his cravat, disliking having to be dressed up. He was far happier in jeans and sweaters or t-shirts. It was bad enough having to wear formal suits at work in The Beeches but at least they were well worn and reasonably comfortable. His wedding suit was brand new, the collar on the shirt was incredibly stiff and rubbed his neck, and his shoes, even though of ridiculously expensive leather, seemed too tight, which was odd as they had been a perfect fit in the shop. With shaking hands, he secured the pin to his cravat and then picked up the solid gold cufflinks, a wedding present from Lucy, from the box on the dressing table. He dropped one and it shot beneath the bed.

"Damn," he uttered, not wanting to get on his knees to scrabble around for it in his wedding attire.

"Let me," said Matthew, entering the room in his underpants and drying his hair with a towel. "I must say, Jeremy darling, you do look a treat in all that get-up."

"So I might but I feel bloody rotten."

"Do you want the hair of the dog?" asked Matthew, on bended knees delving beneath the bed for the errant cufflink.

"No. I didn't mean that. I feel rotten because of Lucy. I really don't know if I can go through with it … it's all … it's all such a bloody mess. I'm in love with you and want to be with you but can't. I don't really love Lucy, don't want to be with her and have to be."

Matthew retrieved the cufflink, handed it to Jeremy, and sat on the bed. "Look, we've been through all this so many times. You will give Lucy the best day of her life today, one that she will never forget. Every girl dreams of her big day and you are going to give her a fabulous one. Then, all you have to do is keep her happy for a couple of years and then file for divorce. You will come out with more than enough to keep both of us in real comfort for the rest of our lives. That way, we all get what we want."

"Well, Lucy might be happy to begin with but what about when she finds out about us? She will be devastated and probably want to divorce me straight away … and declare it's all my fault … and then we wouldn't get very much at all, if anything."

"Oh, I don't think she will. She will be embarrassed and humiliated. She won't want to make it public that her newly acquired husband is having a gay affair and even if she does, we will have to persuade her otherwise … until we are ready and we can do it our way, not hers."

"What do you mean … persuade her otherwise?"

"Look, let's just wait and see what happens … concentrate on today … on getting you safely up the aisle and legally married. Then we'll worry about what comes next."

Jeremy was biting his lip anxiously. "Okay ... but what if she gets pregnant?"

"All the better. She will have something to comfort her when you have left and give us more leverage over her in later years in case we need more cash."

"I don't understand."

"Oh gosh, Jeremy. You can be so dim sometimes. If Lucy has children, they will want to see you and you will want to see them. So, if Lucy wants them to be happy, she will agree to pay you for your time when you visit them or take them out."

"God! You are so bloody devious!"

"I know, darling ... and don't you love me for it? Now. Let's finish getting you ready. You really do have to look your best today," Matthew smiled charmingly as he took Jeremy's face in his hands and kissed him hard on the mouth.

* * *

St. Mary's was packed. All the pews on either side of the church were full and extra chairs had been brought in and aligned at the rear. They were all there in their finery, the family in the front pews; friends, estate staff and villagers behind. The air was heady from expensive perfumes, colognes and the flowers; masses and masses of blooms picked from the Canleigh gardens and the greenery from the woods and the lakeside. The organist was playing Bach's lullaby, 'How Lovely is Thy Dwelling Place', which Jeremy adored and had chosen himself, hoping it would help him relax as he stood at the alter, Matthew at his side.

Nervously he glanced down the aisle, waiting for Lucy to appear and the music to change to the wedding march. He smiled at the family directly behind. Alex looked dapper in his morning suit, his hat on the seat beside him. Ruth, in a pretty pink suit and Vicky in powder blue were as beautiful as ever. They always looked good in whatever they wore but when dressed up, were exceptionally glamorous. Katrina was a bridesmaid, so would be with Lucy. Suzanne had wanted to come over from Australia but didn't want to leave the baby as he hadn't been well and couldn't fly.

Jeremy took a quick look further down the nave. He nodded to those guests he recognised and then froze with shock as he saw a tubby woman spilling out of a scarlet dress waving at him. Luckily, she was sitting right at the back and the remainder of the congregation couldn't see her. Jeremy recognised her instantly. It was bloody Beryl Porter, his mother … his birth mother … from London. What the hell was she doing here? How had she known about the wedding? What the hell did she want? God! She was the last person he wanted to see at this most important moment of his life.

But just as he started to wonder how he could get rid of her before the rest of the family found out she was here, the organist hit the keys for the rousing Mendelssohn's wedding march and everyone shuffled to their feet as Lucy, her arm through Philip's, made her appearance at the church door.

Jeremy watched her walk up the aisle, her face a picture of radiance beneath the veil. She looked incredibly beautiful in her amazing gown and for a second, he wished fervently that he wasn't gay, that he hadn't met Matthew, and that he wasn't going to break her heart in the not too distant future. He didn't love her in the way a husband should and watching her walk towards him, her face wreathed in smiles, knowing that she trusted him completely, he felt a rotten cad. Why hadn't he stood up to Matthew and just refused to marry her? He almost hated himself for what he was about to do. Then Matthew coughed beside him and he turned and felt a wave of desire that surpassed any other. It was Matthew he could never give up and although he had to stand and say his vows to Lucy, he was glad Matthew was by his side.

He turned back to watch Lucy, almost skipping up the aisle towards him. The organ fell silent. Lucy turned to Katrina, close behind her, appearing regal and far older than her thirteen years, with her brunette hair up in a chignon, decorated with tiny yellow roses, showing off her high cheekbones, perfect skin and violet eyes. She was enjoying the attention immensely and looked every inch a budding film star in her full-length deep yellow silk dress, holding a posy of cream and yellow roses from the Canleigh gardens.

Lucy handed Katrina her bouquet, a larger version of Katrina's posy. Philip gently lifted the veil from Lucy's face and laid it back over the sparkling Canleigh tiara keeping it in place and then Lucy turned to Jeremy and smiled.

Jeremy felt another pang of remorse. His fiancée looked stunning. Her skin was flawless, her eyes bright and shining, her lips full and wide. She was the perfect bride, not only in looks but in nature too and he was an exceedingly lucky man but beneath all that, he felt a real rotter, sandwiched in the middle of two people who both wanted him. He had a nasty feeling that it wasn't going to end very well ... not for any of them.

* * *

"Jeremy doesn't want you here. You're not invited ... so please leave immediately otherwise I shall have you escorted off the premises," demanded Matthew forcibly to the woman in red.

They were standing in the churchyard. The photographs had been taken and the happy couple were in the process of being driven across to the marquee in front of the Hall with the wedding guests milling across the lawns after them.

"And who are you to say a mother can't be at her son's wedding? I have more right to be here than you," Beryl Porter spat back. "And this wedding is a queer kettle of fish ... in more ways than one," she grinned knowingly. "I began to wonder exactly who my son was saying his vows to ... was it that pretty young girl ... or was it you?"

Matthew drew himself up to his full height, but the rapid blush spreading across his face gave him away.

"So ... I'm right, am I?" Beryl hissed. "He's been in your bed too ... and by the look of that beautiful girl he has just married, I shouldn't think for one moment she knows ... she can't, can she ... otherwise she wouldn't have gone through with this charade today. My, my. What a pickle my son has got himself into."

"So what?" snapped Matthew. "It has absolutely nothing to do with you. Jeremy doesn't want you in his life, you common old tart ... so be gone ... and

391

never darken his door again … or you will be sorry … very sorry indeed."

He left her, striding fast across the lawns after the wedding party. Beryl stared after him, wondering how her handsome son had managed to get himself involved with such a man. He was a leech was that one. She had seen his sort before and nothing and no-one could shock her now. She had been rolling around with the dregs of humanity in London before she was legally old enough to have sex and considered herself highly experienced in the ways of the world and to know trouble when she saw it … and that man was trouble with a capital T. However, there was nothing she could do about it. Her toffee nosed son had made it quite plain from the looks he had thrown her way, and then sending his paramour to harass her, that she wasn't welcome.

She jammed the flimsy white hat with its floppy brim firmly onto her head, pulled down the scarlet polyester dress over her hips and sashayed out of the churchyard in her red stilettos towards her battered old Mini parked beneath some trees beside the church. She had seen a pub in the village … the Canleigh Arms … she would go in there and drink a toast to the happy couple. There would surely be someone in there who would join her. She might even be able to do some business and get some jerk to pay for a room for the night. There must be some bloke in the village who could benefit from a little fun. She smiled as she got into the car, threw off the stilettos, lit a cigarette, and drove barefoot up the long, winding drive towards the village. She didn't even glance back at the marquee. That pompous lot weren't her sort. She had nothing in common with them … only her son … and she could leave him until another day.

However, stopping in the car park, alongside the cars of the village toffs, she changed her mind about trying her luck. The Canleigh Arms looked expensive. It would be full of snobby people who would only look down on her and it would be doubtful if she could entice a punter in there. Damn and blast. She could have done with some cash as business had been a bit slow lately. She wasn't getting any younger, she wasn't welcome on the streets with the younger, feistier, drugged up hookers, and it was becoming more difficult to make a living inviting punters back to her home. She had never wanted to do that anyway. It was sometimes difficult getting rid of them and the older and less attractive she became, the demand for kinkier and kinkier stuff grew. She had to face it. She was becoming too old for being on the game and would have to start thinking about finding another way of providing for herself … and now she had seen the way her biological son was living, her mind was in a whirl. She had expected opulence and wealth but once she had set eyes on Canleigh Hall and the people he was associating with, she realised she had stumbled on her pot of gold and whether he, or his obnoxious gay friend liked it or not, she was determined he was going to help her out. She had no idea how she was going to get him to agree but agree he would.

She watched a couple leave the pub and get into a brand new Daimler. The woman must be about the same age as her but she looked smart, healthy, slim and well turned out in a pale blue suit, pearls and permed hair. Beryl's heart sunk. That woman had never had to turn tricks to get food on her table. She was probably well educated, had obviously made a good marriage, and had a fancy home somewhere full of expensive furniture and knickknacks. She probably didn't have to work and would spend her days lunching with her friends, attending charity events and generally enjoying herself. Then her husband, who would more than likely have a good job or business, would come home, they would have a beautifully cooked dinner, spend some leisure time together in the evening, go to bed, enjoy warm, pleasurable intimacy and then curl up and sleep, wrapped in each other's arms.

Beryl didn't cry often but she did now. She felt worthless, cheap, and completely alone. She had nothing and no-one. It was doubtful if Suzanne would want to travel all the way from Australia to see her, and that boy, the son who she had just watched get hitched, didn't want to know her either.

She started the car, sniffing hard and wiping the tears away with the back of her hand. Well, he was going to have to. She would leave it alone for now. He would be going off for a fancy honeymoon somewhere but as soon as he was back, she was going to get in touch now she knew where he would be living ... in a stately home no less ... Canleigh Hall. Yes. It didn't matter what that bloke had said, whoever he was. Her son would help her out in her old age. After all, that was what son's did, didn't they? Looked after their old mums ... and his pretty young wife looked nice. She would want to help her mother-in-law, wouldn't she? Of course she would.

Beryl drove the car out of the car park, turning left for Leeds and the M1, hoping the car wouldn't start making the peculiar noises it had on the way up. It was due for an MOT soon and she had no idea how she was going to find the money for that, let alone any expensive repairs.

She debated on trying to find the kind of areas she would be familiar with in Leeds. She would have more of a chance trying to entice a punter to cough up for a night in a boarding house … after all, she might be getting on a bit but she had on her smart red dress which showed off her assets to their best advantage and her legs weren't all that bad. In a dim light the lines and wrinkles on her face weren't quite so noticeable either and she could always apply another layer of make-up. Should she try it or should she head back to London? The decision was made for her as she passed the Elland Road football stadium on the way to the M1. The road signs for Merwood jumped out at her. She had seen it on the television. Merwood was a seedy area of Leeds, full of drugs and prostitutes. She indicated left. She could return to London tomorrow and then if the car broke down, she would be a lot safer in daylight than in the middle of the night.

* * *

"I don't like him," said Ruth to Vicky as they walked into the Hall after waving Jeremy and Lucy off on their honeymoon, strangely accompanied by Matthew.

They had spent hours in the marquee after the marriage ceremony but once the disco commenced at seven o'clock, they both decided they had had enough and were going to leave the younger members of the party to it. Katrina was having a ball, receiving lots of attention from young males, some of whom she knew and others she didn't and Vicky had asked a couple of Lucy's older girlfriends to keep on eye on her and to come and find her if Katrina looked as if she was getting out of her depth. Some of the boys wouldn't have a clue she was only thirteen and they could get into really hot water with her over-confident child if they weren't careful.

Philip and Alex had made their escape much earlier and were settled on the south terrace of the Hall on loungers, enjoying a whisky and the evening sunshine. The music from the marquee was much fainter now they were on the opposite side of the building with a few solid brick walls between them.

"Who?" asked Vicky as the two women entered the library and Ruth walked over to the drinks tray. She ignored Vicky's question for a second. "I've had enough alcohol for one day. I think I'll just have water ... how about you?"

Vicky nodded. Drinking in the afternoon never did her any good. "Water is fine. Who are you talking about?"

"Matthew. He gives me the creeps ... and why he had to accompany Lucy and Jeremy just now, beats me. I thought he was staying here for the night and going back to Oxford by train tomorrow."

"Well, as they are staying at the Randolph tonight, I suppose they felt it churlish if they didn't offer him a lift ... and I know what you mean, I can't warm to him either. I do wish Jeremy hadn't picked up with him."

"Didn't he meet him while he was at Oxford?"

"Yes, so he says, although he never mentioned him while he was there. I didn't know the chap existed until a few months ago. Then, suddenly, he pops up to York every couple of weeks and Jeremy goes over and always spends the night over there."

"Oh?" questioned Ruth, with a raised eyebrow.

Vicky shrugged. "He says he doesn't want to drive back once they have been drinking. I've always taken the view that he's being responsible. Why ... what are you thinking? Come on, Ruth. Let's have it."

Ruth sank down onto the sofa by the fireplace and placed her glass of water on a nearby side table. She was deathly tired, had drunk too much champagne this afternoon and really only wanted to go upstairs and lay down. The strain of talking to so many people and pretending she was feeling jolly had taken its toll and she wanted nothing more than to escape, even from Vicky, who even though she was officially her step-daughter, was her best friend after Philip.

"Oh, I don't know, Vicky. I'm probably not thinking clearly but it's ... it's the way he looks at Jeremy, with that smile of his, as if he knows something we all don't ... and he hangs onto Jeremy's every word and tries to exclude Lucy. Didn't you notice ... during the wedding breakfast ... every time Lucy tried to make conversation, he interrupted and took over. It was so rude and blatantly pushing her out ... as if he's in control of Jeremy."

She pushed her hair back from her forehead. "Oh, forget it, Vicky. I'm just being silly. Seeing something where there is nothing. I'm tired and need to go and rest."

Vicky sat down beside her, took her hand, and looked at her sympathetically. She knew how hard it had been for Ruth to appear happy today. She was still grieving badly for Stephen. After all, it had only been a few short months since he died and how did a mother ever get over loosing a son ... her only child?

"If it's any consolation, I noticed too and I agree ... it's most peculiar. It's as if he has some kind of

397

hold over Jeremy but what it could be, I have no idea."

"You don't believe ...?"

They looked at each other, both knowing what the other was thinking but neither wanting to voice it.

"And who was that woman ... that tubby lady in the awful hat and red dress that was far too tight ... whom Matthew was talking to in the churchyard as we left the churchyard? I've never seen her before and she certainly wasn't on the guest list."

"I was wondering that myself. She looked terribly out of place ... and she ... oh Christ!"

"What?" said Ruth, alarmed at the look of horror on Vicky's face.

"She couldn't stop looking at Jeremy as he and Lucy walked back down the aisle ... I thought for a second she was going to launch herself at him. Her face was wreathed in smiles and she put out an arm to grab him and he pulled away pretty smartly."

"So ... who is she?"

"Oh, Ruth. I've a ghastly feeling she might be his birth mother."

"What! But how ... how did she find him ... and does he know?"

"I've no idea. Absolutely none. He hasn't discussed her with me for years ... but if she is ... and from the way he shrugged her off, I would assume he knows ... but doesn't want anything to do with her. Oh, Lord. I do hope she's not going to be a problem. Not now. Not when he and Lucy are beginning their new lives together. Anyway, I have no idea where she went but at least she didn't come over here after the service."

"So," said Ruth quietly. "Now we have her ... and Matthew to worry about ... along with Delia in the background. Whatever Lucy says about her mother turning over a new leaf, I can never forgive or forget what she has done and if she ever comes here .... Why is life always so complicated, Vicky? Why can't we all just live in peace and harmony? I am so tired of it all."

"Let's get you up to bed," said Vicky. "You look positively exhausted. You can always come down later if you feel up to it."

Ruth rose to her feet. Her body felt heavy ... nearly as heavy as her heart. She just wanted to get upstairs, pull the covers over her head and weep ... weep for her son, who should have been here today ... giving Lucy away ... smiling and laughing with his fiancé, Sarah ... planning their wedding ... planning their lives ... the children that should have been her grandchildren.

She could feel it overwhelming her again, her grief. That dark, black feeling of despair that she would never set eyes on her beloved son again. She clutched onto Vicky's arm for support and they left the library and walked upstairs.

CHAPTER 30

JUNE/JULY 1996

Jeremy and Lucy had left Canleigh for their honeymoon at 6.00 p.m., just before the evening party got under way, although they didn't leave alone. Matthew accompanied them. He had taken the train up to Leeds for the wedding, leaving his car in Oxford and Jeremy insisted they give him a lift back.

"Don't be silly. I can catch the train tomorrow," Matthew had said, with little enthusiasm.

"Don't *you* be silly," Jeremy had replied. "We are going straight there and can drop you off at home. It's no bother at all, is it Lucy?"

Lucy would have liked to refuse but it would have seemed churlish as it was a perfectly logical idea but never feeling at ease with Matthew, she could have wished for a more pleasant travelling companion.

As it happened, it hadn't mattered too much. The drive down to Oxford had been pleasant in the evening sunshine. The traffic was light and Jeremy, who liked to drive fast, made the miles go quickly as they were all tired and wanted nothing more than to arrive at their destination to rest and relax after such an eventful day. They didn't speak much. Jeremy turned the radio onto a classical channel, broadcasting an evening of Chopin and the fabulous sounds of piano music filled the car. Lucy put her head back on the headrest and dozed on and off. Matthew slept and occasionally snored on the backseat.

They dropped him at his flat later that evening.

"I have something for you," said Matthew as he stepped out of the car. "Come in for a moment, Jeremy, and I can give it to you ... night, Lucy. Thanks for the lift and do enjoy your honeymoon," he said, giving her a strange, knowing smile, which made her feel decidedly uncomfortable. What was it about him that she didn't like? He was perfectly polite but then she realised who he reminded her of. Felix, the butler. He had the same smarmy smile and air of superiority ... and he was gay. Was Matthew gay and if he was, what did Jeremy have in common with him apart from that they were at University together?

She sat outside Matthew's flat pondering on the relationship between him and Jeremy, growing chilly now it was getting dark, and wishing Jeremy would hurry up. Desperately tired and impatient to get to the Randolph, she was just about to get out of the car and knock on the door of the flat when Jeremy appeared, looking a little ruffled and smoothing his hands over his hair.

"Sorry. I didn't mean to be so long," he said, starting the car and turning it towards the city centre.

"Where's the present?" she asked.

"Oh. Oh, it was too big for us to take to Southampton. We can collect it on the way back."

"What on earth is it?"

"It's a surprise. You'll see ... now for goodness sake, let's get to the hotel. I don't know about you but I'm totally bushed and want nothing more than to crash out."

Their room at the Randolph was the best, a present from Vicky and Alex, but as comfortable and opulent as it was, neither saw much of it. As soon as they arrived, they dispensed with their finery, showered and collapsed into bed. Jeremy had opened the champagne, generously left by the management, but he only had a few sips, murmured how sorry he was, laid his head back on his pillow and dropped into a deep sleep.

Lucy, expecting to have their marriage consummated but not exactly heartbroken as she was deathly tired too, drank her champagne, curled up next to her husband and joined him in slumber. They had eight glorious weeks with nothing to do but indulge themselves and she wasn't going to lose any sleep worrying about not 'doing it' on their wedding night. They had plenty of time … all their lives in fact. She smiled and slid into oblivion.

The next day they were up early with only hours to go before they caught their cruise ship. They enjoyed a quick breakfast in their room and sped out of Oxford and down the A34 towards Southampton. Feeling brighter and fresher after a good night's sleep, their conversation centered on the events of the day before and the forthcoming honeymoon. It was only when Lucy mentioned Matthew that she noticed a strange look pass over Jeremy's face but arriving in Southampton and seeing the cruise ship made her forget all about it. She nearly burst with excitement as it came into view and once they were aboard and shown to their cabin, she was in perfect ecstasy. It was all as she had imagined, totally luxurious and with a wide balcony where they could sit and watch the world go by.

"How kind of Mother to give us this for a wedding present," she said. "I'm so looking forward to seeing her in a few weeks so we can tell her all about it. We're going to have such a fabulous time, aren't we, darling?"

Jeremy didn't say a word. He just looked out to sea and she was sure she heard him sigh.

* * *

Felix was busy. The Kershaws were moving to Tangles before Lucy and Jeremy returned from honeymoon and there was a lot to do. For all their married life, they had lived at Canleigh, looking after Stephen and Lucy but now the time had come for them to depart and leave Canleigh to the newlyweds.

Felix was excited and pleased. His relationship with the Kershaws had always been a little strained, to say the least, but young Lucy was a pushover and as for Jeremy ... Felix couldn't wait to get his hands on him and help him with his personal needs.

"That's it for the bedroom, I think," remarked Ruth, flipping the zip around the fourth suitcase she had packed that morning. "All the cases can go downstairs now, please Felix, and I'll just pop upstairs to my studio and finish packing up there."

"Very good, Madam," he replied, grabbing two of the cases and leaving the room. She didn't know how much he was enjoying this, seeing her finally leave the Hall and relinquish her position as his employer. Life was certainly going to be a lot more enjoyable and easier from now on, he was determined of that.

The only fly in the ointment was that Matthew fellow. Felix had watched him hovering around Jeremy at the wedding, being far more attentive than a normal best man would. Felix had known instantly, of course. It was obvious there was something going on and that it wasn't over. Felix was overcome with jealousy at first but having eyed Matthew up and down, had realised that the situation could be turned to his advantage. Knowledge was power and he knew the two were having an affair. He could either blackmail them or join in. It wasn't beyond the realms of possibility that all three of them could end up in bed together. Now that would be an interesting turn of events. Felix felt the excitement grow. It was only a couple of weeks before the honeymooners returned and he had a funny feeling young Lucy Canleigh wasn't having the grand time with her husband she had expected.

* * *

Ruth felt very strange. In fact, she didn't really know how she felt if truth be known. She and Philip had planned their departure to Tangles for months. He was really happy to be returning to his old home and she wanted to be happy too but was desperately sad at leaving Canleigh. It had been a major part of her life for so many years.

As she wound her way up to the attic, which she used for a studio for her painting, she remembered the first day she had set foot in the Hall. She had been with Richard, Charles's son and heir and had only come for the weekend to think over her decision to leave medical training. Then she had meet Charles and fell headlong in love with him. Their wedding only months later in St. Mary's had been one of the best days of her life. It had been a daunting experience, becoming a Duchess, but Charles had helped her through it, advising and guiding her on what and what not to do, making it so easy for her. Then there had been the birth of darling little Stephen.

They had been so happy ... until Charles died. Her heart lurched badly and the terrible pain she had experienced when he had left her, shot through her again causing her to double up and almost faint.

She grabbed onto the door handle of her studio and pushed it open, heading straight for the seat by the window. She opened it, took great gulps of fresh warm air and slowly and gradually the faintness receded. She looked around her favourite room in the whole house. She was going to miss it dreadfully. Lucy had said she could come and paint here whenever she wanted but she wouldn't like to. Once Lucy and Jeremy came home, Canleigh would be theirs, she had no further right to it ..., and anyway, she needed to be with Philip. She loved him and wanted to be with him for the rest of their lives. They had been so lucky finding each other after his wife, Sue, and then Charles had died. Their love wasn't of the 'in love' type where passion soon died. They shared friendship and a mutual understanding of what the other had gone through and relied heavily on each other for emotional support. It had worked and their marriage was a good one and if it hadn't have been for Philip, she didn't have a clue how she would have coped with losing Stephen. He had helped keep her sane through the last, ghastly few months when she thought she was going to go mad with grief. It was still raw and painful, but she was coping. The black days would always be there. She knew that. But there was still life to be lived and Philip needed her and it would be good to make a fresh start at Tangles. Here, at Canleigh, she would always be thinking of Stephen and what might have been if he had married Sarah. At Tangles she would be free of all of that and could concentrate on helping Philip ... and there was a room at the top of the house she could use as a studio. It hadn't such a beautiful view as this but it was quiet and peaceful and she could paint to her heart's content.

She picked up the box in which she kept her paints and brushes and started to collect those that were spread out on her painting table next to the easel. She hadn't long. A removal van was supposed to be arriving within the next hour to take everything to Tangles. She had better hurry up.

* * *

The four weeks on board the cruise ship flew by, although to Lucy's surprise, Jeremy wanted to spend as much time out of the cabin as he could. He was strangely restless and only seemed at ease when he was swimming during the day and dancing in the evening on the days when they were at sea. He insisted they participate in all the shore excursions and then collapsed in the evenings in one of the bars or even, to her consternation, spent an excessive amount of time in the casino. Gambling held no attraction for Lucy, and she was concerned as to how much money he appeared to be getting through but reasoned they were on holiday and once they were home, he wouldn't do it again.

He didn't appear to be able to relax or sit still for any length of time and gradually it began to get on Lucy's nerves. She had thought any activity Jeremy wanted to partake in would have involved her and would have taken place in the privacy of their cabin. Not so. They did have sex, on the third night, but

Lucy didn't find the consummation of their marriage particularly enjoyable. It was rushed, with little consideration for her, and when it was over, Jeremy turned over and promptly went to sleep. In the end, she decided not to let it worry her. They were on a cruise ship, sailing around the Mediterranean and their lack of intimacy wasn't going to spoil it for her. Once they were home at Canleigh and got into a proper routine with their daily lives, it would all slot into place and they would be the husband and wife she thought they would be.

So, Lucy threw herself into the excursions ashore with gusto. Most days they stopped somewhere, departed the ship on tenders, and explored the local attractions, sometimes with a guide, sometimes on their own. Absorbed in the history and the flora and fauna, Lucy found she was thoroughly enjoying herself and when Jeremy grabbed her hand or threw an arm around her shoulder, her heart soared and she felt happy again, sure that their lack of intimacy in the bedroom was only a passing phase and he really did love her and everything would turn out all right.

Their cruise ended when they reached the port of Civitavecchia. Their luggage was taken off the ship and they hired a taxi to take them to the Grand Hotel Ritz in Rome where they had the pleasure of residing in a luxury suite for a week, courtesy of Lady Delia Canleigh. Lucy was sorry the cruise had ended but Rome had been on the top of her 'places to visit list' since she was a little girl and she was tremendously excited as the taxi wound its way towards the hotel. Then she noticed Jeremy. He was becoming agitated, fiddling with his watch and wedding ring and cracking his knuckles, a habit she loathed and which he only did when nervous or under stress.

"Are you okay?" she asked, puzzled by his demeanour. He had been looking forward to this visit for days. So why was he becoming jittery?

He didn't answer her but as the taxi pulled up outside the hotel and Jeremy rummaged in his wallet for enough cash to pay the driver, she knew what was the matter. Her heart sank and she flopped back into her seat, dismay written all over her face as she stared at the man standing at the front door of the hotel. He moved towards the car and opened the door for Jeremy to get out. Her husband leapt from the vehicle, embracing him in a hug. Lucy could hear Matthew's rumble of laughter and she felt sick. Her worst fears were being realised. Her husband *was* gay and his lover was here with them on their honeymoon. What the hell was she going to do?

CHAPTER 31

The week in Rome was a nightmare for Lucy. There were so many things she had planned on seeing, so much she wanted to do ... with Jeremy by her side ... but it wasn't to be. Matthew said he was in Rome on business, but exactly what that was, he never divulged and as he wasn't a businessman, Lucy could only surmise that it was a lie and he had only wanted to be here to be with Matthew and upset their private time together.

Jeremy insisted Matthew dine with them every night, which appalled Lucy. She had naturally expected him to decline but after a half hearted protest on their very first evening, with very little pressure from Jeremy, he accepted the invitation with a smirk at Lucy.

As Matthew had little interest in history or art, the conversation seemed to centre on the best restaurants and bars for eating and drinking, with the odd casino thrown in for good measure. The two men made little effort to include Lucy and growing bored, she excused herself after coffee every evening and retired to bed with a book ... and this was supposed to be her honeymoon! Jeremy would fall into their suite in the early hours of the morning, inebriated and apologetic, lunge for the bed and fall asleep in his clothes. Disgusted and upset, Lucy would throw a blanket over him and leave him to it.

Determined to see all the sites she had read up on for months, and giving up on Jeremy, she spent her time exploring Rome from top to bottom. She took a tour bus on the first day, enjoying the informative audio tour and when she had her bearings, ventured down to the colosseum, awestruck by its size and horrendous history. To discover thousands of animals as well as people had been hunted and killed in its parameters, was particularly upsetting and once she had spent a couple of hours exploring the massive building, she was glad to leave.

Even though she was keen to visit the Forum, it was becoming far too hot for exploring outdoors so she returned to their suite at the hotel, had a long cooling shower and dozed on the bed with the air conditioning on full blast. Jeremy had disappeared without even leaving a note for her. She assumed he would be with Matthew and felt dreadfully hurt and forlorn, only managing to raise her spirits a little by planning her next excursions.

Every day she asked Jeremy to accompany her but every day he grunted from the confines of the bed, groaning about his hangover and how it was too hot to go out. Donning sunscreen, a sunhat, and sunglasses, she left the hotel early in the mornings; angry and heartbroken that Matthew encouraged her husband to virtually drink himself senseless every night, spoiling their precious time together.

But even so, she made the best of her time in Rome, spending a day at the Forum, marvelling at the ancient ruins and trying to imagine what it was like in its heyday with people bustling about the streets and the market. She visited the Vatican and its enormous museum, praying quietly in one of the side chapels that her marriage would survive and flourish despite Matthew, and standing awestruck in front of St. Peter's tomb and the fabulous sculptures and art by Bernini and Michelangelo. Entering the Sistine chapel later in the day, she sat on one of the side benches and

410

marvelled at the frescos on the walls and ceiling above her. Then she strolled along to the Spanish Steps and the Trevi Fountain, wishing fervently that Jeremy had accompanied her. Even so, she still threw a coin in the fountain. She loved Rome. She wanted to come back ... without Matthew!

Their week in Rome came to an end and Matthew announced at their final dinner that he was returning to England in the morning, leaving them to journey on to Florence on their own. Although Jeremy appeared stricken with misery, Lucy was utterly relieved and delighted. Matthew had ruined Rome for her; she didn't want the same to happen in Florence and Venice. She left the table feeling a lot more cheerful than she had all week.

Lucy went to bed with a guidebook to Florence while Jeremy ventured out yet again with Matthew. He appeared even more worse for wear when he staggered into their suite at four in the morning. His clothes were in disarray, his hair a mess and he was slurring badly.

"Wish we were going home," he mumbled as he fell onto the bed. "Don't want Mattie to go. He's such fun, Lucy, such fun ... and I'm going to miss him terribly."

Lucy felt as if a dagger had been thrust into her heart. It was true then. He obviously loved Matthew more than her ... and by the look of him tonight, they had probably had sex. She was so revolted, she could have been sick. How was she going to allow him to touch her again ... but that was even if he wanted to. She laid her head on the pillow and cried quietly. Her marriage was over before it had begun.

Strangely, she awoke in the morning, feeling more light-hearted than she had for days. Matthew was gone. His taxi had been booked for 6.00 a.m. and it was now 7.00 a.m, and they were off to Florence today ... to wander around the Uffizi gallery, see the Duomo and explore the beautiful Tuscan countryside ... and she would have Jeremy all to herself.

She wasn't disappointed. Jeremy wasn't too lively on the journey to Florence, hiding his eyes behind sunglasses and taking a couple of paracetomol for his hangover every few hours but after a good nights sleep, he was as bright as a button and enthusiastically joined her to stroll around Florence and the Uffizi. They actually held hands and he even bent down to kiss her at one point and she could pretend that the last few days in Rome with Matthew had never been.

They spent a week in Florence and then moved onto Venice for a fortnight. They rode everywhere on gondolas, Jeremy pretending to sing 'Just one Cornetto' as they slipped past the grand old buildings. They explored St. Mark's basilica, the Doge's palace, they watched glass being blown, dined in St. Mark's Square and enjoyed classical concerts and the opera.

And then it was time to return to the U.K and have a trip up to Scotland to see Delia before driving back down to Canleigh. Matthew hadn't been mentioned by either of them since he had returned to England but Lucy did wonder when he might put in an appearance again, whether he might come to Canleigh or whether Jeremy would meet him in York, as he had before their wedding.

What she had previously assumed was just a night out with his friend had obviously been far more than that and she wasn't sure whether to tackle Jeremy about it or sweep it under the carpet. It was easier to do that but secrets had a way of coming out eventually and she had a nasty feeling that something bad would happen in the future if it wasn't tackled. But what could she say? What could she do? She couldn't ask for a divorce so soon after their marriage, but did she really want to? She still loved Jeremy, even though she was revolted by his behaviour but for the life of her, she couldn't understand why he had married her, knowing he was in love with Matthew and obviously wanting to be with him. It was a mystery and one she was reluctant to delve into. No, for the time being, she would leave it, hope it would go away, hope Matthew would go away and it was just a silly phase Jeremy was going through. Once they returned to Canleigh and resumed their everyday lives ... and Matthew would be down in Oxford getting on with his life ... this silly episode would all be forgotten ... especially when they had children. Lucy wanted them badly. So, she and Jeremy would have to sort their marriage out if little ones were to come along.

* * *

Delia was so excited. Lucy and Jeremy were on their way up to Blairness from Heathrow. They were going to stop at Loch Lomond overnight to break up the journey but tomorrow they would be at the castle and she would be able to hear all about their honeymoon and see the wedding photographs, which had been mailed to them in Rome.

She had a lot to tell them too. Plans for Blairness were going well. The caravan park was open and booked up until the end of the season and all the guests seemed to be very happy with their choice of holiday. Everything was going according to plan for

413

opening the house with the work on the outbuildings being turned into a café, shop, garden centre and toilets nearly complete. Staff had been interviewed and appointed and were in the process of being trained for their various duties. Massive orders had been placed to stock the shop and garden centre by Vera Franklin, who would be managing both, and the new restaurant manager, Kate Wiley, was busy preparing menus for Delia's approval.

A date of 1st August was planned for the grand opening. It was a shame they hadn't been able to open for the whole season but August, September and October would be a good trial run for next year.

Brian had been a tower of strength and Delia could never thank him enough for being so enthusiastic and pulling out all the stops to make all her plans for Blairness a success. He had worked tirelessly to help her and for the last couple of months, joined her for dinner a couple of times a week so they could discuss how things were going. She had loved those evenings. They would have a couple of glasses of wine with dinner and then move to the red drawing room, sitting up well into the night, drinking numerous cups of coffee, while repeatedly going over and over everything to make sure nothing could go wrong. They poured over plans of the estate and the buildings, making long to do lists and filling in forms for various permissions and work to be carried out.

They could have met through the day but finding the time was hard. Brian was busy, overseeing the normal day to day running of the estate and Delia had more than enough to do helping Kate and Vera settle in and deciding, with Crystal, which rooms would be open to the public, what would be on display and tweeking the audio tour for the tourists she hoped would be interested enough to pay Blairness a visit.

So, it was good for them to get together at least two evenings a week to catch up. After dinner, Meg would lie on the rug in front of the fire and snooze while her master and Delia plotted and schemed for the future of Blairness. They would sit close to each other on the old Chesterfield sofa, Brian skimming through information on his laptop while Delia, Parker pen in hand, scrawled notes on her notepad. Occasionally they would smile or laugh, sometimes their fingers touched and once, when she was desperately tired, she had laid her head on his shoulder and slept. Her heart was always soaring when she was with him. She had never felt like this before, not even with Philip. She idolised the very ground this man walked on. He could do no wrong in her eyes. She looked up to him as she had never looked up to a man before. Every word he spoke was of grave importance to her, every look and glance he passed her way filled her with a feeling of delight. He made her feel safe, as no-one had before … and every day, she loved him, more and more. She had no idea where their relationship was going but she knew she couldn't live without him now … and she would kill to keep him.

The days and months following Delia's secret visit to Canleigh flew by in a flurry of hard work, lashings of coffee and high anticipation from all of her stalwarts; Brian, Crystal, Connie and the McFrains. Once the alterations were complete, extra staff would be needed as room attendants, for reception and car parking duties, along with more cleaners, and shop and café staff. Advertisements were drawn up and job descriptions prepared. They all worked like demons to

415

knock it all into shape so as little of the season disappeared before revenue started to trickle in.

Delia woke up every day with a feeling of huge anticipation, eager to crack on and make Blairness *the* most visited attraction in Scotland and maybe even in Britain. Opening the house to the public was just a start. She had plans for concerts, indoors and outdoors, classical and modern, events such as game fairs and dog shows and naturally, the horse trials. They could rival Badminton and Burgley. They had the land. It could work. She could really put Blairness on the map. She was so excited, she could hardly sleep. Her adrenalin was at its highest and she could work for long hours every day, so great was her desire to see Blairness hum with activity and prove to herself that everything she had learned all those years ago, could now come to fruition, albeit not at Canleigh.

The only fly in the ointment now was that dratted little butler, Felix. He had sent her his bank account number so he could benefit from her deposit very month. She hadn't been able to figure out how to wriggle out of it as yet, apart from bumping the damned man off, and unfortunately, that wasn't an option. She really did have too much to lose to go down that route again. No, she would have to pay him for now ... but one day, and she still had no idea how, he would have to be dealt with as she had a sneaky suspicion that his demands would only increase and she wasn't going to see all her hard earned cash from improvements to Blairness go to him. She would just have to bide her time for now and push the horrid man to the back of her mind. She had set up the direct debit, he had his money every month, and that would have to suffice for now.

* * *

Beryl Porter was seriously under the influence of alcohol but then she always seemed to be drunk nowadays. She had bought eleven cider flagons last week but they now stood in her kitchen, all empty. As were the ten packets of cigarettes on the coffee table.

She lay in a stupor on the sofa in the living room, sore, battered, and feeling deeply sorry for herself. A punter had done her over last night. She had bumped into him as she staggered out of the Red Lion and he had insisted on seeing her home, promising her twenty quid for a quickie. Needing more fags, booze and a bit of food from the cheap shop in the next street she agreed but once the front door was closed behind them, he had slapped her around a bit, ripped off her clothes, raped her and then left without giving her a penny. Angry with herself she had drunk what remained of the cider and had curled up in a ball on the sofa, trying to ignore the agony he had left her in. She would have liked to have taken some painkillers but had swallowed the last for a headache two days ago. She had no money to buy anymore, even if the shops were open in the middle of the night, so she had no alternative but to suffer.

Blurrily she looked at a five week old newspaper on the coffee table. It had a picture of the happy honeymooners, Lucy and Jeremy ... her son ... wandering in the ruins of ancient Greece on an excursion from their cruise ship. How she envied them ... not a care in the world ... young, attractive and with pots of money. Bah! Her daughter-in-law certainly wouldn't have to worry about buying painkillers. Beryl turned on her side, trying to ease the pain between her thighs and on her bruised and battered body, wondering if she should make her way to the hospital later. At that moment in time she hated her son. He should have been here, looking after his old mum, not swanning about Europe having a good time. He would have to sort himself out when he came home and do as a good son should. She would have a chat with him. A seriously good talking to. Then it would all be all right. He would look after her. Give her the money she needed to have a decent lifestyle and give up all these bloody punters. She was too old for this now and he would have to look after her in her old age. She was going to see to it. Yes, as soon as he landed back in the U.K, she was going to pay him a visit.

She turned over again and nearly screamed with the pain in her stomach. That bastard had done her some kind of damage down in her nether regions. She needed to drag herself to the hospital. She lay, watching the sun rising in the sky through the torn and grubby net curtains. She would leave it another hour and if she couldn't get off the sofa, she would have no choice but to ring an ambulance.

* * *

"I've never been to Rome," said Delia wistfully at dinner that evening. "I should so like to go. Father took us to Venice and Florence and we stayed in the villa at Lake Como many times but somehow we never made it to Rome. I've no idea why."

"It's utterly fascinating," replied Lucy enthusiastically, trying to remember the sights and the sounds, not the heartbreak of not having Jeremy with her to enjoy it all. Damn Matthew for spoiling it for them.

418

"Did you enjoy it as much as Lucy?" Delia asked Jeremy curiously. "She's taken hundreds of photos of the city and its attractions but none of you ... or of you two together."

Jeremy shifted uncomfortably in his dining chair and studied his empty plate. "Yes ... it was lovely ... but I think Venice was far better."

Delia looked at him. She still couldn't make up her mind about him ... he was an enigma that was for sure. "Well, you certainly looked very happy there."

"It was a fabulous honeymoon," said Lucy, finishing her roast beef and taking a sip of Merlot. "We really can't thank you enough."

"My pleasure ... so ... once you return to Canleigh, what are you going to do with yourselves?"

"Jeremy has decided to do a course in horticulture, haven't you darling? Once he knows what he is doing, he is going to redesign the parterre and the gardens by the lake."

"I do hope you're not going to destroy Granny's rose garden," Delia said sharply. "She laid it just after the war and it's very precious."

Lucy looked at her mother sympathetically. She knew how much Great Grandmother had meant to Delia and the rose garden was spectacular for many months of the year and kept the Hall well supplied with beautiful blooms.

"Definitely not," she said reassuringly. "I love that rose garden. It will never be touched. I promise you."

She patted Delia's hand and Delia smiled with relief. "Sorry, darling. I know Canleigh is yours to do with as you will now but I couldn't bear to think of the rose garden being altered. I'm so glad you love it too."

McFrain entered the room to remove their plates and bring their puddings.

"Homemade vanilla ice-cream drowned in Tia Maria," said Delia, her eyes sparkling. "I know you had it in Italy and loved it and I wanted to try it too. It sounds delicious."

Lucy laughed, remembering how she and Jeremy had experimented with various liquors and spirits on their trip, having seen it on the menu at one of the hotels in which they stayed. It had become a joke, wondering what they should ask to be added to their ice-creams every evening.

"Blimey. It is good," said Delia, taking her first mouthful. "I think we should have this here more often. I should think Brian would love it too. He adores ice-cream. If he sees the van stop in any of the villages, he has to buy a cone with a flake in it. He does make me laugh. He reminds me of a little boy," she giggled.

Lucy looked at her mother, watching her face as she mentioned the estate manager. A rosy glow had spread over her skin and her eyes had a look of knowing a secret, which she was dying to reveal.

"How is Brian?" asked Lucy mischievously. She liked him immensely and did hope he was as keen on her mother as she obviously was about him. Her life had been pretty rotten so far and it would be good if she could find some happiness and stability. It would also make Granny Ruth and Aunty Vicky feel a lot happier if they knew for certain her mother was really settled at Blairness and not hankering after Canleigh or Steppie any longer.

Delia blushed. "He's fine. An absolute brick. I really have no idea what I would do without him ... should we have coffee in the red drawing room?"

420

"If you don't mind … I would like to go up … and I'm sure you two have plenty to natter about," said Jeremy tiredly. Keeping up a conversation with Delia was a real strain. He felt she could see through him and he didn't like it. The longer he was out of her presence the better.

"Of course," said Delia, eyeing him up and down as he gave Lucy a kiss on the cheek and left the room.

The two women stood up, Delia linked her arm with Lucy's and they moved out of the dining room, across the entrance hall and into the red drawing room.

McFrain had placed the coffee on the table between the sofas and Delia poured two cups, handed Lucy hers and then added plenty of Demerara sugar to her own.

"Now then, young lady," said Delia. "Tell me all about the honeymoon … properly … and I want to know exactly why it looked as if you were on your own in Rome … and why Jeremy has hardly said a word since you arrived here.

"He's just tired … the travelling wears him out," Lucy replied, not daring to say how Jeremy had moaned all the way up to Scotland. He made no bones about how he didn't want to visit Delia in her gloomy Scottish castle, that there was little to do, he would be bored to tears and couldn't wait until they were back at Canleigh with Leeds, Harrogate and York not far away. She had listened wretchedly, realising it was more like Matthew he was desperate to see.

"Um. Ok … well how about Rome?"

Lucy shrugged. "There was so much to see … I just didn't think about taking photos of us."

Delia was flicking through the massive book of wedding photographs Lucy had left on the coffee table earlier.

"You looked divine, darling," she purred, stopping to study those which included all the family ... Vicky and Alex whom she hadn't set eyes on for years ... and Ruth and Philip. Her heart skipped a beat, waiting for the searing hate she had felt for them both to manifest itself but nothing happened. She could look at them without feeling anything. She didn't bear them any animosity. It had vanished. Blairness and Brian had seen to that. She didn't envy Ruth and Richard their love or what they had. They were nothing to her now ... just people she had once known and didn't want to know again.

Lucy watched her, knowing what she was looking at, wondering what was going through her head. Did she still bear hatred towards two of the people Lucy loved most? She almost cried with relief when Delia sighed and smiled across at her with no malice in her eyes.

"How smart everyone looks in all their finery ... who is this chap here, darling? Standing next to Jeremy. I presume he was the best man. Is he one of Jeremy's friends from University?"

Lucy couldn't help herself. She shuddered, hoping Delia would think it was because she was cold. She obviously did as she handed Lucy a red woollen blanket. "Put this over your knees darling."

"Thank you ... he's called Matthew ... and yes, they met at University."

"And you don't like him."

Lucy gasped. "How did you know?"

"It's in your tone, Lucy. You sound ... you sound as if you loathe him."

Lucy couldn't look at Delia. She didn't want to talk about Matthew. If she did, it might just come out ... all that hurt he had caused in Rome. All that angst that her husband loved Matthew more than he did her.

"Why don't you like him?" asked Delia puzzled by Lucy's look of distaste when Mathew was mentioned.

"Oh, I don't know ... he's ... he's a bit pushy, that's all. A bit full of himsclf ... you know the type."

"Um. Yes. I suppose I do," said Delia thoughtfully. There was obviously more to this than met the eye but she didn't want to push it.

"Where does he live?"

"Oxford ... he has a flat there and a bookshop... so I don't suppose we'll see much of him now," Lucy replied, hoping it would be true. If Matthew continued to pay regular visits to York, she fully expected Jeremy would still zoom off to be with him overnight. She rubbed her brow and sighed, not realising her mother was watching her closely.

"So," said Delia, "what plans have you for Canleigh ... what are you going to do with it now you own it lock, stock and barrel?"

"Nothing really," Lucy looked up surprised. "I just presumed it would go on as normal."

"Well, surely you don't intend to just rattle around in it, letting it eat up money by the thousands every week. What will you do with yourself all day? I hadn't put you down as wanting to be one of the idle rich," Delia grinned.

"I really hadn't given it much thought," admitted Lucy. "Life has been such a whirlwind in the last few months, what with Stephen dying, Granny Ruth's terrible grief, finding out I've inherited Canleigh, organising the wedding. It's all been pretty unsettling. I had planned on just 'being' once we go home."

"And you're right. You need to become accustomed to being in charge and to get your head around being married. Then you can start to plan … and if you need any advice … you know you don't have far to come."

Lucy raised her head. Was this a bid from her mother to interfere in the future of Canleigh after all?

Delia raised a hand and laughed. "No, darling. No. Don't even think it. I have more than enough to do here at Blairness … I really am not interested in Canleigh any longer. It's yours and I am pleased for you … I am only offering you my wisdom and knowledge if you wish to take advantage of it … although I do think you should consider doing something with the stable block. It's just sitting there, idle and disused. It's a complete waste."

Lucy's expression was incredulous and as soon as the words were out of Delia's mouth, she knew she had made a crazy mistake.

"You've been … haven't you?" whispered Lucy. "Why? You know you could be slung straight back into prison … and when … when did you go?"

Delia slumped back onto the cushions on the sofa and grimaced. She would have to come clean but knew that Lucy would never give her away, especially when she told her how she felt about Canleigh now.

"Yes."

"Oh, God," groaned Lucy. "What a crazy thing to do."

"Yes, it was … but you needn't worry. I shan't do it again."

"But why? Why would you risk it?"

"I just had to, darling. I had to say one last goodbye to the place … to get it out of my system, if you like. I hired a cottage close by and just wandered around one night; around the lake, through the gardens, up to the house and ... and the churchyard."

Lucy's hand flew to her mouth but she was speechless.

"That was all it was, darling. I had to say goodbye to all my memories but my future lies here, at Blairness. I knew that then and releasing all my demons has given me the urge to get on with what I have to do here. Believe me, darling. I am so very pleased that Canleigh is now yours. I don't want it ... I have suffered, and others have suffered so much because I wanted something I could never have. It had to stop and it has. I have finally buried my past and have a really good future to look forward to at Blairness ... and I wish you and Jeremy all the luck in the world with Canleigh. You do believe me, don't you, Lucy?"

Lucy sat still, trying to take in what her mother was saying, trying to imagine her creeping around Canleigh in the dead of the night and none of them being aware of it. Granny Ruth and Steppie would have had a fit if they had known.

"And you won't say anything to anyone, will you? I know it wasn't a bright thing to do but I've felt so much better since I went ... life is really worth living again now."

Lucy studied her mother. There was something different about her. She had puzzled on it all evening. Delia was more buoyant, excited, and happy. Lucy had assumed it was because they were talking about the wedding and the honeymoon but obviously not.

"No," she said slowly. "No, of course I won't say anything. I certainly don't want you to go back to prison either ... but you won't do it again, will you?"

"No. I promise faithfully never to set foot on Canleigh soil once more. Nothing and no-one will get me back down there. I have all that I want here," Delia said, a wide grin on her face.

Lucy knew instantly. It was Brian. Her mother didn't just fancy Brian, she really was in love with him. Every time she had mentioned him this evening, her face had lit up. Lucy's trepidation dissolved. There was nothing more to worry about. Brian was a lovely man and was perfect for Delia.

"It's Brian, isn't it?" she queried with a smile, unable to help herself.

Delia stood up and moved over to the drinks tray on a table at the far side of the room. "Umm. You don't miss much, my girl."

Lucy jumped to her feet and threw her arms around Delia. "I'm pleased for you. I mean it. I really am. You deserve some happiness after all you've been through ... and he's such a nice man ... I do hope he's going to be my step-father."

"Whoa," laughed Delia. "Don't get too ahead of yourself. Brian and I might well have feelings for each other but marriage ... that is another thing entirely."

Lucy grinned. "Well, just remember, I am quite happy to be matron of honour when the time comes."

Delia hugged Lucy closely, feeling an overwhelming sense of love for the daughter she had been apart from for so long. "Thank you, darling. Your support means more to me than you can ever imagine."

426

CHAPTER 32

Felix was excited. The Kershaws had finally moved out of Canleigh and into Tangles and next week Lucy and Jeremy would arrive and take up the reins. He was looking forward to it immensely and had taken extra pains to make sure the Hall looked as good as it possibly could.

As Tina had come down with a bad bout of summer flu and was tucked up in bed in her cottage in the village, he had taken it upon himself to hire in extra cleaning staff to give the place a thorough going over. All the furniture had been polished and the valuable Chippendale commodes, sideboards, tables and chairs shone as they had never shone before. The carpets and furnishings had been deep cleaned, and the windows and mirrors sparkled. The chandeliers had been taken down and washed and the oak floors polished. Then all the crockery and glassware had been checked and rechecked for cracks and chips and the silver cutlery and tableware given an extra polish.

Felix worked with the team of cleaners, supervising and assisting until they went home and then, following a shower and a meal, made himself comfortable on the south terrace on a lounger. He swigged whisky and smoked incessantly, pretending he was the owner of Canleigh and had all the money and time in the world to do as he liked.

However, he *was* on his way to an improved financial future, with Lucy and Jeremy ripe to milk and Lady Delia beginning to cough up. He had known she would. She simply had no alternative if she didn't want to return to a prison cell for many more years.

She had deposited the first £500 into his bank account and as he had nothing much to spend it on, it could mount up nicely every month. In a year, it would be £6000. In two, it would be £12,000. However, it still wasn't enough. He wanted more. Much more ... and next week, when the happy couple arrived back at Canleigh, he was going to start making headway on making more money than he had ever dreamed could possibly be his when he had started his career as a butler to the rich and famous. He smiled, took another swig of whisky, and lit another cigarette. Life was soon going to be good. Very good indeed.

* * *

Beryl woke up with a jerk. Someone was tapping on the door. It was dark. The street lights were on. She could see them through the net curtains. She must have slept all day. So much for visiting the hospital. She tried to move but the pain in her groin was excruciating. Whatever had that bugger done to her?

The tapping came again. More insistent. She froze. What if it was that man from last night, coming back for more? She didn't move, sitting silent as the grave, waiting and hoping that whoever it was would go away and leave her alone. God, she could do with a ciggie and a bloody drink.

"Beryl," someone hissed through the letterbox. "Beryl. Are you in? It's Matthew. Jeremy's friend ... from the wedding. I have a message for you from him."

Her heart was pounding. It was so loud she could hear it clearly and wondered if he could too. Their last meeting hadn't gone too well and why would her son

428

be sending her a message? He didn't want anything to do with her, did he? At least he hadn't on his wedding day. Was there a slight chance he had changed his mind? Perhaps now there had been time to think about it, he was willing to have her in his life … but wait a minute. He was still on his honeymoon. She had the picture in the newspaper to prove it. This Matthew chap must be lying. He had to be. There was no way she was moving off this sofa and opening the door to him, even if she could.

Then her hand flew to her mouth. He was fiddling through the letterbox where the door key hung on a piece of string. She knew from the rattling sound that he had found it and was drawing it up towards him. In a few moments, he would be inside. In sheer panic, she dragged herself to her feet and headed for the kitchen and the back door. Unfortunately, she tripped over a discarded shoe in the darkness, went flying onto the hard tiled kitchen floor and crashed her head against the corner of the cooker door. When Matthew stepped into the lounge seconds later, drew the moth-eaten curtain over the net at the window, and turned on the light, she was motionless, blood pouring from the wound on her forehead.

He took in the scene with delight. He hadn't had to do very much at all. No struggling. No screaming. She was half-dead already. He grabbed a cushion from the sofa and placed it over her face. Her eyes flickered open for a second but soon closed again as he forced the cushion hard over her nose and mouth. In just a few seconds, she was dead.

* * *

429

As the birds began to twitter just before daybreak, Ruth turned over in bed and snuggled up to Philip. It seemed strange, sleeping in the bedroom at Tangles. She missed Canleigh, although she was more than happy to be here with her lovely husband. It was what he had wanted for so long and he was so delighted to be living back at his old family home

"You awake?" he said sleepily.

"Yes."

"Does it feel odd, being here, instead of Canleigh?"

"A bit ... how do you feel?"

"It's wonderful to be home at last," he grinned, turning over slowly so as not to hurt his leg and taking her in his arms. "And even more wonderful that you are here to share it with me ... but this room will take a bit of getting used to ... it's a trifle modern for Tangles."

Ruth smiled. "I like it. It's spanking new ... and as it's a fresh chapter in our lives, that's as it should be."

They had discussed where they would sleep before moving back to Tangles and neither had wanted to use the room where Philip had slept with Sue, his first wife ... or had crazy romps with Delia. Memories for Philip and vivid imaginings from Ruth wouldn't have done their marriage any good, even though they had been together for years and knew each other inside out. They finally decided on Philip's grandparent's bedroom. It was bigger than Philip's and faced east, which was perfect for the early morning sunshine. All the old heavy furniture had been removed and a new, modern fitted bedroom suite in white was installed. They bought a new bed and Ruth ordered furnishings in sage green, which gave the room a wonderful calming feel. A door had been knocked through into the adjacent bedroom and now contained a huge corner jacuzzi bath and a walk-in shower cubicle big enough to hold a party in.

Philip hugged Ruth tighter. He knew she was missing Canleigh and all that it represented. She … they … had both assumed when they left Canleigh it would be in entirely different circumstances with Stephen and, probably Sarah Misperton-Evans, happily married and producing offspring. How differently things had turned out. The whole family had been in shock for the last few months with their lives turned upside down, just because some drugged up idiots had decided it was fun to attack a group of squaddies. They were all in prison now but it would never bring Stephen back. Philip was heartsick at the loss of his stepson. They had been such good friends, ever since the child was small. Philip had taught him to ride and to appreciate the countryside around them and to love and treasure animals. Stephen had been a willing learner and they had formed a firm bond. To lose him was a tremendous tragedy and Philip missed him more than he could say. He had been so proud of him, forging a career in the army, an upstanding, dependable, loyal young man who would have been a huge credit to the country and to the family … especially Ruth.

She had been inconsolable for months. The wedding had helped a bit, although Vicky had dealt with the majority of the preparations, assisted by Lucy. He hoped that moving to Tangles would help even more and he had tried his best to make her feel at home by turning one of the bedrooms into a new studio for her, treating her to new paints and canvases and a whole load of artist's paraphernalia. It wouldn't be the same as the room she had used in Canleigh, which had the most magnificent view of the lake, but it was bigger so she could spread herself out more and would be able to sit and look over the gardens and the woods beyond.

"I think I'll get up and go for a walk ... perhaps do some sketching while I'm out," Ruth said, slowly unwinding herself from Philip and giving him a kiss on the cheek. "You don't mind, do you?"

"No," he yawned. "You go and enjoy yourself. I'm going to stay here for an hour and then I have to get down to the stables. I want to see how Maddy and the new foal are doing."

Ruth smiled. Poor little Maddy had been rescued by the RSPCA last week from a muddy field where she had been on her own for months. The owner had died and no-one had wanted her. They had rung Philip to see if he could take her in and monitor the birth of her foal before the pair were re-homed. Although Ruth had a funny feeling they wouldn't be going anywhere. The mare was exceptionally gentle and trusting and obviously grateful to be near others of her own kind and when recovered from her ordeal, would no doubt make a great addition to the riding school ponies, while her foal would be allowed to grow up with stability and love and probably join her.

"Give her a pat from me, bless her," said Ruth, heading for the shower. "I'll take her a carrot or two later."

Philip grunted, turned over and went back to sleep. Ruth hurried through her ablutions, keen to get outside. It was a gorgeous morning, not a cloud in the sky and lovely and warm. Not hot. She didn't like it really hot. It was too exhausting and made her feel irritable. This was perfect. About 20 degrees. She didn't want breakfast but grabbed a banana in case she became hungry, along with her canvas shoulder bag containing her sketchpad and pencils.

She left the house by the back door and walked down the lane towards Canleigh. She could have turned another way but her footsteps always took her towards her former home. Former home. Sadness engulfed her but she mustn't let it get to her. She had a new beginning now ... at Tangles, and it was a grand old house, full of history, full of love and she would be happy there ... with Philip. Of course she would. It was perfectly natural she would miss Canleigh. She had been there for so many years, loving Charles, coping with him dying, bringing up Stephen and Lucy, having to endure the loss of Stephen and then celebrating Lucy's wedding. Then there was all the time inbetween, in charge of the estate. The estate manager, David Berkeley, had been a marvellous help, as had the solicitors, the accountants, and the staff inside and outside of the Hall. However, although she was relieved to have such a huge responsibility taken off her shoulders, it was going to be exceedingly odd to have so much more free time on her hands. She would help Philip if he needed her to but as much as she liked horses and to ride occasionally, it wasn't a real passion and that side of his business was best left to his staff. She had offered to help with the paperwork but he insisted on doing it as he liked to keep a strict eye on things, although he used the services of Alison Parfitt, the estate office secretary at Canleigh, when he wanted letters and documents to look official.

Still, there was all her charity work which took up quite a bit of time and she could always join things and perhaps they could get away more. Philip wasn't keen on holidays but she would have to persuade him.

433

Perhaps a trip somewhat warm and dry would be good during the winter, which would help his aches and pains. Then there was her art. She hadn't done much since Stephen had died. The passion had left her but now, with the sketchpad in her hand, she felt the old familiar itch to fill it and then go back to her new studio at Tangles and paint. Vicky and Philip had been on at her for years to do an exhibition. It had never appealed to her before but perhaps it was something she should think about now.

She turned a corner in the lane and there before her, was Canleigh in all its glory, bathed in morning sunshine. It looked so beautiful; her heart ached with love for it and for what might have been. Stephen, her darling son, married to the lovely Sarah, playing on the lawns with their children. She could see it, just as if it were real. She could see herself and Philip, sat in chairs beside them, laughing at the children's antics, enjoying a picnic, playing with their toys. Tears rolled down her cheeks and she pulled a tissue from the bag slung over her shoulder. She hadn't been able to go anywhere without a good supply since Stephen had died, so often had she burst into tears since that dreadful day when she had been told what had happened to her son.

A blackbird suddenly burst into song in a tree beside her and she smiled at him through her tears. He sounded so cheerful and full of hope and she should too. She might not have Stephen and his family to cherish at Canleigh but she would have Lucy and Jeremy and, hopefully, their children to look forward to. It wouldn't be the same but they were family and she loved Lucy as if she were her own.

She just wished she didn't have this weird feeling about Jeremy. She didn't know what it was but she had never really liked him, ever since Vicky had brought him home as a child. Suzanne, his sister, had been a much nicer, easier going child and it was a shame she had decided to settle so far away with her family now she was grown up. It would have been lovely to have them closer ... but Jeremy? What was it about him that disturbed her? But whatever it was, s+he just had to put her feelings aside and pray that any misgivings she might have would be unfounded. Lucy loved him, that was what mattered, and time would tell. Ruth signed. Families. What a worry they were.

* * *

In her bedroom at The Beeches, Vicky was thinking the same thing. She was alone, as Alex had disappeared down to Cardiff for a few days to settle in a new club manager. She missed his presence in the bed beside her. That was the only drawback to having businesses all across the country. It meant Alex had to be away so often and she couldn't help feeling insecure when she was without him. He was her rock and had been from the day he discovered her after Barrie and Delia had launched that dreadful attack on her at the flat above the London club in Kensington, following Delia's court case for the murder of Richard and Rocky.

She still had the occasional nightmare, waking up crying and sweating. Alex, knowing what the dream was about, would cuddle and soothe her until she went back to sleep. He was so wonderful, so steadfast, making her feel safer than she had ever done, and even though their work entailed coming across some very beautiful and vivacious women, he had never given her cause for concern. His looks, smiles and touches were all for her and she felt the same. No man, no matter what they said or did, could ever compare with Alex. She was utterly devoted to him and wished they could just concentrate on The Beeches so that he could stay at home. They had enough money in the bank to keep them comfortable for the remainder of their lives and if they sold all the clubs, would be exceedingly rich and then they *could* stay here, near Harrogate, near to the rest of the family at Canleigh and Tangles and be together all the time. It was a tantalising thought and one she hadn't voiced to Alex as he so enjoyed the cut and thrust of having clubs all over the place but his frequent absences were beginning to make her miserable and she would have to say something soon and this was Wednesday and he wouldn't be back until Monday. Six whole days to get through before they were together again.

He was very good and rang her at least twice a day but it wasn't the same, not having him here, especially at night. She hated sleeping alone; terrified someone would enter her room when she was asleep and attack her. Before going to bed she would check the door to their flat at least three times, making sure it was double locked and the chain was in place. She didn't like to tell Alex she also kept a knife under her pillow, removing it with relief on the day he returned.

She had confided how she felt to Ruth and had been touched when she offered Vicky and Katrina rooms at Canleigh when Alex was away. Vicky declined. She couldn't desert The Beeches and upset Katrina's routine. She really had to grow up and not be so silly ... but even though she told herself she was being totally irrational and no-one would want to attack her, she was still nervous and uneasy and never relaxed until Alex was safely back home.

She slid out of bed and looked out of the window, over the beautiful gardens and the countryside beyond. It all looked so peaceful and pleasant. It was hard to believe what it had been like when they took over ... a complete wilderness ... and taken a long time to tame.

She stretched and yawned. She should get a move on. Katrina had to be woken and taken to school and that was another problem. The headmistress of Thistledown Girls was on the warpath because Katrina had been accused of bullying by one of her classmates. Vicky had been invited to pop in and see Mrs. Robins this morning to discuss it, which wasn't something to look forward to and she was cross with her daughter for placing her in such a position but then Katrina was becoming a problem at home as well as at school. She was a bit too bolshy for Vicky's liking; difficult to please and to discipline, dodging out of her homework and actually disappearing into Harrogate two weeks ago, plastered in make-up and coming home drunk ... and she was only thirteen years old, although she appeared much older, with her tall and willowy figure and beautifully chiselled features. With her hair up and a smattering of eyeliner, mascara and lipstick, she could easily be taken for eighteen. Vicky and Alex had grounded her but it only led to more resentment and bad behaviour and Vicky was beginning to wonder how long it could go on.

The disturbing signs that Katrina was mirroring Delia's teenage behaviour were daunting. Delia had been a bit of a bully; at school, with poor Richard and

437

herself and then, of course, Philip. Katrina had an unhealthy interest in Delia, often asking questions about her evil aunt and pouring over old photographs and press coverage which she found on the internet … and that was a real worry. The child was determined to have a successful acting career but Vicky had a sneaky suspicion that, like Delia, she would do anything and everything to attain her dream, no matter who stood in her way or got hurt … and that was simply terrifying.

* * *

Delia was up early too. She had jumped into the shower at seven o'clock and then went for a long walk up to McCullen Top. It was fast becoming her favourite viewing point on the estate. She could see for miles; the mountains, the heather, the forests and the castle. She could sit on a boulder, gaze on the scene with awe, and feel freer than she had ever done. It was a good place to come and think. Usually she was alone but occasionally Brian and Meg joined her as she was within sight of his cottage and if he were around, he would march up the hill and sit beside her. They rarely spoke. Just sat and stared, comfortable in each other's presence, knowing there was no need for unnecessary conversation but this morning he didn't come. The Landrover was missing so he must be out and about too. It made her a little sad. This morning she was going to Edinburgh for a couple of nights with Lucy and Jeremy so unless he came up to the castle before they left, she wouldn't see him again for two days.

Delia grinned. Whatever was the matter with her, missing a man for two days? Brian really did affect her badly. It would have been nice if he could have accompanied them but she knew he was too busy and wouldn't be able to get away. She didn't really have the time either but Lucy and Jeremy would be gone in a few days and she wanted to make their visit to Scotland a memorable one. Lucy, at least.

Delia still couldn't take to Jeremy, even though he had been politeness itself during the last few days and did his best to ingratiate himself with her, offering compliments on the castle, the estate, even her attire but it didn't seem genuine and she didn't trust him ... and wished fervently Lucy hadn't married him. Delia had a very nasty feeling that her daughter was going to regret that decision for a long time to come but there was absolutely nothing to be done about it. Like other parents, she just had to wait it out and be there to pick up the pieces ... and there was going to be many of them, of that Delia was fairly certain.

CHAPTER 33

Matthew was tense with anticipation. Jeremy and Lucy would be back at Canleigh very soon and he wasn't going to leave it long before he made an appearance and welcomed home the happy couple. Oh, he would make it seem casual but he wanted to make sure Jeremy was still up for what they had planned and was going to show his gratitude for the despatching of his mother.

His thoughts turned to their time in Rome and how much he had enjoyed it. Night after night with Jeremy, while dear Lucy slept alone, probably not having a clue as to what her errant husband was up to. It had been as if he and Jeremy were on their own private honeymoon. They left the hotel every night, following dinner with Lucy, then visited bars and casinos, drinking recklessly and throwing money away on roulette and blackjack as if they were multi-millionaires. It had been heady, exciting and crazy, especially after they had partied the night away and then headed back to Matthew's room for rampant sex before Jeremy sneaked back to the suite he shared with Lucy.

She never questioned it, which was a puzzle. If it had been him in her position, he would have gone ballistic but she said nothing. She spent her days visiting all the attractions that Rome had to offer so he didn't set eyes on her until dinner every evening. She would then be quiet, rarely joining in the conversation between him and Jeremy, pick at her food and then make the excuse that she was tired and return to the honeymoon suite straight after pudding, insistent she would prefer coffee upstairs.

Ridiculous woman. She was a real pushover and he didn't care a jot for her feelings. If she was upset because Jeremy spent so much time with him, it was her own fault. She should have been much more vibrant, sparkling and forceful but it was just as well she wasn't. He was going to enjoy sucking every penny out of the silly woman he could and it was all going to start with Jeremy telling Lucy that she had to offer him a rent free cottage on the estate. Then, once he was in situ, he would be able to idle his time away as Jeremy would make sure he wanted for nothing. He would pay all the bills ... until the time came to divorce Lucy. Yes, he was looking forward to the next couple of years and after that, well the world would be their oyster. He and Jeremy, would be able to disappear into the sunset forever and he would never have to entertain the idea of working for a living again. Oh, joy. Oh, bliss. No wonder he couldn't sleep. He sat up, turned on the light and lit a cigarette. He grinned at himself in the mirror opposite the bed. The headmaster at his grammar school had told him more than once he had a good head on his shoulders and would go far. How right that man had been.

* * *

Jeremy was relieved to leave Blairness. Watching Lucy give Delia one last hug was the best part of the week and he jumped into their car eagerly, desperate to be on the road, heading for Canleigh and the commencement of their new life as owners of one of the richest estates in England.

441

"Drive carefully," warned Delia, venturing around to the driver's side of the car and looking at him sternly. "And don't forget to let me know when you arrive."

Jeremy nodded and started the car, impatiently waiting for Lucy to buckle up.

Delia waved; he could see her in the rear view mirror as they drove away, down the long straight drive towards the village and onto the main road. Lucy waved back but as they turned out of the main gates, she burst into tears.

"What the hell is the matter?" he asked abruptly, surprised by her reaction to leaving Blairness.

"I don't really know," Lucy sobbed. "Take no notice of me ... but then, you don't most of the time, do you?"

Jeremy changed gear. The main road was clear of traffic and he could put his foot down. "Now what are you talking about?"

Lucy hadn't wanted a row but suddenly a wave of anger and disappointment engulfed her. "You. You've been a right misery since we came to Blairness. You've hardly spoken to mother and haven't wanted to be with us. Just skulking about on the estate on your own ... it's been nearly as bad as it was in Rome ... when you left me to my own devices because of *darling* Matthew. I'm beginning to wonder why you married me, Jeremy, because you certainly aren't acting as I expected you would."

A coldness crept over him and he turned the heating up. He would be bloody glad to get out of Scotland and back to slightly warmer climes. Yorkshire wasn't known for hot weather but it was certainly preferable to all this mist and damp.

"I don't know what you mean? I just wanted to give you and your mother some space ... you don't see each other very often ... and I like wandering over the countryside on my own. You know I do."

"But you didn't need to make it so obvious you preferred your own company," sniffed Lucy.

"Well, I'm sorry," huffed Jeremy. "I was only trying to be considerate."

"And what about Rome?"

"What about Rome?" he asked, trying to put off answering a little longer because he truly didn't know what he was going to say.

"Leaving me ... spending all your evenings and nights with ... with ... Matthew," she virtually spat out his name.

The road was becoming busier and Jeremy had to concentrate on driving. He played for more time, indicating, changing gear, and passing a trundling tractor.

"You could have come with us ... you didn't have to go to bed early every night," he blustered.

"You didn't have to go out with him. You should have been happy to go to bed early with me ... your wife ... it was our honeymoon, for goodness sake ... and why would I want to go out drinking and gambling? You know that's not my style."

"Well, I'm bloody sorry," Jeremy raised his voice. "I can't help it if you're so damned boring and don't want any fun."

"Fun!" Lucy shrieked. "I don't believe you just said that! How can you be so horrid? *We* should have been having fun together, in the bedroom ... but you've hardly touched me since we've been married. How many times have we had sex? Twice ... and that was at my instigation. What the hell is the matter with you, Jeremy? Are you regretting marrying me ... what have I done ... don't you love me any longer ... was this all just a ghastly mistake?"

Jeremy sighed. "Don't be so melodramatic. Of course I love you and no, it's not been a mistake. It just takes a lot of getting used to ... being married ... and the last three months have been ... well, a bit unusual. We're used to working regular hours ... to suddenly have all this leisure time and money addles one's brain." He tried to smile reassuringly. "I'm sorry, darling. I really am. Once we get back to Canleigh and get into some kind of routine, I'm sure it will all be a lot better."

Lucy sniffed again. "And Matthew? You're not going to spend a lot of time with him, are you? I don't like him, Jeremy. He's got a peculiar air about him and he's very dismissive of me, always putting me down and making me feel inferior."

"No. He'll be down in Oxford and we'll be at Canleigh so I doubt we'll see much of him now."

"What if he keeps coming up to York? Will you go and see him?"

Jeremy sighed. "Only now and again ... he's my ... friend." He had nearly said 'lover' and just stopped himself in time, "and you won't ever have to see him. There. Will that satisfy you?"

Lucy dabbed at her eyes with a tissue and looked in the mirror in her sun visor. She looked a wreck now she had cried and it was too difficult to apply fresh makeup in a moving car.

"I suppose it will have to," she said, slightly mollified. Jeremy was probably right. The honeymoon had been lovely but it hadn't been real life and within hours, they would be commencing their new one, back at Canleigh. Things would be

444

different then and although they had only had sex a couple of times, she had a slight suspicion she might already be pregnant but now was not the time to say anything. She wanted to be sure. She would visit the doctor this week and obtain confirmation. Then there really would be cause for celebration and joy and if Jeremy became more attentive and rarely saw Matthew, there was some hope for their marriage. She settled back into her seat and shut her eyes. She didn't like watching Jeremy drive and they had a long way to go yet.

* * *

Felix saw the car, heading along the drive towards the Hall. He grinned. They were back!

* * *

The car pulled up on the gravel outside the Hall and Lucy smiled. It was good to be home. She had always loved this old place, remembering how when she was a child and visiting with Delia, she would trot up the front steps, pretending she was a princess going to visit her prince in a fairy castle but that prince, Stephen, was dead and Canleigh was all hers. She still couldn't believe it.

Felix had opened the front door and was assembling the staff on the front steps; Pru, the cook, with a big grin on her face, Tina, the housekeeper, looking pale following her nasty bout of flu, and Olive and Molly, the two cleaners.

Felix approached the car and opened Lucy's door.

"Welcome home, Madam," he said with a smile that didn't reach his eyes.

"Thank you," she replied, moving towards the rest of the staff and shaking their hands. With the exception of Felix, they had all been employed at the Hall while she was growing up and they were as good as family, especially Tina who had helped look after her as a child. They all gave her beaming smiles before looking down the steps at Jeremy who was standing by the car with his phone in his hand and a shocked expression on his face.

"Is something the matter, darling?" asked Lucy, concerned to see the blood draining from his face.

"It's my ... my mother ...," he stuttered. "She's dead."

For a second Lucy felt as if she was going to faint. "No! Not Aunty Vicky! She can't be."

"No ... not her ... that woman ... that woman in London. My real mother," he shouted, turning on his heel and heading down towards the lake.

"Jeremy! Wait!" cried Lucy. "I'll come with you."

She ran after him, trying to grab his arm as he strode faster and faster. He shrugged her off and glared at her furiously. "Leave me alone. Just leave me alone. Do you hear?"

Lucy stood still, watching him stride away and disappear down the lakeside path. He was doing it again, shutting her out but this time all of the staff had seen and heard him shout at her. She turned to look at them as they moved indoors while only Felix remained on the steps, his face a mask, and she had no idea what he was thinking, only sensing his amusement and pleasure in her humiliation. She had never liked the man and neither had Granny Ruth. She had always been on the edge of giving him the sack but never did because he was so good at his job. Perhaps now was the time for a change. Lucy walked past him with as much dignity as she could muster, into the Hall and through to the library to pour herself a drink but she realised with a start that she couldn't. Not if she were pregnant.

"Coffee, Felix," she ordered. "And I want it now."

* * *

Jeremy made his way down to the lake and to the nearest bench. He knew he shouldn't have spoken to Lucy like that. It had been unkind and unnecessary, especially in front of all the staff but he was in shock and had to get away from her to think.

He sat down and looked at his phone again ... at the text from Matthew. 'I am pleased to inform you that Beryl has died and will bother you no longer. I look forward to your gratitude. Xx'

God! That last sentence. It could only mean one thing. Matthew must have killed her. That awful, dreadful woman, who laid claim to being his mother. He would never have to see her again or worry about what she might do or say ... or what she expected to receive from him now that he was the husband of a very wealthy woman. He was thankful to have her out of his life but why, oh why, had Matthew killed her? Bloody hell! And how and where had he done it? Had he managed to cover his tracks? Could it be connected to him? The damned woman had come to the wedding ... then there was his own visit to her ... what if someone had seen him? What if someone made the connection? As far as he knew, only Matthew and Lucy had known he had gone down to London to see

447

her. Obviously Matthew wouldn't say anything but Lucy might if the police came asking questions. Bloody, bloody hell!

He rang Matthew's number immediately but there was no answer. He deleted the text in case Lucy happened to check his phone. Not that she ever did but he wasn't going to chance it. He groaned. How was he going to explain to her how he had known his mother had died? He couldn't tell her he had received a text from Matthew. She would think it very strange and start to ask awkward questions. How could he have known? Think, Jeremy, think. He pressed his hand up to his forehead as if to help his brain come with up a solution but he was stumped. Who else would he know in London who would know his mother, his telephone number and text him? Who, who, who?

"Jeremy ... are you okay?" asked Lucy tremulously by his side. "I'm worried about you ..."

He sat stock still, staring broodily out over the lake, which looked stunning with the sun shining above, turning the water a fantastic shade of blue.

"Jeremy ..."

"Yes. Yes. I'm fine. It was the shock. After all, I didn't want her in my life, did I?"

"No. I know you didn't but ..."

"Look, Lucy," he said, desperate to get her away from him before she asked the inevitable question as to who had told him. "Thank you for caring and I'm sorry I reacted the way I did just now but please ... would you mind leaving me alone for now. I just want to be on my own."

She patted his hand. "Okay ... I understand ... I'll be indoors if you want me ... will you ... will you go to the funeral?"

"Funeral?" The sun was in his eyes as he gazed up at her. He hadn't thought that far ahead. "No. No. After all, I didn't really know her, did I?"

She turned and walked slowly back up towards the stable and the Hall, leaving him to sit and mull over his problem. He pressed Matthew's number again but it went straight to voicemail as it had before. Where the hell could he be? What the hell was he doing? How dare he send a message like that and then not be around to explain himself?

He tried Matthew a number of times during the next hour but with the same result. Throwing caution to the winds, he walked back to the Hall. The day was warm, far warmer than Scotland and he was desperately thirsty and growing hungry. His bodily needs had to be seen to and he would just have to try to dodge Lucy as best he could, as the only solution he could think of was to say that a neighbour or the police had found his number from when he had paid her a visit a few months ago and had rung him. That was it! But then they would have told him how she died ... and he didn't know. Lucy would ask. Oh, God. Blast Matthew!

He reached the stables, puffing a little as the climb up from the lake was steep. He stopped to catch his breath and tried Matthew again, astonished when he answered.

"Matthew, where the bloody hell have you been?" he hissed. "And what the hell have you done?"

"Just as you asked, darling. You wanted the old slag gone ... that's what you told me at your wedding when she turned up unexpectedly in that dreadful outfit. Get rid of her, you said. Well, I did. I went down to London two days ago but didn't have to do much. The silly bitch was trying to get away from me

449

and tripped. She banged her head on the cooker and knocked herself out. There was blood everywhere."

"So it was an accident then?"

"Well, yes and no."

"I think you better expand on that."

"She was still breathing, so I finished her off with a cushion … held it over her face."

"Oh, Christ! You *did* murder her! You'll go down for it … and I might get dragged into it too."

"Don't panic. The police aren't going to find out, are they? Why should they? She obviously had punters all the time, in and out … no pun intended," he laughed. "It could have been any one of them."

"Did you go in the day or at night?"

"Late."

"And no-one was there apart from her?"

"No … and if there had have been, I had a good excuse for visiting her all lined up … a message from you. Don't worry. No-one saw me. I made sure of it … and I didn't touch anything, apart from the cushion, and as I was wearing gloves, they won't find my fingerprints."

"Christ!"

"What? What's the matter? I've done you a huge favour, darling … and don't you forget it."

"And what's that supposed to mean?"

"Just that and it goes to show how devoted I am and how far I will go for you … so … when are you free now you are back at Canleigh? I can come up to York at the weekend … or you can invite me to your new home. After all, we have to scout around and see what cottage would be best for me to reside in for the next couple of years."

Jeremy wanted to be sick. Suddenly the thought of being with Matthew wasn't so enticing. There would always be his mother's death between them now and the hint from Matthew that Jeremy was beholden to him. The desire he had felt for Matthew began to fade.

"Jeremy?"

"Yes. Yes. I'm still here. I'll see. I think Lucy is having the family over at the weekend ... being our first at Canleigh as husband and wife. I don't think I will be available or can get away."

"And how is the delicious Lucy? Don't forget, you have to keep her sweet for a good long while yet."

"She's fine. Glad to be home, I think. Anyhow, Mathew, I must go. I can hear her coming down the path. I'll ring you."

He snapped his mobile shut quickly and thrust it into his pocket. Lucy wasn't coming but he had to find an excuse to end the conversation so he could think. He walked slowly towards the Hall, up to the south terrace, through the French windows into the library, poured a large amount of brandy into a glass, drank the lot in one go, and went back outside, where he sunk down on one of the loungers and shut his eyes against the glaring sun.

At least he knew what had occurred now and how his mother had died so his idea of the police contacting him would cover it if Lucy asked. Relief flooded over him but he was still sickened by Matthew. It was the glee in his voice that he had helped someone to die. It was the way he had laughed. Christ. Had he bitten off more than he could chew getting involved with Matthew ... and his schemes for getting his hands on Lucy's money?

* * *

Felix followed Jeremy back to the Hall. He had been in the stables, checking he hadn't left his mobile phone in the Rolls Royce when he had been cleaning the car the day before. He hadn't seen it for over twenty-four hours and had searched the Hall high and low but without success. The only other place he could think of was the car. He could remember putting it on the driver's seat when he had started hosing the car down as he didn't want it to get wet but couldn't remember picking it up when he had finished later.

He heard Jeremy on the phone and from what he said and the way he was talking, it could only have been Matthew with whom he was conversing. Felix stood silently behind the big car, listening attentively to the conversation and liked what he heard. Something was badly up and it sounded as if it had something to do with Jeremy's so-called mother, who he had found out just a short while ago, had died. Felix couldn't hear what Matthew was relaying but from Jeremy's questions and replies, it appeared he could have been responsible and could implicate Jeremy. Interesting, very interesting. Felix grinned to himself as he watched Jeremy return to the Hall and cross the parterre to the south terrace and enter the library. Not wanting Jeremy to know he had been overheard, he took a detour around to the back entrance to the Hall, quite forgetting he had been down to the stables to look for his mobile. He had other things on his mind.

CHAPTER 34

JANUARY 1997

Lucy was uncomfortable. Whichever way she turned in bed, her bump got in the way. She was becoming totally exhausted by lack of sleep, her ankles were swollen, she seemed to have permanent heartburn, had no energy to do very much at all, and began to long for the day she could hold her child in her arms.

Granny Ruth and Aunt Vicky, both of whom had been over the moon that she was expecting her first baby, had been great, taking turns to visit and keep her company during the day when Jeremy was at college. He had enrolled for a course in horticulture at Askham Bryan College and commenced his studies in September, which kept him occupied for most of the week. He had some impressive ideas for re-structuring Canleigh gardens and sometimes in the evenings, he would haul out his plans and pour over them with her. It gave her enormous pleasure to see that his final choice of career provided him with such satisfaction.

Their marriage had improved since returning to Canleigh. He made a gigantic effort to make her happy, although sex was a very rare occurrence. The image in her mind of him having sex with Matthew, whether he actually had or not, turned her off, even when he did make half-hearted overtures, and when she received confirmation from her doctor that she was pregnant, it gave her the perfect excuse to be left alone. Jeremy had been more than happy not to have to perform his marital duties but did become far more attentive, making sure she had everything she wanted. He even took her for little trips in the car in the evenings when he had no assignments to complete, before the winter set in, when they would find a country pub and enjoy a drink or two, albeit non-alcoholic as he was driving and she was pregnant.

They grew a little closer, both looking forward to the impending arrival of their first child. Lucy was particularly happy that Jeremy, as far as she knew, had only seen Matthew once, a week after they had arrived home from visiting her mother after the honeymoon but he hadn't stayed away all night. He had been home by midnight, which was unusual. He had also been in a foul mood the following day but she hadn't said anything, just waited for it to pass and kept out of his way. Matthew hadn't been mentioned since and for that, she was glad. Jeremy was obviously settling down at Canleigh and the world was beginning to look rosy ... at least it would when she finally delivered this baby.

* * *

Jeremy was far happier and more content than he could ever have imagined. He and Lucy rubbed along reasonably well and were both excited at the impending arrival of the baby and he was actually pleased and looked forward eagerly to helping care for his newborn.

He had taken the news that he was to be a father with surprise, considering they had only 'done' it a couple of times. He knew it only took one sexual act but it was still a shock ... but a good one, and it made the perfect excuse not to have sex with his wife. It also gave him the advantage of having his own room so he didn't disturb her, especially as he had to be up early to attend Askham Bryan every weekday.

He was thoroughly enjoying his course, couldn't understand why he hadn't thought of it before and had wasted so much time on reading law in Oxford, and then struggled with hospitality. However, when he thought about it, there had been no opportunity in his earlier life to gain an interest in his newly acquired passion. They had lived in the flat above the club in Kensington for years, with no garden, and although The Beeches had big lawns and flowerbeds, Vicky and Alex employed a gardening contractor to tidy it up every week and the most Jeremy had done was sit on a bench and admire it.

It wasn't until he had paid a visit to Canleigh a year or so ago and started a conversation with Roy Fitzgerald, the head gardener, and listened to his enthusiasm for his chosen career, that Jeremy began to take an interest. Roy was a mine of fascinating information. He knew all the Latin names, the history and how to care for all the fabulous plants and trees growing at Canleigh and was more than willing to instil his formidable knowledge in others. The more Jeremy talked to Roy, the more he was attracted to a career in horticulture and where better to experiment than Canleigh and once he knew what he was doing, there was more than enough land for him to potter around and re-landscape. Lucy was quite happy to indulge him, provided the precious rose garden was left untouched.

So, his life was a busy one. Up early to drive to Askham Bryan every day, assignments to do in the evenings, chatter to Lucy over dinner and then fall into bed, and do it all again the next day … and he loved it. He loved Canleigh. He loved his life … and didn't miss Matthew one little bit.

That surprised him too. He had fallen so heavily in love with Matthew but once he had admitted to killing Jeremy's mother, the passion died instantly and he wanted nothing more to do with him. Jeremy arranged to meet him once more, a few days after he and Lucy had returned from honeymoon, so that he could tell Matthew to his face that it was all over.

They had met at the hotel in York, as usual. Matthew had wanted to come openly to Canleigh but Jeremy had been adamant they meet in York.

"God, I've missed you," cooed Matthew as soon as Jeremy crept into his room, glancing down the hallway to make sure no-one had seen him.

Jeremy shut the door behind him and stood looking at Matthew, reclining on the bed wearing a look of expectation on his face and little else.

"Well," said Matthew. "Come on darling, I've been waiting."

"Sorry but it's not going to happen."

Matthew's look became one of surprise and his voice harder. "Oh no! Don't tell me the delightful Lucy has got to you."

"It's nothing to do with Lucy, although yes. I do feel an obligation to her now that we are going to have a child."

Matthew's eyes narrowed. "Oh. A child. That will be it, then. You are planning on playing happy families … and what about me? What about all the promises you made? All the plans we had. Are you chickening out now you have your little wifey pregnant?"

456

"Lucy has nothing to do with it."

"Oh," said Matthew, sitting upright, lighting a cigarette, and taking a deep puff. He pulled the sheet up to his chest and stared hard at Jeremy. "So if it's not Lucy, what the hell is it?"

"You. I'm sorry but I just can't do this any longer."

"But why? What have I done?"

"You killed my mother."

"Bloody hell! You wanted me to! You told me to … at your wedding. You told me to deal with her and I did!"

Jeremy sat on the bed and held his head in his hands. "I didn't tell you to kill her … I never said that. I would *never* have said that. I just wanted you to talk to her … get her to leave me alone … bribe her if necessary … I don't suppose she would have wanted much … and Lucy has millions and wouldn't have missed it … but not this … not murder."

Matthew didn't look at him as he blew smoke rings at the lampshade above his head. "I didn't go there with the intention of killing her. I told you it was an accident … she fell and hit her head."

Jeremy turned to face him, his face full of anguish. "Yes, but you finished her off! You didn't have to put a cushion over her face."

"Oh, yes I did. If she had survived, she would have told the police I had tried to kill her, that she was trying to get away from me and if she had, that wouldn't have looked too good for you either. Everyone saw me arguing with her at your wedding. She stood out like a sore thumb. Everyone must have noticed her. If it had come out that I had been in her house at the time of her death, it would have been curtains for both of us. I had to do it. I had no choice. Come on Jer, see sense. You know I'm right."

"Okay," sighed Jeremy. "I suppose you probably are but even so, I think we should stay away from each other for the foreseeable ... just in case."

"Why?"

"Because I need to get my head around it ... because I am busy ... because I have a child coming ... because I'm not in love you any more ... there ... I've said it now."

"Wow."

Jeremy looked at him sadly. "I'm sorry ... I really am but it's over. Please ... please don't contact me again."

He stood up and walked over to the door as Matthew dropped his cigarette into the ashtray beside the bed and leapt across the room. He grabbed Jeremy's arm and turned him around to face him.

"You can't do this to me. You can't. I love you, Jer. You know I do. That's why I killed her. I wanted to please you ... make you happy ... make you secure, to know that she could never hurt you again."

Jeremy shrugged off Matthew's hand and opened the door, striding down the corridor towards the fire exit. It was when he was on his way down the back stairs that he realised Matthew was behind him, doing up his dressing gown, running to keep up.

"Jer. Wait. Please, Jer. We need to talk about this."

Jeremy reached the door to the car park and flung it open, just as Matthew came up behind him and almost threw him against the outer wall. His head came down and his lips pushed hard against Jeremy's. "You'll not do this to me, Jer. You are mine, do you hear. You will always be mine ... and I will be coming for you. When it's time, I will be there and you will divorce Lucy and we will be together ... for ever ... do you hear me?"

Jeremy didn't see Vicky, standing by her car, in the dim lights of the car park, watching them with horror written all over her face as she recognised the two of them, appearing to be kissing passionately. She dived into her car and drove hurriedly onto the main road. She didn't see Jeremy pull his arm back and punch Matthew on the jaw, sending him flying to the ground and she didn't see Jeremy heading towards his car as Matthew writhed around in agony. All she knew was that her son, her adopted son, was definitely gay ... and what the hell would that do to Lucy's marriage? Vicky was a very worried woman.

* * *

"It's good to see Jeremy buckling down at Canleigh," said Alex, over dinner in their apartment at The Beeches. "I never did think he was suited for hospitality. He's much better off in the fresh air fiddling with his plants."

Vicky laughed. "You do have a nice turn of phrase."

"Well, it's true. He was like a fish out of water here but he just looks so right in dungarees and wellies, digging up Canleigh soil ..., and he seems to be so much healthier. He was always so pale and wan. He's broadening out too. Looks like a real man."

'A real man'. Vicky looked up at her husband who was pouring them both another glass of wine. "What do you mean, a real man?"

Alex put down the bottle and glanced at her. "What I say. He's always appeared so ... I hate to say it, but effeminate ... and I did wonder if he was gay ... but then he married Lucy so that put that idea out of my head."

"I'm not that sure," Vicky uttered quietly, fiddling with her napkin. "I saw them, you know."

"Who?"

"Jeremy ... and ... and Matthew. Remember ... I attended that hospitality conference in York, just after Lucy and Jeremy returned from honeymoon. When I left the hotel, I saw them ... Jeremy and Matthew ... in the car park. They had slipped out of a side door and were hugging each other."

Alex grinned. "Well, men do hug occasionally. It doesn't mean they are gay."

"It didn't stop there."

"Oh?"

"They kissed. I saw them, Alex. It was disgusting. It made me feel sick. Our Jeremy, pressed up against a wall, being kissed by that ... that man."

Alex sat up and stared at her. "Oh Christ!"

Vicky, feeling relieved now she had told him, picked up her wine glass and took a large sip. "I don't know how I've managed to stop myself saying something. I was about to but then we got the news that Lucy was pregnant and I hoped it was all a mistake and what I saw would never happen again."

"Blimey." Alex put his glass to his mouth but didn't drink. This put a whole new light on things. "Do you know if they've met again?"

"No ... but then, how would I? We don't keep tabs on him now. He's free to do as he wants and I don't think Lucy will stop him. She's a lovely girl but she's not exactly dominant. Jeremy could walk all over her if he wanted to. He's always had a petulant streak about him ... and after seeing that awful woman,"

460

Vicky shuddered, remembering the scene at the wedding, "we now know what his mother was like … and he has her genes."

"Um. She was pretty ghastly. It was so embarrassing for Jeremy, her turning up like that … and it was patently obvious she only wanted to know him because of who he was marrying and what he will be worth."

"Well, at least she's out of the picture now," sighed Vicky.

"Funny old business, that. The police couldn't make up their minds whether it was purely an accident or murder … didn't the coroner return an open verdict?"

"I believe so. Ruth mentioned it. She saw a piece in the London Standard when she was down for a weekend."

"How terribly sad … whatever happened to the woman. Anyhow, it's the living who are our priority and if your suspicions are correct and although everything at Canleigh seems reasonably okay at the moment, I do think we should keep an eye on Jeremy … I would hate to see Lucy badly hurt by him, especially now she's about to have their child.

Vicky put her knife and fork together, leaving a large amount of salad and salmon untouched. Her appetite had suddenly deserted her. If Alex was concerned, then she should be too. The niggling sense of unease she had endured since seeing Jeremy and that … that friend of his, was growing by the second and she hoped, with all of her heart, that Jeremy had finally seen sense and where his future should be … with his wife and child.

* * *

Felix was happy. It was much nicer working at Canleigh now Ruth and Philip Kershaw had departed for Tangles. Lucy had no idea how to be firm with staff. He could run rings around her, lying through his teeth more often than not when she queried any of his tasks, or asking where he had been when he had slipped off for a few quiet moments on his own, and as for Jeremy ... well, he was putty in his hands.

Felix had worked hard on getting Jeremy to trust and like him. He had been subservient, sycophancy being second nature to him, and Jeremy had lapped it up, having someone look up to him for once. Felix had made Jeremy feel important ... a person of consequence and standing and Jeremy was beginning to show his gratitude. In little ways at first and then, slowly, the gifts became bigger and more expensive. It had started with a couple of tickets to the theatre ... Jeremy had no idea Felix hadn't anyone to go with and that he went alone. Then there was a new television for his room, then the latest mobile phone, followed by a laptop.

Felix was thrilled. His plan was working, it had been far easier than he thought, but then he hadn't expected Matthew to be out of the way. Jeremy only left the estate to go to Askham Bryan these days. The visits to York ceased months ago, just after his wedding. So, Felix could only assume that the affair with Matthew was over and the path was clear for him.

Ruth and Lady Victoria still turned up frequently, especially since Lucy had announced she was pregnant. They came and fussed and petted her, which made his skin crawl. He wasn't keen on babies and wasn't looking forward to this one making an appearance. However, Tina would be taking on more duties once it was born. Since her housekeeping only entailed a few hours every day, she had plenty more in which to help with the child in the nursery and as that was a part of the house Felix had no reason to visit, hopefully, he wouldn't have to see very much of the new arrival.

So, all in all, Felix was content, working on Jeremy, gaining his trust, gaining his love. He reckoned it wouldn't be long before they were in bed together. Smiles of affection had been exchanged, the odd touch on the shoulder, the arm, the hand. It was going to happen, it wouldn't be long now ..., and then he really would have Jeremy under his thumb.

As he prepared the dining room table for dinner, he smiled. His bank balance was looking healthy, thanks to Lady Delia's deposits and he was about to embark on an affair with Jeremy. Oh, yes. He was a very happy bunny!

* * *

Matthew was cross, bored and broke. The bookshop was doing badly. He had barely taken enough this month to pay the rent on his flat and he was beginning to grow concerned that he wouldn't be able to cover it at all next month. The blasted Inland Revenue had been after him for overdue tax and once he had settled that, along with their fine for late payment, he barely had enough to buy food. He had tried tapping up his parents but they were skint too.

"I'm sorry, my boy," puffed his elderly, sick father, from his tatty chair with threadbare arms, when Matthew had paid them a visit last week, "but since I've been ill, your mother and I have had a real struggle to survive. If it wasn't for our Social Security benefits, I don't know how we would manage."

His parents had run a successful grocery store ever since Matthew could remember; the family had never wanted for anything and it had paid for Matthew's time at university. Then, a couple of years ago, his father had begun to have heart problems, along with the onset of Parkinson's disease, and the shop had to be sold as he couldn't work and Matthew's mother was placed firmly in the role of his carer. The proceeds from the shop paid off the mortgage on their house and for a new car but now they were entirely reliant on the State to keep them, with nothing spare to give to Matthew.

"But ... but there must be something ... surely you have savings?" Matthew blustered.

His father shook his head. "No, son. Don't forget we spent a considerable amount getting you through University ... what with your fees, accommodation and living expenses, not to mention books. There was always something you needed."

"Oh, hell!"

"Please don't swear, Matthew. We didn't pay for you to have a decent education just to hear you use foul language."

Matthew banged out of the house and drove furiously back to Oxford, having to stop for petrol on the way and appalled to discover he didn't have enough in his wallet to pay for it. He had to rummage beneath the seats and in the glove compartment, trying to find the ten-pound note he knew he had shoved in there for emergencies. After a few moments of panic, thinking he must have spent it another time, even though he couldn't remember when, he found it, buried between two old Rolling Stones cassette tapes. It paid for his return to Oxford but the fuel needle on the dashboard was pointing virtually at zero when he pulled up outside his flat. The car wouldn't be going anywhere in the near future.

He went indoors and headed for the drinks cabinet. There wasn't much there to console him either. He'd drunk all his whisky and the decent wine and all that was left was vodka, which he wasn't keen on but he was desperate, poured a large amount in a glass, and topped it up with lemonade. He downed it in one ... then poured another, ripped off his tie, threw himself on the sofa and pulled out his mobile phone. It hadn't much credit. Oh, God! What was he going to do? Things were becoming pretty dire now. Blast the Inland Revenue! Blast the people who didn't come to buy books in his shop! Blast his father for being ill and not being able to bail him out! Blast, blast, blast!

He had no option. He would have to ring Jeremy.

CHAPTER 35

FEBRUARY 1997

It happened two weeks later. Lucy had gone to bed early, feeling particularly exhausted, and her body as heavy as lead now she only had another couple of weeks to go. She was irritable and emotional, desperate to get the coming ordeal over with and hold her baby in her arms.

Jeremy, tired from another hectic day at college, dozed in the library over coffee after dinner. He hadn't intended to fall asleep but the fire was crackling in the grate, the drapes were drawn and the sofa was comfortable. He took off his slippers, lay back to read the paper and within minutes was enjoying a wonderful dream as he wandered around the most beautiful garden he had ever seen.

It was Felix who woke him at 11.30 p.m., touching his shoulder and speaking to him softly.

"Sir. It's getting late and you know you like to be in bed early in the week."

Jeremy shook himself awake and smiled up at the concerned face of the butler. "Thank you, Felix. You're right. I should be in bed. I've had a hard day today and tomorrow isn't going to be much better. I'll go up now. I wonder … would you mind bringing me some hot chocolate, please. Now I've woken up, I'll probably find it difficult to get back to sleep and that will certainly help."

"Very good, Sir. I'll be up with it in a few minutes."

Jeremy left the library and went upstairs. He had showered before dinner so he only had to undress, put his pyjamas on and clean his teeth. It didn't take long and he was in bed, wondering whether or not to have a look at his latest gardening magazine when Felix knocked on the door and entered with a silver tray on which sat the mug of steaming hot chocolate.

The butler set it down on the bedside table and looked down at Jeremy. "Will there be any thing else, Sir?"

Jeremy stared at him and gulped. It was the way the man was actually ogling him, the wry smile on his face, the knowing look. Jeremy's knees went weak and he felt a rising excitement in his stomach. He couldn't help himself. He patted the empty space beside him on the bed.

"You look as if you are in dire need of a rest, Felix. Why don't you join me?"

* * *

They were in the throes of passion. Felix was doing things to Jeremy, Matthew hadn't. There was no love between them but the sex, God it was wonderful. Jeremy was in seventh heaven. Where the hell had Felix learned to do what he did? It was blissful. Jeremy hadn't experienced such pleasure for a very long time and the joy of it was that he didn't have to go anywhere to meet a lover. He would have him here now, under his very roof, to do what he liked with, when he liked. He had been happy before tonight but now he was ecstatic. He had it all. He really had it all.

467

Felix had thrown the covers off the bed and they both lay naked, devouring each other's bodies in the soft glow from the bedside lamp. They were both panting and groaning as they mated, Jeremy unable to prevent himself from crying out with delight. "God, Felix. Go for it!" he yelled, his eyes shut tight so he could concentrate wholly on what Felix was doing to him.

The bedroom door opened. Jeremy, with his eyes closed, didn't notice but Felix did and grinned at Lucy widely, continuing to bugger her husband as she stood, horrified, on the threshold, cradling the huge bulge in her stomach protectively with her hands.

"You bastard!" she screamed. "You bloody awful bastard!"

Jeremy's eyes flew open as Felix slid off his back and Lucy disappeared rapidly into the corridor, running as fast as she could away from the dreadful scene she had just interrupted. She didn't know where she was going. She only knew she had to get away from both of them. She was crying uncontrollably, taking in huge great gulps of air, making her heave and sway. She was wearing a long floaty negligee, which was loose and comfortable. It swirled around her legs as she stumbled towards the stairs. She wanted Granny Ruth. She would know what to do. She had to get to her.

She could hear Jeremy coming after her, shouting her name, calling for her to stop. She reached the top of the stairs. She knew the car was just outside the front door. She had left it there earlier and Felix hadn't put it away. She would drive over to Tangles. She just had to get to Granny Ruth … and now … before Jeremy caught up with her. She didn't want to hear his excuses and his lies. She hated him. She

468

hated him more than anything. It had been bad enough in Rome, with Matthew, but this … with the butler … that vile little man. Ruth had expressed she was uneasy about him more than once. She had been right. He would have to go. She couldn't bear him to remain in the house another day but for now, she had to get to Granny Ruth. She had to. She wouldn't feel safe until she was with her. She didn't want to stay another minute at the Hall with only those two perverts for company.

Gasping and crying, she reached the top of the stairs. Jeremy, followed by Felix was pounding after her. She turned to see them bearing down on her, Jeremy looking aghast and Felix still with that nasty grin. She turned, looked down the stairs, and felt dizzy. Her baby was kicking, obviously unhappy at the stress she was under. She placed her foot on the first stair and everything suddenly went black as she tripped on her negligee and flew down the stairs, the garment floating around her body gracefully as she fell onto the hard tiled floor below.

* * *

Lucy was in a bad way. She was unconscious, had a dislocated shoulder, a badly bruised neck, and two damaged ribs … and her waters had broken.

Jeremy, belting down the stairs after her was horrified, rushing to the phone in the entrance hall to call for an ambulance, terrified Lucy was going to die but also scared that if she didn't, she was going to blame him if she lost the child. Felix fetched him some clothes while he stayed with Lucy, after dashing into the library for a cushion to put under her head and a blanket to cover her. He felt the tears run down

469

his cheeks as he rung Ruth straight after he had called for an ambulance.

"It's Lucy," he sobbed. "She's fallen downstairs. Ruth ... I don't know what to do ... the baby is coming ... the ambulance is on its way but it might not get here in time."

"I'm on my way," Ruth gasped and slammed the phone down.

Jeremy scrambled into the clothes Felix presented him with, not taking his eyes off Lucy, while Felix, who had also dressed in a hurry, stood by the front door, waiting for the ambulance. He didn't know whether to be pleased or worried. If the blasted woman came round and remembered what she had seen, she could make it her business to get rid of him as soon as she recovered. Just as things were going his way. He turned to stare at her. Jeremy was kneeling by her head, holding her hand, and sobbing pitifully, telling her how sorry he was. Shit! Shit, shit, shit!

The ambulance roared down the drive, Ruth in hot pursuit in her car. Philip had wanted to accompany her but it took too long for him to get dressed so he had stayed at Tangles, desperately concerned about Lucy and insisting Ruth contact him as soon as she had any news.

"I don't know if anyone has told Vicky and Alex," she had yelled at him as she dashed outside to get into her car. "Can you ring them, please, darling."

An hour later, Lucy was in surgery, undergoing a caesarean section as her injuries prevented an attempt at a normal birth. She had come round in the ambulance, her large eyes full of fear for her unborn child and for some reason, and Ruth couldn't figure out why, had ignored Jeremy and pushed his hand away. She wanted Ruth by her side so she had to

470

change places with Jeremy. Lucy held onto Ruth's hand while the ambulance rushed through the deserted streets of Leeds. It was nearly 1.00 a.m. in the morning on a Wednesday and it was raining, making it possible for the ambulance to steam ahead without worrying about drunken hoards of people falling out of nightclubs and bars as they did at weekends.

Selena Seymour was born soon afterwards, a healthy balling infant ... apart from the fact that she had Downs syndrome. Ruth and Jeremy had waited outside the theatre while the operation took place and were ushered into a side room as soon as it was over.

"The baby is fine," said the female doctor who had delivered Selena. "She's suffered no lasting damage from what we can tell from the fall downstairs. However ..."

"Yes?" said Ruth and Jeremy simultaneously.

"You are aware that the baby has Downs?"

"No," whispered Jeremy, sinking onto a nearby chair.

"Didn't Mrs. Seymour have the test?" the doctor asked, with surprise.

"No. She wouldn't. She said that whatever happened she was going to love this baby whether it had problems or not," said Jeremy, shaking his head in disbelief. "But she ... we ... never thought it would."

"Can we see Lucy ... and the baby?" asked Ruth.

"Mrs. Seymour is having her injuries seen to so not just yet but as soon as the checks on the baby are complete, a nurse will bring her out to you."

The doctor patted Jeremy's shoulder, smiled sorrowfully at Ruth, and left them to see to another patient.

471

Jeremy and Ruth sat, side by side, silently waiting to see the child. There was nothing to say, just a terrible sadness for the baby and for Lucy ... for them all, although Ruth was still puzzled as to why Lucy hadn't wanted Jeremy by her side in the ambulance. She hadn't thought about it much at the time, in the panic of the situation but now she did. Lucy and Jeremy's marriage had seemed to be fine so why wouldn't she have wanted him next to her, holding her hand and reassuring her?

She looked at Jeremy. He was cracking his knuckles repeatedly. It was driving her mad. "What made Lucy fall downstairs? She's always so careful ... especially since she's been pregnant."

Jeremy cracked his knuckles again, making Ruth want to hit him. He was staring at the floor, seemingly deaf to her question.

"Jeremy!" Her voice was rising, "why did Lucy fall downstairs? You must know."

He took a deep breath, knowing he had to answer her question otherwise she would assume, quite rightly, something untoward had happened.

"I don't really know," he said quietly. "She was wearing that long negligee she is so fond of. She must have tripped over that."

Ruth didn't know whether to believe him or not. Her heart was telling her to but her head ... that was another matter. Lucy hadn't wanted Jeremy anywhere near her in the ambulance and that was very, very odd. However, Ruth's anxieties were dismissed when a smiling nurse pushed open the door, carrying little Selena in her arms, wrapped up in a cream blanket.

Jeremy took her. He didn't know what to say or to think. This was his child ... his little girl ... but she wasn't perfect. She was going to have problems. She might be bullied. She might not live to old age. He had very little experience of children, let alone those who had very real problems, like this one. He racked his brains to remember what he knew about Downs but it was virtually nothing.

"She's absolutely beautiful," whispered Ruth, running a finger down the baby's cheek. "Little Selena. Welcome to the family."

Jeremy, with a sudden movement, thrust the baby at Ruth and dashed out of the room. He couldn't bear it. He was so ashamed. It was all his fault. He was gay. He had no right to have a perfect child. It was justice. God had punished him and he deserved it.

Shocked by Jeremy's reaction, Ruth sat down, holding the baby tightly, feeling a rush of deep love for her. She was so beautiful. A true little angel for Canleigh. Even so, Ruth felt a terrible sadness for her and for Lucy, who would be devastated ... and as for Jeremy ... she had no idea what to think about his appalling behaviour.

An hour later, Vicky and Alex dashed into the hospital and hurried up to the maternity wing to find Ruth waiting for Lucy in the private room provided for her and watching over Selena who was in a cot beside the bed.

"Where's Lucy?" asked a breathless Vicky. "Is she okay?"

"Yes. She has some nasty injuries which will take a while to recover from but nothing life threatening. She'll be brought in here as soon as they have seen to her."

"And this little one," cooed Vicky, moving to the cot and staring down at the child. "Oh! Oh, ... I had no idea. Lucy and Jeremy ... they never told me."

"They didn't know. Lucy didn't have the test."

Vicky's eyes filled with tears as Alex moved to her side and put an arm around her shoulders. "That's such a terrible shame ... but she's lovely. Look at her little fingers, her lovely skin and her hair ... she has lots of it. She's so pretty."

Ruth smiled. "Yes, she is ... and she has the most beautiful big blue eyes. Just wait until she wakes up."

At that moment, the door was pushed open and Lucy was wheeled in. She was awake but drowsy and as the staff tucked her up in bed, she gave a vague smile to Ruth then drifted off again.

"She should sleep for now. She's had a lot of stuff pumped into her one way and another," explained the staff nurse. "But she will be fine. Just let her sleep. We'll leave the baby with you now but if she wakes, let us know and we'll take her down to the nursery to be fed and changed."

"Where's Jeremy?" asked Alex as soon as the nursing staff had left.

"I have no idea," replied Ruth with a grimace. "He held Selena and then literally bolted."

"Oh, no! Don't tell me he's rejected her," said Vicky with shock.

Ruth shrugged. "I don't know. I really don't. I certainly hope not as Lucy and little Selena are going to need all the support they can get ... especially from Jeremy. I hope he's not going to let them down."

* * *

Jeremy had dashed out of the hospital and hailed the first taxi he saw. He couldn't stay a moment longer, not with Ruth watching him and with the impending arrival of Vicky and Alex. He felt so ashamed, so cross with himself for giving Lucy such a

474

shock, fornicating with Matthew, and he felt so sorry for the baby. The poor little baby.

The taxi drew up outside Canleigh Hall, Jeremy threw some notes at the driver and ran up the steps and through the front door. Felix wasn't around and for that he was thankful. He wanted to be alone. He strode through to the library and poured a huge glass of neat brandy. The room was cold. The fire was out. He shivered uncontrollably, letting the brandy gradually do its job of warming him up and calming his nerves. He poured another and with the glass in his hand, went upstairs to his room and turned on the light.

Felix had made the bed and there was no sign anything untoward had happened in this room only hours before. He closed the door, sat on the bed and finished the brandy. He was beginning to feel tiddly now, relaxed and mellow. The shock of the night's events was wearing off and the guilt was beginning to fade. It would be all right. Lucy was going to be fine. As soon as he could talk to her alone, he would apologise profusely. They would make it up. Of course they would. They were a family ... a proper family now and he and Lucy would love the child and give it everything it needed. Everything would be okay. It would. He was determined about that.

A soft knock on the door made him look up. Felix, in just his underpants, stood looking at him. "Can I make you feel better, Jeremy?" he said, moving towards the bed. "I can make all your problems go away, you know I can. Just let me help you ... let me soothe you ... you know you want me to."

Jeremy closed his eyes as Felix stood beside him and began to massage his shoulders. It felt so good. He could feel all the tension in his body flowing away

475

and then it stopped and he opened his eyes. Felix had pulled off his underpants and was ready for action.

CHAPTER 36

"I don't want to go home," announced Lucy, two days later. "Could I ... please could I come and stay with you for a while?"

Ruth was sitting beside Lucy's bed in the private room at the hospital, cuddling Selena after giving her a feed and changing her nappy. Lucy was finding it hard to hold her baby and breastfeed due to her painful ribs, neck and shoulder and had reluctantly agreed for Selena to be fed on formula.

She looked up in surprise. "Of course you can ... but why, darling? I thought you would want to be at home with Jeremy?"

"No! ... no," she repeated a little less emphatically when Ruth's look of surprise turned to shock. "It's just ... just that I shall be in that great big house, stuck in the bedroom for a while, and Jeremy will be occupied at college and in the grounds and ... and I'm a little frightened about taking full responsibility of Selena ..."

"But Tina will be there to look after you both ... and you know how dependable she is."

"Yes, I know but she won't be there at night and Jeremy is always so tired when he gets home and won't want to be bothered by Selena ... please Granny Ruth. Please can I come and stay with you ... just until I feel stronger?"

Ruth laid Selena in her cot beside the bed. The child, clean and replete, was nodding off and within minutes would probably be sound asleep. Ruth turned to Lucy. "You will be very welcome, you know that

477

..., and you can stay as long as you like ... but what about Jeremy ... won't he be upset? Won't he want you home?"

Lucy sighed, tears not far away. She wanted so badly to tell Ruth what had happened but she couldn't. She didn't want to talk about the horror of what she had seen in Jeremy's room, of her fear as she had run down the corridor trying to get away from her husband and his lover, the terror when she had fallen down the stairs. It was like some horrible dream. She wished it was but knew perfectly well it wasn't. She had the injuries to prove it, leaving her so weak and vulnerable. She just wanted to feel safe and protected and returning to Canleigh with Jeremy and Felix in situ, while feeling so fragile, was an alarming prospect. No. She had to stay away until she felt stronger and able to deal with the situation. Because deal with it, she would have to. Felix would be dismissed immediately she stepped foot back inside Canleigh ... in fact, as soon as she saw Jeremy again, she would tell him that Felix had to go before she returned.

Filing for divorce had also crossed her mind but the scandal would be terrible. She was a prominent figure now she owned Canleigh and was considerably wealthy and the tabloids had been interested in her ever since poor Stephen's death. Divorcing Jeremy, only months after their marriage and birth of their baby because he was having an affair with their butler, would really give them something to yell about. God, she could see it now ... all over the News of the World ... journalists crushing at the gates trying to take photos and obtain titbits from the villagers. She could vaguely remember what it had been like when she was a child and her mother had

478

tried to kill Granny and Steppie and had been arrested. The estate had been under siege from the press for weeks. She couldn't face that. She really couldn't.

"He'll understand. He has exams coming up soon and will need peace and quiet so it will suit us both."

Ruth looked puzzled. "Canleigh is quite big enough for him to distance himself if he wants to concentrate on his studies."

"I know but ... oh, please, Granny Ruth ... Jeremy and I ... we're not getting on too well at the moment. I just think we need a break from each other for a while."

Ruth held up her hands. "Okay. Okay. Don't distress yourself. Of course you can come to Tangles. Philip and I will look after you and Selena, and Jeremy can visit until you feel well enough to go home. Now, I have to love you and leave you. Philip has finally agreed to allow me to help with his paperwork as he's snowed under. It seems everyone in Yorkshire wants to learn to ride at Tangles and he's spending so much time teaching, he just hasn't the time to deal with administration at the moment. He needs a secretary really but until we get one, I will do my best to sort out his messy office.

I'll pop back to see you tomorrow. Hopefully, you can be discharged in the next day or so and we can make arrangements for you at home. We'll have to bring the cot and all the baby things over from Canleigh but I can discuss that with Tina later. Bye darling. Have a good rest. Selena shouldn't disturb you for a while now," she said, glancing fondly at the sleeping baby.

She kissed Lucy's cheek and left the room, leaving Lucy to sink back into the pillows, crying with relief now she wouldn't have to return to Canleigh just yet.

* * *

It was dark outside but the hospital car park was well lit as Ruth made her way to her car, glancing up at the maternity ward she had just left. She was more than puzzled by Lucy's reluctance to return to Canleigh. It was most odd. Even though Selena had Downs, she was a gorgeous baby, and Lucy should have been eager to return to Canleigh, with Jeremy, and become a little family. Instead, she wanted to bolt to Tangles. Ruth recalled how Jeremy had scarpered after Selena was born and since then, had only visited his wife and child once, and according to the nurse Ruth had asked, only stayed a short while, leaving Lucy in tears. Ruth began to feel very worried about the whole situation. It just wasn't normal and something was badly wrong. However, there wasn't much she could do about it until Lucy was at Tangles, they could talk freely, and Ruth could worm it out of her.

It was a bitterly cold evening. Snow had been forecast but had so far held off. She was glad her car had heated seats as even though she had on a thick wool coat, gloves and a hat, she was still freezing. She settled herself into her seat and started the engine, intending to head back to Tangles and tackle that paperwork but as she joined the rush-hour traffic on the main road, she had a better idea. She was going to go to Canleigh, tackle Jeremy, and find out exactly what was going on between him and Lucy. She would no doubt be told not to interfere but this was Lucy, the girl she had brought up since she was four years old and was like a daughter, and Ruth was anxious about her.

It took a while to thread through the city traffic with everyone eagerly heading home at the end of the day, no doubt seeking warmth and a hot meal. All Ruth wanted was answers. Jeremy should be at Canleigh by now. He was normally home around five o'clock and it was nearing six as the signs for Canleigh came in sight. She turned off the Harrogate road and along the drive, pulling up sharply on the gravel in front of the Hall next to Jeremy's car. He was definitely at home.

Felix appeared as if by magic as she ran up the front steps. He stood, holding open the front door for her, with that damned knowing smile on his face that she hated so much.

"Madam," he said.

"Would you tell Mr. Seymour that I'm here to see him please, Felix? I'll be in the library."

"Very well, Madam … can I get you anything?"

"No," she said sharply. "Just tell Mr. Seymour please. I haven't much time."

Felix nodded and disappeared upstairs while Ruth marched into the library. A huge fire had been lit, the curtains were drawn, and the lamps dotted around the room gave it a warm and welcoming glow. She stood in front of the fire and smiled at the portrait of her former mother-in-law, the Dowager Duchess, above the mantelpiece. Ruth had never met her but had always gained comfort from her picture. It was a shame they had never met. Ruth was pretty sure they would have been good friends from what everyone who had known her, said about her.

"Ruth?" said Jeremy behind her.

481

She turned to stare at him. He looked ill at ease and shifty. He had recently had a shower as his hair was still wet and he was dressed in jeans, a dark brown cashmere sweater and thick woollen socks. He hardly looked as if he intended going out. More likely, he was going to spend the evening relaxing at home.

"Jeremy," she replied, looking him up and down. "I take it you're not going to visit Lucy and Selena."

"Err ... no. I thought I would give it a miss this evening. I have exams to prepare for and ... well, I'll give her a ring instead."

Ruth sat down on one of the sofas by the fireplace and looked up at him. "What's going on, Jeremy? You're both behaving very oddly and I want to know why."

Jeremy turned his back on her and headed for the drinks cabinet. "Drink?"

"No, thank you. Please, Jeremy. What's going on?"

Jeremy poured a brandy, adding a dash of lemonade, drawing the action out, giving himself time to think. The last thing he had expected was to be tackled by Ruth and he had no idea what to say.

"I'm waiting," said Ruth impatiently tapping her fingers on the arm of the sofa.

Jeremy took a large gulp of brandy and turned to face her. "I don't know what you're talking about. There's absolutely nothing going on and Lucy and I are fine."

"Well, you can't be that fine as she doesn't want to return to Canleigh when she's discharged. She wants to stay at Tangles. I find that very peculiar ... I also find it very odd that you aren't spending as much time as you possibly can with your family ... and why you

482

bolted as soon as you set eyes on Selena ... what the hell is the matter with you, Jeremy?"

Jeremy shook his head. "Nothing. Truly. It's all been such a shock ... Lucy's accident ... the baby not being ... as we had expected ... and it's true, I have an awful lot of work to do in readiness for the exams next term ..."

"I see," murmured Ruth, not seeing at all. She'd never particularly warmed to Jeremy but his behaviour now was disgusting her. She wished so much that Lucy hadn't married him. She deserved far better than him.

"So you don't mind if Lucy and Selena come to stay at Tangles for a while?"

"No. That's fine by me," he smiled, throwing a glance at Felix who had made an appearance at the door. Felix had obviously heard Ruth's question as he grinned back at Jeremy and she knew instantly, with a flash of realisation, what was going on. She stood up abruptly, making the coffee table in front of her wobble. She couldn't understand why. Then she noticed one of its four legs was slightly wonky.

"This needs seeing to before someone has a nasty accident with a hot drink," she instructed, her mind in turmoil as she was trying to take in what she now knew ... and more to the point, what poor Lucy was probably aware of. She had to get out of here ... now. She couldn't bear to be in the same room as the two men who stood silently watching her. Jeremy did have the decency to look somewhat ashamed but Felix, as usual, stared at her, challenging her to say something but knowing she wouldn't ... and as she had no jurisdiction over what when on in Canleigh any longer, she couldn't dismiss him. That threat was over

483

for him. He had control over Jeremy and he looked at her confidently, knowing she couldn't touch him.

"I'll let you know when Lucy wants to come home," Ruth muttered, diving for the door, unable to get out of the room fast enough. As she dashed across the entrance hall, she looked up at the stairs which Lucy had fallen down. Had she fallen or had she been pushed? God. The thought was terrifying, the reality even worse. Surly Jeremy wouldn't stoop that low ... no, she didn't think he would ... but Felix ... he was another matter entirely.

* * *

"What do you think?" Ruth said, pushing Philip for an answer. She desperately wanted his opinion on her thoughts, hoping he would make her see sense and that her suspicions were completely nonsensical.

Philip relaxed in the old rocking chair by the agar in the kitchen at Tangles and sipped his coffee. It was too hot, burnt his tongue and he placed the mug on the table.

"To be honest, darling, I don't know. I respect your judgement and I think you're probably right about Jeremy and Felix ... but why Lucy fell down the stairs in the middle of the night, remains a mystery. She still maintains she wanted a drink from the kitchen and tripped on her negligee and we have to believe her, until she tells us otherwise. We certainly can't go accusing Jeremy or Felix of pushing her."

Ruth spooned three sugars into her coffee. She didn't care. She needed it. She was in shock. "I know. I know you're right but I'm scared for her, Philip. The atmosphere at Canleigh is bad. That odious butler has a definite hold over Jeremy, I'm sure of it, and he's going to use it to his full advantage. Why on earth didn't I get rid of him years ago? It was so foolish of me."

"Don't blame yourself."

"Well, I do. If I had employed a nice, solid couple, just like the Hardys, we wouldn't be having this discussion now ... and I don't like the thought of Lucy returning to Canleigh while he's still employed there ... to be alone at night with only him and Jeremy ... and Selena. They will be so vulnerable."

"Are you saying you want to move back?" said Philip with a resigned sigh. He had so loved being at Tangles, just the two of them. He had treasured the last few months more than he could say. Ruth was still grieving for Stephen but she had shown signs of being able to be happy, continuing with her charity work, taking up her art again, helping him with his paperwork and she was producing wonderful, appetising meals here in the kitchen with the help of his grandmother's old recipe books. He had envisaged them remaining like this for the rest of their days, not having to relocate back to the Hall.

"No, darling. I couldn't do that to you. You so generously gave up residing here for years to be with me while Stephen and Lucy were growing up. I can't ask you to do that again. I know how happy you are to be back here ... and I am too. It has such a lovely feel, this place. It really is a home, unlike Canleigh. I love that too but it's grand and formal and not exactly cosy."

Philip touched her hand and smiled. He was more pleased than she would ever know. "Thank you, darling ... that means a lot. Now, don't despair. We'll

485

look after Lucy and Selena until they are strong enough to return. You'll have the time and opportunity to wheedle it out of her if something is awry and if it is, we can go to the police. We can also persuade her to dismiss Felix before she goes home and you can help her advertise for another butler."

"Huh. I didn't do too well last time, did I?" said Ruth glumly.

"Well, Felix did come with impeccable references and he has been faultless in carrying out his duties. Anyhow, with another butler in place, Lucy should feel more secure. Tina might be persuaded to do more hours as well and perhaps some more live-in staff could be hired. After all, Lucy can certainly afford it."

Ruth smiled. "You are so wise, darling."

"Feel better now?"

"A little ... although I'm still disgusted with Jeremy but there's nothing I can do about him until Lucy confides in me. So, as you have a lesson in the indoor ring in half an hour, I'll throw the dishes in the washer and then get cracking with your paperwork."

She stood up, kissed the top of his head, and set to. She did feel better as she always did whenever she discussed anything with her husband. He kept her sane. Thank God she had found him.

* * *

"Do you think she'll say anything?" asked Felix.

"Who, *Granny* Ruth or Lucy?"

"Either of them, I suppose," said Felix pouring two large brandies, handing one to Jeremy and sinking down onto the chair at the old Chippendale desk by the window.

486

"I've no bloody idea," murmured Jeremy, gulping down his brandy. "Sod them. Sod them all."

"She doesn't like me, you know. She never has."

"Who?"

"Ruth. I know she appointed me in the first place but she was always on the verge of giving me the sack."

"Why? You're a damned good butler. That doesn't make sense."

"I am, aren't I," laughed Felix, downing his brandy and placing his feet on the desk. "That's why she couldn't do it ... but I have a funny feeling she's going to try and persuade Lucy to get rid of me."

"I won't allow it!"

"That's all right then," winked Felix wickedly. "Now, then, *Sir*, the whole evening stretches in front of us and I have a very good idea of how to fill it ... how about you ... are you up for it?"

Jeremy stood up, walked over to Felix, and pulled him to his feet. "Oh yes. Yes, yes, yes."

* * *

Lucy sat propped up by pillows. The rain was lashing down outside and even with hospital heating, she felt a bit chilly and pulled the bedclothes up to her neck, glancing at Selena in the cot beside her.

The baby was fast asleep and looked so innocent, so sweet and so completely dependent on her mother for absolutely everything. Lucy's heart filled with love for her. She was desperately sad that Selena had Downs but even so, was determined she was going to be given every chance to lead the best possible life she could. The doctors had warned that Selena might not live to old age so every day with her was going to be precious and would be filled with love, fun, and experiences. Her darling child would want for nothing … apart from a decent father.

She looked at the clock on the wall. It was seven thirty. Visiting time would be over in half an hour and still Jeremy hadn't turned up. Admittedly, he hadn't said he would but he could have made the effort. Vicky had visited in the morning and Ruth in the afternoon, leaving the evening free for Jeremy but Lucy wasn't surprised he hadn't turned up. On the previous evening, he had only stayed about ten minutes, making the excuse he had college assignments to complete. He had brought a peace offering, a teddy bear for Selena, and a bunch of mixed flowers for her but it hadn't been enough. He hadn't wanted to talk, or apologise, or even make an excuse for his appalling behaviour … and she hadn't known what to say either. She was physically too weak, sore and mentally crushed to be able to deal with it. That's why she wanted so much to get to Tangles. Let the lovely old place soothe her; allow her body to heal and her mind to sort out exactly what had happened and what she was going to do about it.

She wanted to tell Ruth and Philip but couldn't. It was too raw, too vivid. She didn't know if she could ever tell anyone. She felt so ashamed, so humiliated that her husband of only months, could do what he had done … in their own home … with their butler. She didn't know how she would ever face that man again … and he would have to go now. She couldn't return to Canleigh if he were there.

A terrible sadness for herself and Selena flooded over her. They should have been so happy, going home to a loving husband and father. Instead, Lucy was fearful of the future and of returning to the Hall with her baby. What a terrible dilemma.

With a start, she thought of her mother. A nurse had kindly sent Delia a text message on Lucy's phone to say the baby had been delivered safely. An enormous bouquet and a beautiful card arrived from Scotland this morning with a message to say that as soon as Selena and the baby were fit to travel, Delia wanted them to go up to Blairness for a week or so as she couldn't wait to meet her granddaughter.

Without thinking further, Lucy picked up the telephone beside the bed. She wanted to speak to her mother more than anything in the world, although she didn't know if she dare tell her what had happened. With Delia's reputation, it might not be wise. Lucy had seen her mother's rage with her own eyes all those years ago when she had attacked Granny Ruth beside the lake with Demon. She didn't want to give her cause to be angry with anyone again but she wanted to hear her voice. After all, Delia was her mother.

* * *

Delia had just finished dinner, carried her coffee into the red drawing room, and was debating on whether to read a book, watch television or just sit and listen to music. In an effort to keep herself from worrying about Lucy, following a phone call from the hospital two days ago to say Lucy had fallen down the stairs at Canleigh and was in labour, she had buried herself in work in between constantly ringing the hospital to keep abreast of what was happening. The relief had been immense when she knew Lucy was

489

not in any immediate danger and the baby was safely born, although Delia was distressed to hear the poor little thing was going to have some problems.

She flicked on the television. The Bill was on. Yuk. Police and criminals. She had had enough of all of them. A boring documentary was on BBC1, a cookery programme on BBC2 and after a quick run through of all the other channels, there was nothing to attract her interest for more than a few seconds. She turned it off, just as her mobile rang.

"Mother?"

"Lucy, darling! How are you ... how is the baby?"

"We're okay ... Selena is absolutely fine ... she's doing well, eating and sleeping and she hardly ever cries. She's a real poppet."

"That's good. You can get some rest then but how are you really, darling? I've been so worried but naturally, I can't come and see for myself. Whatever happened? How did you manage to fall down the stairs? Did you faint or something?"

Lucy drew in her breath. This was an opportunity to spill it all out but she couldn't do it. Not on the telephone and not to her mother. It was too dangerous. She might explode with anger, come down, do Jeremy an injury, and end up back in prison. No, she had to keep her mouth shut and not tell her mother anything that would arouse her suspicions. She began to regret the call.

"Yes. I think I must have. I can't really remember too well. One moment I was walking towards the stairs, the next I was at the bottom, and all I was concerned about when I came round was the baby. Thank goodness she didn't suffer any damage."

"Yes. I agree … and how do you feel … about her having Downs … I am so sorry about that, darling. It must have been a dreadful shock for you."

"It doesn't matter," said Lucy defiantly. "Not one bit. She's a little individual in her own right. She's absolutely beautiful, I love her to bits, and she's going to have the best possible life I can give her."

"I'm so pleased to hear you say that, darling. I really am … and I can't wait to meet her and fuss over you both. When are you being discharged? When can you come up … I presume Jeremy won't be able to come with you due to his college commitments … will he mind if you come with Selena?"

"We'll be allowed to go home either tomorrow or the next day … but I'm not going straight to Canleigh … I'm going to stay at Tangles with Granny Ruth and Steppie for a few days … just till I feel a little stronger … and well enough to drive. Then I'll come up to you."

Delia pushed down the rush of jealousy at the idea of Lucy going straight to Ruth although it made perfect sense and she should be glad Lucy had Ruth to look after her.

"That's wonderful, darling. I can't wait to see you both. Just let me know as soon as you're fit enough … or even if you want to come sooner. I know I can't come down and fetch you but we could get your butler or someone to drive you."

Lucy closed her eyes and shuddered, pushing the thought of driving all that way with only Felix for company. It was terrifying. She could see his eyes as she ran away from him along the corridor that night. He had looked positively evil, full of hate for her. He intended her harm. She was sure of it. He might not have pushed her down the stairs but he might do

491

something equally as bad in the future if he was allowed to remain at Canleigh. But he wouldn't. She was going to have him fired as soon as she could get hold of Jeremy and tell him to do it.

"Lucy … are you there?"

"Yes. Yes. I am. Sorry, Mother. I'm suddenly feeling really tired. Do you mind if I go? I'll ring you as soon as I'm feeling better."

"Ok, darling. You get as much rest as you can. I'll wait to hear from you."

Lucy put down the phone and burst into tears. It was so wonderful to know that her mother, Granny Ruth, Steppie, Aunt Vicky and Uncle Alex cared so much about her but the one person who should have been here, by her side, was missing and she didn't know how she was ever going to forgive him.

CHAPTER 37

APRIL 1997

Jeremy dreaded his daily visits to Lucy. He drove over to Tangles every day once his wife and daughter were discharged from hospital and he brought flowers on every visit. He chatted amiably about his studies and smiled and cooed over the baby in front of Ruth and Philip but when he and Lucy were alone, he clammed up, unable to think what to say, until she mentioned dismissing Felix.

Life at Canleigh was much more pleasant without Lucy. He was at college through the day but in the evenings, once he had got his trip to Tangles out of the way, he could go home. Felix would be waiting to serve him a delicious dinner and then they spent the best nights of Jeremy's life, exploring each other's bodies endlessly, revelling in their coupling. Jeremy had never enjoyed himself so much, even with Matthew. The passion and the knowledge that Felix possessed of how to make another man swoon with delight, were excessive. Jeremy didn't want it to end. He didn't want Lucy to come home and he was more than pleased to hear she was off to see Delia as soon as she felt fit enough to drive such a long distance.

He knew Philip and Ruth were watching him on his visits to Tangles and he had to be careful not to let slip how he really felt, trying hard to make a real show of how much he loved little Selena, expressing his wish to have his family at home as soon as possible.

Then, on the evening before Lucy was driving up to Scotland, she dropped her bombshell. Ruth was in the kitchen and Philip was teaching in the indoor arena, leaving Lucy and Jeremy alone in the lounge, Selena in the pram beside them.

"We'll probably be at Blairness for a couple of weeks and while we are away I want you to give Felix four weeks notice. He can treat the last two weeks as holiday as I want him out of the house by the time we return."

She was looking at him sternly. Her strength was returning and she was calmer and clearer headed than she had been for a while.

"No," Jeremy gulped.

"I'm sorry, Jeremy," she hissed quietly, hoping Ruth was way out of earshot. "But I'm adamant about this. If you think I can tolerate being in that man's presence again, you are deluding yourself. He is to leave *MY* home. Do you understand?"

"*YOUR* home? Don't forget, Lucy, we are married and it's my home too and I have a say in what goes on in it and I don't want Felix to leave. He is an important part of the establishment and I don't know how we can manage without him."

"Huh! How *you* can't manage without him, don't you mean?"

Jeremy couldn't meet her eyes. He cracked his knuckles and stared at the floor and his next words struck the death knell in her heart that any hopes of a normal marriage between them would ever happen.

"Yes, you're right. I can't. You see, I love him … and if you want to avoid any hint of scandal, you will allow him to remain. We promise to be utterly discreet and never give you any cause for concern and

I will play the adoring husband and father. No-one need ever know."

"I'll divorce you then," Lucy snapped, her eyes flashing, angry that he was trying to manipulate her.

"I don't think so. What would the grounds for divorce be, may I ask? This family have endured enough scandal in the past to last it for a lifetime. Do you really want to drag it through the mud once again? And you will look so foolish my dear. Everyone will wonder why you didn't realise your husband was bisexual when you married him. After all, we have known each other since childhood. Surely you must have guessed."

Lucy was rendered speechless and felt nauseous. He was right. She was perfectly aware she couldn't go ahead with a divorce. It would be simply ghastly if it came out that he was having an affair with the blasted butler. She shuddered, glancing at innocent little Selena, who had just woken up and was gazing up at the ceiling with her big blue eyes. Poor, poor little Selena. Not only did she have massive problems of her own, she was also going to have to live with a father who was no good for either of them. God. What a mess.

"And another thing," he continued, his eyes darkening ominously as he played his trump card, "I believe your mother made a visit to Canleigh not so long ago."

Jeremy grinned. Felix had told him how they could keep Lucy quiet when they had been discussing their future a few nights ago. Jeremy had laughed his head off to hear how Felix was blackmailing the evil bitch in Scotland. How she must be loving that!

Lucy gasped with dismay, looking at him with horror in her eyes. How did he know. How had he found out?

"Felix told me a while ago ... he saw her ... in the churchyard in the middle of the night. He was out for a walk, down by the lake and followed her up to the stables, to the Hall and then over to the church."

"He must ... he must have been mistaken. It couldn't have been mother," Lucy blustered.

"Yes, it was. Apparently he got a good look at her in the moonlight as she was hovering around the family graves. She was taking a hell of a risk coming here and it was a bit of luck Felix saw her. So, my darling wife, if you breathe a word to anyone, anyone at all, about my relationship with Felix, or try to obtain a divorce, until I am good and ready, I shall very quickly alert the authorities of your darling mother's visit and have her thrown back into prison forthwith. We will have a divorce by the way ... but when I decide to, not you. In a couple of years maybe ... perhaps longer. We will have to see how it goes and how much I can wangle out of you at the time. It will have to be enough to give Felix and me a bloody good lifestyle, I can tell you."

Lucy couldn't speak. She sat, in complete shock, unable to take in the enormity of what he was saying.

Taking her silence for acquiescence, Jeremy finished the coffee Ruth had given him on arrival and picked up his car keys. "Right. Now we understand each other, I'll return to Canleigh for dinner. Have a lovely time at Blairness, darling, and give my love to your mother ... and don't forget to let me know what day you will be home and I'll make sure Pru makes a fabulous welcome home dinner."

He stood up, brushed his mouth against her hair, tickled Selena under the chin, and walked swiftly around the house to get to his car which was parked on the front forecourt, eager to get back to Canleigh and tell Felix he had it all sewn up.

Lucy, watching him depart, began to shake. She didn't know whether it was from fear or rage but she couldn't stop. It started in her hands and worked its way all over her body. She wanted to cry. She wanted to scream. But nothing would come out. Just this awful juddering and a dreadful moaning and whimpering as she began to rock backwards and forwards in the chair, hugging her body with her arms and tucking her hands in her armpits ... and then the crying started. Huge, great sobs of despair hit the evening air and made Selena look at her mother. Lucy didn't notice. Her eyes were full of water and she wept piteously for the mess of her marriage and for her afflicted child.

* * *

Delia was enormously pleased to see her daughter and granddaughter. They rolled up at Blairness in Lucy's car just before six o'clock the following evening. Lucy had taken the drive steadily, having stopped regularly to feed and change Selena and to give herself a break. Her ribs were healed but she still tired easily. She had considered staying the night somewhere near Loch Lomond as she had with Jeremy but that would have brought back memories of their honeymoon and she didn't want to go there. So she journeyed on, arriving at Blairness exhausted but delighted when Delia, Crystal, and Connie cooed over Selena and literally took her over but it was Delia who noticed how frail Lucy appeared and took her aside.

"Now. You're not to do anything while you are here. Do you hear me? You are to let us look after Selena as much as possible and you are to rest. Your room is all prepared. I've had a cot put in there but I also have a spare in my room so if you want to leave Selena with me at night so you can sleep properly, that is absolutely fine by me."

"That's so kind," murmured Lucy, moved by her mother's thoughtfulness.

"It's what mother's are for ... and I have a lot of making up to you to do for all those years you didn't have me."

"I know ... and thank you," said Lucy, feeling an overwhelming sense of relief. Granny Ruth and Steppie had been wonderful and shouldered most of the burden of caring for Selena while Lucy had been growing stronger, physically and mentally, but since that last conversation with Jeremy and her reaction to it, all her confidence and self-esteem had disappeared rapidly.

"Now ... get yourself upstairs and have a rest. I assumed you would be desperately tired tonight so you can have dinner either in your room or on a tray with me in the red drawing room. We'll have a proper celebration dinner tomorrow. Crystal, Connie and her husband and Brian are going to join us ... I hope you don't mind."

"That sounds lovely ... how is Brian?" Lucy asked, glancing over at Connie and Crystal who were sat on the sofa, taking turns to hold Selena, who was

498

loving the attention and making funny noises of appreciation.

"He's fine," murmured Delia with a wry smile.

"Oh?" quizzed Lucy. "Have you two finally got it together?" she asked boldly.

"Lucy!"

"Sorry, mother but I'm pretty sure that on my last visit I detected a growing attraction there. You do spend a lot of time together ... and get along so well."

Delia actually blushed and Lucy couldn't help but smile. She had never seen her mother colour up before and it was intriguing.

"Well, of course we spend a lot of time together ... he is my estate manager after all. We have a lot to discuss and yes, we like the same things but it doesn't mean we're going to jump into bed together."

"Oh, I see," laughed Lucy, making Delia smile. "You can't fool me, mother dear. You really can't ... and I shall watch this space with great interest."

"Get up the stairs, my girl and have a rest. Your brain is addled," Delia teased. "McFrain has already gone up with your things. Leave Selena down here with us. We'll see to her ... we'll see you later."

Lucy did as she was told. It would be good to have a shower, relax for an hour or two before dinner, and have the responsibility for Selena taken away from her. She smiled at the three women who were cooing over her baby and left the room, grateful for the opportunity to be able to put Canleigh, Jeremy and Felix firmly out of her mind.

She badly wanted to tell her mother about the threat that hung over them both from Jeremy and Felix but it wouldn't do any good, in fact it would probably rile her mother enough to do something about it and that would never do. No. She had to keep her own counsel for now and see what happened. It was going to be damned hard but when she did return to Canleigh, she would just have to keep busy, concentrate on Selena and keep away from Jeremy and Felix as much as possible. She certainly wasn't looking forward to returning to Canleigh very soon.

* * *

The fortnight sped past too quickly, for Lucy because she didn't want to go home and for Delia, because she didn't want her to.

"You can stay longer if you like. There's nothing you have to go back for is there, apart from Jeremy, of course. He must be missing you," remarked Delia as they ate breakfast in the dining room two days before Lucy was due to return home. Selena, having been fed and changed, was asleep beside them in the latest Silver Cross pram Delia had generously purchased for her first grandchild.

"Well, he's busy … he has a lot of assignments to do in the evenings so I don't see much of him as he's out all day and at weekends, he's outside with our gardeners. He's become obsessed by horticulture," Lucy replied, thinking how he was also enraptured by the dammed butler.

"Well, there you are then. Stay another fortnight. Please, darling. We all love you being here."

Lucy grinned. It was Selena they all loved. She'd hardly had to lift a finger for her baby since she had been at Blairness as all the staff took turns to fuss over her and relished the chance to feed her or take her for long walks in the pram. They only brought her back when she needed changing, which highly amused Lucy.

"I'll ring Jeremy and see what he says. If he's happy for me to stay for longer, then I will."

Delia finished her toast, picked up her coffee and looked at Lucy. "Um. If he's that busy, I don't expect he'll worry too much."

"No, I don't suppose he will," said Lucy sadly.

Delia raised her eyebrows but didn't say a word. She had watched Lucy closely over the last couple of weeks and she was sure the girl was miserable about something … something to do with bloody Jeremy but no matter how she tried to get her to open up, she wouldn't say a word against him. But something wasn't right and Delia wouldn't rest until she found out what it was.

A knock on the dining room door made them both turn. Brian stood on the threshold, holding a couple of folders under his arm and wearing a warm smile on his face.

"Good morning … do you have a few minutes to spare, Your Ladyship, please? I just need your signature on a few things."

Lucy grinned. Brian always called Delia by her title when they were in company but she had overheard him say Delia on more than one occasion when they thought no-one could hear.

Delia felt her face flush with Lucy's scrutiny and could have kicked herself. Brian always made her feel like a silly schoolgirl these days and they still hadn't 'got it together' as Lucy had described it. It certainly wasn't because the desire wasn't there. It was. In spades. But as kind and friendly as Brian was, and how close they were becoming, he still kept a distance, a barrier between them and Delia didn't

501

know what to do about it. She wanted him badly ... and it was more than just sex. She wanted him. All of him but for once in her life she was too shy to do anything about it. It was too important this time. Whatever she did, she didn't want to frighten him away from Blairness. If he left, she would be in bits. It just didn't bear thinking about. So, until he made some kind of move to further their relationship, she was stumped.

Brian walked over to the pram and tickled Selena under the chin. She thrashed her arms and legs about and gurgled happily.

"What a lovely child she is," he remarked. "She always seems so content."

"Yes. It's very rare to hear her cry," said Lucy.

"Right," said Delia, having regained her composure. "Sit down and have a coffee, Brian, while I look at the papers."

"I'll go and ring Jeremy now," said Lucy, rising to her feet. "I'll just catch him before he leaves for college. Can I leave Selena with you for a few minutes please?"

"Lucy is staying another fortnight," said Delia once Lucy had left the room. "Quite frankly, I wish she could move in permanently. I don't think she really wants to go back to Jeremy. There's something wrong there. I know there is."

"Until she tells you, there's nothing you can do ... she knows you're here for her and if she wants to, she will tell you. Just give her time."

Delia smiled. "I love your wisdom."

"Do you?" he asked, his eyes boring straight into hers.

She could feel her face going crimson again and bent her head to sign the papers.

"We need to talk," he said quietly.

She lifted her head. "Do we?"

"Yes. I think we do. We both know how we feel about each other ... and have done for a while but we need to decide what we are going to do about it. Don't you agree?"

Delia cleared her throat. She hadn't expected this declaration this morning. She didn't know what to say. She fiddled with the pen he had handed her to sign the documents, turning it over and over in her hand.

"Is there anything else you require, Your Ladyship?" asked McFrain from the doorway.

"No. No, thank you, McFrain."

The butler disappeared and Delia glanced at Brian, who was sitting with a questioning look on his face, waiting for her answer.

"Yes. You're right," she said firmly. "When are you free today?"

"After lunch."

"Good. That's perfect. Lucy and Selena always take a nap after lunch. I can meet you then. Where?"

"Come to the cottage. We can be quite alone there and no-one will disturb us."

He stood up, shuffled the signed documents back into his folder, touched her shoulder, and left. Delia placed her hand on the same spot, wanting to keep the connection. What was he going to say this afternoon? Was he going to tell her he was going to resign ... and needed to get away from her and Blairness? She couldn't see what else it could be. He didn't want to further their relationship. Of that, she was certain. It was obviously making him feel uncomfortable and he had finally made up his mind and was going to tell her. Her heart flipped over with sadness. She couldn't imagine what she would do without his firm shoulders to lean on. He knew Blairness inside and out. His experience and expertise were invaluable. She couldn't do without him in her life. She just couldn't. He had to remain and if it meant she would have to just dream about being in his arms, having him make long, delicious love to her, so be it. He just had to remain at Blairness. It was nothing, she was nothing, without him.

* * *

"I'm sorry, Madam, but Jeremy has already left for Askham Bryan," announced Felix.

Lucy gripped the telephone in her hand tightly. Just hearing that odious little man have the audacity to use Jeremy's first name instead of calling him Mr. Seymour was enough to make her want to wretch. How the hell was she going to bear being in his presence?

She closed her eyes and took a deep breath, pretending it was anyone but him she was speaking to. "Well, could you please tell him when he returns, that I ... we ... Selena and I ... we are going to stay at Blairness for another fortnight."

She could visualise the grin that was spreading over his face, the pleasure he was taking from her decision. She wanted to slam the phone down but daren't. She had to remain dignified until she had decided what, if anything, she could do about this ghastly situation she found herself in.

"Very good, Madam. Do enjoy your extended time away, although we are all missing you."

"Goodbye," Lucy said smartly, replacing the receiver. She sat down on the bed. The dreadful shaking was coming over her again. She sat on her hands to stop the trembling. She wasn't going to let it take her over as it had last time. She had to get a grip. She had another fortnight. Another two whole weeks to try to steady her nerves and she had to do it because she had to go back at some time. She couldn't skulk up in Scotland forever.

* * *

Delia and Lucy enjoyed the spring sunshine, wandering around the lake, taking turns to push Selena in her pram.

"What did Jeremy say about you staying with us for a little longer?" Delia asked.

Lucy bent over the pram to check Selena, not wanting Delia to see the expression on her face. "I didn't speak to him. He had already left for college. I left a message."

"Well, I'm sure he will be okay about it, especially if he is as busy as you say … and it's only another two weeks. He will have you both for a lifetime."

Lucy didn't answer as she straightened up, allowing her hair to fall over her face, hiding it from her mother.

There it was again, thought Delia. That ominous silence when Jeremy was mentioned. She was really becoming worried now. For a new mum, Lucy was acting a little strange, not wanting to share the first precious weeks of her baby's life with the father. She was naturally pleased Lucy was in no hurry to leave Blairness but it was still odd and she desperately wanted to find the underlying cause of what was wrong before Lucy finally left for Canleigh.

"Didn't you say you were seeing Brian this afternoon?" said Lucy, saying the first thing that came into her head, wanting to change the subject.

"Um. Yes. We have a meeting."

"Perhaps you wouldn't mind taking that novel I borrowed from Connie back to her please. I've left it on the coffee table in the red drawing room. You know the one ... 'Tender is the Night'," Lucy grimaced. "Not quite my taste but it was nice of her to lend it to me."

Delia laughed at Lucy's expression. "No. I didn't think it was. Connie always has her head in the clouds. She's obsessed by romance. Just as well her husband dotes on her ... but I'm sorry, darling. I'm not going to the office today. I'm meeting Brian at his cottage."

"Oh? That sounds intriguing ... and what might you be up to in Brian's abode," Lucy teased.

Delia tensed. "I've no idea. I just hope ... oh, I don't know ... I'm just worried he might be about to tell me he wants to leave Blairness."

"Why? He loves it here ... he told me on one of my earlier visits. Why would he want to leave? You haven't done anything to upset him have you?"

"Not as far as I know. Quite the opposite. I've done everything I can to make him want to stay."

Lucy caught Delia's eye. Her mother did look worried.

"You do love him, don't you?" she asked gently.

Delia nodded. "I fell *in* love with him the first day I set eyes on him but that's changed as we have grown closer. I'm not in love with him any longer. I actually love him. Intensely ... but in a good way," she said hastily, seeing the wary look Lucy gave her. "It's not like I felt for Philip ... don't worry, darling. This is so different. A more mature kind of deep love. Oh, I don't know. I can't explain it but if Brian leaves Blairness, I'm going to be totally devastated. Quite frankly, darling, I couldn't bear it."

* * *

Delia took her time walking down to Brian's cottage. Lucy and Selena had headed up to Lucy's room not long after lunch, leaving Delia to have a quick shower, change into fresh jeans and a vivid red, long sleeved, top. Her hair gleamed after she washed it. She applied a layer of foundation and finishing powder, followed by a flick of mascara and a light lipstick. A couple of squirts of Chanel 19 and she was ready to face him, praying hard he wasn't going to resign. She didn't know what she would say. She could hardly go on her knees and beg him not to go. Whatever happened, she would have to maintain her dignity.

It was surprisingly warm for an April day in Scotland and Brian was waiting for her in the garden, sitting on the bench outside the door, dressed in faded jeans and an open necked white shirt. Meg was at his feet. Delia's heart missed a beat as she opened the gate and walked towards him. He looked divine. His gorgeous thick hair, the strong chin, the fabulous azure blue eyes, and that muscular body. Oh God, that body.

Meg ambled to her feet and crossed the lawn, wagging her tail in greeting. Delia covered her confusion by making a fuss of her.

507

"Drink?" asked Brian, pointing at the bottle of white Chardonnay and two glasses on the wooden table beside him.

"That would be nice."

She sat down next to him and took the glass he offered her.

"Here's to a successful outcome of our meeting this afternoon," he grinned, tapping his glass next to hers.

Delia was tongue-tied. She didn't know what to say. She felt unusually shy and drank the wine quicker than intended. It began to go to her head almost immediately, which was unusual. She could usually sink a few before she felt any affects.

He allowed her some respite, amused by her lack of confidence. This wasn't the Delia he knew and loved. She was usually forthright and bold but not now. She looked positively uneasy and apprehensive and suddenly he took pity on her. He placed his glass back on the table, and did the same with hers. He turned back to her, pulled her hands in his, and looked her in the eyes.

"Delia, it's time we were straight with one another. I think you know how I feel about you … and I think you feel the same … about me."

Delia felt her whole body tense and she bit her lip. Here it was. He was going to let her down gently and put the boot in. After all, no man would want her after all she had done in the past. She was a murderer, an ex-con, a dangerous person to know, let alone love. No. She was destined to be on her own forever. Her heart bled and she desperately hoped she wouldn't start to cry and disgrace herself.

"I'm not sure if you have ever been made aware of my ancestry," Brian was saying, "which might make my position here a little clearer. I'm the son of the Earl of Glentagon. The second son actually, not the first ... he ... my older brother ... is now the Earl as our father died a couple of years ago."

Delia nodded. Her solicitors had informed her of his family background, along with details of his education and career when he had been appointed.

"That's why the position here was of such interest to me," he was continuing. "I shall never inherit Glentagon and I wouldn't want to as I love my brother dearly and I hope he has a long and happy life and as he has a wife and three male children, I am firmly out of the picture as far as inheriting the estate is concerned.

I'm not going to go into details about my army career as the last few years were in the S.A.S and as you know, we are sworn to secrecy. However, it was a traumatic time and I saw and had to do things which impacted badly on me. When I was finally discharged, I wanted nothing more than peace and quiet, a steady job, and to live in the countryside. The opening here was a golden opportunity for me, to be involved with a large estate, to be left pretty much to my own devices and to give me the breathing space I needed to recover from the trauma of my army career ... and it has. I've loved every moment of my employment here and the last thing I want to do is leave. "

It was coming. The excuse for him to get away. What would it be? Would his brother need him to assist with Glentagon?

Delia pulled her hands away from his but he reached out and pulled them back.

"Delia ... Your Ladyship," his eyes twinkled. "I want you to know how much I love you. I'm hoping upon hope that you do feel the same as I am putting everything on the line here. As much as I don't want to leave Blairness, I will if I have read you wrong and I've made a ghastly mistake."

She couldn't believe what he was saying. He didn't want to go. He didn't want to go … and he loved her! He had actually said he loved her!

Delia looked up at him, seeing it in his eyes. She shut hers. She couldn't believe it. She cried with sheer joy as he took her in his arms and kissed her scar, her hair, her eyes, her lips. His mouth was soft and tender and she felt faint with desire.

"I love you, Brian. I really love you," she murmured, "and I don't ever want you to leave Blairness … I couldn't live without you."

He picked her up, carried her into the cottage, through into the bedroom, and laid her on the bed. They looked at each other, their hearts pounding with sheer joy and excitement. Neither had felt so happy in their lives.

CHAPTER 38

MAY 1997

Two weeks later, Lucy drove Selena back to Canleigh, having contacted Tina first to make sure everything would be in ready in the nursery.

She didn't want to leave the lovely cocoon at Blairness. Her mother was so happy, it radiated from her like light from a beacon. There had been no need for her to inform Lucy what had happened at Brian's cottage that afternoon. It was written all over her and she couldn't stop smiling at everyone who crossed her path and was even heard to sing when she thought no-one was listening.

During the day, she and Brian were formal, as they had always been, apart from the odd touch and smile, which all the staff and Lucy noticed, even though the pair assumed no-one had. Then, in the evenings, Brian was invited for dinner and kept them both amused with tales from his earlier army days, before he joined the S.A.S, along with snippets of information about Glentagon where he had been born and grew up. He made a special effort to include Lucy in the conversation, even though it was obvious he only had eyes for her mother, who wasn't quite as giggly as a schoolgirl but very near.

It was just as well Lucy liked to read because as soon as they had enjoyed coffee in the red drawing room, she would make her excuses and go up to bed to check on Selena and read one of the many books

Crystal and Connie kept finding for her. Brian and her mother would remain downstairs for a while but inevitably Lucy would hear them head along the landing to Delia's room.

She was delighted for her mother. It was good to see her so animated and as lovely as Brian was, she wouldn't be able to twist him around her little finger. He was forthright and determined, and obviously possessed nerves of steel according to the titbits of his army life he had revealed, serving in Northern Ireland, the Falklands and many other dangerous places in the world. After what he had been through, dealing with Delia would be a piece of cake.

But, finally, it was time to go home. She couldn't stay away from Canleigh forever. It would look most peculiar and she had responsibilities towards the estate. She said a tearful goodbye to Delia, Brian, Crystal, and Connie and flung her arms around darling Meg, who she could easily have taken home with her. She had fallen in love with the soppy old dog and would miss her. Perhaps it was time to have a dog of her own. She would think about it on the way home.

The drive down to Canleigh seemed endless, probably because she was in no hurry to get there and kept religiously to the speed limit but eventually she headed into the village, past the Canleigh Arms, the petrol station, the village shop, and swung into the main gates of the Hall. Minutes later, she drew up outside the front door and switched off the engine. Nothing stirred. No-one came to the door to greet her, even though she had left messages about what time she was likely to arrive.

She got out of the car and breathed in the air. She had forgotten how much she loved Canleigh. The lawns in front of the house had been trimmed today and the air was heavy with the wonderful smell of cut grass, mingled with scents from the rose garden to her right. Pigeons could be heard calling to each other in the trees by St. Mary's, the odd car could be heard in the distance, travelling along the main road. It was all so peaceful. So calm. What a wonderful place to bring up a child. She opened the rear door, unfastened the buggy, and lifted Selena out, holding her in her arms.

"Just look, darling. This is your home. This is where you are going to grow up and where you will be very, very happy," she said with determination, still surprised no-one had appeared to greet her. Where the hell was Felix? Where the hell was her husband?

Suddenly the door opened and Tina ran down the steps. "I'm so sorry, Lucy. I heard the car coming along the drive but I was talking to Mr. Seymour on the phone. I'm afraid he and Felix have gone out for the evening and won't be back until late. He told me to give you his apologies and he will see you in the morning."

Lucy's mouth dropped open. She was utterly stunned Jeremy could so blatantly treat her like this. She had brought his daughter home for the very first time and he couldn't even be bothered to be here … he was out with *Felix*. How dare he? How could he? She was so angry she could burst and was glad Tina had taken Selena from her arms and was making a huge fuss of her. It gave her time to compose herself but although she was angry, she was also relieved the inevitable meeting with both of the men was now put off until the morning. At least she could go to sleep in peace, especially as Tina was staying the night and would care for Selena.

"Prue has prepared you a meal and will serve you in the dining room when you are ready, unless you want something on a tray upstairs," Tina said helpfully, skilfully holding Selena with one arm and taking one of Lucy's suitcases from the boot. Lucy took the other and followed Tina and Lucy up the steps and into the entrance hall.

"Perhaps you would ring down to Pru and tell her I'll have dinner in my room, please Tina. Ask her to bring it up in around an hour, after I've freshened up. After I've eaten, I'll pop up to the nursery to say goodnight, then I think I'll have an early night. I'm exhausted after that drive."

Tina expertly whisked Selena and her suitcase up the stairs and disappeared towards the nursery while Lucy dumped her luggage in the entrance hall, pleased to see the Silver Cross pram had journeyed safely down to Canleigh via a courier, as it was too big to place in the car. She went through to the library to have a look at the post Susan Armitage always left in a big file on the desk. Lucy knew there was nothing urgent as Susan would have alerted her and sent it up to Blairness but even so, she wanted to have a quick look and familiarise herself with her home at the same time.

The library smelt musty and she threw open the French doors, breathing in the lovely heady smell from the recently trimmed box hedges, much preferable to the whiff of tobacco inside. She looked around the room. Dirty glasses sat on the coffee table, along with cigarette butts in the ashtray, there were ashes in the grate and dead flowers in a vase on the mantelpiece. The room, usually pristine and welcoming, felt jaded and unloved. What was going on? Why hadn't Felix tidied up? Why hadn't the room been cleaned?

She quickly flicked through the papers Sue had left her. Nothing needed dealing with now and she was desperately tired. Her brain would work better in the morning. She shut the French windows and went back out into the entrance hall, leaving her luggage at the bottom of the stairs. She didn't need anything in her suitcase and it was much larger than Selena's and she didn't want to drag it upstairs. Felix could do that in the morning.

She mounted the stairs slowly, feeling fear rising in her stomach, as she recalled the last time she had been here. It all came flooding back. Standing in Jeremy's doorway, seeing ... oh God ... seeing Felix on top of her husband, buggering him ... the look on their faces, Jeremy's enraptured and Felix ...Felix ... dominant and triumphant.

She remembered how she had gasped, then turned and fled along the corridor, Jeremy and Felix pounding after her, Jeremy yelling her name. She had reached the top of the stairs and looked back at them ... terrified, sickened, fearful for what they were going to do to her ... to her unborn child ... then the fall ... the awful sensation of travelling at speed through the air, banging down the stairs and then nothing. She vaguely remembered coming to for a short while in the ambulance but then it all went blank until she had woken up in hospital.

The grandfather clock at the bottom of the stairs struck, bringing her back to the present. She was standing midway up the stairs, gripping the handrail with both hands. They had started shaking. She had to get to her room before it took over her whole body. She had to get a grip.

515

She managed to reach the bedroom she should have been sharing with Jeremy, stumbled to the bed and dissolved into tears. She was more frightened than she had expected. It had to be tiredness. It had been a long, stressful journey even though Selena had been a little angel. She would feel better in the morning. She had to.

However, her appetite seemed to have left her. In the absence of Felix, Pru brought up one of Lucy's favourite meals, a plate of salad, cold chicken and boiled potatoes sprinkled with cheese, a pudding dish containing a slice of apple and blackberry pie with whipped cream, and a pot of coffee. Lucy, enormously pleased to see her cook again, thanked her profusely but once she was on her own and tried to eat, as tasty as the meal was, she could only pick at it.

Finally giving up on trying to force it down, she made her way up to the nursery to say goodnight to Selena and Tina, then returned to the bedroom and lay in bed, listening and waiting for Jeremy and Felix to come home, dreading it, fearing it, terrified of it. She had locked her door and positioned a chair beneath the handle so if anyone tried to get in, she would be forewarned.

They arrived home just after 3.00 a.m. Lucy was wide-awake and heard the car meander down the drive and pull up outside the house. She heard them laughing loudly, banging the car doors and the front door. She heard them come upstairs. She lay and trembled, hoping desperately they wouldn't attempt to come near her. She needn't have feared. Their footsteps went past her room and down the corridor to Jeremy's. The door slammed and that was the last she heard. The tension in her body slowly receded and she drifted off into sleep, neither caring nor wanting to know what was going on in her husband's room. She just wanted them to leave her alone.

* * *

Nothing improved. In fact, Lucy's situation grew worse and was becoming untenable. Jeremy made no pretence that he loved her or had any feelings for her any longer. He was obsessed with the gardens and he was obsessed with Felix. Even when they knew she was looking, they would fawn over each other, touching, kissing and generally behaving in a way to make her feel inferior, useless and unloved.

It didn't help that she was suffering from postnatal depression, although that gave her the excuse she needed not to have to say what was really wrong with her. Ruth insisted Lucy visit the doctor and she was placed on ante-depressants, which just made her feel sick. She stopped taking them, telling herself that she would get over it. Millions of women must have suffered from this in the past without the help of pills and potions and she would be the same but it ground her down, the depression, and her marriage.

She managed to be as normal as she could when she was with Selena and was more grateful than she could say that Tina was there to help look after her. As every child did, Selena adored Tina, who adored her in return and Lucy often felt Selena was better off with Tina than with her.

For most of the day, she could pretend everything at Canleigh was as it should be. Jeremy was at college or out in the gardens and Felix was busy with his butlering duties, and she made sure she kept out of his

517

way as much as she could. When she wasn't having meetings with David Berkely, the estate manager, or Roy Fitzgerald, the head gardener, or dictating letters to Susan Armitage, she spent her time with Tina and Selena.

It was when Jeremy appeared at the end of the day that the reality hit home that things weren't right. She couldn't bear to have Felix wait on them over dinner. He was always touching Jeremy, making snide remarks and innuendos and smirking at her all the time, knowing she wouldn't say or do anything and that she just had to put up with it for her mother's sake. Just watching him fawn over Jeremy made her feel sick and nervous. She took to eating evening meals upstairs in the nursery and then carried her baby down to her bedroom where she would either watch television or read.

She badly wanted to talk to Granny Ruth but visits to Tangles became less and less frequent as it was obvious her grandmother knew something was up from the looks she gave her. She didn't actually say anything outright but kept asking if Lucy was okay and if there was anything worrying her.

But how could she admit that her marriage was in such a terrible mess and that she was frightened, for not only her mother's freedom but also her own life and possibly Selena's. Neither man had actually said they wanted to kill them but Lucy's nerves were in shreds and her imagination was running wild. If Jeremy was definitely planning to divorce her in the future, would he be content to just accept a settlement? If she and Selena were dead, he would get far more ... he would get Canleigh and all that went with it. Stupidly, even though Derek Rathbone had urged her to, she hadn't made a will. She would have to see him as soon as she could and do it. If Jeremy and Felix were told the estate would go to someone else in the event of her death, that would take away any reason for them to kill her or Selena, who would certainly never be in a position to run Canleigh but would need a lot of money to cover her care costs in the future.

But who? Who could she leave it to? Naturally, her first thought was her mother but that would be a huge mistake and anyway, she was perfectly happy at Blairness now. Granny Ruth wouldn't want to have the responsibility again since she was happily settled at Tangles. Aunty Vicky then. She and Alex would be perfect. They would probably turn it into a hotel.

Desperately needing solace, Lucy took to visiting St. Mary's nearly every day, gaining strength from sitting silently in the family's pew, gazing at the alter with the huge brass cross resting on it and the wonderful stained glass window behind. It was rare she was disturbed in the week as there was only the Sunday service still carried out as the Vicar was now in charge of three other parishes and had his work cut out to get round to see to everyone who needed him.

She prayed for help. She prayed for forgiveness of any sin she might have committed, she prayed for Selena ... that she would grow up, well and happy, in a secure and loving environment. She prayed Felix would leave Canleigh.

She would wander around the churchyard after her talk with God, visiting the graves of the family she never knew. They were all there, generations and generations of the Canleigh family, some with elaborate tombstones, some with less ornate ones. Lucy hadn't known any of them, apart from Stephen. She often hovered over that of Richard, the Marquess of Keighton, her mother's twin. The man she was supposed to have murdered. Had she? It was difficult to imagine it. Lucy knew what Delia had done to Ruth and Philip. She had witnessed the attack on Granny Ruth and would never forget it; the look of demented rage on her mother's face as she made Demon rear up and lash out at Granny. She also knew how Philip had suffered with his health since her mother had assaulted him but the question over whether she actually did kill her own twin, whom she had grown up with, and also the man purported to be her brother from America, with a gun, shooting them down in cold blood, was another matter entirely. It had to be as her mother said. Rocky turning the gun on Richard and then she struggled to get it off him and shot him in the process. The trial had been dismissed, so there it was. She hadn't done it and Lucy wasn't going to give it another thought. She had more urgent present day things to concern herself with.

* * *

Jeremy was livid. He had received another letter from Matthew. One came every day and had done for over a month. All were begging and pleading for Jeremy to see him. Mathew was in financial trouble and had no-one to turn to bar Jeremy. He only needed a few thousand pounds and he would leave him alone.

"It won't stop there," warned Felix, watching Jeremy reading the latest, ripping it up, and throwing it in the bin. "He's still ringing constantly. Fourteen flaming calls yesterday. I always tell him you won't speak to him but he still rings, no doubt hoping you will pick up the phone instead of me. You're going to have to do something about him."

"And what do you suggest?" Jeremy growled. He was heartily sick of Matthew, whingeing and whining. He had told him to leave him alone after that debacle with his mother. He never wanted to set eyes on the damned man again but Felix was right. It was obviously just going to get worse. He wasn't going away and something would have to be done ... but what?

The opportunity came sooner than expected.

* * *

Matthew couldn't understand why Jeremy wouldn't speak to him, especially after what he had done for him with his mother, that horrid old slag. He had watched the papers avidly in the days following her death but the police had concluded she was killed by a punter or an intruder but with police cuts, and the apparently large amount of clientele she enjoyed, they were stretched to find the culprit and probably didn't even care too much. After all, she was only a common prostitute. As the months wore on and he received no knock on the door, he relaxed and almost forgot it had ever happened. Apart from now. It was an ace card he held, he could use it against Jeremy, and he'd have to do it soon as time and money were running out.

Last week he was evicted from his flat for not being able to pay the rent. He had sold all his possessions, scraping up enough to pay the rent on the bookshop for another month and leaving the flat with nothing but his stereo and his clothes. He managed to find enough cash to buy a single mattress from a second-hand shop and have it delivered to the bookshop. He would have to live there for the time being but as it was doubtful he could make enough to pay the rent in the future, he would probably be slung out pretty soon and would end up either on his parents' sofa or, at the worst, on the streets. So much for an expensive education!

He slept badly on the mattress, convinced the last owner must have had fleas as every morning he woke up with bites on his legs and ankles. He had to wash in the tiny kitchen at the rear of the bookshop and as he had no money for takeaways and no method of cooking, had to live off cold tinned food and salads. He had never been so unhappy and desperate in his life and there was only one way out of his dilemma, only one person who could assist him out of it and treat him to the life he deserved. Jeremy. Jeremy was going to have to pay for the help he had received with getting rid of his mother.

With his letters unanswered and his phone calls ignored, Matthew decided there was nothing for it but to visit Canleigh. He would see Jeremy in person and sort his life out. It had to be done ... and quickly. He couldn't leave it much longer or else he really would be dossing on the streets and to do that was unthinkable, especially in a city such as Oxford where he had arrived with such high hopes just a few short years ago and knew so many people.

His car had been repossessed and he couldn't afford the train fare up to Yorkshire. With only a ten-pound note in his pocket, he walked to the Oxford ring road and thumbed a lift. He was lucky. It was raining and a man pulled over almost immediately, obviously feeling sorry for him. He took him to Sheffield, apologising that he could go no further.

Matthew thanked him and stood on the slip road for the M1 with his little placard, indicating he wanted a ride to Leeds. He waited for an hour and a half, growing increasingly tired and hungry and badly needing a pee. Cars shot past, heading up the slip road to the M1, ignoring him, uncaring whether or not he obtained a lift. Finally, a couple of male students in a tatty, rusted up old van, slowed down beside him and offered their services. Matthew was truly grateful, especially when they stopped at the next service station and treated him to a hot coffee and a ham and cheese roll, allowing him to keep tight hold of his ten-pound note.

His luck held out with them. They were heading to Harrogate to attend a pop concert, and as they had to drive right past Canleigh, they dropped him off, leaving him with only the drive to the Hall to negotiate.

It took him half an hour and it was six in the evening when he eventually stood outside the front door of the Hall. He stood for a moment, remembering how things had seemed so different only a year or so ago at Jeremy and Lucy's wedding, when he had been the best man, in his posh suit, looking forward to a posh life in the future. How wrong it had all gone but it wasn't going to remain like that. He was here now and Jeremy would have to see him. He pressed the doorbell and waited, his breathing becoming faster as his tension increased.

* * *

Lucy was in the nursery and didn't hear the doorbell. It was Selena's bath and bedtime and as

523

Tina had the night off to spend it with her husband, Lucy was in sole control of her child.

"There you are, darling," she said softly, towelling her baby dry, applying powder and cream, and after adjusting the nappy, dressing her in a pretty little pink and white sleepsuit.

Without Tina in attendance, Lucy didn't intend leaving Selena to sleep in the nursery one floor above her. She would carry her baby down to the bedroom and place her in the cot beside the bed, where she always slept when Tina didn't spend the night. Lucy didn't like to think of Selena all alone upstairs, even though she had a baby monitor. She wanted to have her near so she could keep an eye on her, and it was easier for feeding too. She certainly didn't want to keep trailing upstairs in the middle of the night. She felt much safer behind a locked bedroom door.

She carried Selena carefully down the stairs from the nursery floor to the first, coming out near to the main stairs which she had fallen down not so very long ago. She could hear arguing below in the entrance hall ... Jeremy and another man's voice she knew but didn't immediately recognise. Then it hit her. It was Matthew. Oh God. What did he want? That was really going to set the cat amongst the pigeons. She shuddered and hurried along to her room, holding Selena close, and locking the door firmly behind them.

CHAPTER 39

Felix had answered the door at Matthew's ring. His look of astonishment had pleased Matthew and he pushed past him, demanding to see Jeremy.

"He's not available," Felix said firmly, regaining his composure, reeking of alcohol.

"Rubbish! He'll be skulking somewhere … in the library is he?" demanded Matthew, crossing the entrance hall and pushing open the library door.

"Ah. The very man," he said, seeing Jeremy reclining on the sofa holding a glass of brandy. "I've been trying to contact you for weeks. Did you not receive my letters or my phone calls?"

"I thought I told you I didn't want any further contact with you," growled Jeremy. "Now get out of my house immediately or I'll have you thrown out."

"You're not going to do that," Matthew replied. "You're going to listen to me and then you're going to help me."

"I don't think so," Felix had interjected. "You heard Jeremy. Now move," he pointed to the front door.

"Back off, little man," Matthew warned, noting the way Jeremy was staring at Felix. A look of desire. In an instant, Matthew knew what was going on. These two were having an affair. It was why Jeremy had thrown him over, why he had finished the one good thing Matthew had in his life.

Felix moved angrily towards him. Matthew stepped back as Felix's fists lashed out and the butler went flying onto the rug in front of the fireplace. Jeremy sprang up to help Felix rise to his feet and sat him on the sofa, fussing over him like a mother hen. Matthew felt sick watching them. Sick with anger and sick with jealousy.

Jeremy turned to him, his eyes glinting with rage. "Now get out of here. This instant … or you'll be sorry."

"No. Not now … especially now I know what's going on here."

"What *are* you going on about now?" asked Jeremy.

"You two … you've got it together. You're having an affair. Does Lucy know?"

"It's bloody well nothing to do with you what I do in my own house," yelled Jeremy, thumping his fist on the mantelpiece and knocking off a glass rose bowl. It smashed on the marble, and red and white roses scattered over the rug.

"Well, I think the public would be pretty interested," smiled Matthew, knowing he had the upper hand, although he knew he was playing a dangerous game. These two would do him harm if he got it wrong. He was damned sure of that. "Wouldn't it look good in the newspapers? New husband of Lucy Canleigh involved in an affair with the butler. I bet they would pay a nice sum for that little piece of gossip, don't you?

Jeremy turned away, trying to give himself time to think, and walked to the drinks cabinet. He poured two glasses of brandy, handed one to Felix and drank the other in one.

"And don't forget you still owe me for doing away with your mother," Matthew added.

"That was nothing to do with me. You did that while I was on honeymoon."

"On your orders."

"How many more times? I didn't bloody well tell you to murder her! You know I didn't. I only told you to frighten her off."

"Okay but you still owe me for getting her out of your life ... and don't forget it would be very easy to implicate you in her demise, very easy indeed ... conspiracy to murder I think they call it. So, if you want to continue with your cosy life here and your sordid little affair, I suggest you finally pay up."

"And how much is it you want exactly," sneered Felix, having recovered from his tumble. The brandy had helped. He stood up, trying to regain his dignity.

"Oh, around £250,000. That should set me up nicely. I can head for sunnier climes, just as we were going to do, Jeremy. I can buy a nice little bar ... perhaps in Spain or similar and set myself up nicely for the rest of my life ... and you would never hear from me again."

Jeremy sat down at the desk, whipped out a chequebook from a drawer, and waved it in the air. "I presume a cheque won't do?"

"Not on your life. I want cash. I realise, of course, that you won't have enough sitting around here and the bank will think it is suspicious if you withdraw so much all in one go but I'm quite happy to return in a few days time to collect what you owe me."

Jeremy snorted. "I don't know about the bloody bank but Lucy is going to go nuts when she finds out. After all, it is her money."

Matthew smiled wryly. "Well, that's your problem. It certainly doesn't concern me what dear Lucy makes of it all. Anyhow, what cash do you have on you now? I'm completely out of funds and need to find somewhere to stay until you obtain all the money. You can pay for a few nights in a hotel for me, can't you, Jeremy dear? The Canleigh Arms in the village do rooms, don't they? That should do nicely ... oh," he glanced at Felix who was clenching and unclenching his fists, eager to plant a good blow on him, "I'm damned hungry. If you could trot down to the kitchens and make me a sandwich or two to take with me, that would be much appreciated."

Jeremy nodded to Felix. "If you would, please, Felix. We could all do with some refreshment. Leave me to talk to Matthew alone for a while."

Felix adjusted his shirt, glared furiously at Matthew, and left the room. Jeremy stayed where he was, flicking the chequebook against the desk, his eyes fixed firmly on Matthew's face.

"Do you promise? That you won't contact me again if I give you what you want."

Matthew nodded and suddenly feeling extremely tired, walked across to the sofa opposite Jeremy, and sat down. "I promise. I just need a new start and this can be it. I can make a go of it in Spain. I know I can ... it's much cheaper to live there ... unlike flaming Oxford."

"I'm sorry it's turned out the way it has," Jeremy said quietly. "I did think a hell of a lot of you but that business with my mother ... and then Felix." His eyes lit up. "I really love him, Matthew. He's made a hell of a difference to my life."

"He's only out for what he can get."

"Aren't we all? You want my money. I want Lucy's. We're all the same under the skin."

Matthew began to relax. Jeremy was coming around, as he had guessed he would once they met in person. It was going to work. He was going to get his money and set up a new life in the sun. He saw a nice little bar, by the sea, lots of happy, sun-seeking patrons, all spending lots of money in his establishment. He would be able to hire staff and retire, spend his days on the beach, maybe even find another partner. He smiled at Jeremy, pleased he had come. He was going to get what he wanted. He could spend a few nights at the Canleigh Arms, collect his money by the end of the week and then he could catch the train down to Oxford instead of hitching, put the money into his bank account, wind up the shop, buy a few new clothes and head off for pastures new.

A movement behind him made him turn. To his horror, he saw Felix brandishing a cricket bat. Before he could move out of the way, it came crashing down on his head.

* * *

Delia was in bed, smiling at the Jacobean plastered ceiling of her bedroom at Blairness. Brian was fast asleep beside her, his arm thrown over her waist, his head buried in her neck. She couldn't believe how happy she was. For the first time in her life, she was content, really content, superbly content. She wanted to scream to the world just how she felt ... and it was all down to this wonderful, handsome, kind, generous, loving man. He had helped her on her road to recovery from all the rejection she had suffered ever since she could remember, from the very first time her father had told her sternly that Richard was to inherit Canleigh and although she was the eldest twin, she was a girl and had no rights over the home she loved.

After all that she had suffered at the hands of her family and Philip, she still found it hard to put faith and trust in any human but Brian had superseded all that. She had worked with him for nearly a year now and she trusted him totally in all things, especially with the opposite sex. He seemed to sense her unease when they were in the company of other women and politely answered any questions and moved on, always smiling knowingly at Delia as if to say that none of them could compare to her and he was hers and hers alone.

He had proved himself time and time again, especially since they had commenced sleeping together, which turned out to be the most glorious nights of passion Delia had ever encountered, as it wasn't just sex, it was making love, real intimate love, such as she had never experienced before, not even with Philip.

Everything in her life was good now. Blairness was coming along nicely. It was going to be difficult getting used to the house being open to the public in August, just in time for the school holidays, and would, at times, be damned inconvenient, but it would bring in much needed revenue and keep Crystal happy and busy. She was going to be a huge asset. Her skills with the public, her knowledge of art and history were of paramount importance and what she didn't know, she did her best to find out as speedily as possible so that she would be ready to impart her knowledge to the hordes of visitors that they hoped would arrive every day.

The café would also be up and running. The caravans were booked up for the whole season. The work on the stable block was finished, two companies had already taken up office space, and Brian had appointments to conduct viewings with four more this week. More cottages, as they came on sale, were being bought up speedily, to prevent people buying them for second homes and instead, were rented out to the locals, which really placed Lady Delia Canleigh on a pedestal. With the promise of more jobs as all the plans for the expansion of the estate came into fruition, the population of the nearby villages were delighted and quite keen to begin overlooking all her past misdemeanours. She had done her time, paid her dues and was a changed woman. She was beginning to be liked, admired and respected and she was revelling in it.

And to top it all, there was Brian. Their relationship was cementing further as each day passed and Delia felt herself relying on him more and more. He was taking total command of her mind and her body and she was loving it, just as she loved him.

She had wondered if he would ever ask her to marry him, not that it mattered to begin with. As long as he was here and she saw him every day and slept with him every night, she was more than happy. However, it had begun to trouble her, never having had the security and stability of a marriage and she began to wish for a solid commitment. It started as a mere thought and then grew to a constant nagging. Brian had said sadly one day that he would have liked children but at forty-six years old, Delia's days of procreating were over so there was no need to rush into anything anyway as far as he was concerned but his status as estate manager and her lover was beginning to concern her. She wanted him elevated. She wanted them to be equal and there was only one way. Marriage.

Then, when curled up on the sofa in the red drawing room last night, Meg snoozing and snoring in the basket beside them, Delia bit the bullet and prayed hard that her gamble would pay off. Brian was telling her how much he loved her, stroking her hair, her damaged cheek, and her lips. Tingles were running up and down her spine but before they left the sofa for the bed upstairs, she wanted an answer to a very important question ... and if he said no, she didn't know what she would do but she had to ask. It was driving her crazy not knowing if he would say yes.

The astonishment on his face nearly made her laugh, as she suddenly broke free from his arms and knelt on the floor beside him.

"Brian Hathaway. I simply can't tell you how much I love you too, how much you mean to me, how much I want you in my life for as long as I have breath in my body. Please, please will you marry me? I love you. I can't live without you ... and if you will have me, I shall be the best possible wife you could ever want."

"Oh, Delia, Delia," he murmured, pulling her back up to the circle of his arms. "What am I going to do with you? I would like nothing more than to marry you but I want you to be really sure before we go any further."

"I am," she sighed. "I want you more than anything I have ever wanted in my life. I want to wake up with you every morning, I want to go to bed with you every night. I want to see your lovely, kind, smiling face every day over the breakfast, lunch, and dinner table. I just want *you!*"

He pulled her closer, placing his mouth over hers. Their kiss was long and lingering and then she pulled away.

"You haven't said yes," she said, terrified he was going to reject her. She couldn't bear another major blow, especially from him. She started to tremble with fear. "I quite understand if you don't want to ... with my reputation ... my ghastly temper. You'll probably never feel safe, wondering if I'm going to whack you over the head with something if we fall out, but if the answer is no, please, whatever you do, don't leave Blairness. I need you so much. I couldn't go on without you here."

"Delia, I simply don't care about what you might have done in the past. You've served a considerable amount of your life in prison for what you did and you are still on licence for a few years, so no, darling, you've paid for your crimes and the woman I have grown to know and love since you arrived at Blairness, is not the woman she once was. It was years ago, Delia. You've atoned for your sins. You've made a good life for yourself here. You have a great relationship with Lucy and are making up for lost time with her. I've watched you, listened to you and love you. I have huge respect for the way in which you have turned your life around and I want to share it with you ... forever. So yes, my darling. The answer is yes."

She had cried. Tears of tremendous joy had flowed. She had soaked herself and she had soaked him as he held her close. He would never know what he had done for her, this man, restoring her faith in a human being. Then, they had come up to bed and made heavenly love, tender but passionate and then fallen asleep entwined in each other's arms.

"Today we are going to Edinburgh," he murmured beside her now, opening his eyes and kissing her neck.

"Oh? What for?"

"A ring. I am going to buy you the biggest diamond we can find ... that's if you want a diamond ... you might prefer something else."

"A diamond is absolutely fine," she grinned with delight as he pulled her around to face him.

"Well, Your Ladyship, you better show me just how appreciative you are going to be."

* * *

Ruth was packing quickly, following an early morning phone call from her father. Her mother was ailing and calling for her. A well educated woman, a general practitioner for all her working life, she had succumbed to the early onset of dementia. Her husband, riddled with arthritis in his neck, back and knees, had been unable to care for her for a long time and she had been placed in an excruciatingly expensive care home near to their residence for the last two years. However, Mrs. Barrett had gone down with a bad cold last month, which she hadn't been able to shake off. It had turned to pneumonia, she had been hospitalised, was now at death's door and her husband was distraught.

"I wish I could come with you," said Philip, watching Ruth throw things into a suitcase.

"There's nothing you can do darling and it's better this way. I can look after Father … and if the worst happens, I can bring him back here."

"Of course you can. We've plenty of room."

"Will you try and visit Lucy if you have time?" she asked, zipping up the case. "We haven't seen her for three weeks now and she sounds so tired on the phone but whenever I invite her here or suggest I go over, she says she is in the middle of something and is too busy."

"Well, so are you," said Philip proudly. "Preparing for your Harrogate exhibition next month … which I am so thrilled you finally agreed to doing, although it's taken up most of your time."

"I know. Thank goodness I have all the artwork finished, as I've no idea how long I am going to be away. If Mother does die, I shall have to stay to help Father arrange the funeral."

She walked over to him and wrapped her arms around his waist. "I shall miss you."

He kissed the top of her head. "And I, you."

"You won't forget Lucy, will you darling? Invite her and Selena over for tea one day to keep you company. If she thinks you are lonely, she's bound to come … and you've always been so close to her. She might just tell you what the matter is. Although I could guarantee she is going to say Jeremy or Felix … or both."

* * *

Selena was crying in her cradle. She was hungry but her mother was still asleep in the bed beside her. Having spent most of the night wide awake, listening for sounds from downstairs, puzzling as to what Matthew was doing at Canleigh and dreading the furore it was going to cause, Lucy had dozed off at daylight and her crying baby couldn't wake her.

"Shut that blasted kid up," shouted Felix, banging loudly on her door, and rattling the handle. "If you don't I'll do it for you."

The commotion woke Lucy sharply. She sprung up the bed, shaking with terror, looking at the door with horror, expecting Felix to barge through at any

535

moment. He gave the door an almighty thump and then it all went silent. He must have gone back to Jeremy's room.

She moved quickly, jumped out of bed, wrapped herself in her dressing gown, picked up Selena, unlocked the door, and scurried along the corridor to the stairs to the nursery. Selena had stopped crying as soon as she was picked up but Lucy couldn't risk her starting again on this floor. Up in the nursery, Felix would never hear her.

Once in the safety and calmness of Selena's domain, Lucy managed to stop shaking, and placed Selena in her cot while she warmed up her milk. She looked out of the window. It was promising to be a grim day, raining hard and as the sky was filled with dark, swirling clouds, it didn't look as if it was going to clear up at any time soon. So, it would be another day in the confines of the Hall. Then she remembered it was Saturday ... Tina didn't work weekends, Jeremy would be at home all day and so would Felix. Depression engulfed her. She had no idea how she was going to fill the time, dodging them, unable to take Selena out for a walk. She considered a drive but wherever they went, it was going to be pretty miserable in this weather. She could go over to Tangles but she was desperately worried she would pour all her worries and fears out to Granny Ruth and had been avoiding her for weeks. There was Aunty Vicky at The Beeches but the same there. She would soon worm it out of her. No, she had to stay away from family. She couldn't even have a trip up to Scotland as she was being so worn down by it all, her mother would probably get it out of her and that would be the utmost folly if her temper was riled.

Lucy sat in the rocking chair, feeding Selena, pondering on what to do … how to fill her time that day and how to sort out her life.

* * *

Matthew came round on the hard wooden floor of the Bothy as dawn was breaking. He didn't have a clue where he was. His head hurt like hell, he had difficulty opening one eye, and he touched his battered face gingerly. Felix had given him a good whack last night, sending him reeling on the library floor at the Hall and the teeth on that side of his mouth were feeling distinctly loose and excruciatingly painful. His feet and hands were also tied up with a rope.

He started to panic as scenes from last night came flooding back and he fervently wished he hadn't come up to Yorkshire. He could have kicked himself. He had completely under-estimated Jeremy and hadn't planned on having his lover to contend with too … and now, from what he could remember of what happened last night, they were planning to murder him

He shifted his position, shuffling painfully across the floor to a battered old sofa, managing to put his weight on the seat with his elbow and push himself up onto it. It might be old and tatty but the comfort after the bare floor was a massive relief to his sore and aching body.

He was terribly cold and even more hungry than he had been yesterday, standing on that roundabout, waiting for a lift to Leeds. How foolish he had been. He should never have come up to Canleigh. As the minutes wore on, fragments of last night's conversation came back to him and he began to shake with fear, fully aware he had to get away as fast as he could. His very life depended on it.

They had manhandled him down to the Bothy. He could vaguely remember being dragged along the path around the lake, coming to and then sinking back into oblivion.

"Let's just throw him in the lake," Felix had muttered at one point when Matthew had regained consciousness.

"No. We don't want his body showing up here. Let's just leave him in the Bothy for now. No-one will use the place over the weekend. Roy, the Head Gardener, has a few days off and all the other gardeners work Monday to Friday. Hopefully, he'll die anyway. There's no heating in there, it's damned chilly tonight, and he hasn't eaten. He looks in pretty bad shape, obviously starving himself for ages by the look of it. If he dies of natural causes in the Bothy, we can just report it to the authorities and they will assume he was just another vagrant. His clothes are much the worse for wear and we can find him some more old rags."

"What about all his bruises and that bang on the head? They'll know he's been assaulted."

"Oh, Christ! That's true ... and when they discover he was my friend and best man at the wedding, we'll be straight on the list of suspects. We have until Sunday to decide what to do with him. Let's leave him here until then, hope he dies, and if he hasn't, we'll have to finish him off somehow, and then dispose of the body ... but not on the estate ... we'll have to get him in the car and drive him somewhere ... a hell of a long way from Canleigh ... probably down to Oxford ... dump him in Wytham woods. Anyhow, we've a bit of time to decide what we're going to do. Let's just get him in the Bothy for now."

"What if he gets out?"

"We'll just have to find him pretty damned quickly and deal with him … properly … but we must think it all through. We don't want any repercussions. We've got it cushy here … although I could do with getting rid of Lucy too … I've been thinking a lot about that lately. I'm fed up with her questioning everything I do and spend. If she were dead, I would be sitting really pretty. Selena can't inherit as she is not of sound mind and it will all come to me as Lucy's husband. Then we really will be free and can do as we please."

"Let's bump the two of them off at the same time then," suggested Felix, puffing and panting as he dragged Matthew. Jeremy, used to manual labour now that he was spending so much time digging and planting, didn't seem to find it an effort but Felix was finding it a real strain.

"Don't be ridiculous. We couldn't. It would look too obvious. We'll have to plan Lucy's demise meticulously … we can't afford any mistakes as I would certainly be in the frame."

They had reached the Bothy by now and placed Matthew on the ground while Jeremy unlocked the door.

"Thank God he decided to come up on a Friday night and this place will be deserted for a couple of days. With a bit of luck if we leave him until Sunday, tied up so he can't get to the sink for water and we'll take the biscuits with us, in the state he's in, he should be dead by then."

They threw him on the floor inside, checked the ropes around his wrists and ankles were still secure, and left him to die.

CHAPTER 40

"Ruth has travelled down south to be with her mother, who is dying, I'm afraid," announced Philip on the phone to Lucy. "And I'm lonely without her. Would you come to tea, please Lucy, and bring Selena ... or would you prefer lunch? We could go to the Canleigh Arms after you've fed Selena and then she'll sleep through it."

Lucy agreed readily. Even though she was close to Steppie, he didn't study her as hard as Granny did. It would be far easier to relax and anyway, she hated to think of him being on his own. He relied on Granny so much and would be lost without her ... and it would be an enormous relief to get out of Canleigh for the day and not be stuck indoors with her husband and Felix.

"I'll be over as soon as Selena has had her mid morning feed."

Selena was sleeping and Lucy, with the baby monitor in her hand, made her way downstairs to the library to collect her handbag, which she had left beside the desk the night before. The door was open and Jeremy was sitting on the sofa facing her, looking tired and worried, but stirred himself when he realised he was not alone.

"Morning," he muttered, avoiding her eyes.

Lucy studied him. He looked shifty, more shifty than usual. What had he been up to now? She remembered the commotion she had heard just a few hours ago and felt the fear rising in the pit of her stomach.

"Was Matthew here last night? I thought I heard his voice," she said quietly, dreading the answer but wanting to know. It was bad enough having Jeremy and Felix to deal with but if Matthew had moved in as well ... she shuddered ... her life really wouldn't be worth living. For an instant, she could have cursed Stephen for leaving her Canleigh and all his millions. She had been far better off without them now the world and his wife were trying their best to benefit from her inheritance. All she had really wanted was a great career in the hotel industry and to be married to Jeremy ... a much kinder, loving, totally heterosexual Jeremy. Instead, here she was, terrified of him and his sexual partners in her own home.

"Um. Yes. He popped in briefly. He ...um ... he looked dreadful. He's lost a lot of money, been kicked out of his flat and he came up here, hoping I could help him out."

"And did you?"

"Well, I gave him all the cash I had on me ... and he left. I said I would send him some more ... when I had spoken to you."

"If he's struggling, it's his own fault," Lucy retorted. "He can fiddle. I'm not giving him a penny."

Jeremy gave a wry smile. "I had a feeling you would say that. Anyway, he's gone so hopefully that will be the last we hear of him."

"Well, I certainly hope so," Lucy retorted. She saw her bag, sighing with relief that at least Matthew wasn't going to be a problem. She opened it, checking her car keys were inside.

"Going out?" asked Jeremy.

"Steppie is on his own ... Granny has had to go down to see her mother ... she's dying apparently. Selena and I are going over to Tangles to keep him

541

company. We'll probably be there for most of the day."

"That's nice, darling. Have a good time … and don't you worry about Matthew. I'm sure that's the last we will see of him."

* * *

Lucy stayed longer with Philip than she had intended. They had enjoyed a delicious meal at the Canleigh Arms, chatted to all the villagers, and allowed them to coo over a contented Selena. They then returned to Tangles, Philip banked up the fire in the lounge and they watched a couple of films on the television, threw a few salad sandwiches together for tea and idled most of the evening away watching another film.

With all the chatter in the pub and then the films and playing with Selena back at Tangles, Philip hadn't found the opportunity he was seeking to sound Lucy out about her life at Canleigh. However, when he waved her off just after 8.00 p.m., he felt she was far happier than when she had turned up a few hours ago.

Lucy arrived home, left the car in front of the Hall, carried Selena inside and went straight up to the nursery to give her baby a bath, not wanting to bump into Jeremy or Felix. She didn't dally, wanting to get back down to the bedroom as fast as possible and just relax on her bed with a good book and Selena at her side.

It only took half an hour and then they were in the relative safety of her room and Lucy did as she always did these days, locked the door, and placed a chair against the handle. What a way to exist she thought but until something occurred to her as to what she could do to change things, this was how they would have to live.

At least it was Sunday tomorrow so she and Selena could go to church and then perhaps they could go back to Tangles and make Philip a nice lunch. That was a nice thought. Something to look forward to and she sank onto the bed hoping they could get through the night without any drama, which made her think about Matthew. She wondered where he was. What he had done when Jeremy sent him on his way with just a few pounds? It must be awful to be in such a position but it was his own fault and she had no sympathy for him. He had certainly not needed to live the life of Riley in Rome and gamble as he had, and as he had ruined her honeymoon, she would never look upon him favourably. It served him right and jolly good riddance. It was such a shame she couldn't say the same about Felix. Oh, God! When was it all going to end?

* * *

Earlier in the day, Matthew had found a knife. Still tied up, he had managed to pull himself upright from the sofa and slither across the room to the tiny kitchen at the rear of the Bothy, opening the drawer in the one and only unit with the tips of his fingers. The knife wasn't particularly sharp but it was all there was and had to do. He shuffled back to the sofa, sat down, positioned it between his knees, and sawed and sawed at the rope. He had to keep stopping as he felt dizzy and sick and his fingers were numb with cold but he kept at it and eventually the tendrils came adrift, one by one and suddenly snapped apart, leaving him to rub his wrists and hands and try to get the feeling back. Then he set to untying the ropes around his ankles. Again, it took him a long time. His fingers still felt like blocks of ice and didn't want to work. He was shaking and shivering, couldn't stop sneezing and his throat felt raw. He had a cold coming on. It always started with a sore throat and he wasn't surprised, stuck in this little hellhole for hours on end. Jeremy was right. The Bothy was cold and damp, and positioned down by the lake and being surrounded by trees, it never caught the sun to dry it out properly. Weak and desperately hungry, aching and sore, he knew he had to get out, as fast as possible before he did keel over and die, let alone wait for Jeremy and Felix to come back and finish him off.

With his body free of shackles, he returned to the kitchen and boiled the kettle. At least he could have a hot drink, which would warm him up. There was nothing to eat and he had to have black coffee as there was no milk but it warmed him, sending waves of heat through his frozen body. All he had to do now was get out of here. It was getting dark again and he daren't put on the light. If they saw it from the house, they would come down here and probably finish him off. He had been terrified they might come back throughout the day but they hadn't, obviously hoping he would have passed away by now.

The windows had bars across and the door was locked but it was old wood and going rotten. It wouldn't take much to batter down and revived by the coffee, he put his full weight against the door and pushed it hard. It began to give. He rammed himself against it twice more and it splintered, enough so that his fingers, warmed up by wrapping his hands around

544

the hot mug, could pull the wood away and make enough room to climb out.

He landed on the grass outside. At last, progress was being made. All he had to do now was get away from here but he had no money and didn't fancy a return to hitching. He needed a car and there were some in the stables. It only needed one to have the keys inside and he could escape easily and get away before anyone realised.

He crept up to the stables, keeping as much as he could off the main path and behind the trees, just in case his tormenters were on their way down to the Bothy. Three cars were there, the Rolls Royce, Jeremy's Mini-Cooper and a Range Rover. All were locked.

Lucy. Lucy had a car. Where the hell was it? He remembered seeing a blue estate outside the Hall last night. That must be hers but surely she wouldn't leave the keys inside. He crept up to the Hall, keeping a wary eye out for signs of Jeremy and Felix. He slid silently along the south terrace towards the French windows of the library. They were shut and the drapes were drawn but he could hear the pair laughing and talking loudly, no doubt pleased as punch with the way things were going for them.

He went round to the front of the house, secure in the knowledge that the enemy were occupied in the library. He checked Lucy's car. It was locked, as he guessed it would be. He had to get the keys. Where did women keep their car keys? They either had to be on the hall table or in her handbag … and her handbag would be in her room. Bugger, he didn't want to disturb her if he could help it and to enter the house was really bordering on foolish but he had little choice. He felt too fragile to walk back up the long drive to the main road and then try to get a lift, and that would be doubtful as he must look a complete fright, wild and rough. Who would want to let him into their car? He hadn't enough cash for a train or bus so he was truly stumped. The car he was standing beside was his only hope. He moved towards the front steps to the Hall, trusting the front door would be unlocked and the keys, any car keys for that matter, would be on the Hall table. They weren't.

He stood in the entrance hall, listening to Jeremy and Felix laughing their heads off in the library. Luckily, the door was shut and they couldn't see him. With a thumping heart, he crossed the floor and headed up the stairs. He knew which room Lucy would be in from when he had stayed here for the wedding. He would have to surprise her and if she kicked up a fuss, he would have to take her with him. He still had the knife from the Bothy kitchen in his jacket pocket. He would use it if he had to.

He tried Lucy's door. It was locked but she was inside. He could hear her talking to the baby. He knocked, a soft gentle tapping so as not to alert those two downstairs but loud enough for her to hear.

"Go away," she called. "I've gone to bed."

"Lucy," he hissed. "It's me ... Matthew."

"What? What the hell do you want? Go away or I'll ring the police."

"Lucy. You must let me in. They're trying to kill me ... Jeremy and Felix ... and they want to do away with you as well, you and the baby. We have to get away ... in your car ... I need your keys. Please. I'm telling the truth. We're both in terrible danger."

Lucy stood, transfixed on the other side of the door, not knowing what to do. Was it some kind of ruse? She didn't trust Matthew. She had no reason to

546

but then she had no reason to trust her husband and Felix either and to have someone actually say they were planning to kill her and Selena was confirmation of her fears. Her heart pounded. She could hear it clearly. Oh, dear God. She was so frightened.

"Lucy ... please. We have to get away from here ...now ... quickly! Hurry! Let me in!" His voice was rising with panic. Why was the stupid woman being so reluctant?

Then he heard the handle rattle as she removed the chair and unlocked the door. He pushed inside quickly, shutting it behind him.

Lucy looked at him, shocked by his appearance and the smell of him ... he reeked of mould and dirt. He was filthy, unshaven and his hair was matted with something dark. It looked like blood. His eyes were wild with fear and he was shaking like a leaf in the wind.

"Where are the keys ... your bloody car keys," he hissed.

Lucy's hands began to tremble. She glanced at Selena asleep in her cot, instinct making her move towards it to protect her child at whatever cost.

"The keys, woman! The bloody keys!" he hissed again, glaring at her savagely.

Lucy pointed at her handbag on the floor beside the bed. "In there."

He fumbled through the bag, finally emptying it onto the bed. The keys fell out and he grabbed them. He looked at her. "You better come with me. If they find out you've helped me, they'll not hesitate to kill you. Believe me, I heard them talking about it. You're no more safe than I am. They battered me last night and left me to die in the Bothy and then they were going to dispose of my body while they planned what to do with you."

"I'm ringing the police," Lucy cried, dashing across the room to the telephone beside the bed.

"No! Don't! They'll take ages getting here ... it's Saturday night and they will all be busy in Leeds sorting out the drunks ... and anyway, Jeremy will tell them I murdered his mother ... the one in London ... and they will arrest me."

Lucy gasped. "Oh my God! Did you ... murder her?"

Matthew shook his head and lied through his teeth. "No, of course not. Why would I? It was probably Jeremy. He wanted rid of her ... look Lucy, we're wasting precious minutes discussing this. Are you coming or not?"

"No," she said, in a daze. She didn't know what to do for the best but getting in her car with this half crazed, disgusting man, who she disliked intensely anyway, would be tantamount to madness.

"Go," she said quietly. "I'm not coming with you ... I'll ring my step-father. He'll come and get me ... and Selena."

"Promise you won't ring the police?"

Lucy nodded. She didn't owe him anything but she still didn't know whether to believe him or not. She sat down heavily on the bed and gestured to the door. "No ... just go ... save yourself. I shan't tell them. I promise," she stuttered.

"You better not ... or else I shall come back for you at some later date," he growled. Taking one last look at the items on the bed, he grabbed her purse and emptied the notes, stuffing them into his jacket pocket.

"Any more money in this room?"

"No."

"Jewellery … I'll have your rings," he pointed to the wedding and engagement rings on her finger, waiting impatiently for her to pull them off. He strode across to the dressing table and rummaged through her jewellery box, taking out a diamond necklace and earrings. "I'll have these too."

"Go," she pleaded. "Please. Just go."

"Okay. I'm gone. Look after yourself Lucy. I don't envy you living here with those two. Best of luck but before I go, just check there's no-one in the corridor … and keep your mouth shut!"

Lucy poked her head outside the bedroom but all was quiet with no sign of her husband or Felix. She nodded to Matthew and he brushed past her, made his way stealthily to the stairs, and disappeared. Relieved to be rid of him, Lucy quickly shut the bedroom door. She was going to have to explain how he had taken her keys but she would give him a few minutes before she raised the alarm. He was obviously telling the truth about them wanting to kill him but whatever he said about Jeremy, she really didn't think he had it in him to kill her. Although Felix might. Perhaps she had been stupid after all, not getting away while she could. If there were any truth in what he said, she was in real danger now, and so was Selena.

She heard her car start. Only seconds later, she heard Jeremy and Felix charge out of the library and shout at the departing car. Then someone was thundering up the stairs, towards her room. She rushed over to Selena and picked her up, cradling her closely in her arms, fearing for their lives.

Jeremy burst in, stopping with surprise when he saw her. "I thought it was you doing a bunk … so who the bloody hell is in your car?" he shouted.

549

Her voice came out as a squeak. "Matthew ...he came in, he threatened us ... he had a knife ... he took my car keys. He said you were going to kill him ...he said you were going to kill us."

"Christ," he yelled, heading back out of the room. "It's bloody Matthew. He's taken Lucy's car. We've got to get after him ... and I'll come back and deal with you!" he shouted at Lucy.

Lucy heard Jeremy and Felix crash out of the front door and tear down to the garage. Within seconds the Range Rover was in motion, hurtling past the house and along the drive at full speed, the tyres screaming as the vehicle screeched around the winding bends until it reached the main road.

Lucy sank onto the bed, still cradling Selena in her arms. She was totally alone at Canleigh and more scared than she had ever been in her life. What would happen when they caught up with Matthew? Would they kill him? Would they come back for her? With shaking hands, she picked up the phone and rang Tangles. Philip answered.

"Steppie. Please ... come and get me and Selena. I think Jeremy and Felix are going to kill us."

* * *

The cars roared down the main road, heading for Leeds. The Range Rover was more powerful than the estate car and caught up quickly. There was little traffic about but the odd car that did appear on the opposite side of the road prevented Jeremy from overtaking.

Felix sat beside him, seething and mad, urging him on to drive faster, to overtake.

"We've got to get the bastard. If he gets away, he's going to tell the police we were going to let him die and don't forget, he regained consciousness last night, when we were dragging him to the Bothy. He probably heard us saying we were planning to kill Lucy. We're going to be in serious shit if we don't get him and finish him off," he muttered. "We'll end up in bloody prison."

"I know. I bloody know," shouted Jeremy, gripping the steering wheel and turning his lights onto full beam in order to dazzle Matthew who was driving like a lunatic in front of them. He was all over the road and had almost hit the kerb twice. They were fast approaching the outskirts of Leeds and if they didn't get him in the next couple of miles, they would be in the suburbs and could be seen. They just needed a straight bit of road with no-one coming the opposite way. Then they could get in front of him and make him stop.

The cars screeched around the corners at speeds far above the legal limits, Matthew guessing what the Range Rover was trying to do, weaving all over the road to prevent it overtaking whenever they hit a straight bit.

"God," said Jeremy. "I do hope we don't see any damned police cars."

* * *

Matthew was thinking the opposite. To see a police car would be the best thing that could happen to him now because he knew damned well those two in the car behind him were definitely going to kill him. He had known it was Jeremy's Range Rover as the lights were higher than the car he was driving and anyway, he had seen it hurtle out of the Canleigh gates in his mirror as he was disappearing down the road. It had caught up with him rapidly, roaring behind him like some gigantic battleship, trying to pass him at every opportunity, the horn blaring and the lights flashing on and off on full beam.

How he managed to keep Lucy's car on the road was a mystery. It was sheer luck and determination but he wished the engine was bigger and had more power. It could never outdo the Range Rover so he had to keep his wits about him. He didn't really know where to go once he hit the ring road but had to make a decision fast. He knew there was a police station a couple of miles further along but it was a dual carriageway. They could easily overtake him but what choice was there? He didn't know Leeds well enough to know where there was another police station. Unless he just crossed the roundabout on the ring road and drove straight into the centre of Leeds. There were bound to be loads of people about. It was Saturday night. They wouldn't dare to do anything to him in the city centre and he could dump the car and disappear into the crowds.

He was nearing the outskirts of Leeds now. He could see traffic lights at a crossroads. They were on amber. He only had yards to go before they turned red. He put his foot to the floor. The car took off like a rocket. There was a man walking his dog off the lead on the far side of the road and it had seen a cat creeping along a wall opposite them. The dog, his eyes gleaming in the car lights, couldn't resist the urge to chase. He charged in front of the car. Concentrating on the animal, Matthew swerved right to avoid it, not registering there was a little Fiat with a young couple inside approaching him in the opposite direction. He hit it at sixty miles an hour. Both cars spun over and over. The Range Rover behind, doing exactly the same speed as Matthew, couldn't stop in time and crashed into both of them, rupturing the Fiat's petrol tank. The explosion could be heard for miles around.

When the police, fire brigade and three ambulances arrived minutes later, alerted by residents of the houses overlooking the scene, they found no-one alive. Five people, all dead. Five people, their lives destroyed in a flash and the only person who could tell them what had happened was the man with his dog.

THE END

EPILOGUE

The wedding was held in the great hall at Blairness Castle on the evening of Monday 22nd December 1997.

Lucy and Selena were there, along with Katrina, who shouldn't have been but had begged to be allowed to come. She had so desperately wanted to meet her evil old aunt, which had amused Delia greatly and terrified Vicky and Alex. However, with assurances from Lucy that she would keep a strict eye on the youngster, permission from the probation service, and a special invitation from Delia who was delighted that at least one other member of her family would be at her wedding, Katrina now stood at Lucy's side, totally in awe of the castle and her aunt.

Lucy smiled at Katrina's expression as she looked around the entrance hall, decorated beautifully for Christmas and the wedding. A huge fir tree, cut down from the estate, covered with white lights and silver balls, stood one side of the fireplace, to the other was a table adorned with an enormous display of cream roses and greenery.

The hall table, which normally sat in the centre of the room, had been moved to the wall between the front door and the office door. It was covered with a white damask cloth and rose bowls filled with more cream roses. Following the ceremony, it would be laden with a delicious finger buffet brought in by the specially selected caterers. Mouth-watering aromas were already wafting their way up to the hall from the kitchens at the rear, mingling with scents from the roses, and beeswax from all the hectic polishing the cleaning staff had undertaken the previous day.

The centrepiece, already in place, was the three-tiered wedding cake, on top of which sat a tiny replica of Blairness castle. Small figures of a bride and groom, with a remarkable resemblance to Brian and Delia, stood by the front door.

Fifty chairs were arranged in the centre of the room, facing the fireplace. The guests, who were now all assembled, were mainly staff members and their families, along with Lucy, Katrina, and little Selena, who was asleep in her pram by Lucy's side. Brian had hoped his brother, the Earl of Glentagon, and his family would make an appearance but not exactly keen on welcoming such an infamous woman into their clan, His Lordship had declined the invitation for his family, with the excuse that they were spending Christmas in America. Brian knew they had never gone away at this time of the year before but as he and his brother had never really seen eye to eye over anything, it didn't come as much of a surprise that they weren't helping him celebrate one of the most important days of his life.

Press interest in the Canleigh family, rekindled with the awful crash on the outskirts of Leeds when Jeremy, Felix, and Matthew had been killed, had now switched to Scotland, with the marriage of the evil Lady Delia Canleigh to her estate manager, the son and brother of an Earl. Brian was positive that was another reason his brother had declined to attend the wedding, as anyone remotely connected with the Canleigh family was hot news.

A quartet of musicians, along with Melanie Jenkins, the famed harpist, in an emerald green dress, was positioned on the landing above the entrance hall, softly playing something from Mozart. Lucy wasn't sure what as a lot of his work sounded very much the same to her but it was beautiful and fitting and she liked it. Hamish McTafferty, the Scottish Piper brought in to pipe Lady Delia down from the top of the stairs to where her bridegroom was waiting, held his bagpipes at the ready.

The registrar and Brian, in his full Scottish regalia, including his kilt in the Glentagon tartan, stood beside the small table by the fireplace, along with the gorgeous looking Gerry Wilson, an army colleague, who was acting as best man. They talked quietly amongst themselves, patiently waiting for Delia to make her grand entrance. Lucy was finding it hard not to giggle as she noticed Katrina and Crystal both ogling Gerry, just as they had at dinner last night. Lucy could almost have felt sorry for him if he hadn't seemed to lap it up, albeit being extremely kind to Katrina as she was so young.

Lucy smiled at Selena, who sighed, moved about a bit, opened her eyes, and then went straight back to sleep. Lucy's heart filled with love for her. Their lives had been somewhat of a roller coaster since she had married Jeremy, and Selena had been born ... until the night of that terrible crash.

Lucy had been in shock for weeks and not wanting to remain at Canleigh, even with a new butler and housekeeper in situ, she and Selena had moved back to Tangles to be with Granny Ruth and Steppie, and spent the odd fortnight up at Blairness. Safe in the knowledge that none of the three men killed that night could do any more harm, she told her mother that Felix had seen her at Canleigh and Jeremy had threatened to reveal it to the authorities if Lucy made a fuss about his affair with Felix, or tried to divorce him. Delia had been furious, railing loudly about what had happened but thankfully, it was too late for her to do anything about it and she had to be content with knowing her trip to Canleigh would never be discovered. Brian and Lucy could be trusted explicitly to never say a word.

However, Lucy still had the remains of Felix to deal with. He had no family. His parents were dead; he had no siblings and had never married or had children. Following the crash, the coroner asked Lucy, as she was his employer and Felix had lived at Canleigh, if she would see to his affairs. In the midst of trying to decide, along with Aunty Vicky and Uncle Alex, on what to do with Jeremy, Lucy agreed reluctantly but refused to have him buried in Canleigh churchyard. Felix was taken to Leeds crematorium and his ashes scattered in the grounds. There were no mourners and no wake.

Once the funerals were over, what was left of Matthew having been taken down to Thame for his parents to bury, Lucy gathered up all the paperwork she would need and made a start on finalising Felix's affairs. On checking his bank statements, she was shocked to discover monthly amounts of £500 had been paid in for quite a while from Lady Delia Canleigh. Realising instantly that Felix had been blackmailing Delia, she withdrew the amount he had purloined from her mother and gave it back to her. Delia was contrite but grateful it was only Lucy who had found out. It was never mentioned again. Lucy took what remained in Felix's bank account and gave it to the Dog's Trust situated in Leeds. Everything else she shredded and his possessions were given to charity shops. That horrid little man was finally out of her life and would never intimidate or frighten anyone ever again.

Jeremy wasn't buried at Canleigh either. Vicky and Alex had been utterly horrified to learn what he had put Lucy through and agreed he could also be cremated in Leeds and his ashes buried at The Beeches. Whatever he had done, they had still loved him and mourned his loss.

It had been a horrid few months for the whole family, coming to terms with what had occurred, although Lucy never revealed to anyone about the threat to Delia's freedom.

Then, like a breath of fresh air and to Lucy's delight, two months ago, an invitation to Delia and Brian's wedding had accompanied the post. She was absolutely thrilled for them both and hoped that with this wonderful event, life was going to take a much better turn for the whole family.

And here they were, ready and waiting to witness the wedding of Lady Delia Canleigh and Brian Hathaway. Lucy, Katrina and Selena, had travelled up to Scotland yesterday, arriving just before dinner. It had been a truly happy occasion, with Brian, Gerry, Crystal, Connie and her husband, all invited, although no-one had stayed late, all wanting to be fresh for the wedding this evening.

Once all the guests had departed, Lucy had accompanied Katrina to her bedroom to make sure she had everything she needed.

"Gosh, she is amazing," Katrina whispered to Lucy. "I would never have guessed Aunt Delia had murdered people."

"Katrina! Please. She didn't," Lucy had said forcefully.

"But if she didn't, she nearly did … after all, that's why she spent so much time in prison."

"We don't need to talk about this now," replied Lucy crossly. "We have come up here for her wedding. Now, get all that out of your head. We are celebrating, remember?"

Thankfully, Katrina hadn't mentioned Delia's lurid past again and Lucy had relaxed today, enjoying helping with the preparations, watching and listening to her mother, high on excitement and happiness. It had been wonderful seeing her so animated. It was a shame that due to the restrictions of her licence, she and Brian were unable to travel abroad for a honeymoon but they seemed quite happy to spend a couple of days down at his cottage, totally alone, apart from Meg, and would return to the castle on Christmas Eve. Lucy, Katrina and Selena were all staying until after New Year and Lucy had a feeling it was going to be a really joyous occasion.

Then she would have to go home … to Canleigh. She couldn't stay with Ruth and Philip forever and had to take up the reins of her life again. However, things were going to be different from now on. A new butler had been appointed, Reginald Miles, he was called, with a lovely wife named Virginia, Gina for short, who was taking over the housekeeping duties from Tina, so she could concentrate wholly on assisting with Selena.

But Lucy didn't want to just live at Canleigh. It wasn't her. She didn't want to be one of the idle rich. She had ambitions. She had a degree in business. Over the past few months while resting at Tangles she had thought long and hard about what she was going to do and had come up with a plan that would allow her to live at Canleigh feeling safe and secure, surrounded by people, and with the type of business she had wanted to run for a long time.

She was going to turn Canleigh into a fabulous stately hotel and she was going to run it. She had discussed the idea with Aunty Vicky and Uncle Alex, who thought it was brilliant and offered to support her in any way they could. Granny Ruth and Steppie were also of the opinion that she could make a real go of it and her mother had been ecstatic.

"I can't think of a better plan for the Hall," she said with enthusiasm. "It needs people, the sort who will appreciate it and love it as we do. Well done, darling, and I wish you all the success in the world with it."

"Wow!" Katrina suddenly exclaimed, staring at the landing above. "Just look at Aunt Delia."

Meg, who had been laying at Lucy's feet, looking particularly adorable with a couple of cream roses attached to her collar, saw the woman she adored standing at the top of the stairs and thumped her tail hard on the floor.

Lucy smiled up at her mother, who looked absolutely divine. Her hair was tied loosely back with a knot of cream roses. Her cream dress, covered with pearls, shimmered in the dappled light from the hundreds of candles dotted around the hall. Hamish filled his bagpipes with air and began to play and Delia's tall, slender figure in the long, elegant organza gown, swept down the remainder of the stairs and across the decorated entrance hall to where the registrar, Gerry and Brian were standing to the right of the fireplace. Her eyes were sparkling with happiness as she looked at the man who was about to become her husband. He beamed back and reached out to take her hand as she approached him.

Lucy's eyes filled with tears to see her mother look so happy. She had never thought to see the day when Lady Delia Canleigh would marry such a special man and find peace at last. She was overjoyed for her mother … and her heart filled and ached with love for her.

* * *

The small light plane heading over the Grand Canyon contained Lord and Lady Glentagon and their three children. They were enjoying a spectacular sightseeing tour but twenty minutes into their flight, something went wrong with the engine. It started to splutter and cough and the pilot was doing his best not to panic his passengers. Three minutes later, the plane was at the bottom of the canyon and Brian and Delia had no idea they had now become the Earl and Countess of Glentagon.

LAST WORD

Thank you for reading Delia's Daughter, the second book in the Canleigh series, which I do hope you have enjoyed and if you have a few moments in which to leave a short review on my Amazon page, this will be so helpful, not only to me, but also to future readers.
UK: www.amazon.co.uk/dp/B076YZQW57/
US: www.amazon.com/dp/B076YZQW57/

Don't forget to visit my website,
www.carolewilliamsbooks.com and sign up for your first free story, a thriller entitled 'Yes Dear', further free stories, news of competitions and future novels.

I also have a dedicated author page on facebook if you would like to be added.

My email address is
carole@carolewilliamsbooks.com and I would welcome your comments and feedback.

Many thanks!

Carole Williams.

11842995R00300

Printed in Great Britain
by Amazon